Named a favorite book of 2011 by NPR,
The Seattle Times, and the *St. Louis Post-Dispatch*

~

Praise for *The Dovekeepers*

"Beautiful, harrowing, a major contribution to twenty-first-century literature."

—Toni Morrison, Nobel Laureate in Literature

"In her remarkable new novel, Alice Hoffman holds a mirror to our ancient past as she explores the contemporary themes of sexual desire, women's solidarity in the face of strife, and the magic that's quietly present in our day-to-day living. Put *The Dovekeepers* at the pinnacle of Hoffman's extraordinary body of work. I was blown away."

—Wally Lamb, author of *The Hour I First Believed*

"I am still reeling from *The Dovekeepers*—from the history Alice Hoffman illuminates, from the language she uses to bring these women to life. This novel is a testament to the human spirit and to love rising from the ashes of war. But most of all, this novel is one that will never be forgotten by a reader."

—Jodi Picoult, author of *Sing You Home*

"*The Dovekeepers* is a stunningly crafted work about a tragic and heroic time. It also showcases Hoffman's immense gift for telling stories about women, magic, and complex relationships. Perhaps *The Dovekeepers* is the masterpiece she has been working toward all along."

—*The Seattle Times*

"Alice Hoffman weaves fiction and fact in *The Dovekeepers*, a thrilling, passionate saga. . . . The book pulses toward its stunning climax. Hoffman's fiction is always compelling, but the history within *The Dovekeepers* makes this novel haunting."

—*USA Today*

"First-rate historical fiction, an epic saga of war, passion, and the ferocious instinct of survival. . . . The beating heart of the story is one that pulses through the author's body of work: a celebration of women and their wondrous ways."

—*People*

"Magisterial . . . an intricate literary tapestry interweaving history and compelling dramatic narrative."

—*Hadassah Magazine*

"Vivid and visual . . . Intricately crafted, replete with the foreshadowing and symbolism of classic myth, *The Dovekeepers* will join Marion Zimmer Bradley's *The Mists of Avalon* as one of the great feminist reimaginings of war epics."

—*Ms.*

"Ancient times come to shimmering life in this superb novel. . . . Hoffman re-creates in spellbinding detail the community's fight to survive."

—*Parade*

"Striking . . . [Alice Hoffman] grounds her expansive, intricately woven, and deepest new novel in biblical history, with a devotion and seriousness of purpose that may surprise even her most constant fans."

—*Entertainment Weekly*

"Splendid . . . thrilling . . . fueled to fever pitch by a rich imagination . . . remarkable."

—*The Boston Globe*

"Hoffman makes ancient history live and breathe in this compelling story. . . . This is both a feminist manifesto and a deeply felt tribute to courageous men and women of faith, told with the cadence and imagery of a biblical passage."

—*Booklist*

"Powerful . . . true to the history of Masada . . . [Alice Hoffman is] one of our best novelists."

—NPR's *All Things Considered*

"The suspense keeps you barreling forward . . . but moments when Hoffman's characters come to a full stop—registering what it's like to be running out of options, experiencing their probably already false bravado evaporating in the arid mountain air—pack a timeless emotional punch."

—*Elle*

"Immersive . . . An enormously ambitious, multi-party story, richly decorated with the details of life two thousand years ago . . . Dramatic and engaging."

—*The Washington Post*

"[It's] as if a wind has blown through and animated the lives on the page."

—*Newsday*

"Ambitious . . . sure to appeal to Hoffman's core readership."

—*New York* magazine

"[*The Dovekeepers*] tells of the historic siege of Masada as only the bestselling author of *Here on Earth* and *The Third Angel* could. . . . A page-turner."

—*The Miami Herald*

"An enthralling tale rendered with consummate literary skill."

—*Kirkus Reviews*

"A gripping, masterful narrative."

—*The Daily Beast*

"Hoffman's prose is vivid and unforgettable, scorching like the desert heat, and will stay with you long after you finish the last page."

—Amazon.com

"Powerful and gripping . . . Hoffman finds poetry and beauty, dignity and honor, even in those perilous, blood-soaked times."

—*Library Journal*

"Brilliant . . . Read [*The Dovekeepers*] for Hoffman's fine sense of narrative, history, and detail."

—*St. Louis Post-Dispatch*

"Alice Hoffman embraces the account and the woman who gave it. . . . Her master work."

—*The Newark Star-Ledger*

"Bold . . . an in-depth and preternaturally empathic fictionalization of the months-long Roman siege of the mountain fortress of Masada."

—*The Kansas City Star*

"Hoffman creates a vividly detailed world. . . . Mesmerizing."

—*Minneapolis Star Tribune*

"A powerful voice for women amid war."

—*The San Diego Union-Tribune*

"Carefully researched . . . Alice Hoffman brings history to life."

—*The Christian Science Monitor*

"Beautiful, intriguing, and compelling."

—*The Vancouver Sun* (Canada)

"Hoffman is at the peak of her powers as a writer."

—*The Globe and Mail* (Canada)

"Hoffman's most ambitious and mesmerizing novel to date."

—*The Guardian* (UK)

"*The Dovekeepers* is a book as monumental as its subject, magical, moving, quite beautifully written. . . . A genuine masterpiece."

—*Daily Mail* (UK)

"A real tour de force."

—*The Independent* (UK)

"Incredible creative power and intense imagination . . . *The Dovekeepers* shows just how far and deep historical fiction can go."

—*The Observer* (UK)

ALSO BY ALICE HOFFMAN

The Museum of Extraordinary Things
The Red Garden
The Story Sisters
The Third Angel
Skylight Confessions
The Ice Queen
Blackbird House
The Probable Future
Blue Diary
The River King
Local Girls
Here on Earth
Practical Magic
Second Nature
Turtle Moon
Seventh Heaven
At Risk
Illumination Night
Fortune's Daughter
White Horses
Angel Landing
The Drowning Season
Property Of

YOUNG ADULT NOVELS

Green Heart: Green Angel & Green Witch
Green Witch
Incantation
The Foretelling
Green Angel
Water Tales: Aquamarine & Indigo
Indigo
Aquamarine

NONFICTION

Survival Lessons

The Dovekeepers

A Novel

ALICE HOFFMAN

SCRIBNER

New York London Toronto Sydney New Delhi

Scribner
A Division of Simon & Schuster, Inc.
1230 Avenue of the Americas
New York, NY 10020

This Scribner trade paperback edition March 2015

Manufactured in the United States of America

1 3 5 7 9 10 8 6 4 2

Library of Congress Control Number: 2011018099

ISBN 978-1-4767-9038-1 (pbk)
ISBN 978-1-4516-1749-8 (ebook)

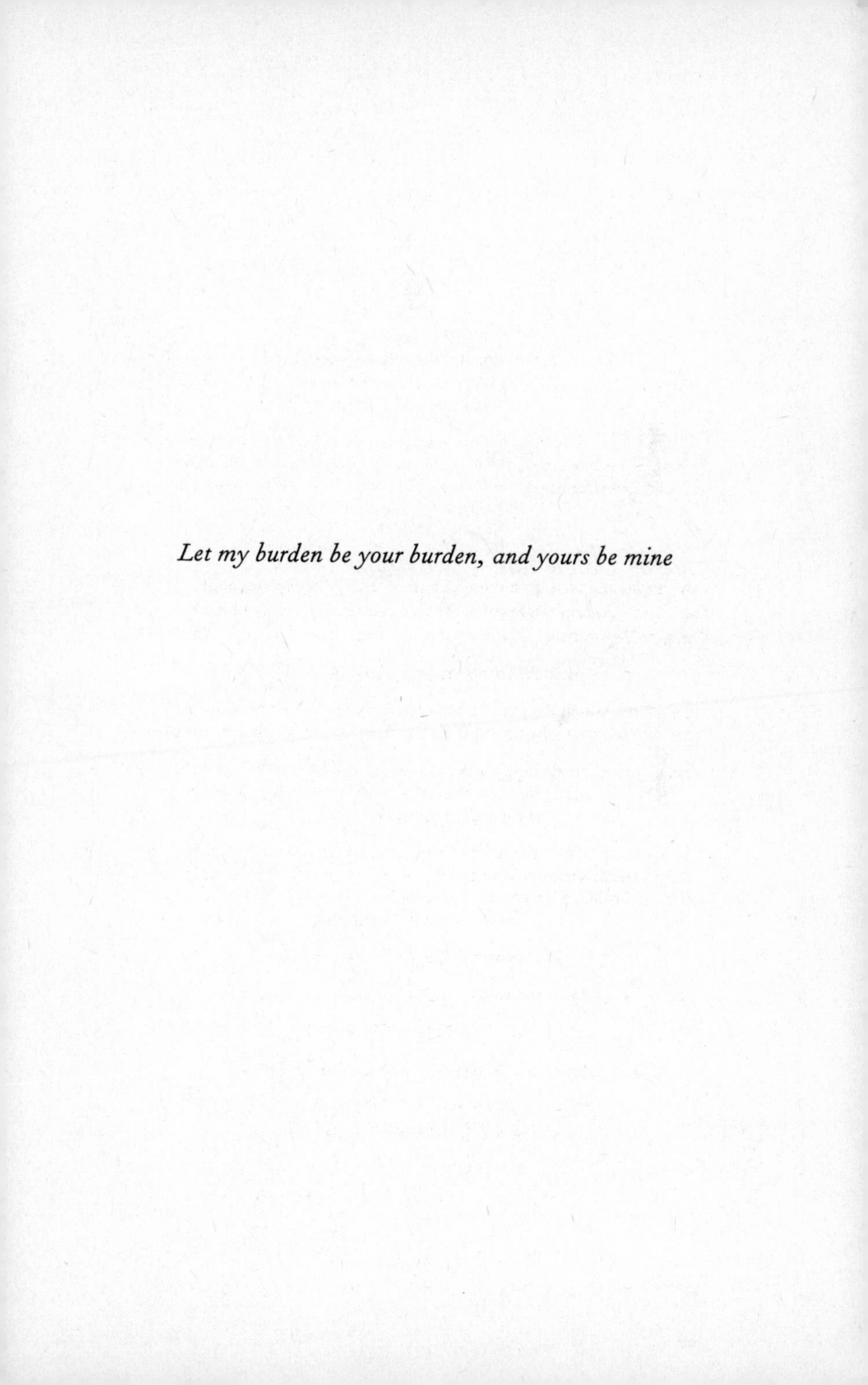

Let my burden be your burden, and yours be mine

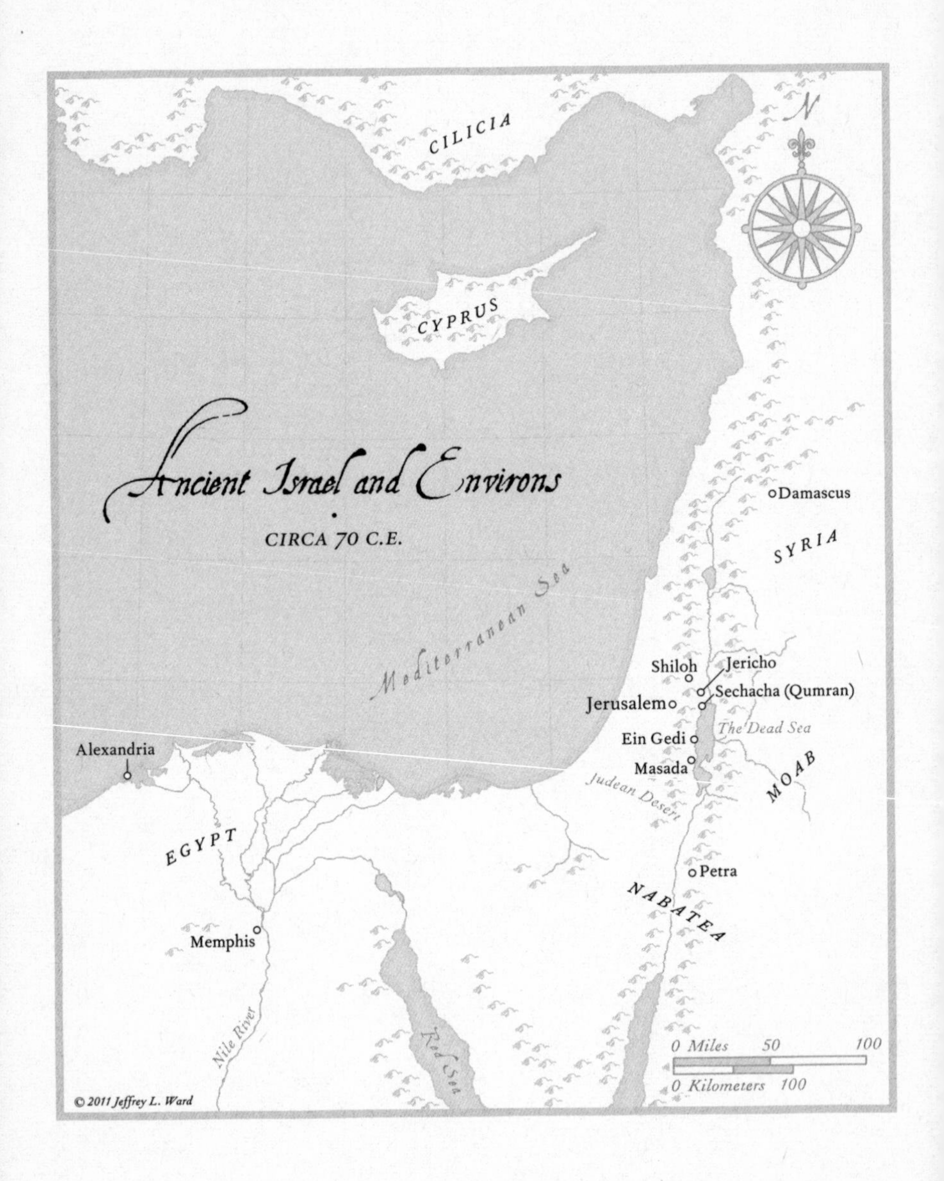
Ancient Israel and Environs
CIRCA 70 C.E.
CILICIA
CYPRUS
N
Mediterranean Sea
Damascus
SYRIA
Shiloh
Jericho
Sechacha (Qumran)
Jerusalem
The Dead Sea
Ein Gedi
Masada
MOAB
Judean Desert
Alexandria
EGYPT
Petra
NABATEA
Memphis
Nile River
Red Sea
0 Miles 50 100
0 Kilometers 100
© 2011 Jeffrey L. Ward

Part One

Summer 70 C.E.

The Assassin's Daughter

We came like doves across the desert. In a time when there was nothing but death, we were grateful for anything, and most grateful of all when we awoke to another day.

We had been wandering for so long I forgot what it was like to live within walls or sleep through the night. In that time I lost all I might have possessed if Jerusalem had not fallen: a husband, a family, a future of my own. My girlhood disappeared in the desert. The person I'd once been vanished as I wrapped myself in white when the dust rose into clouds. We were nomads, leaving behind beds and belongings, rugs and brass pots. Now our house was the house of the desert, black at night, brutally white at noon.

They say the truest beauty is in the harshest land and that God can be found there by those with open eyes. But my eyes were closed against the shifting winds that can blind a person in an instant. Breathing itself was a miracle when the storms came whirling across the earth. The voice that arises out of the silence is something no one can imagine until it is heard. It roars when it speaks, it lies to you and convinces you, it steals from you and leaves you without a single word of comfort. Comfort cannot exist in such a place. What is brutal survives. What is cunning lives until morning.

My skin was sunburned, my hands raw. I gave in to the desert, bowing to its mighty voice. Everywhere I walked my fate walked with me, sewn to my feet with red thread. All that will ever be has already been written long before it happens. There is nothing we can do to stop it. I couldn't run in the other direction. The roads from Jerusalem led to only three places: to Rome, or to the sea, or to the desert. My people had become wanderers, as they had been at the beginning of time, cast out yet again.

I followed my father out of the city because I had no choice.

None of us did, if the truth be told.

I DON'T KNOW how it began, but I know how it ended. It occurred in the month of *Av*, the sign for which is *Arieh*, the lion. It is a month that signifies destruction for our people, a season when the stones in the desert are so hot you cannot touch them without burning your fingers, when fruit withers on the trees before it ripens and the seeds inside shake like a rattle, when the sky is white and rain will not fall. The first Temple had been destroyed in that month. Tools signified weapons and could not be used in constructing the holiest of holy places; therefore the great warrior king David had been prohibited from building the Temple because he had known the evils of war. Instead, the honor fell to his son King Solomon, who called upon the *shamir*, a worm who could cut through stone, thereby creating glory to God without the use of metal tools.

The Temple was built as God had decreed it should be, free from bloodshed and war. Its nine gates were covered with silver and gold. There, in the most holy of places, was the Ark that stored our people's covenant with God, a chest made of the finest acacia wood, decorated with two golden cherubs. But despite its magnificence, the first Temple was destroyed, our people exiled to Babylonia. They had returned after seventy years to rebuild in the same place, where Abraham had been willing to offer his son Isaac as a sacrifice to the Almighty, where the world had first been created.

The second Temple had stood for hundreds of years as the dwelling place of God's word, the center of creation in the center of Jerusalem, though the Ark itself had disappeared, perhaps in Babylonia. But now times of bloodshed were upon us once more. The Romans wanted all that we had. They came to us as they swarmed upon so many lands with their immense legions, wanting not just to conquer but to humiliate, claiming not just our land and our gold but our humanity.

As for me, I expected disaster, nothing more. I had known its embrace before I had breath or sight. I was the second child, a year younger than my brother, Amram, but unlike him entirely, cursed by the burden of my first breath. My mother died before I was born. In that moment the map of my life arose upon my skin in a burst of red marks, speckles that, when followed, one to the other, have led me to my destiny.

I can remember the instant when I entered the world, the great calm that was suddenly broken, the heat of my own pulse beneath my skin. I was taken from my mother's womb, cut out with a sharp knife. I am convinced I heard my father's roar of grief, the only sound to break the terrible silence of one who is born from death. I myself did not cry or wail. People took note of that. The midwives whispered to one another, convinced I was either blessed or cursed. My silence was not my only unusual aspect, nor were the russet flecks that emerged upon my skin an hour after my birth. It was my hair, the deep bloodred color of it, a thick cap growing, as if I already knew this world and had been here before.

They said my eyes were open, the mark of one set apart. That was to be expected of a child born of a dead woman, for I was touched by *Mal'ach ha-Mavet*, the Angel of Death, before I was born in the month of *Av*, on the *Tisha B'Av*, the ninth day, under the sign of the lion. I always knew a lion would be waiting for me. I had dreamed of such creatures ever since I could remember. In my dreams I fed the lion from my hand. In return he took my whole hand into his mouth and ate me alive.

When I left childhood, I made certain to cover my head; even when I was in my father's courtyard I kept to myself. On those rare occasions when I accompanied our cook to the market, I saw other young women enjoying themselves and I was jealous of even the plainest among them. Their lives were full, whereas I could think only of all I did not have. They chirped merrily about their futures as brides as they lingered at the well or gathered in the Street of the Bakers surrounded by their mothers and aunts. I wanted to snap at them but said nothing. How could I speak of my envy when there were things I wanted even more than a husband or a child or a home of my own?

I wished for a night without dreams, a world without lions, a year without *Av*, that bitter, red month.

WE LEFT the city when the second Temple was set in ruins, venturing forth into the Valley of Thorns. For months the Romans had defiled the Temple, crucifying our people inside its sacred walls, stripping the gold from the entranceways and the porticoes. It was here that Jews from all over creation traveled to offer sacrifices before the holiest site, with thousands arriving at the time of the Feast of Unleavened Bread, all yearning to glimpse the gold walls of the dwelling place of God's word.

When the Romans attacked the third wall, our people were forced to flee from that part of the Temple. The legion then brought down the second wall. Still it was not enough. The great Titus, military leader of all Judea, went on to construct four siege ramps. Our people destroyed these, with fire and stones, but the Romans' assault of the Temple walls had weakened our defenses. Not long afterward a breach was accomplished. The soldiers entered the maze of walls that surrounded our holiest site, running like rats, their shields lifted high, their white tunics burning with blood. The holy Temple was being destroyed at their hands. Once this happened, the city would fall as well, it would be forced to follow, sinking to its knees like a common captive, for without the Temple there would be no *lev ha-olam*, no heart of the world, and nothing left to fight for.

The desire for Jerusalem was a fire that could not be quenched. There was a spark inside that holiest of holy places that made people want to possess it, and what men yearn for they often destroy. At night the walls that had been meant to last an eternity groaned and shook. The more the Romans arrested us for crimes against their rule the more we fought among ourselves, unable to decide upon a single course of action. Perhaps because we knew we couldn't win against their might we turned on each other, riven by petty jealousies, split apart by treachery, our lives a dark tangle of fear.

Victims often attack one another, they become chickens in a pen, bickering, frenzied. We did the same. Not only were our people besieged by the Romans but they were at war with each other. The priests were deferential, siding with Rome, and those who opposed them were said to be robbers and thugs, my father and his friends among them. Taxes were so high the poor could no longer feed their children, while those who allied themselves with Rome had prospered and grown rich. People gave testimony against their own neighbors; they stole from each other and locked their doors to those in need. The more suspicious we were of each other, the more we were defeated, split into feuding mobs when in fact we were one, the sons and daughters of the kingdom of Israel, believers in *Adonai*.

*

IN THE MONTHS before the Temple fell, there had been chaos as we labored against our enemies. We made every effort to win this war, but as God created life, so did He create destruction. Now in the furious red month of *Av*, swollen bodies filled the *kidron*, the deep ravine that separated the city from the glimmering Mount of Olives. The blood of men and beasts formed dark lakes in our most sacred places. The heat was mysterious and unrelenting, as if the wickedness of earth reflected back to us, a mirror of our sins. Inside the most secret rooms of the Temple, gold melted and pooled; it disappeared, stolen from the most holy of places, never to be seen again.

Not a single breeze stirred. The temperature had risen with the disorder, from the ground up, and the bricks that paved the Roman roads were so hot they burned people's feet as the desperate searched for safe havens—a stable, an abandoned chamber, even the cool stone space within a baker's oven. The soldiers of the Tenth Legion, who followed the sign of the boar, planted their banners above the ruins of the Temple with full knowledge this was an affront to us, for it threw in our faces an animal we found impure. The soldiers were like wild boars themselves, reckless, vicious. They were coursing throughout the countryside, killing white cockerels outside synagogues, meeting places which served as *bet kenesset* and *bet tefilliah*, houses of both assembly and prayer, as an insult and a curse. The blood of a rooster made our houses of worship unclean. Women scoured the steps with lye soap, wailing as they did so. We were defiled no matter how they might scrub or how much water they might pour onto the stones.

With each violation we understood the legion's warning: *What we do to the rooster, we can do to you.*

ONE EVENING a star resembling a sword arose over the city. It could be spied night after night, steadfastly brilliant in the east. People trembled, certain it was an omen, waiting for what was to come. Soon afterward the eastern gate of the Temple opened of its own accord. Crowds gathered, terrified, convinced this occurrence would allow disaster to walk inside. Gates do not open if there is no reason. Swords do not rise in the sky if peace is to come. Our neighbors began to trade any small treasures they had, jostling through the streets, determined to escape with what little they possessed. They gathered their children and began to flee Jerusalem, hoping to reach Babylon or Alexandria, longing for Zion even as they departed.

In the ditches that filled with rainwater during times of sudden flooding, there was soon a river of blood running down from the Temple. The blood cried and wept and cursed, for its victims did not give up their lives easily. The soldiers killed the rebels first, then they murdered haphazardly. Whoever was unfortunate enough to pass by was caught in their net. People were torn from their families, herded off streets. There came the evening known as the Plague upon Innocence. Any illusion that our prayers would be answered vanished. How many among us lost our faith on this night? How many turned away from what our people had always believed? A boy of ten had been taken in irons, then crucified because he had refused to bow down to the soldiers. This boy had been afflicted with deafness and had not even heard the command, but no one cared about such things anymore. A world of hate had settled upon us.

The sin of this boy's death rose like a cloud, evident to us all. Afterward, twenty thousand people panicked in the streets, trampling each other in a frenzy, forsaking their dignity as they flocked onto the roads.

By the time morning had broken, nearly all had abandoned Jerusalem.

*

AS FOR ME, my world was over before the Temple began to burn, before stone dust covered the alleyways. Long before the Temple fell, I had lost my faith. I was nothing to my father, abandoned by him from the moment I was born. I would have been neglected completely, but my mother's family insisted a nursemaid be hired. A young servant girl from Alexandria came to care for me, but when she sang lullabies, my father, the fearsome Yosef bar Elhanan, told her to be quiet. When she fed me, he insisted I had eaten enough.

I was little more than a toddler when my father took me aside to tell me the truth of my birth. I wept to discover the circumstances and took on the burden of my entrance into this life. My name was Yael, and it was the first thing about myself I learned to despise. This had been my mother's name as well. Every time it was spoken it only served to remind my father that the occasion of my arrival in this world had stolen his wife.

"What does that make you?" he asked bitterly.

I didn't have an answer, but I saw myself reflected in his eyes. I was a murderer, worthy of his indignation and wrath.

The girl hired to care for me was soon enough sent away, taking with her all consolation and solace. I knew what awaited me upon her departure, the stunted life of a motherless child. I sobbed and held on to her skirts on the day she left us, desperate for her warm embrace. My brother, Amram, told me not to cry; we had each other. The servant girl gave me a pomegranate for luck before she gently unwound her skirts from my grasp. She was young enough to be my sister, but she had been like a mother to me and had given me the only tenderness I'd known.

I gave my gift of the pomegranate to my brother, having already decided to always place him first. But that was not the only reason. I was already full from my portion of sorrow.

*

AS I GREW, I was quiet and well behaved. I asked for nothing, and that was exactly what I received. If I was clever, I tried not to show it. If I was injured, I kept my wounds to myself. I turned away whenever I saw other girls with their fathers, for mine did not wish to be seen with me. He did not speak to me or take me onto his lap. He cared only for my brother, his love for Amram evident at every turn. At dinner they sat together while I was left in the hall, where I slept. There were scorpions secluded in the corners that soon grew used to me. I watched them, fearing them but also admiring how they lay in wait for their prey on the cool stones without ever revealing themselves. I kept my sense of shame deep inside, much the way the scorpion hid its craving. In that we were alike.

All the same, I was human. I longed for a lock of my mother's hair so I might know its color. In that hallway I often wept for the comfort of her arms.

"Do you think I feel sorry for you?" my father demanded one day when he'd had enough of my wailing. "You probably killed her with your crying. You caused a flood and drowned her from the inside."

I had never spoken back before, but I leapt up then. The thought that I might have drowned my mother with my own tears was too much to endure. My chest and throat burned hot. For that instant I didn't care that the man before me was Yosef bar Elhanan and I was nothing.

"I wasn't the one at fault," I declared.

I saw a strange expression cross my father's face. He took a step back.

"Are you saying I am the cause?" he remarked, throwing up his hands as though to protect himself from a curse.

I didn't answer, but after he stormed out, I realized that we did indeed have something in common, more so than the scorpion and I, even if my father never spoke to me or called me by name. We had killed my mother together. And yet he wanted me to carry the blame alone. If that was what he wanted, then I would take on the mantle of guilt, for I was a dutiful daughter. But I would not weep again. Nothing could cause me to break this vow. When a wasp bit me and a red welt rose on my arm, I willed myself to be still and not feel its pain. My brother came running to make certain I hadn't been harmed. He called me by the secret name he'd given me when we were little more than babies, Yaya. I loved to hear him call me that, for the pet name reminded me of the lullabies of my nursemaid and a time before I knew I'd brought ruin to my family.

I burned from the sting of the wasp but insisted I was fine. When I looked up, I saw the glimmer of tears in Amram's eyes. Anyone would have thought he'd been the one who'd been wounded. He felt pain more easily than I and was far more sensitive. Sometimes I sang to him when he couldn't fall asleep, offering the lullabies from Alexandria whose words I remembered, as if I'd once had another life.

ALL THE WHILE I was growing up I wondered what it might be like to have a father who wouldn't turn away from the sight of me, one who told me I was beautiful, even though my hair flamed a strange red color and my skin was sprinkled with earth-toned flecks as though I'd been splattered with mud. I'd heard my father say to another man that these marks were specks of my mother's blood. Afterward, I tried to pluck them out with my fingers, drawing blood from my own flesh, but my brother stopped me when he discovered the red-rimmed pockmarks on my arms and legs. He assured me the freckles were bits of ash that had fallen from the stars in the sky. Because of this I would always shine in the darkness. He would always be able to find me, no matter how far he might travel.

When I became a woman, I had no mother to tell me what to do with the blood that came with the moon or escort me to the *mikvah*, the ritual bath that would have cleansed me with a total immersion into purity. The first time I bled I thought I was dying until an old woman who was my neighbor took pity on me and told me the truth about women's monthly cycles. I lowered my eyes as she spoke, shamed to be told such intimate details by a stranger, not quite believing her, wondering why our God would cause me to become unclean. Even now I think I might have been right to tremble in fear on the day that I first bled. Perhaps my becoming a woman was the end for me, for I had been born in blood and deserved to be taken from life in the same way.

I didn't bother to ring my eyes with kohl or rub pomegranate oil onto my wrists. Flirtation was not something I practiced, nor did I think myself attractive. I didn't perfume my hair but instead wound the plaits at the nape of my neck, then covered my head with a woolen shawl of the plainest fabric I could find. My father addressed me only when he summoned me to bring his meal or wash his garments. By then I had begun to realize what it was that he did when he slipped out to meet with his cohorts at night. He often wrapped a pale gray cloak around his shoulders, one that was said to have been woven from the strands of a spider's web. I had touched the hem of the garment once. It was both sinister and beautiful, granting its wearer the ability to conceal himself. When my father went out, he disappeared, for he had the power to vanish while he was still before you.

I'd heard him called an assassin by our neighbors. I frowned and didn't believe this, but the more I studied his comings and goings, the more I knew it to be true. He was part of a secret group, men who carried the curled dagger of the *Sicarii*, Zealots who hid sharp knives in their cloaks which they used to punish those who refused to fight Rome, especially the priests who accepted the legion's sacrifices and their favor at the Temple. The assassins were ruthless, even I knew that. No one was safe from their wrath; other Zealots disowned them, objecting to their brutal methods. It was said that the *Sicarii* had taken the fight against Jews who bowed to Rome too far, and that *Adonai,* our great God, would never condone murder, especially of brother against brother. But the Jews were a divided brotherhood, already at odds in practice if not in prayer. Those who belonged to the *Sicarii* laughed at the notion that God desired anything other than for all men to be free. The price was of no consequence. Their goal was one ruler alone, no emperors, no kings, only the King of Creation. He alone would rule when they were done with their work on earth.

MY FATHER had been an assassin for so long that the men he had killed were like leaves on a willow tree, too many to count. Because he possessed a skill that few men had and claimed the power of invisibility, he could slip into a room as a shadow might, dispatching his enemy before his victim was even aware that a window had been opened or a door had closed.

To my sorrow, my brother followed our father's path as soon as he was old enough to become a disciple of vengeance. Amram was dangerously susceptible to their violent ways, for in his purity he saw the world as either good or evil with no twilight space in between. I often spied them huddled together, my father speaking in my brother's ear, teaching him the rules of murder. One day as I gathered Amram's tunics and cloak to wash at the well I found a dagger, already rippled with a line of crimson. I would have wept had I been able, but I had forsaken tears. I would not drown another as I had drowned my own mother, from the inside out.

Still, I went in search of my brother, finding him in the market with his friends. Women alone were not often seen among the men who came to these narrow passageways; those who had no choice but to go out unaccompanied rushed to the Street of the Bakers or to the stalls that offered pottery and jugs made from Jerusalem clay, then, just as quickly, rushed home. I wore a veil and my cloak clasped tightly. There were *zonnoth* in the market, women who sold themselves for men's pleasure and did not cover their arms or their hair. One mocked me as I ran past, her sullen face breaking into a grin when she spied me dashing through the alleyway. *You think you're any different than we are?* she called. *You're only a woman, as we are.*

I pulled my brother away from his friends so that we might stand beneath a flame tree. The red flowers gave off the scent of fire, and I thought this was an omen, that my brother would know fire. I worried over what would happen to him when night came and the *Sicarii* gathered under cedars where they made their plans. I begged him to renounce the violent ways he'd taken up, but my brother, young as he was, burned for justice and a new order where all men were equal.

"I can't reconsider my faith, Yaya."

"Then consider your life" was my answer.

To tease me, Amram clucked like a chicken, strutting, his lean, strong body hunched over as he flapped imaginary wings. "Do you want me to stay home in the henhouse, where you can lock me inside and make sure I'm safe?"

I laughed despite my fears. My brother was brave and beautiful. No wonder my father favored him. His hair was golden, his eyes dark but flecked with light. I saw now that the child I had once mothered had become a man, one who was pure in his intentions. I could do little more than object to the path that he chose. Still I was determined to act on his behalf. When my brother rejoined his friends, I went on through the market, making my way deep within the twisting streets, at last turning in to an alley that was cobbled with dusty, dun-colored bricks. I'd heard it was possible to buy good fortune nearby. There was a mysterious shop spoken about in whispers by the neighborhood women. They usually stopped their discussion when I came near, but I'd been curious and had overheard that if a person followed the scrawled image of an eye inside a circle she would be led to a place of medicines and spells. I took the path of the eye until I came to the house of *keshaphim*, the breed of magic practiced by women, always pursued in secret.

When I knocked on the door, an old woman came to study me. Annoyed by my presence, she asked why I'd come. As soon as I hesitated, she began to close the door against me, grumbling.

"I don't have time for someone who doesn't know what she wants," she muttered.

"Protection for my brother," I managed to say, too unnerved to reveal any more.

At the Temple there was the magic of the priests, holy men who were anointed by prayer, chosen to give sacrifices and attempt miracles and perform exorcisms, driving out the evil that can often possess men. In the streets there was the magic of the *minim*, who were looked down upon by the priests, called charlatans and impostors by some, yet who were still respected by many. Houses of *keshaphim*, however, were considered to engage in the foulest sort of magic, women's work, evil, vengeful, practiced by those who were denounced as witches. But the *min* who performed curses and spells would have never spoken to a girl such as I if I had no silver to hand over and no father or brother to recommend me. And had I gone to the priests for an amulet, they would have denied me, for I was the daughter of one who opposed them. Even I knew I didn't deserve their favor.

The room behind the old woman was unlit, but I glimpsed herbs and plants draped from the ceiling on lengths of rope. I recognized rue and myrtle and the dried yellow apples of the mandrake, what is called *yavrucha*, an herb that is both aphrodisiac and antidemonic in nature, poisonous and powerful. I thought I heard the sound of a goat, a pet witches are said to have, from inside the dim chamber.

"Before you waste my time, do you have shekels enough for protection?" the old woman asked.

I shook my head. I had no coins, but I'd brought a precious hand mirror with me. It had belonged to my mother and was beautifully crafted, made of bronze and silver and gold, set with a chunk of deep blue lapis. It was the one thing I had of any value. The ancient woman examined it and then, satisfied, took my offering and went inside. After she shut the door, I heard the clatter of a lock. For a moment I wondered if she had disappeared for good, if perhaps I'd never see her or my mirror again, but she came back outside and told me to open my hand.

"You're sure you don't want this charm for yourself?" she cautioned, insisting there was only one like it in all the world. "You might need protection in this life."

I shook my head, and as I did my plain woolen veil fell. When the old woman saw the scarlet color of my hair, she backed away as though she'd discovered a demon at her door.

"It's good you don't want it," she said. "It wouldn't work for you. You need a token that's far more powerful."

I snapped up the charm, then turned and started away. I was surprised when she called for me to wait.

"You don't ask why?" The market woman was signaling to me, urging me to return, but I refused. "You don't want to know what I see for you, my sister? I can tell you what you will become."

"I know what I am." I was the child born of a dead woman, the one who couldn't bear to look at her own face. I was immensely glad to be rid of that mirror. "I don't need you to tell me," I called to the witch in the alleyway.

I WENT HOME and delivered the gift to my brother; it was a thin silver amulet to wear around his neck, the medallion imprinted with the image of Solomon fighting a demon prostrate before him on the ground. On the back of the charm, *The Seal of God* had been written in Greek along with the symbol of a key, to signify the key Moses had possessed that had unlocked God's protection. So, too, would this amulet protect my brother in the blood-soaked future he was set upon.

Amram was delighted with the token. He claimed I had the ability to know his mind, for he had been praying for guidance and wisdom, the smallest portion of that which God had once granted to Solomon. I kept from him that it was the woman who dabbled in magic who had known what he'd desired, not I.

The demons, my brother pledged, must never win. That was the mission of the *Sicarii,* and they could not fail. He opened his heart, and when he spoke, I believed in him. Amram had a way of convincing a listener to accept the world with his vision, making it possible to see through his eyes. When I gazed upon my brother, all that was before me was the kingdom of Zion and our people free at last.

In very little time, my brother surpassed my father at their dark task. He was the best not by chance but by choice. He learned the ways of the assassin from my father and also from a man named Jachim ben Simon, who had become his teacher. Ben Simon was said to know death better than most and was revered for his use of a double-edged knife made of silver. Under his tutelage, Amram was determined to go forward with his skill, to rise above all others. My brother was devoted, practicing with the intensity of a master craftsman. But as he did so, his moods and tempers changed before my eyes. I watched the boy I knew disappear and a cold, fearless assassin take his place. From our father he learned to slip through the night unseen and climb towers using a single strand of rope wound around his waist. He practiced silence, not speaking for days on end, becoming so still that even the mice in our garden failed to notice him. He went barefoot to ensure there was no sound when he approached, only the suddenness of the blade, taught by Ben Simon, taken even further by Amram's own natural grace.

Before long, my brother was called upon for the most dangerous assignments, all of which carried the chill of death. Although he hadn't the cloak that was said to grant invisibility, his great gift was his ability to disguise himself. He dressed as a priest or as a poor man, hiding himself in borrowed garments, gaining access to whomever was considered to be a traitor. He could make himself appear ancient, his face transformed by etched lines of charcoal, or seem a mere boy, eyes shining. People whispered that he was invincible, and it was soon rumored that the amulet of Solomon around his neck protected him from evil. His friends adored him and called him Hol, the name of the phoenix. They vowed that he resembled this mystical bird that arose from fire and ash; he escaped from every attempt the officials made to catch and murder him.

Because of my father and brother, other men were afraid to speak to me. The *Sicariis'* deeds were mysterious, but there were some secrets everyone knew, especially in Jerusalem. The men of my family were pointed to in the street, whispered about, both revered and despised. No wonder no one would have me as his wife, not even the brute who drove donkeys to the market. I was a young woman, but I was treated like a beggar, scorned, my reputation tarnished. It was only when men saw the unusual color of my hair that I noticed their curiosity and, often, their desire. Their gazes were disconcertingly sexual, obvious even to one as inexperienced as I. I knew I would enter their dreams when they couldn't control what they yearned for. But a dream is worthless in the world. What good did their desire do for me? In the light of the day, they walked right by. I wanted to shout out *Take me* to every man who passed by. *Rescue me from what has happened, from the pillar of bitter salt I have become, from the crime I committed before I was born, from the men of my house, who lurk outside the Temple seeking only revenge. Take me to your bed, your house, your city.*

I removed my veils in public places. I did not bother to braid my hair but let it shine, seeking salvation from my loneliness.

Still they all turned away, unable to see me, for I was no more than red air swirling past them, invisible to their eyes.

BEFORE LONG there were posters with my brother's likeness set upon the walls. The Romans would pay for information, more if he was captured, even more if he was found guilty of his crimes and crucified. Amram no longer came home and instead was resigned to moving around the city in the dark; he belonged to dreams rather than to the routine of our daily lives. My father and I were the only occupants in our house. Though we didn't speak to each other, we both looked out into the darkness as it began to fall. We knew that was where Amram was. Once again we shared something. We could not hear of a capture without wincing. We showed each other flashes of raw emotion every time the door rattled. But it was never him, only the wind.

One terrible night it was not the wind but rather a troop of soldiers at the door. My father shrugged when Amram's name was brought up; he insisted he had no son. It was his bad fortune to have only one child, a worthless daughter.

When even Amram's friends, those who had praised him as the unconquerable phoenix, dared not help him, my brother knew his life in Jerusalem was over. He had no choice but to escape. There were fortresses in the desert our people had commandeered. If he could reach one, he might be safe. Before he left, he took the risk to come and say good-bye. After he and my father embraced, Amram motioned me aside. He had brought a farewell gift. A blue scarf. It was far too beautiful for me, more than I deserved, yet he insisted I take it.

"There are worms that spend their lifetimes spinning such threads, and now you refuse to honor their destiny?"

"No worm made this." I laughed to think of such heavenly fabric being spun by insects. It was the opposite of my father's spider-made cloak, which had been woven of fabric so pale it faded into air. This blue silk announced itself with a splash of unexpected color.

Amram vowed it was true, insisting that while the worms had spun their silk in the boughs of mulberry trees, they had been devoted to me, as he was. Upon completing their task, each worm had turned into a blue butterfly, arising into the heavens once its work on earth was done.

I looped the scarf over my hair. I would think of heaven every time I wore it and of my brother, who was so steadfast in his faith. I stood at the gate of our house, remembering that he had said the freckles on my skin were like stars. Like the stars above they would lead him to find me again.

THERE WERE FEW of us left in the city. We rummaged through ruins, cautious, in fear for our lives. At night we heard the screams of those who were taken to the Temple, captured by soldiers prowling the alleyways in search of anyone of our faith. The members of the legion drank wormwood, a dangerous, nearly lethal brew which made them vicious as well as drunk. No woman was safe. No man's life was his own. Whoever was able had fled to Alexandria or Cyprus, but my father insisted we stay. He had more work to do, and that work was the knife that he carried. In time, Jerusalem would awake, and like a lion it would free itself from the nets of slavery. *Teeth and claws*, I heard him say, *that is what our future will bring*. But I knew what he really meant was flesh and bones.

I knew from my dreams what it meant to come face-to-face with a lion.

*

SMOKE DRIFTED from fires set throughout the city, and the murk acted as a screen so that our people could escape from the marauding soldiers. I could smell olive wood, burning willow. Scorched remnants ignited palm-thatched roofs and haystacks. On the pallet where I slept, in our small house, I covered my head and wished I lived in another place and time. I wished I had never been born.

One afternoon while I was at the market searching the nearly empty bins of the venders for peas and beans for our meager supper, the Romans appropriated our home. I stood watching from a hidden place in my neighbors' abandoned courtyard, for their house had been ruined months earlier. The soldiers ransacked our house before they burned it to the ground and our belongings were strewn in the chalky dirt. Sparks flew up like white moths, but when they fell down upon the earth, they smoldered bright crimson, like the petals on the flame trees.

If I had little before, I had close to nothing now. I went through the rubble and took only what could fit in my two hands, a small griddle to cook flatbread, a lamp made of white Jerusalem clay to burn oil on the Sabbath, my father's prayer shawl, singed at the fringes on the four corners, his leather flask, a packet of salt that would taste of smoke when used in cooking. I waited for my father, hidden behind a wall. My skin was dusky, and there were ashes in my hair. If my father didn't come back, if he had been murdered or had fled without telling me, I thought I might simply stay behind the wall, planted there like a flame tree.

Finally my father appeared, slinking through the twilight, wearing the cloak that allowed him to make his way without being detained. When he saw the prayer shawl in my hands, he knew the time to flee had come. I wondered if he would leave me there to be the beggar woman I'd always feared I might become, to scrounge through the garbage. But he motioned for me to follow as another man might signal a dog. I resolved to do as I was told and trudged after him. Perhaps our blood relation meant something to him after all, or perhaps he took me with him because he feared how my mother in the World-to-Come might respond if he abandoned me there in the street. Or he may have simply remembered it was he who had gotten her with child, and that I'd been correct to consider him a partner in my crime. If my tears had drowned her from the inside out, he was the one who had ushered my life into hers.

AT NIGHT we went from house to house, pleading to be let in. There were fewer and fewer of our people in the city every day—they had fled or were in hiding—and it became difficult for us to find those willing to help. I was a dog and nothing more, asking no questions, unable to think for myself. I hovered in the shadows as people turned us away. Even those who believed in my father's politics were wary, unwilling to leave themselves at risk. Only a few left their doors open, and even they made sure to look the other way and not greet us with an embrace. Often we slept on straw pallets, grateful for a shelter meant for goats. We shared the animals' chamber and slept restlessly with the sound of beasts breathing beside us. I had the same dream again and again. In my dream there was a lion sleeping in the sun, one I dared not wake. One night I dreamed that the lion was eaten whole by a snake that devoured everything in its path. I stood barefoot in my dream, on a stretch of rocky earth that was so blindingly white I couldn't open my eyes. I felt compassion for this wild beast, the king of the desert, for in my dreams he had given in to the snake without a fight. He had looked at me, beseeching me, staring into my eyes.

That night my father shook me awake. My feet were bleeding on the rocks in my dream. Before me there was the coiling black viper of the desert that wraps itself around its prey and refuses to let go. He had devoured the lion and now had come for me. In my dream I offered the scaled beast almonds and grapes, but it had a taste for human flesh. I begged for it to release me as I mourned for the lion. I yearned for that beast in the way that a person yearns for her own destiny. What happens is already written, and the lion had been written beside my name.

"We must go and not look back," my father said when he woke me.

If I wasn't quick enough, my father would doubtless leave me behind. I didn't argue, though I felt a tide of dread in that dark chamber. There was blood on the assassin's robe, and his eyes were shining. Something had happened, but I dared not ask what it was. I rose from my pallet on the floor, ready in an instant. I gathered the belongings I had carried with me from house to house. The blue scarf my brother had given to me, the griddle and lamp I had found in the rubble of our home. We left with another family, that of the assassin Jachim ben Simon, the man who had apprenticed my brother and taught him how to kill with the curved, double-edged knife. This assassin was known to be terrifying when he struck his enemy, a whirlwind who sought only vengeance. He had been a priest once, the oldest son of a family of priests, and had spent his youth in study and prayer. But he'd seen how gold lined the pockets of only a few, how the poor were trod upon and used and enslaved. He'd seen his own father agree to make offerings and sacrifices on behalf of the Romans in our Temple on the Day of Atonement, insisting that Roman sins could be laid upon our altars and be forgiven by our God.

He'd taken up the knife of the *Sicarii* and excelled at his work. He was a truly dangerous man, all sinew and muscle. I saw his big, distinctive head and cast my eyes down, not wanting to glimpse a man who was so feared. His wife was named Sia, his young sons Nehimiah and Oren. I heard the wife crying as she clutched her sons. Their family had little more than we did, but they did have a donkey, which Ben Simon's wife and sons rode upon. I walked behind them, like a woman in disgrace. In truth, I was used to being an outcast, more comfortable on my own. Jachim ben Simon looked over his shoulder once and seemed startled, as if he'd forgotten about me and now spied a wraith.

As we made our way out of Jerusalem, I was already trying to decipher who among us would die and who would live, for surely we would not all survive. Without brute strength, even our escape would be difficult. The streets were mayhem. All Jews had been expelled from the city, and any found would be instantly murdered. That was the new edict and therefore the law. Many of the priests had plunged into the sewers, hoping to escape the city undetected. But their collusion could not help them now; they were in the realm of the rats, struggling for their lives along with the rest of us.

We could hear what sounded like a roar as the Temple was torn down. It was *Tisha B'Av,* the ninth day of the month, the day on which I'd been born. In the years to come, people would swear that six angels descended from heaven to protect the walls of the Temple so that it would not be entirely destroyed; they vowed those angels sat there and wept and are weeping there still. The Romans used battering rams that weighed one hundred tons, and more than a thousand men were needed to swing them so that they might loosen, then pull down the huge stones upon which King Herod's mark had been etched. Ropes were hoisted by hundreds of men, some of them ours, enslaved, cursing themselves for their fate and for the wretchedness of their own deeds. Stone should last forever, but on that night I came to understand that a stone was only another form of dust. Streams of holy dust loomed in the air, and every breath included remnants of the Temple, so that we inhaled that which was meant to stand throughout eternity.

Once again the fires that had been set created a smoke screen and this helped in our escape. For that we were grateful, despite the smoldering heat. The air was thick and gray. I held my scarf to my mouth and tried not to breathe in sparks. I guessed that my father had killed someone that night and that was why his robe was spattered red. I was thinking about such matters when Ben Simon's wife, Sia, came to walk beside me. She pitied me because I followed behind in the clouds of dust that had been stirred up. She was perhaps ten years older than I, with a mass of black hair set into coils. Her eyes were dark with gold flecks. She might have been beautiful had she not been the devoted wife of an assassin, worn down by fear. Assassins should not marry, I decided then, or have daughters, or allow anyone to love them.

"Would you like to ride with my sons for a while?" Ben Simon's wife suggested.

I could see she was tired, and I was used to walking. I thanked her and said no, I was happy to follow. I hoped she would leave me alone.

"I'm so glad to have you here," she blurted. "Leaving would be so much worse without another woman beside me."

I glanced at her, wondering what she wanted of me. She smiled, taking my hand, and then I understood. She wanted a friend.

I urged her to return to her sons. She should leave me to tread last, as I was invisible to most people, even without a cloak such as the one my father wore. Perhaps I had inherited that ability, or perhaps I had learned its secrets from watching my father. Either way, the Romans who searched for us would see only a swirl of dust wherever I walked.

Sia wouldn't hear of it. "You're wrong," she remarked. "You would be the first one they'd see. Your hair is so beautiful it makes me think of flame trees."

I wondered if her words were a curse, for I had been standing beside a flame tree when my brother admitted he was an assassin. It was not possible for her to know, but on those rare occasions when I dreamed of my mother, she came to me as a flame tree, and in my dreams I bowed my head before her and wept.

When I studied Sia, I could see that her intention was to be kind on a night pierced by danger and uncertainty. We walked close, drawn together by the peril around us. We were journeying through the Valley of Thorns, under a sky hung with so many stars they made me think of stones in the desert, countless, too white to look upon. They say the face of our Creator is like that, so bright that a single glance brings blindness. I kept my eyes downcast. I would have preferred to walk alone, but Sia set her pace with me, her arm linked through mine.

She confided that my father and her husband had killed an important Roman general and that was why we had made haste to flee. She herself had cleaned the blades of their knives, washing the metal in pure water, reciting a prayer as she did. She was obliged not to ask questions, and to do as her husband demanded, but she had an urge to confess that she had handled a knife streaked with human blood, a confession made to me as we trudged after the men. Her voice broke as she spoke of it.

"How will God punish me?" she murmured.

I hushed her—women were not to speak of such matters—but it was too late. Ben Simon had overheard and turned to glare at us. He was a tall, imposing man, with dark olive skin, fearsome, a deep scar etched across one side of his face. Once again I gazed at the ground in an attempt to avoid him. He called sharply for Sia to be quiet.

"Let us not speak of this," she said then. "Sometimes it's better not to know what men must do."

WHEN WE could walk no farther, we stopped at a resting place, an oasis the assassins' friends had spoken of in glowing terms. Every Zealot had a plan should disaster come, a direction in which he would run if need be. This was the first stop, a small green space where camels who had run off during the chaos had gathered. The beasts ran when we approached, kicking up dust, afraid that we would throw ropes around their necks, as unwilling to be slaves as we were. There was a citron tree growing there. The fruit of the tree is called *pri etzhadar*, the lemony *etrog* that is made into a jam. These specimens were bruised, sour without honey to sweeten the taste, but we didn't care. We were starving and thirsty. We ate in silence, wolfing down our meager supper. In the distance, we could see Jerusalem burning. The smoke rose up in a funnel cloud, then disappeared. I counted stars, so bright above us. Sia sat beside me and whispered. She insisted it was a good omen to find the citrus on the first night of our journey, and although I did not argue with her, I knew otherwise. This bitter tree was nothing more than a key to a door and that door opened into the desert.

I had overheard my father speaking with Ben Simon. We were not headed toward Alexandria, or toward Cyprus. Instead we were taking the ancient route that led toward the Salt Sea, the route of the doomed. In the month of *Av*, the birds were unable to fly where we were going, even at night. It was too hot, the air unrelenting, an oven. You could bake bread on a stone. We would roam as far into the desert as we could, for it was there my father believed we would find the Zealots and their fortresses, my brother among them.

On the night we fled, as the Temple burned and the sky was ringed with fire, there was a light breeze. This would be the coolest time we would know before we entered into the wilderness. But there was to be something more that cast me into a burning world on the night we left Jerusalem. I walked down to a well that had been abandoned long ago. There was no longer any water. That wasn't really a surprise. People often lied about water, promising pools where there were none, dreaming of water in a world composed of dust. All the same, if someone crouched on hands and knees to dig, it was possible to find mud. Drained through clenched fingers, water would well up, there for whoever was willing to sink to her knees. I wasn't too proud to do so.

Determined to get what I wanted, I managed to fill half a jug with silty water, strained first through my fingers, then through the fabric of my blue scarf. When I was done I rose, greedy with thirst. I turned away from the well, then gazed up in alarm. I didn't see the night sky filled with stars, or the fires of Jerusalem, only the other assassin, Ben Simon, who had been watching me. My arms were covered with mud, my tunic cast open. I felt myself flush with heat. I didn't understand why he had appeared out of the dark or why he stayed. He didn't even know my name. I thought he would turn away, but he stared at me for a long time, the way a man looks at a deer to gauge if it's too far away to chase, or just near enough to catch. He nodded, and then I knew. I wasn't invisible after all.

I COUNTED OFF the days in the desert by cutting my leg with a sharpened rock. Our people were not allowed to injure ourselves; that was the practice of pagans and nomads in their time of mourning. *Do not cut your bodies to mourn for the dead, nor tattoo any marks on you,* the Lord commanded us in the Fourth Book of Moses. But I heard only the voice of the desert, not the words of the Almighty. I hid the cuts beneath my shawl. In the life we led, pain was something to get used to, to inure yourself against. I would rather hurt myself than be hurt by someone else, and so I took up this practice with a sense of purpose and without remorse.

It was the first time I broke our laws. After that, the rest came easily to me.

I was thrown together with Sia and her children when I would have preferred to be alone. Still, she was kind to me and I became accustomed to her. Because she was older and married, I thought she would expect me to be deferential, but instead she considered me a sister, and I grew to enjoy her company. There were days when we laughed and made our rough life into a game, even though the men threw us sullen looks. We worked well together, collecting the few greens we could find, making stews of our dwindling supply of oil and olives, dried figs and lentils. We cooked bread on the hot stones of our fire, covering the loaves with ashes so they might bake. Sometimes the men went off to hunt, bringing back an occasional partridge, which we added to our stews.

I was deeply affected by what a good mother Sia was to her sons, how uncomplaining when they clamored for her attentions. Her boys were little more than babies, and she sang them to sleep every night, determined not to relinquish all of the loving-kindness they'd known in the world we had left behind. Each time she sang I thought of the girl from Alexandria who had cared for me when I had no mother. I often fell asleep beside the children, imagining that Sia's lullabies were meant for me. My new friend had tirelessly combed out the ashes that had fallen into my hair during the burning of Jerusalem. When we found a shallow pool, we rushed into it as soon as we spied the glittering water, able to forget, however briefly, what our circumstances were, splashing each other as if we were indeed sisters.

Secretly, I continued to record my time in the desert by etching each day into my flesh. I kept to myself, but I couldn't help but be aware of Ben Simon, taking note of the scar on his face. Whenever I saw him watching me, I quickly covered my leg. I didn't want him to know who I really was, a neglected, ugly girl with callused hands. And yet something connected us, perhaps because we were both scarred. Clearly he saw me as no one else ever had. I could see his face transform as he stared at me; there was something burning and reckless in his glance. It came to be that the only time I felt alive was when he looked at me. His very presence was like bee stings, riveting my attention. I began to brood over him, wondering how he had been scarred and what dark matters he had attended to in Jerusalem. I had persistent, slow-burning thoughts of him jumbled inside my head, ones that embarrassed me and made me feel that I was a traitor, though I'd done nothing wrong.

Once, when there was a pale moon, I went to the pool where Sia and I had bathed. During my time of monthly bleeding, I had sequestered myself away as was our custom. Now it had ended and I needed to cleanse myself. In Jerusalem, we had gone to the *mikvah* to bathe. Here there was only the pool in the *nachal,* the ravine where birds came to drink in the evenings, flocks of ravens, larks, and huge griffon vultures, the strong, fearless creatures we called *nesher* that nested in the cliffs. I found that the water was fast disappearing with the rising heat of *Av*. Still, I took off my tunic and splashed myself and felt some relief. I heard a rustling in the tamarisk trees, a variety that can be found growing in the harshest of places. Quickly, I drew on my cloak, fearful that one of the leopards whose territory we had entered might be stalking me, hungry enough to consider me his prey.

There was an echo of footfalls, and I froze until they vanished. I returned to our camp, cleansed but on edge. Everyone was sleeping inside our small goatskin tent, which was fastened to the ground with bolts made of horn. Only Ben Simon was awake. He seemed restless. I flushed to think perhaps he had seen me at the pool. He called me to him, and I went, my eyes lowered.

"It's dangerous," he warned.

He had never spoken to me before. I didn't know if he meant there was danger in walking in the wilderness alone or in raising my eyes to meet his. I felt outraged that he might think he could tell me what to do, treating me as he would a child, or worse, his slave, and yet I felt a flicker of pleasure when I noticed the spiky green leaves in his hair. They were from the tamarisk that grew by the pool, a tree that lifted its boughs toward heaven in a place where nothing else could survive.

TWENTY-ONE CUTS and then the night when it happened. Afterward I wondered if I had been marking off the time until it did.

Was that what I was waiting for? Was that where my desire had led me? Perhaps I had peered into the Book of Life, which metes out fate, and while in the depth of my slumbers I had seen his name written there. Or perhaps it was only that I was an envious girl who had nothing, and was therefore willing to take what belonged to another woman, one who was my only friend.

I was building a fire to cook our meal of lentil cakes on the griddle I'd brought with me from Jerusalem. He crouched down next to me. The sky paled with heat. The larks were flying in the dim light, and great colonies of bee-eaters were calling, their brilliant blue feathers slicing through the hazy air. Jachim ben Simon was more commanding than most men and I could feel the heat of his presence beside me. He didn't look at me this time. Instead he reached down and ran his hand along my leg, lingering over the cuts I had made until my skin seemed on fire.

"You're not afraid of the things other women fear," he said.

I realized this was true. He still wasn't looking at me, but he seemed to know me, even though I was hidden inside my veils. Most women feared for the lives of their children and husbands. Their concerns were starvation, illness, demons, enslavement. I feared the lions in my dreams, half-believing I would be devoured by one of the creatures that stalked through my sleep. I was afraid an angel would be waiting for me in the desert, sent there to tell me that my life was a ladder of mistakes, that I was born a murderer, responsible for the death of my own mother before I took my first breath, that my crime was worse than that of any assassin, for I was guilty not only in the eyes of my father but in the eyes of God.

Ben Simon took his hand away, but I could still feel the heat of his touch. I felt it for days. Did that mean he was an angel, hidden among us, there to judge me? Or was he only a man who wanted to satisfy himself?

*

WE WERE nearly going blind in the white light that pierced through our tent during the most brutal hours. Travel was impossible in the heat of the day, for the winds were merciless and could cut a man to pieces. We were city people who had strayed in the wilderness, wanderers with no direction, stranded in the territory of robbers, and thieves, and holy men. Emptiness was the name of the desolate land we crossed. We saw no one. When the pool of pale water disappeared into the sand, when even the mud left behind became hard-baked and dry, there was no reason for us to stay in our camp.

We packed up our few belongings—the goatskin tent, the handheld spindles we used to spin wool, our knives and the griddle, a jar in which there was still some oil, the lamp that we burned to mark the Sabbath, though there was little enough oil to do so. We moved on, searching for water. We ventured onward beneath the inky sky in the early mornings, during hours that were less brutal, before the sun emerged from the dark. Our route led us to a well, but it was dry. It led to an orchard, but it was barren. Olive trees had withered here, their silvery bark turned to empty shells. It was said that the nomads who crossed this wilderness were often forced to kill their camels and drink hot blood when their thirst could not be contained. There was no grass, and even the herds of ibex, wild goats who were unafraid to race across the rockiest cliffs, didn't often venture into this harsh land. Only the leopards came here. Though they were mysterious and rare, we occasionally spied paw prints. These were the fastest animals in all creation, unearthly in their beauty, but they journeyed alone. Only those who lived cut off from all others of their kind would come here.

We went forward, believers with nothing to believe in. Our lips were so dry they cracked and turned white. Sia rubbed the last of the olive oil on her sons' mouths, so their lips would not bleed. The days piled up like twigs, bent and useless. At last we found a cave to shelter us from the light and wind. There was a pool of still water, murky, with a lacy film across the surface, unclean, yet we put our faces into it like dogs. The east wind, *Ruach Kadim,* came up from Edom, flaming with heat. We wound ourselves in linen scarves, thin fabric made from flax, cooler than wool, perhaps because the reeds from which this fabric was made from had grown in marshes and carried water in the thread. We veiled our faces, making sure to keep our hands over our ears. Even then we couldn't drown out the sound of the desert; the howling railed against us like a living being.

WE STAYED in the cave for days on end, too spent and parched to go on, afraid of meeting with the Roman garrison that patrolled the desert. We burned bits of the thornbushes we found to frighten away the jackals. A drift of white smoke rose from the mouth of the cave, the ash catching in our eyes and throats. The assassins hunted, but they found no game. They prayed, but there was no relief. I still cut my leg with a sharp rock. If I didn't keep track of my life, no one else would. As time passed we began to starve. Again I wondered who among us could outlast the others. Our hunger kept us rapt and exhausted. We slept so many hours I could not tell the difference between my waking life and my dreams. I dreamed of Jerusalem and of my mother and of the flame tree in the marketplace. Those images were more real to me than the foul stink of the cave. Secretly, I had begun to eat the damp earth where moisture gathered near the rocks. My skin turned dusky, and it appeared that the desert was spilling out of me, the way they say sand pours out when you stab a demon with a knife that has been blessed and cleansed in pure water.

One night my father and Ben Simon slit the donkey's throat. There are those who say animals have no spirits, but I heard the donkey scream. It had a voice like any man or woman, one that begged for breath and life. When I ran out to the cliffs, I could still hear its echo. The men said a prayer thanking God for what they had convinced themselves had been an easy death for the poor creature, for they'd used a ritual knife; then they made a fire out of a pile of twigs and roasted the meat. I could see pools of the donkey's dark blood on the hillside below our cave. The stars were above us in the sky. Some could be seen quite clearly, others were hidden in the murk of the darkness. We waited for the morning star, which we named *Cochav hashachar* and others called Venus, looking for it to break through the sky in bands of pale, shimmering light and give us one more day.

After we ate, I felt defiled. The donkey's bones simmered in a pot over the fire so that we might have food until the next Sabbath if we doled it out in scraps that we wolfed down. We were like people who had gone backward, barbarians in the desert. There were nomads who lived in this way; we saw evidence of them sometimes. They were wild men, pagans, their faces painted, their spears double-edged, their calls to each other the bleating of savages. Their lives depended on their camels, who gave them meat, and milk, and shelter when the tanned hides were stretched into tents. Their women gave birth in the sand, staining it slick and black; their dead were left on the rocks for the carrion; their men were exceedingly dangerous, for they had their own codes. No one who got in their way was spared. Some of these men had six wives, and the women were kept like donkeys, mistreated, used for bargaining.

Ben Simon had come upon the bodies of two of these wives. They were little more than children, likely not yet old enough to bleed with the moon. They had tried to run away from their circumstances and had fled as far as the desert would allow. Ben Simon discovered them when he was out hunting; they were buried beneath drifts of sand and stone, holding hands, their eyes staring, open to the World-to-Come. Both had coils of long black hair and wore the indigo-tinted scarves of their people. They had lain down to wait for death the way a bride waits for her bridegroom, the palms of their hands and the soles of their feet adorned with henna in intricate patterns of the *thania* ceremony, so that they might bring luck to the man they married. Perhaps they had been misused by their husband with no recourse or he had cast them aside. Perhaps they had run off together before the wedding ceremony and had lost their way.

I was cleaning out the cooking pot when Ben Simon signaled to me. I followed him even though we hadn't spoken since he'd warned me of danger. He brought me to see the two wives. We did not speak, or even look at each other. I wondered why he'd chosen me to share this knowledge, why he had revealed to me that when the dust rose up and the dead were before him, this fierce assassin, who had murdered so many, who had washed the blood from his hands night after night, whose face was torn in two by a ragged scar, had tears in his eyes.

We stood under the darkening sky at the hour when the earth turns deep blue. It was the time when those who wander often see mirages, swearing the rocks they walk upon have become the sea. Perhaps the two child-wives had thought themselves rescued by the sea of the dead, preferring it to the lives that they led, in which they were kept like beasts, traded like pieces of silver. I suddenly understood that Ben Simon was telling me he would never drive me to such an end. He would protect me and care for me. My fate was revealed as he tenderly buried those two sister-wives as surely as if the Book of Life had fallen open before me.

I would never want to run away from him.

EVERY NIGHT I curled up in the cave, awake long after the others had fallen asleep. I was not the only one who kept my eyes open. Jachim ben Simon came to me late one night. He lay down beside me, his arms around me. I had been waiting for him, but now I was too stunned to move or cry out. He looked at me even more deeply than he had at the well where there'd been no water or at the grave of the two wives. I knew that he truly saw me. He saw that I was accustomed to doing whatever a man told me to do, that I had followed my father out of Jerusalem without a single question. But there was more inside me, and he saw that, too. He saw that I was burning, and that I was alone, that I was trapped by the lion in my dreams, and the angel I was waiting for, and the burden of my birth.

We would probably die before long. Our bones would be white upon the white rocks. We would be clawed at by eagles, taken by jackals. We would rise into the wind and become ashes. But not now. Not yet. We were still alive. Ben Simon slid his hand inside my tunic. There were deep blue veins in his arms that I could see through the dark. I could feel his sex against me, aroused. I was terrified that he might tear me in two. All the same, I didn't try to stop him. I was burning the way the leaves of the pomegranates burn in the month of *Av*. They're green one instant, in flames the next. Sia had been right. I was like the flame tree: the more I burned the more alive I became. If she'd leaned closer to me, she would have noticed the scent of fire and been forewarned, instead she took me to be her friend.

Ben Simon moved his hand between my legs. I heard myself gasp. He quickly covered my mouth with his free hand. The others were on the far side of the cave; they must not hear. He whispered that silence was the only thing he would ever ask me for. I nodded, and he moved his hand away from my mouth. My lips were hot from his touch. I wanted to know one thing before my vow of secrecy, before my words were swallowed and my promise kept. I could feel the spell of silence claiming me, but before it was complete I had only one question. I wanted to know how he had come to have a scar on his face. It seemed a secret to me, and if I knew his secret, I might know him, and then he might belong to me even though he was Sia's husband.

He said it was the mark of a lion. He flinched when he spoke of the memory. The Romans had captured him outside the Temple when he was young and unmarried. He was tall and well muscled, with strong arms, exactly the sort of man they wanted. They were searching for gladiators and had therefore devised a test. They locked ten men in a room with a lion. Whoever survived would be sent to Rome. The first nine were killed, but when it came to this man who lay beside me, the lion had cut him once across his face, then fallen at his feet. The creature had died a sudden death, collapsing all at once, splayed out upon the tiled floor. Perhaps the lion had been wounded in his other encounters, but Ben Simon announced to the soldiers that he had slain his foe with one look. It was such a strange sight that the Romans, now puzzled and confused, took to discussing the possible causes of this odd circumstance. It was then Ben Simon managed to escape, though his wound still bled.

He was appalled that he had killed such a beautiful beast, when he would have much preferred to murder the soldiers, for one of the nine who might have been gladiators and had died before him was his brother.

"The truth is, I was bitter," he confided, whispering in my ear, in order to explain why the lion had collapsed at his feet. "The lion didn't like my taste."

I ran my hand over his features in the dark, wondering what it might be like to come face-to-face with a lion. Perhaps the creature had sensed something in him, a lion of a man. I would have cried over Ben Simon's humiliation and suffering at the hands of the Romans, but the desert had taken away my tears. Perhaps I was bitter, too.

He took his time with me that first night. He did things to me I didn't know even existed. He kissed me everywhere and bade me to do the same to him. After a while my pleasure was in hearing his, in making him hold me tighter and want me more. When he entered me, my eyes were open. I saw the scar the lion had left and knew my dreams had been telling me the story of my own life all along, both what had happened and what would come to pass. He was someone's husband, but on that night he was mine, the lion I had always known would find me. I was meant to save myself for my own husband, but I already knew there would never be a young bridegroom whose family would want to see my first blood after our marriage. Instead, there was only this man who told me I was beautiful. He told me in such a way, I believed him.

WE BECAME PEOPLE of the desert as the month of *Elul* passed, wrapped in cloaks to hide from the sun, searching through the day for sustenance. We forgot feast days. Even the Sabbath was a day like any other, though it was beautiful and holy and should have been remembered with joy and with praise. All hours were white, all flared alike. Soon enough my father was the only one who prayed three times a day, and before long he joined Ben Simon in simply praying daily at dawn, facing toward Jerusalem.

One fortunate afternoon Ben Simon caught a young, wild she-goat. Because the beast walked right to me when he brought her into our camp, he gave her to me as a gift. The goat seemed devoted to me from the start, begging to be petted, following at my heels. I was so flattered, I couldn't bring myself to relinquish her to the one to whom she rightfully should have belonged. Sia was Ben Simon's wife, the elder of the two of us, yet when she called the goat to her, waving and beckoning, the she-goat refused to come, shying and darting away.

I kept my pet tied with rope so we could drink her milk and make the yogurt we call *lebben* and others call *homes*, using my scarf to strain the curds, skimming off some of the buttery *chem'ah* we often ate plain before it was turned into cheese, for in our current circumstances we found this simple dish to be a feast. I dug in the shade where there was a single ancient olive, stunted from the wind. There I found mud that I strained for some dark, salty water. I could then make cheese, *haris halab*, wrapping the mixture in cloth until it was hard and ready to eat. The more dishes we had for our meals because of the goat's milk, the more Sia seemed to suffer and burn with envy. One day I saw her lean down to speak to the goat, trying her best to convince this wild creature to change its allegiance, but the goat merely scampered to my side. Afterward I wondered if this was the moment when Sia knew. Although she masked her eyes, I could later hear her sobbing. Somehow in this desert where there was not enough moisture for tears, she still could cry.

BY THEN I had too many cuts to count, they crossed each other, moths floating along the surface of my skin. We now saw a few stray travelers on our journey, and we traded whenever we could. Whatever we had that might be considered precious—my father's fine leather water flask, Sia's marriage bracelets—was exchanged for salt and cumin. Once we procured several scrawny chickens and we feasted like kings, but when we were done we were left with only the feet and the bones. Such a meager dish would have to serve us for a long time. We went hungry, and in our hunger, we grew careless, as people who are lost often do. We had so little we seemed to have no tie to this world, had we not been tied to one another.

When my time came and I bled, I used the torn hem of my tunic as a rag between my legs. There was nothing else. We were becoming savages, much like the barbarian tribes who lived in the desert and obeyed its brutal laws. Live if you can, or be left behind with the old and infirm, an offering to the creatures that prowl at night. I wound the blue scarf my brother had given me around my head, even though blue had been the color worn by the sister-brides we had found buried in the wilderness. All that we had was carried on our backs. All that we were was illuminated by the bright light of the Almighty. We lived because He allowed us to do so. Every breath belonged to our Lord, who had given us another day on earth.

NOW whenever I went to walk beside Sia she quickened her pace. The intimacy between us had been pierced to the bone. When we cooked together she didn't speak. Sometimes she faltered when I was beside her. Once she became flustered and she burned her hand on the griddle set atop the fire. When we found a shallow pool at our next camp, I asked her to bathe with me. She declined, insisting she would bathe alone, but she never did. Instead she watched me reproachfully from behind the rocks, my young body an affront to her. I could hear her crying. I might have wept myself if I hadn't lost the ability to do so, but I had decided long ago, in my father's house in Jerusalem, I would never cry again. The goat soon became my only company. I found myself talking to her, until I recalled that was what witches were said to do. Then I only whispered, so no one would overhear.

WHEN AT LAST we found a place where we might stay for a while, with clutches of mint and a few yellow onions managing to grow in a gorge nearby, I searched out a cave that was higher on the cliff in order to seclude myself when my time came with the moon. A woman who bled was unclean, what was called *niddah,* and must remove herself from others for seven days. Even a single drop of blood that fell forced a woman to retreat from the world of men, until she had cleansed herself in a *mikvah,* water that was pure, running directly from God.

I went off by myself because it was our law, but there was

another reason as well. I could no longer sleep in the same space as Sia. I had begun to imagine that she lay awake in the dark when her husband came to me, insistent now, as though claiming something he was owed. I wondered if she covered her ears, or worse, if she listened to us. I set myself apart to escape her prying eyes. In truth, I preferred my aloneness. I streaked my skin with mud to keep cool. I unplaited my hair. The stars were brighter on the ridge where I camped, they flecked the darkness to fill the night. I had seen women following the nomads, second and third wives who were banished to walk only with other women. They, too, covered themselves with mud. Though they should have walked in shame, they were even more beautiful than the first wives, for their skins had been turned white and yellow and red with mud, and their hair was loose, falling down their backs like water. They seemed oddly proud, for if there was nothing to quench the men's thirst, then there was at least this available, their bodies, their souls.

We celebrated *Rosh Chodesh*, the rising of the new moon that marked the start of the month of *Tishri*. *Blessed is He who spoke and the world came into being.* Every month began as a reflection of the first words of the Torah, with new life, marked by the reappearance of the moon. By then we had been wandering nearly fifty days, avoiding any sign of Roman troops. On the Day of Atonement I found myself guilt-ridden, appalled to think God knew what I did at night, aware that I had stolen something that didn't belong to me, as though I were a common thief, as well as the murderess my father had claimed me to be. My father and I had little to do with each other, though we were often confined in a small space and took our meals together. We turned our backs to one another. He had little choice but to eat the food I managed to set before him, though I'm sure he considered it to be unclean. I had heard him recite a prayer over his bowl, as men may do to chase away demons.

"Do you think I might kill you from the inside out?" I asked recklessly one noontime as he muttered over the greens I had prepared.

He shot me a filthy look. He was hunched over, frail, suddenly an old man. For the first time I saw him for who he was despite his cloak of invisibility. I knew he was broken. I realized then it was the prayer for the dead he had been murmuring, the words one is to say when a passing occurs: *Blessed are You, Lord our God, King of the universe.* Since the time of my birth he had been in mourning and he was mourning my mother still. All at once I was ashamed. He was my father, no matter how cruel, and I had not honored him.

We celebrated the glory of God on the Feast of the Tabernacles. The men prayed, but we had no grapes on the vine, no red pomegranates to split open so that the juice rained down our mouths and arms and this day differed little from any other day. Soon enough, the weather began to change. At last there were birds again. I hadn't realized how silent the world was in the months of great heat until the flocks returned as they journeyed above us. This was the route they took so they might spend the winter in the south, where the nights were not so black and chill. The entire sky swelled with flocks of larks and scarlet rosefinch. There were buntings, turtledoves, brilliant Abyssinian rollers, glossy ibis. There were whole colonies of glorious yellow and turquoise bee-eaters, who called to each other, even in the night. A huge expanse of color drifted above us, all moving south, searching for grasslands. Sometimes they were like clouds along the horizon and other times they became the entire sky. To see the vibrant waves of birds in shades of red and blue above the white desert was a miracle. I no longer counted off the days with regret but rather with joy.

Even when I was unclean, when I had removed myself from the others, even though his wife might wake in the dark and find him gone, Ben Simon didn't stay away. Men were supposed to avoid women during their time of the month, it was written in the Fourth

Book of Moses, and so it was the law. But we broke every law it was possible to break in the desert, that was where cutting my leg had brought me, for it was the first rule I had ignored. I had no mother to call out cautions, but in truth, I would have disobeyed even if my mother had been alive to warn me. One broken law led to another. Ben Simon became unclean, covered with my blood the way he'd been covered with Roman blood when he struck his enemies in the courtyard of the Temple. He was used to committing crimes. His attitude was both tender and coarsely male. When he sank down beside me, his hand on the curve of my hip, his sex hard against me, I could see no guilt at all in his eyes. He said God could distinguish a sinner from a sin, and what we did was beyond judgment.

Whenever I came down from the cave, I could tell Sia knew where her husband went each time he vanished from her side. I knew by the uncomplaining way she went about her work, by her frown. I couldn't meet my friend's eyes. Everything I might have been had disappeared. The girl who walked to the oasis on the night the Temple burned no longer left footprints. She, who had ashes in her long, red hair and wept for the loss of her city and her home, had been left behind where the citron tree had grown. The key that had opened the gate into the wilderness had opened Sia to my betrayal.

I tasted grit between my teeth. I was a woman of the desert now, no longer the shy outsider, a city girl frightened of scorpions. I had become fierce, willing to do anything to get what I wanted. This was the way hunters were born. I felt that savagery inside of me, a dark glimmering of will that resolved to survive. If I wanted something, it became mine. I sneaked up on migrating birds and caught them in my scarf, sometimes in my bare hands. I was cunning, a lioness. I had watched how the black desert viper could hypnotize a bird, slowly wrapping itself around its prey before the final bite rendered it motionless.

Our people believed every creature had a spark—*nitzotz*—that which was holy, and we were to show kindness and compassion to all beings, what we called *baal chayyim*. All animals praise God, as we do, with their songs and their voices. In midwinter, we dedicated a Sabbath to the birds, to offer our gratitude and acknowledge that it is their songs that have taught mankind how to chant and praise the glory of our Creator. We were even obliged to chase the hens away before we gathered their eggs so they would not see what happened to the unborn beings which might have been their offspring. When we needed meat, we were to make certain to sever the throat of an animal in a single perfect cut to allow its spirit to rise in a steady stream of light. We were not to eat blood in any manner, but to let it drip from the necks of our prey, returning to the earth from whence it came.

But I had witnessed the way death came in the desert each time the viper who waited in the speckled shadows of the rocks partook of his meal. I had learned my lesson. I broke the birds' necks, but I did so quickly, and I always said a prayer. I lay the bodies of these flightless creatures across my knees and plucked their feathers and ignored the fact that I had taken the lives of such wondrous things. What was I not capable of? What bitter, brutal thing would I not be willing to do? In the cave I had grown teeth and claws, exactly what my father had said would come to us in the desert. Reckless, I no longer cared who might hear us at night. It didn't matter if Sia's eyes were swollen or if my father spat on the ground when he saw me, to protect himself, clearly convinced that I could manifest ill will and bring about curses. Let them believe they heard lions, come down from their lair in the mountains to make such wild noise late at night. Sia was nothing to me. Her children were not mine. Who survived depended on sinew and muscle and a crude sort of will. I possessed all three. I stopped returning to the tent to sleep and remained in the cave.

It was now *Cheshvan*, what some call the bitter month, the time of Noah, when rain flooded the world as my passion flooded my head. I allowed Ben Simon to observe my nakedness when I stood on the rocks atop the cave. I allowed him take me right there for the hawks above to view, for the Lord of all things to witness, for his wife to watch if she dared to look upon the cliffs that I favored. My beloved would approach only so far, making it clear I must be the one to sin. Every man is tempted by evil urges; he would not be a man if a swollen flicker of desire did not rise within him. But a woman who allows herself to swoon before such humiliations would be judged harshly, for she would be repeating the first sin of paradise as one of Eve's daughters, betraying God's laws for her own fulfillment. I accepted this. I was already a criminal, the murderer of my own mother; desire was nothing compared to evil such as that.

When Ben Simon bade me to him I would run to him like a dog, but at least I was now a dog who chose my own master. I let him take me the way dogs take each other, and then the way lions do, face-to-face, entwined. When he insisted he was obliged to leave, I wouldn't let him go. I satisfied his every urge, offering any favor to convince him to stay. I burned with him, hot and liquid in his grasp, our bodies a dark tangle, for we had become beasts for whom this was the only language. Salt tears stung my eyes, but they did not fall. Ours was a destroying sort of love. When he felt humiliated by his own needs, Ben Simon would heap insults upon me, then he would weep and take me again in his arms. I couldn't get enough of him because I knew as soon as he left me he would return to his family. He belonged to them. He never lied about that. I would watch his footprints when he went and mourn him before he was gone.

IT WAS THE TIME when we remembered the reconsecration of the Temple after the Syrians were driven off, when *Adonai* allowed a single day's oil to burn for eight nights to mark our faith and our triumph. But now the Temple was lost to us, and our oil burned with plumes of black smoke. The rocks were our ovens as flames leapt from the few twisted boughs we could find. A pale rain fell and spattered our fire so that even cooking was difficult. Our feast was a dove I had trapped in my scarf. The creature sang *tirr tirr,* a lovely song that sound like *tor,* our word for turtledove. I looked upon a bush of myrtle and saw the dove's mate waiting there. Later in the season when the turtledoves would migrate south, I wondered if the one perched on the branch would leave alone, or if she would stay and mourn. I thought of Solomon's words to his beloved, *Behold thou art fair; thou hast doves' eyes.* I saw grief staining the dark eyes of the one perched in the bushes, and a tenderness I had never seen in humankind. I walked toward the lone dove, wondering if I should do away with its loneliness, but it flitted off to a higher branch, its pale feathers gleaming, too lovely a creature for me to destroy.

A portion of water served as our wine that evening, for there were no grapes, and no time to try to ferment the figs we occasionally found growing wild. I had become accustomed to the way we lived and found solace in silence. I'd grown to love the scent of the desert at night, fragrant and harsh at the same time. We went from place to place, following the possibility of finding water, chasing after the tracks left by quail. I continued to live removed from the others so that Ben Simon could easily come to me while his wife and children slept. Once, when Ben Simon was off hunting, my father came up to me and asked if it was my desire to be a *zonah.* I felt that he had slapped me. He compared me to the prostitutes who lived at the edge of Jerusalem and were willing to pull off their cloaks for anyone who would pay them, even Roman soldiers.

"If that's who I am, then that's who you made me," I informed my father, the man who had murdered so many with his curved dagger, who had ignored me and used me as he would a dog, who hadn't flinched when he brought me into the desert, where I could have no future other than the one that had already been written.

I HAD STOPPED counting off days. I did not wish to be elsewhere, even though there was still no sign of my brother and the fortresses of the rebel Jews. The heat had lifted and the rains had begun in earnest. Soon there would be pools forming in the *nechalim;* the ravines between the cliffs would rush with iridescent waterfalls. I was like the leopard that roamed the desert, thinking only of survival and what I might need to get through each day. I saw prints in the sand, always a single cat, never two together. They were such solitary creatures that when they met their mates they would begin to scream, for they were drawn to each other, yet were enemies still. They were nothing like the lions, who were bound for life and rested in each other's embrace.

Once I had come upon a leopard, though such a sighting was extremely rare. I was silent beside some rocks where birds were nesting, waiting for one to find its way closer so that I might fall upon it. I glanced up, and there stood the leopard, dun-colored with black spots, large, surely powerful enough to kill me. My heart thudded. I was seized by the sheer desire to live. I stood upon a rock and lifted up my shawl and made myself fierce, my red hair blowing out behind me, my face snarling, my scream the scream of a leopard. The creature glanced at me, startled, then darted away. It disappeared between the rocks, then burst onto the flatland, where it glided over the earth. I was shivering, stunned by my own ferocity. That was who I was now. A creature who cared nothing for another's hunger, who thought only of her own.

I would have been happy to live this life forever. To wait for the dark and have Ben Simon when I could, but that was not the way it had been written. At the end of the month of *Kislev,* when clouds gathered and the nights grew cool, Sia's sons fell ill. Bad fortune had been lurking every time we ate food that had not been blessed or when we drank from still pools. We had left a place where there were demons, and perhaps some had followed us through Zion's gates. The children were sweet boys, always ready to tag along to search for figs in the fertile soil of the ravines, at least until their mother protested and would no longer allow them to accompany me. When I asked if I could help with their illness, Sia let me know there was nothing I could do. They weren't my children, she told me. I saw grief stamped upon her, but I did not offer to share it for I had helped to cause her despair. Of course she wouldn't want me near.

Day after day the boys' skins flamed hot, though the air grew cooler. Soon the children made rasping sounds when they tried to breathe. Faint red marks were scattered over their flesh. I could hear Sia weeping when they refused the soup of blanched vetch she offered them. She cried out to *Adonai* for Him to take her instead of her children. In my deepest heart I had wished for the very same thing. It was terrible, but it was true. I felt my disgrace, yet I wanted her gone from us. This was who I had become and what my craving had done to me. Now when I thought about who would be the first to die, I guessed it would be her.

If you cannot be brutal in the desert, you will never survive. This is what I told myself and what I believed. I was not a donkey or an innocent girl or a worried mother or a boy with a high fever. I was a red-haired woman who had stared down a leopard. I spoke to a goat on a mountainside. I saw that Ben Simon sat watch over his children, the raw planes of his face transformed by worry. I went to him and bowed before him and begged to nurse his children. A curl of a smile formed on his mouth and he stroked my hair, but he said their lives were in God's hands, not mine.

Sia was watching, her face ashen.

"Let me show you what I can do," I insisted.

In a single day I caught three wild hens and cooked them over a fire. I found water in a spring that fed an Egyptian sycamore and plucked the orange-colored fruit. I made a hearty soup for the boys, then cut the sycamore fruit into thin, cool slices to hold against their fevered lips.

Sia could not reproach me. She had no choice but to nod blankly and accept my gifts. I plunged into survival. I made it my calling and my art, unlike my father, who spent his time idly gazing toward Jerusalem as the sky edged from white to blue. He, who had killed a dozen Romans, who was a rebel and a renegade, was being bested by Judea, by the wind and the hunger that had claimed him and how helpless he had become. Now that the children had fallen ill, he was terrified, chanting to the Almighty throughout the day. It wasn't that he cared about the boys, it was his own flesh that concerned him. He insisted that demons could move from one person to another in a touch or a breath. I had contempt for him and turned away. When he asked me for water to wash his hands, I told him to find it himself, to paw through the sand as I had done.

I cared about only one man, the one who had faced a lion. But I feared he was too tenderhearted and had been reclaimed by his wife and family. He had stopped coming to me at night. In my cave I shivered, alone. I suffered and watched from behind the rocks. He sat with the children beside a fire made of the twigs I'd collected, eating the soup I'd made, drinking water I had dug from beneath the sycamore. I was healing them for each other. Once I saw him take Sia's hand in his own large hand and press her palm to his mouth. He had the right to do so, she was his wife, but I burned with a haze of jealousy. I couldn't eat the soup I'd cooked. I didn't drink the water I had found beneath the roots of the sycamore tree.

I knew from the talk of women at the well in Jerusalem that it was possible to bind a man to you and keep him from straying. It was a blood act, they'd said, fearful of such things, but blood did not frighten me. I went off alone to a place where I had seen black adders, where there was a grove of yellow Sodom apples, whose long, fibrous seeds served as wicks when we had enough fat from a partridge to use for the Sabbath light. I crouched down on my haunches and drew the face of a lion in the dirt with a stick, then circled it with stones, which I streaked with my own menstrual blood. I wanted to keep my lion caged, and in this way I imagined I might do so. I had no mother to teach me the simplest cures, but my spell proved successful. Ben Simon came to me that night. He still wanted me. I tied up my hair with my blue scarf. I was careful, and silent, grateful beyond measure. Everything seemed breakable now. What was between us had grown until it was a flower, the red blossom of the flame tree, which stains your fingers when you pick it, twisted onto a vine that pricks your skin.

"I shouldn't be here," he said.

The same was true for me, and I should have said as much. Instead I went to him and we denied ourselves nothing. None of us was meant to be in this wilderness, but as it had been written that we should journey here, it had been written that he would come to me. All I wanted was his hands on me, his mouth on mine, his body and mine becoming one. That was when I was alive. I wondered if perhaps I'd set the spell upon myself and if it was a curse I'd have to pay for eventually. I should have allowed Ben Simon to care for his wife and children, but I didn't let him go. A leopard knows who she is; she does not calculate her prey's agony and fear, she runs because she is made to do so, she takes what she must.

Perhaps it had been better when I was invisible, when men walked past me and looked away, when I stayed at home like a dog. I barely knew myself now. But I knew what I wanted. When I went walking among the rocks, barefoot, I left a trail. He always followed to find me. Even so, this was not his sin to carry, for when he came to me, I never once said no.

THE NIGHTS grew cooler and the air was blue, sweeping in from the Great Sea, bringing rain in the banks of clouds. Yet the boys' fevers still hadn't broken. They had been sick for too long a time. Their lips were swollen and white. Their eyes rolled back, and they talked to spirits. We watched them, uneasy, fearing the worst. It had come to the point where they would not eat or drink. And then one day, when the branches of the tamarisk bloomed with pink flowers and there were clutches of sage rising between the rocks along the cliffs, Sia herself fell ill. She swore there was nothing wrong with her, but she shivered and refused to eat. In the evening she lay down beside her boys, and when the next morning came, she did not rise from the ground. When I brought her water, she accepted it, but the way she looked at me was terrible. Once she clasped my hand and I thought she was about to curse me. Instead, she gazed into my eyes with a fevered intensity. I don't know if she found what she was searching for, but perhaps she did, for she asked then if I would take care of him should she die. I knew who she meant. I bowed my head and promised I would.

"Yes, of course you will," she murmured. She didn't sound angry, rather she appeared to be a woman who had surrendered and no longer needed to bother with the details of those who would remain on earth, except to make certain that the husband she loved would be loved in return.

After that I couldn't look at her, my only friend who'd been so kind to me. I helped as best I could, crouching beside her with a dampened rag to cool her burning skin. I boiled a tea of nettles and mint, but she couldn't drink. I made a broth from the bones and meat of a partridge, but she shook her head and turned me away. I had never nursed anyone, nor had I attended to the ill or the dying. She lay there uncomplaining, as did the children, who moaned softly. In Jerusalem the *minim* could be paid to come with their secret chants. They would pray for cures from the Infinite One, and as masters of *pharmaka* they had access to medicines that could cure blindness, headaches, fever. The root of the peony could be crushed and digested by those who had seizures; hot wax could stop bleeding. The *minim* wrote the Almighty's name a thousand times, the scroll slipped inside a roll of leather, prayers with mysteries so private they could only be whispered to God alone. If I could have, I would have gone to one of the women in the alleyways such as the one I'd turned to for Amram's amulet, for they often had access to darker spells and could bring back a life the Angel of Death seemed poised to snatch away.

But we had no one to whom we might plead for a cure. We had nothing but dust. Time passed, but the fevers did not. Even I knew a body could contain such demons for only so long.

One evening Ben Simon did not come to me. I went to the place where the tamarisk grew. The rocks I'd placed so carefully had been jumbled up, perhaps by wild camels or by jackals making a den for the night. Either way, the spell had been broken. I came back to camp and found him holding his children, weeping. Now I knew I had been wrong. A person could indeed cry in the desert, even one marked by the bite of a lion. At that moment I understood who I was to him. I did not come first, or second, or even third.

It did not diminish the way I felt or who he was to me.

But I knew.

There was only one thing I could do to please him. When I told Ben Simon I would journey to search for a cure, he embraced me. I drank in his gratitude as though it were water. I wanted to set forth alone, but he not would allow it. A woman in the desert was like a bird in a snare, there for anyone to catch. He insisted my father go with me, and although my father thought little of me, he agreed to be my companion, perhaps only to flee from those who were so ill.

Ben Simon gave me his knife, the one he had used to murder so many. There were rusty stains upon it, but the silver blade was so sharp that when I grazed my hand against it blood sprang from my thumb. I kept the knife in my tunic, wrapped inside a flat piece of wool, tied with a string made of my goat's threaded hair. Ben Simon made certain I took my pet along, so that her milk would give us sustenance if we found nothing else. He gave me the flask in which he carried water and the last of the barley cakes. I took these things, though I was seized with the impulse to give it all back. As a gift marked a beginning, so, too, did it signify an ending. Something was happening as we said good-bye. He was giving me all he had, and yet a curtain had been drawn between us. I could feel my throat closing up, my heart hitting against my chest. I looked upon my beloved's face, but he no longer saw inside me. I had become transparent, no more to him than air. It was as it had been on the day we left Jerusalem, before he spied me sifting through the mud for water, before he knew my name. I thought perhaps this was the way an assassin said farewell, fiercely and with dignity. I had no idea that he could already read what had been written.

WE LEFT when the morning was dark and there were hawks spiraling across the sky.

My father and I went without knowing how long it might take to find a cure or if there was indeed anything for us to find. Mistrust was everywhere, and for good reason. We were as likely to be murdered as we were to reach a settlement. Bands of robbers occupied caves all across Judea. There were escaped slaves, thieves, rebels with nothing more to lose. The wilderness was enormous. Every limestone cliff resembled ones we had already passed. We circled, lost, for several days to avoid soldiers from the Roman Legion, the goat that I led mawing to warn us of our mistake. There were those who wandered here for all eternity, who were never seen by civilized people again. I had heard stories from the women at the well in Jerusalem of a lost young girl who lived with the hyenas, who would run with them, and eat carrion, and sleep among them, and who, when she was found, had sharpened teeth, for she was no longer human.

When we passed the same cliffs for the third time, I had no other choice; I took the scarf my brother had given to me and tore off strips of silk. I tied the flares of blue to the thorn trees to help guide our return.

A few days into our journey, my father surprised me by speaking to me. I shouldn't have wished for such a thing, for he had nothing good to say. He ranted, blaming me for entrapping Ben Simon, as though convinced that I was the lion who had devoured this man, taking him from his wife. I looked at my father, defiant, wondering what he would think if I walked away and left him to fend for himself. He went on to inform me that if Ben Simon's two boys survived they would owe me their lives and would be my sons as much as they were Sia's. His eyes blazed with anger. "Maybe then God will forgive you."

I didn't defend myself. I often ran my hand over the cuts etched into my flesh that marked off our time in the desert, stopping when I reached the day Ben Simon first came to me. In truth I had walked into the wilderness to search for a cure as a way to bring him back to me. I had not thought of the boys or Sia until this moment. God wouldn't forgive me for that.

My father and I made camp as dusk fell. In this season the nights were cold, and I gathered twigs along the way to make a fire at night. When there was no other fuel, we burned our own excrement and that of the goat, and the smoke reeked foully. Surrounded by that dreadful blaze, I feared we had wandered out of God's sight. At night we slept sitting up, back against back, our cloaks around us, the folds of the cloth burdened with grime. We heard creatures in the dark, wild dogs and jackals, once a bear lumbering toward its cave. This was a route not many walked, for we were without a glimpse of water. We had heard of the fate of Sodom, a place which had been burned to the ground by lightning. People said there were trees filled with beautiful fruit, but once plucked the fruit turned to smoke and ash in your hand. In the daylight hours our every breath burned. We dared not visit any oasis for fear the Romans would find us. The goat had not had water for so many days, she could no longer give milk. She huddled beside me. There were stones in her hooves which I did my best to pluck out. All the same, when I insisted we go on, I thought I heard her crying.

We had come so far that a single small section of my scarf remained. Behind us a map of blue charted our way through the wilderness, back to Ben Simon. Our journey seemed hopeless, for we could see nothing more than the white cliffs before us. My father scowled, vowing he could have predicted as much, for I brought only bad fortune. But then we came to the top of a cliff and spied a sight in the distance that made our hearts lift. It was the Salt Sea, a horizon of vivid azure. The water was changeable; one moment it was blue and then green and then a flat slate color. When clouds approached, the surface turned black, so that the Romans called it Lake Asphaltitis, for it threw up black clusters of tarlike asphalt. But for us, it resembled heaven, so blue we had to blink back tears.

The sea appeared to be so close I imagined I could reach out and touch it, but my father said it was a walk of several more days. He warned that distance was an illusion that had tricked many men, even great sages, into walking to their death. They were certain they were moments from the sea and started off beneath the brutal sun on a course that would bring them directly to *Mal'ach ha-Mavet*, the Angel of Death who was said to have a thousand eyes, never losing sight of a single one of his victims.

Days slipped away under the burning sun as we remained on the ancient path that led toward the sea. We passed the ruins of a settlement where it was possible to see the moon doubled when it was reflected in the Salt Sea. The settlement had been destroyed by the Romans. It was intended to be paradise built by the Yahad, a group of believers from the Essene sect, Jews who practiced strict codes with fixed hours of prayer. It was said that our people had been cut into four quarters, each with their own philosophy, and then cut up four more times for good measure. Truly righteous, the Essenes had indeed cut themselves off from all others.

The Yahad's name for their oasis was Sechacha, our word for cover, for their houses were domed with the broad leaves of the date palm trees. They had come to the desert as true believers, forsaking their comfortable lives in Jerusalem. They had foreseen the fall of the Temple and had fled here to await the End of Days, so that they might spend their last hours in chanting, their scribes at work on rolls of parchment to assure that their truth would not be lost when this world ended. The Essenes forbade idols, as we did, but they were far stricter in their practices and would not even touch a coin with an imprint upon it. They believed no man should be king. Still they would not lift up arms or fight their oppressors. We were in the hands of *Adonai,* they insisted, therefore arrows and spears were meaningless. There were children of darkness and children of light and the true battle on earth was to remain in the light and praise the one who knows all, *Elohim*.

We saw the crumbling ruins of their aqueduct, and the dam under a waterfall, which we drank from deeply, though the pool was cluttered with the remnants from the settlement the Romans had destroyed: oil lamps and broken glass vessels, clay inkpots, piles of *ostraca*—broken pottery shards used for writing upon. There were still tall oaks and laurel trees to offer dappled shade, but anything made by human hands had been crushed. Fallen wooden beams hewn from palm trees and the leaves used for roofs were in brown, crinkled heaps. I wandered through the scriptorium, a library whose shelves and columns littered the ground. Bits of torn scrolls on goatskin or papyrus lay in the dirt, rotting and falling into shreds. I went along the cobblestones to see the ritual baths lined with wide plaster steps. There were snakes in these baths now, nesting beside pools of fetid water.

At last I came to piles of bones, the remains of the faithful. Though I was unworthy, I tore my ragged clothes in the act of *keriah,* as a sign of respect and mourning, and murmured a prayer for the dead. *May His great name be honored. Blessed be He, forever and ever.*

I found my way back to the fire my father had lit. We spent the night at this oasis, knowing the Romans would avoid this place and the ghosts of those they'd murdered, but starving jackals would be called to us by the fear in our scent. Surely they had been here before, for the bones of the dead were scattered so widely we could not collect them and store them in a stone container as was their due. We looked at each other, my father and I, and perhaps we saw each other in a different light as the stars hung overhead and the bones glimmered before us. My father did not berate me on this night. Instead, he told me I should be the first to sleep, having decided he would stay awake to watch for any beasts who might come to surround us. It was the first kindness he had ever offered me.

WE WENT FORWARD early the next day. Perhaps an angel led us on our journey. We found our way south, the direction of the springs. It was here the Essenes from Sechacha had come to haul water back to their settlement. We turned onto a path edged by brambles. The goat, now famished, chewed leaves that were prickly and brown. But as we ventured farther, there were green shoots among the rocks. The breeze rose up, carrying the fragrance of balsam and the soft, nearly undetectable scent of water. All at once I recognized the sound of bees. It had been so long since I had heard their honeyed song I nearly swooned. We had come to an oasis where a spring arose from the ground and huge date palms towered. The air was a cool balm, so sweet it seemed we had stepped inside a cloud filled with perfume, rich with the scents of myrrh and coriander. We had found a group of the Yahad people who had survived, settling here to wait for the End of Days.

In the clearing their grapevines and gardens were brilliant against the white-hot sky. The beauty of the world burst forth in every growing thing. There was a field of wheat and flax, yellow and gold, ablaze with sun. We heard bells that were hanging from the trees on twists of black rope, ringing as they moved with the breeze. There were dozens of mulberry and olive trees circling a stone well, alongside a grove of pistachios that turned the haze green. A pen of forty goats was set up in the shade, another forty sheep dozed in the sun.

Many among the Essenes had been priests, some lived without women in the limestone cliffs, their caves marked by *mezuzoth*, containers holding scrolls in which prayers to God were enclosed. These men were too pure for the entanglements of life in this world, but there were also men who had arrived with wives and daughters, their women dressed in white linen, heads covered at all times. They resided in large tents with their families, some of them having fled from Sechacha, others having arrived only recently from Jerusalem after the fall of the Temple.

People peered at us as we walked through the settlement. There were stone common houses, and ritual baths, and libraries where scholars set to completing documents, dividing themselves into groups of three, so that the men could work on scrolls written upon animal skins or papyrus throughout the day and the night. Perhaps my father and I looked like demons, made of sand rather than flesh. Our eyes peered out of our filthy faces. My hair was like blood twisted down my back, so long it reached past my waist. Some of the women blinked when they saw me, but no one jeered. The people of the Yahad sect practiced kindness in what they believed to be our last days in this world. What belonged to one man also belonged to his neighbor.

The women came to greet us. The fabric they wove on their

looms was so light their garments flowed around them. I yearned for sheets of linen to wrap around myself so no one would see me. Perhaps then I would be able to withstand the intensity of God's bright light when He could not forgive me for all I'd done.

Although these holy people had lost many of their own at the hands of the Romans, for they revealed that the settlement of Sechacha had been conquered and ruined even before the Temple fell, the Essenes weren't willing to carry daggers, which they considered an affront to the greatness of God. Quickly my father made the decision not to tell them he was one of the *Sicarii*. These people considered the *Sicarii* to be on the side of darkness, snakes who defied *Adonai*. We merely announced that we were among those who had been expelled from Jerusalem, a poor father and daughter who had become wanderers. When we spoke of the mother and children traveling with us who had been stricken with fever, the Essene women had compassion and quickly resolved to help us. One among them, who identified herself as Tamar bat Aaron, escorted my father to a learned man, a priest whose followers called him Abba—father—a teacher of righteousness whose people did his bidding out of joy rather than duty.

Abba was so old he had to be brought everywhere in his chair, carried by four strong men; so pure Tamar whispered we must sit sixty arm spans away, the distance kept by all of the women, their heads covered, their eyes downcast yet shining, for although women were not included in the strict Essene ways, they were radiant when they heard the great man speak. Another priest of Abba's magnitude would have turned us away, too enmeshed in prayer to be bothered with our pleas. Or perhaps such a powerful man might have agreed to hear us if we had brought silver in exchange for his favor. But Abba was convinced that every man was his brother. He was a follower of a teacher from Galilee who taught that peace was the only hope for mankind. Without it, we were like the jackals in the desert, nothing more.

Beside me, Tamar whispered that Abba had had ten wives and outlived them all; he now spent his days giving glory to God and teaching the ways of peace. The men here prayed three times a day; in the morning as they faced in the direction of Jerusalem, then again at sunset, and once more after nightfall. They carried what was holy within them, for every man was a temple, and every prayer spoken could be heard by our Father above us.

When told of our plight, Abba presented my father with a fever charm, a prayer slipped inside a metal tube that was to be attached to the arms of the afflicted. He offered a length of blessed rope, to tie into knots in the children's tunics and bind them to good health, as well as a precious bulb of deep purple garlic to keep away demons. We were to recite the name *Adonai* a hundred times over a cup of water and garlic that had been boiled three times atop a hot fire, then instruct those who had sickened to drink while they prayed for grace from God.

WE WERE GIVEN pressed dates and barley cakes and allowed to spend the night. A light rain was falling, and the earth quickly flooded with puddles. My father was led to a common house to stay among the men. I tied my goat to a tamarisk tree and went with the unmarried girls, who looked at me with puzzled expressions. I must have appeared as a wild beast to them. When I uncovered my hair before them, they were shocked by the knots and set to work on them with wooden combs. They brought me to bathe in their ritual pool, where the water turned black all around me. Even I could see it was a bad omen, but the Essene girls laughed and said holy water took away all sin. Their people believed immersing themselves brought them closer to God, and they bathed several times a day. There was a double staircase into the bath; one flight of the limestone steps to enter, the other for the pure who had been cleansed so they might walk out of the water without touching those who were still unclean. Indeed, when I stepped out of the water, I felt truly cleansed for the first time since leaving Jerusalem. My hair was so red that the bees came to me, circling round. The Essene women laughed, suggesting that my hair must appear to be a field of roses. I had to run from the swarm and shout out that I was a woman, not a flower.

I was given a tunic by Tamar. It was a simple white garment, with a goat-hair rope to tie at the waist. I said it was too great a gift, but Tamar insisted. "Possessions are nothing, for they will be worthless in the World-to-Come," she told me. "You cannot take any of it into the house of the Lord."

The past seemed like a distant dream. We were far from the carnage we'd known in Jerusalem, several days' walk from the caves where we'd found shelter. But what I'd done and what I'd come to know had been more than a dream. When I narrowed my eyes, I could see beyond the orchards to the pocked limestone cliffs and the path I'd marked with bits of blue. I could feel a pulse at the base of my throat, a flush of panic at having left Jachim ben Simon behind. I feared what had bound us together might disappear if I were no longer in his sight. Perhaps he would come to believe that I, too, was only a dream from which he had now awakened.

I wondered what our hosts would think if they knew the truth about us. My father continued to bide his time and keep our secrets. He believed these pious people to be fools, convinced that those who sat and waited for the End of Days were creating it for themselves. But of course it was inevitable that he would think so. Every man engaged in war tells himself he can alter what has been written, that it is he, not God, who is the maker of destiny, free to change what is meant to be.

ON THE MORNING we left, Tamar brought me to her house and gave me a portion of cheese, salty white *haris halab,* that would last several days and keep us well fed, along with some sweet pressed dates. She had four young sons, unused to strangers, their mouths agape at the sight of me until their mother shooed them away. When we were alone, she warned that we must take care on our journey. There had recently been a raid at another settlement, called Ein Gedi, an oasis where four springs met with each other to cause great waterfalls, one of which formed a pool where King David was said to have hidden from his enemies. It was here that the *Moringa Peregrina* grew, a bloom with magical powers that had allowed David to write his songs with such purity. There were flowering acacias growing beside the waters, and jujube trees, whose orange fruit attracted birds from Greece and Egypt, and there were groves of balsam, whose sticky gum formed the incense that was more valued than gold. Ein Gedi was a place of plenty in a time of hunger. Because of this, it had called out like a lamb to those who were starving. The attackers had come in the night. Seven hundred people had been killed or held captive by the *Sicarii* who had raided the settlement's warehouses. The Essenes knew these were the culprits because the curved knife, the weapon that finds its mark, then pulls out the soul of its victim, had been used. The thieves had stolen everything, grain and wine and water, along with the lives of the innocent.

My heart dropped at the mention of the *Sicarii*.

"The murderers won't find you if you're careful," Tamar told me. "Should anyone approach you in the wilderness, hide as best you can. Perhaps now you understand why we are certain the end is near. With such treachery on earth, the angels will surely come to us and guide us into the World-to-Come."

I nodded, even though I knew that my father believed that daggers and not angels were the answer to betrayal. I didn't blurt out that my brother might have been among those who had raided Ein Gedi. We made haste to leave, and as we readied ourselves one of the men came to deliver a last message from Abba. My father's eyes were hooded, his heart closed, but he listened, for he was a guest in this settlement, and must at least pretend to have manners. I overheard what was said and quickly lowered my eyes. When the messenger had finished speaking, my father nodded a farewell, but he never offered his gratitude. That was my father's character, silent and heartless; exactly what I expected of him. He signaled to me with the wave of a hand, and like his dog I went with him, following at a distance, my eyes cast down.

As we set off, several of the women escorted us, waving, wishing me well, calling out how pretty I looked in my new garments. They knew nothing of me, only the little I had revealed, some of which felt like a lie. My father and I were strangers to each other as well. We knew as little of each other as the Essenes knew of us. We had many days to walk, and, although my father had ceased to humiliate and berate me, we had nothing to say. I knew nothing of my father's life before he'd taken up the dagger, though I had heard rumors that he'd had a brother who'd been sold into slavery. If a man sees his brother tied with ropes and dragged down the cobblestone road, does he ever see anything else? If ten men are kept in a room with a lion and only one survives, what does that man become? If a woman with red hair keeps silent, will she ever be able to speak the truth again?

As we journeyed, we looked back in order to see the ever-changing colors of the Salt Sea. We could spy the sails of the flatboats that traveled across the sea to the country of Moab, ruled now by a fierce people called Nabateans. In this fertile land Moses was said to be buried, yet no one had ever discovered where that holy place might be, though many had searched. Perhaps this was best, for Moses held the key to secrets that were too immense for men to absorb, a gift and a burden too heavy for our people to bear.

One day, after we had climbed the tallest cliffs, the sea disappeared from view, sinking into the earth as though it had been swallowed. Waves of blistering heat rose above the spot where it had been, for its waters were even hotter than the air. Soon even that disappeared. We trudged on. I did not think about the fact that I was a young woman in the desert, alone and on fire. I refused to let my thoughts dwell on roaming beasts or robbers. Most of all, I did not allow myself to imagine what might have occurred at our camp in our absence, how a fever can burn like a flame until there is nothing left but ash, how it spreads the way fire does, leaping from one victim to the next.

We had Abba's blessing and his medicine. We needed only to find our way. I hurried my father along, collecting scraps of blue as we followed the map they made, grateful to my brother for his gift. The fabric was tattered. Some of the squares had been carried off by hyenas or by the wind, so all that remained were the threads cast from silkworms that had turned into butterflies. One day there was a heavy rain. My father wanted to wait out the rain, taking refuge in a limestone cave, but I insisted we walk on, though our skins glistened with water and our garments were sodden. My father had little choice. He would be lost without me, for I alone knew the direction we must head toward. As we walked on, my father raved and complained, but the rain ended, a little at a time, so that we walked through the drops and then through the fresh, cool air.

The campsite was empty when we arrived. There was the fire pit and the basket I used to collect mint and greens. There were the bowls for our meals, and the ax which had cut the thorns from our path. A fine layer of grit covered everything, and I thought of the two girl-brides Ben Simon had showed me and how he had cried and how I had fallen under his spell. We had stolen our time together, time that had seemed endless in the dark. I felt something sharp in my throat. I didn't know it was the beginning of my grief until my father silenced me. I had been wailing, the way the leopard does, suddenly and without regard for any other living creature.

We discovered them in the dank cave, searching for comfort and shelter in their final hours. They were together, as they deserved to be. All had the red marks of illness pocking their skin, all had wasted away so that bones showed through their flesh. Ben Simon had set his wife and children onto a stone ledge before he lay down beside them. The veins in his arms were still blue, but they were fading, and his skin had grown cold. I fell to my knees and clutched at him, desperate for any last warmth. I put my mouth upon his, but there was no breath, no life. I could taste the World-to-Come.

I would not move when my father shouted at me, or when he raised his hand to me. In the end my father had to bury them. It was a woman's place to ready bodies for the Angel of Death and chant lamentations, then to set herself aside until the specter of death was no longer with her, but I refused. Welts rose across my back and shoulders when my father beat me, but I would not be his dog on this day. My father shouted out that I was a coward, afraid to see to the needs of the dead, but he was wrong. I wasn't afraid to be unclean any more than I was frightened of the dead. I only feared that if I held Ben Simon for too long, I wouldn't be able to let him go.

My father carried the bodies to the highest cliff and set rocks atop them so hawks and vultures and jackals couldn't get near. He said prayers of lamentations, having folded Ben Simon's prayer shawl around his own shoulders to honor him. For seven days after this ritual, my father had to sit in the sun to cleanse himself because he had been so close to death and was considered *tamé*, impure. He sang the lamentations that a woman was meant to sing because I would not allow those words into my mouth. I would not recognize Ben Simon's death or see him walk into the World-to-Come. When I closed my eyes I could envision the natural grace of his strong body, the sharp planes of his face, his deep glance of appraisal which cut right through me. I did not want to let him go, yet I could hear my father's laments and prayers even when I covered my ears with my hands. His chanting sounded like the wind, and like the wind it wrapped around me until I heard nothing but a single song.

I wondered if in his illness Ben Simon had been like the lion who had fought so hard against nine warriors, only to lay down his head and die before the tenth. I wondered if he had lasted until the day when it rained, when we were so close, only moments away, and if that rain had been made of his tears, for he had not been ashamed to weep.

I remembered the words I'd overheard before we left the Essenes when Abba had sent his messenger to my father. *Even for the righteous, it is only up to Adonai to punish*. Perhaps this holy man had known who we were all along. Now the assassins' punishment had fallen upon us. If one of the *Sicarii* carried all the men he had murdered on his back wherever he went, did the dead not wish to eventually take their revenge? Perhaps their spirits had followed Ben Simon, and when he was weakened by grief, when he sank down, eyes shining wet before the still forms of his children, they had burned through his flesh and overtaken him.

I buried the Essenes' cure, for it was worthless now, as they said things of this world always were. As I dug in the hard, white earth, I wondered if perhaps I was the one being punished, if I was now meant to suffer as I had made my friend suffer when I stole what belonged to her.

During the seven days my father was away to cleanse himself from his nearness to the dead, I did not eat or drink. I tied the goat to a low bush and didn't listen when she called to me. On the dawn of every day I cut a mark of my sorrow into my leg, each more deeply than the last, for I now used Ben Simon's sharp knife. Every wound was like a kiss to me, a dark slash of passion. The scent of blood emanated from my skin, a film that covered me. A leopard came one night and sat on the other side of the fire pit, watching me. I did not rise to chase it away. *Come and devour me. See if I care.* My eyes met with his, and I saw the yellow glimmer of violence in his glance. But in the end he must have deemed me worthless, for he slunk away.

When my father returned from his days of purification, he was shocked to see my condition. I could barely rise from the ground, as ashen as the dust I would someday become. I had nothing in my life but to wait my turn for the World-to-Come. What was this earth to me now? A prison cell, a lash of rope. My father had always told me I was nothing, and that was what I had become. Later he admitted that, when he saw me before him, he thought of my mother at the hour of my birth, already gone from this world. On the day he found me wasting away, he thought of what she would have done had she been there with her only daughter. She would have wished to save me. That was why he convinced me at last to take a sip of water.

On the eighth day after Jachim ben Simon was buried under stones, I broke my fast and drank from the leather goatskin that had belonged to him. I did so not for myself but for my beloved, for he was not yet gone from me. Though the Angel of Death had snatched him, a flicker of his spirit remained.

By then I knew I would not bleed again.

SOON AFTER, my father had a powerful vision. He awoke with tears running down his face and his faith renewed. He had dreamed that my brother was waiting for us in a tower. The dream was so real he could hear my brother speak to him. *Look, and I will come to you,* Amram had said. My father vowed that when the clouds lifted he would see his son.

Believing this to be so, the assassin took a staff so that he might climb the highest of the crags, where he believed it would be possible to witness on earth what he had viewed in his dreams. I did not argue with him, but I was skeptical. My father might have faith, but I had none. I saw us as we had become: a man too old and frail to be a worthy assassin, his ruined daughter who was unable to weep or bleed. I thought perhaps someone had put a hate curse on me, perhaps it was Sia before she died, perhaps it was all I deserved in this world.

The rains came now with great force. The air was blue and wet with heavy downpours. My father and I sat for days in the cave to escape the flash floods in the *nachal*, the goat our only company. This fetid cave was the last place that Ben Simon had been in this world; he had breathed in the damp, chalky scent of the limestone and had breathed out his soul inside the cobwebbed confines of this cavern. I thought I might feel closer to him here, but it was Sia's spirit that hovered close by. I felt her pinch me as she tried to get my attention. She pursued me in my dreams. *Did you think it would be any other way? Did you think you would get what you wanted?* When I awoke, panting for air, I sometimes believed I could hear a burst of her laughter, as if we'd had a battle and she had been the one to win and was now pleased with the results.

The months of winter were upon us. I wanted to run away, but the rains that had fallen in sheets made for a world I couldn't flee. All at once the desert was a sea. Where there had been only the rattle of the wind, now all we heard was the rushing water in the *nachal*. What we had longed for we now had in abundance. There were pools everywhere; at the bottom of every ravine the floodwaters ran so fast that any goat or deer making a misstep could easily be carried away. Flying insects rose up in swarms, borne from the water in funnel clouds. Ibex came to drink and were refreshed. My little goat tugged on her rope; she'd always followed at my heels, but now she seemed maddened by the scent of rain. She kicked and raced in a circle, and her milk was fresh and tasted like grass. I wept to think that life went on even when so much had been lost, that rain still fell and myrtle grew between the rocks.

I found a clear pool that had gathered in a gulley. I realized I hadn't been cleansed since I'd gone to the ritual bath of the Essene women. I took off my garments and saw that I was bruised and thin. I barely recognized my own flesh. And yet my belly appeared thickened, bulging, so that I looked like a woman who had satisfied myself with too much water. I saw how deeply I had gashed my leg, scars that would never fully heal. I'd had to restrain myself from cutting myself to shreds, for the knife against me made me feel I was being taken by Ben Simon, and I longed for that blood-brimmed connection.

Darkness was falling as I bathed in the pool. Stars would soon be appearing in the sky. When I heard the sound of sobbing, I pleaded with the ghost of my beloved's wife to leave me be, certain that she was beside me, torn apart by all of her sorrow. Sia was the tender one, always ready to cry.

I was certain these were her tears that I wept, not mine.

BY THE END of *Shevat* the wildflowers were blooming with vivid color; the willows had filled with strands of tender green leaves. My father and I made do. We did not complain about our circumstances, or discuss the past. But each night I climbed to the cliff where the bones were. I knelt as the light floated away and the day ended. I was praying for something that could never be granted; another life, the one I had already lived and lost.

I was there late one day, watching the light fade into bands of pink and gray, when I spied two men coming across the desert. They were young warriors. I called to my father, and he scrambled up beside me, using a branch from the tamarisk that he'd smoothed into a staff to help him make his way. Together we stood on our perch, watching as the strangers approached, the plumes of dust rising before them like clouds.

"This is my dream," my father said, his expression joyous. "Those are the clouds that will reveal where we should go. These men will lead us to the tower where Amram is hidden."

We had been alone in the desert for a long time, our only company the bones beneath the rocks. But the bones spoke to me. They told me that my prayers would not be answered. I would never be forgiven. I would have to pay for my sins. I wanted to escape from the voice that sounded like Sia's. If I went elsewhere, perhaps it would be rendered mute. I wanted to believe in my father's dream. I was more cautious than he, yet I, too, felt my brother near to us.

"We cannot yet trust," I said, and for once my father did not disagree. Dreams came to men for many reasons, both as oracles and as warnings.

I watched the men approach, curious, my shawl wrapped around me. My father prepared in case those who came forth were enemies pretending to be our saviors, ready to fight should they turn against us and prove his dream to be a false prophecy. He took hold of his dagger, then murmured a prayer asking God to be on his side.

The men stopped in the canyon below. They called out to my father, vowing they were Zealot warriors. My father answered their call. He was still holding the dagger concealed in his cloak. Though he was weakened and no longer young, he could throw a knife from a great distance and strike a man dead. I had seen him do as much when a soldier cornered him in an alleyway near our home. He had then walked away without a look back, as though he hadn't taken a life.

The young warriors shouted that Hol had sent them. They knew the phoenix, the warrior who managed to rise each time another would have fallen. At the mention of the pet name known only to my brother's closest friends, my father dropped his weapon. Tears brimmed in his eyes, and his weathered face, so aged since we had left Jerusalem, broke into a grin.

"Bring me to him," he commanded.

I noticed that my father did not say bring *us* to him. I was nothing, as I always had been. Only when he needed me to guide him, to feed him, to be his only sustenance in the wilderness, did he remember that I, too, was his child.

The men who'd come for us were no older than my brother, young in years yet hardened by what they'd seen and done. I recognized one, Jonathan, from Jerusalem. He'd been a serious prayer student. People thought he would be a rabbi or a scholar, then he'd joined with my brother and picked up the knife. The other was called Uri, which meant light. He was a lumbering, warm-hearted young man whose good humor dominated every discussion. I shied away, reluctant to make my presence known, but my brothers' friends rejoiced in finding me and called me to join them. Amram had told them about me, the sister called Yaya, who had cared for him as a mother would, who had made his meals, sewn his tunics and his mantle, listened to plans so secret he hadn't dared tell anyone else. The one called Jonathan took out a blue square of silk that the wind had carried to my brother's path. This was how they'd found me.

WE WOULD take a route that would lead us to the southernmost part of the Salt Sea. I knew that, if I went, I could not look back. I would be abandoning Ben Simon, the only man who had ever known who I was. His bones would not be gathered on the anniversary of his death, as had always been our custom, to be secured in a stone ossuary. But if I stayed, the desert would claim me. I could not falter now, or give in to my impulse to lie down beside my beloved.

We would be going through the harshest part of the wilderness, a place of salt and sorrow, a land even more difficult to traverse than the valley where we'd found the Essenes. There were said to be troops from the Roman garrison scattered throughout, and we would need to take care to avoid their camps, backtracking when necessary. I thought of my poor little goat, whose milk was the only thing I could stand to drink. It is said there is a goat demon in the desert called the *Sa'ir*, but if anything I had found a goat who was an angel. She had saved our lives when we had nothing; she had been wild and I had kept her captive and she had forgiven me; she had been my only friend when I was alone.

Before we left, I let her free. I tied a string of red around her throat and led her to the highest cliff. "Go on," I said as I cut the strand that bound her. She was so accustomed to following me, she didn't flee back into the wilderness. My pet merely stood there, looking at me. I smacked her rump to get her moving. I thought of Ben Simon's dark eyes, his olive skin, the curl of a smile whenever he spied the goat trailing behind me so meekly. "Stay away from me," I insisted, waving her on.

I knew that although I was shouting at the goat, I was speaking to Sia's ghost.

AT THE START of our journey, the cliffs were so high the men had to tie ropes around my waist, and around my father's waist as well, then help pull us up the sheer sheets of limestone. Because of the season there were herbs and wild asparagus sprouting in the *nechalim* between the cliffs. The air was scented with mint and tangy scallions. Every bit of green was a delight to see. There were the yellow blooms of mustard as well, like fallen stars upon the ground. The sycamore fruit had turned bright orange, and wasps were drawn to its ripening odor. We relished the sound of such abundant life, but soon enough we went on, higher, to where the air was pale, shimmering. We tramped across fields of rocks so sharp even the ibex could not run here. Our feet were bleeding by the second day.

At twilight, no matter where we were, I went to sit quietly by myself. In this way I would procure our evening meal. Each night I would watch for birds. Once I discovered the delicate lattice of twigs where they nested, I sat nearby in silence. They came to me, thinking I was cast of stone, seeing me as a part of the desert and nothing more. I covered their eyes when I broke their necks. I should have let their breath rise all at once and given them a clean death with a single knife stroke. I always carried Ben Simon's knife in my tunic, kept close to my skin, but I didn't use it unless I turned it on myself to mark my leg. I held the birds close and listened to their hearts beating, and then I did what the desert had taught me.

We roasted the birds over a fire the warriors had made. They applauded me as they ate the food I cooked. They said I had a talent. I was a huntress, they joked. My father glared when they sang my praises. "It was nothing," I insisted. "The birds came to me."

The warriors seemed like boys when they teased me about my hunting skills; all the same, I tried to make myself invisible, as I had been in Jerusalem. Boys became men at night, when their pulses beat and the forbidden seemed possible. Though I had no gray cloak, I knew how to vanish. I could make myself disappear and seem like nothing as I hunched over cleaning the cooking pot with sand, my eyes elusive. But in the firelight my scarf slipped from my head, and my brother's friends saw that my hair was red. They could tell I wasn't a girl anymore. They looked away, uneasy, shamed by their own thoughts. They should not even have been sitting at the fire with a woman who was not their mother or their sister or their wife, let alone taken food from my hands. I was considered a *niddah,* impure and unclean, for there was no *mikvah,* not even a silty pool of water. But we were in the desert, and they had little choice. They ate the birds I killed, they helped me up the cliffs, they led me toward my brother. As they did so, they recounted stories of the fortress they had commandeered, tales I found preposterous.

The fortress was impenetrable, they said, the surrounding land so fierce no attack upon them would prove successful. The retreat had once been a palace built by King Herod, a place of unearthly beauty concealed by clouds. I knew of that king, whose cruelty was so legendary it was said he had once slit open a hedgehog, then turned the poor beast inside out to place upon an enemy's face so that he might blind his foe. He had betrayed those around him and been responsible for the murder of his wife, Mariamne, whom he accused of trading in *philtrons* and *pharmaka*—medicines and love potions and spells. She was so beautiful the Roman general Marcus Antonius became maddened at the sight of her and was desperate to have her. Because of this Herod sentenced her to death. Soon after, his son was accused of having a poison concocted from the venom of asps, prepared by a woman from Edom who was a practitioner of *keshaphim*. The son's execution followed his mother's.

Every betrayer knows his fate is to have the misery he once doled out to others returned to him in kind, yet Herod had dreams of outrunning the page on which his fate was written. He built his stronghold on the western slope of the mountain called Masada, completed a hundred years before our time. The Queen of Egypt wanted Judea for herself, pleading with Anthony and with Rome to grant her this desert as a gift, for she yearned for the treasures it possessed: the route to the sea, the fields of salt, the balsam forests that lay beyond in Moab, troves of myrrh and frankincense, riches beyond measure.

Those who awaited us at Masada were said to be more than nine hundred strong, three hundred of them warriors. Five winters ago they had taken Herod's great fortress from the hands of a small group of Roman soldiers lodged there. They had done so easily, in the cover of night, winding along the back of the mountain, a feat the Romans had thought impossible. Nothing was impossible, they had discovered. They had managed to climb into the sky, closer to God.

I thought it was a dream when my brother's friend vowed that the old king's Northern Palace was more beautiful than the hanging gardens of Babylon, one of the wonders of mankind. The black and white columns had been transported from Greece, lashed onto boats that crossed the open sea, then hauled by ropes and pulleys across Judea on the backs of slaves. The glimmering mosaics had been brought into the wilderness from Italy to be laid down one tile at a time by the finest masons. The baths, heated by ceramic columns set beneath the floor, were made of quartz of such high quality the stones shone with red light when the sun was high. Floors were patterned in shades of rose and green and black, and frescoes had been painted by hundreds of Italian artists using the finest pigments from Rome, aquamarine and sapphire and carnelian, gemlike, gleaming as jewels do. The only colors I knew now were those of the white desert, the black night, the red stain of my own blood on the soles of my feet as we climbed over stones.

As the men spoke of such wonders, we huddled in damp caves where scorpions gathered, seeking shelter from the raging windstorms. I thought of the scorpions which had nested in the hallway when I was a child. They were so still they might have been an illusion until they suddenly leapt to attack their prey and prove otherwise. Guilt was like that, I had discovered. Remote, until it struck. I heard her still, the friend I'd had, the woman I'd betrayed. When I slept I could feel the curve of her hip against mine. I'd heard that demons could attach themselves to a person. Once this was accomplished, it was impossible to leave them behind or dismiss them. At night they closed their hands over yours with a predatory ownership. They whispered a single word in your ear: *Mine.*

Remorse engulfed me in this wasteland, as did my silence. It had risen around me as the thorn trees grew, wild, their limbs a tangle of treacherous sticks. There were hyenas where we camped; we heard them calling. At night we saw them forming a circle in among the stark black trees. We picked up stones, ready should the beasts' hunger cause them to attack. My hands were filthy, my scarves shredded as if by knives. I held on to the single square of blue. It was all I had left of my brother and the life I had led before I'd come to this place.

I found it impossible to imagine that if we journeyed deeper into the wilderness we would come upon frescoes that could rival any in the empire and the palace of a king. Still my brother's friends swore on the name of Yehuda of Galilee, the man who had begun the Zealot way of life and the rebellion against the priests who bowed to Rome, that ahead of us there were a thousand oil lamps to light up the night, all burning so fiercely they equaled the stars in the sky. When I asked how long it would take to reach this miraculous place, they laughed and said it would take time, for the fortress could only be found at the end of the world, and we must be careful not to stray. One step and we might fall off the edge of all eternity.

Mild air washed over us. Fortunately it was winter, so we didn't roast alive. From the west the cold sea wind called *Ruach Hayam* came to us in clouds, and we shivered in its chilly grasp. The wind flew inside my tunic and reminded me of things it would be best to forget. The touch of Ben Simon, the way we were one, how he had possessed the ability to see me when I was crouched in the darkness. Though I listened to the stories of Herod's palace, I was not compelled by thoughts of the future and of miracles. I longed for what I'd once had, all that I'd lost in the space of a single day, the hour when he was taken from me.

My life in the wilderness had been turned to ash. I had the punishment I deserved. Just as I had not let go of her husband, Sia would not let go of me, no matter how far we might journey. I thought I could leave her behind, but if anything, the distance had helped her ghost to grow stronger. Her spirit wrapped itself around me every time I tried to eat, pecking at me. I couldn't swallow more than a mouthful of food. If I did manage a bite, I would have to run off and bring it up again. When I closed my eyes to sleep, she was there, waiting. She gazed at me with the same doleful look she'd had when she asked if I would take care of Ben Simon, though she knew what we did together in the dark and what he was to me. It was he I longed for, but it was she who wrapped her arms around me, who slid her fingers over my skin, who whispered in my ear. I could feel her fever all over my flesh.

ONE NIGHT we were so near to the Salt Sea I rose from sleep to discover that salt had wound through my hair and turned the edges hard and white. I had been dreaming of a path of stones and a snake so huge it could devour a city. I tried to talk to the slithering creature, pleading for it to go away and leave us in peace, but the serpent wouldn't hear of it. *Come closer*, it whispered. I longed for the lion in my dreams. I missed him and yearned for him, despite the danger in doing so. I reached for the snake, but it disappeared, leaving me with a handful of black dust.

The shouts of the warriors who led us roused me. Groggy, I pulled myself from the tangle of my sleep. I stood and rubbed the salt from my eyes. All at once I saw a miracle before me. If a thousand blue butterflies had risen from the ground it would have been no more of a marvel. Herod's fortress was suspended in air, jutting out from the edge of a white cliff, exactly as the warriors had promised, a wonder of the world.

There was the path that led to Masada, winding up the sheerest cliff imaginable. One misstep, one moment of doubt, and anyone who made his way here could easily careen to his death in the valley below. The wilderness had made me a disbeliever, but as I climbed what was called the serpent's path, which wound like a snake up the side of the mountain, I felt something open inside me. This was where the snake in my dream had led us. I recognized it as surely as though it was a path I had walked a hundred times before: the small willows and clusters of bent olive trees, the chalky white earth beneath the limestone rocks. It had been written in the Book of Life that we would come to this path, and so it was meant to be.

Above us there were birds of prey, falcons and hawks. I knew they would be upon me if I were to stumble. They would take their revenge for all the birds I had killed in the desert, all the feathers I'd plucked, some with my fingers, some, when I was starving, with my teeth. I had wished for another's death and taken a man who didn't belong to me. I had given myself to the desert to become what I now was, a woman possessed by a ghost, mourning an existence that would never be again, carrying a secret that would ripen and expose me for the thief I had become.

I paid attention to the path and did my best not to think about the way I might appear to others, a barbarian, my skin powdered white with rock dust, my garments filthy, my hair turned to straw and salt, white at the edges but scarlet at the roots, my eyes empty except for the reflection of the desert. I was a lioness without claws or teeth, bent over like an old woman as I maneuvered along the rocks, so far from the girl I had been I could barely recall my own name. I thought of how I had given Ben Simon my promise to be silent. Now silence was all I had. The wind was howling as we rose higher on the cliff; that was the single voice we heard.

The serpent's path appeared endless. Stones fell and echoed when they hit the ground below. The world looked smoky and distant from this vantage point. I took the rope from around my waist and said I wanted to make my own way. I walked on without assistance, even at the steepest part of the path. I could hear the rattle of my breathing, sharp, like a dagger. The fortress before me was like a dream, and like a dreamer I went forth, marveling at the sight of what I beheld. It was everything they said, all the more brilliant for the desolation around us.

We had been found and brought to this place so near to the sky we could hear the voice of the King of Creation. The Lord had saved us and delivered us, as the Torah vowed He would. I would have been willing to do anything for the glory of God as I walked through the gate, except forgive Him for what I had lost.

*

BENEATH HIS CLOAK, my brother wore armor to protect him on those occasions when he went out in the night. A dagger would not suffice. He needed heavier weapons now: a bow, arrows, an ax, a lance of wood and brass. He resembled a dragon with scales or a silver snake, creatures feared by men, known to God alone. There were indeed three hundred warriors, but I instantly recognized my brother across the field beneath the pink bower of almond trees, planted high on this plateau above the rest of the world. I knew the swagger of his walk, the shining light that came from deep within him. Even armor couldn't hide that. My father had been brought to him right away, but I met with Amram after I was cleansed. I was taken to one of the *mikvahs,* of which there were several, for women and for men. In the largest bath, there was a line down the stairs for the clean and the unclean. The water pooled black where I was, and the other women left the bath lest they become unclean once more. I was not surprised. What I had done could never be washed away.

I dressed in the torn tunic and scarves Tamar had given me, then ran to meet my brother in the field. If I closed my eyes and breathed in the scent of almonds, I could imagine I had entered into another life. Perhaps we might one day return to Jerusalem and find the world that had been stolen from us. Perhaps all these months had been a dream, like my dream of the lion. Then I heard my brother shout to me, and it was quite clear there was no way to go back. He called me Yaya, my childhood name. I knew that girl was gone.

"It took long enough for you to come here," Amram said, embracing me, then letting me go so he could have a look.

Only months had passed since our last meeting, yet it seemed ten summers had gone by. Before this day Amram had always seemed younger than I—now he seemed a true warrior, fierce, sure of himself. For once I felt myself to be the little sister. My brother made me think of steel, metal that has been transformed through flame.

I didn't want to know how many men he'd killed or what cruel deeds he had accomplished. I was appalled to think he might have been one of the warriors who had taken Ein Gedi and slaughtered people of our own faith.

"I'm here now," I said.

My hair was clean and oiled, plaited atop my head. I could tell from my brother's gaze how different I appeared to him. He studied me, searching my expression, not quite seeing what had happened but aware that something had changed. I'd been bitten by a lion, but you had to look inside me to see the scar.

"I thought I would find you long before this. You must have been hidden, Yaya," Amram teased.

I thought of the caves where we had camped and what I had done there and of that last sorrowful place where Ben Simon had died. If he had gone with me to the Essenes, he might have lived. I had come to think that he knew what would befall him if he chose to remain behind, and still he had stayed. I should have seen it in the manner in which he glanced away from me, as if we had already been separated while I stood before him to say farewell. I should have known when he gave me his knife.

I didn't want my brother to see my shame. I sank onto the grass, beneath a canopy of pink almond blossoms, so that I might avert my face and be unreadable beneath Amram's curious glance. It was said that the almonds of pink trees were bitter, whereas those on trees where the blossoms were white would always be sweet. I lowered my eyes so I might seem like any other young unmarried woman.

"We did as best we could," I said simply.

"The others were unlucky," he replied. "I was sorry to hear of their passing. I thought Jachim ben Simon would take care of you. That was why I left you in his hands."

"It was their fate to enter the World-to-Come," I told him. That and nothing more.

My brother came to sit beside me joyfully, for a moment a boy once more rather than a warrior. He had scars I hadn't seen before, including a deep gash on his neck where he'd been pierced by an arrow. When he unclasped his armor, I noticed the constant pressure of the bow he carried had etched itself into his skin; there was now a crescent on his back and chest even when he did not shoulder his weapon.

He had grown his hair long and braided it tightly as warriors did. His face was still beautiful, but burned by the sun, thin. The openness of his youth was gone. He was no longer a boy learning rebellion in the dappled red shade of the flame tree.

"We are among the last holdouts in all of Judea," he told me. "Fortress after fortress has fallen. We haven't run and we never will."

There were only two routes to Masada, the way we had come, through the heartless desert which stretched on toward the mountains of Moab on the far side of the Salt Sea, or along the dusty route that connected Edom and the Arava Valley to Ein Gedi and Jerusalem. Either route was visible from this perch.

"We're safe here," my brother promised.

He told me that when the rebels first arrived they'd pulled down the golden eagle Herod had installed on the huge gate of the palace. There were to be no idols here, no great shows of wealth. All men were equal in this domain, no kings, only the kingdom of God. No man needed to bow to any other, not even to Eleazar ben Ya'ir, their leader, a great man and a great warrior.

My brother showed me that he continued to wear the amulet of Solomon I'd given him, strung around his throat. He took great pride in it still.

"Where's your scarf?" he asked then.

I showed him the single section of silk that remained. I told him how the scarf had saved my life and the life of our father, how it had become a map to guide us through the desert, tied to the thorn trees. To my great surprise, my brother brought forth a matching bit of blue. It had come to him on the wind, he told me. He'd thought it was a bird at first, and had held out his hand. It had come to him as if called. That was how he knew I was still alive, and that he would find me, and that our presence in this place so close to God was meant to be.

WE WENT WALKING through the orchard, toward terraces where ancient olive trees and huge, twisted grapevines grew. In the gardens there were onions, chickpeas, cucumbers, melons, all made possible by King Herod's amazing use of cisterns and pools which brought water to this mountain. Beyond us rose a field of emmer and barley, with sheaves tied together with rope. A plow drawn by donkeys cut what was left, the blade attached to a long piece of wood; two boys shouted at the donkeys to keep them going. As the chaff rose up, the air glowed yellow, like honey poured into a bowl.

Amram told me of the huge storerooms from the time of Herod, filled with enormous porcelain vessels of wine and oil shipped from Rome and Greece, many with the king's stamp still upon them. Through the Water Gate and the South Water Gate, donkeys brought up wooden barrels filled from the pools in the ravines below, enough for four baths and twelve cisterns, one a well so enormous fifty people could fit inside, shoulder to shoulder. It was no trouble to fill the pools and baths, even in the dry months. A market had grown up inside the fortress walls, much like the one in Jerusalem. There were bakers and tanners and weavers in small shops that had been set into narrow stalls between Herod's wall and the open ground of the plaza. Tents and houses made of wood had gone up against the fortification of the wall.

The warriors made their homes in what had been the Roman garrison's living quarters, while the priests and wise men had taken up residence in the small palaces where Herod's kin and advisers had lived long ago. There were mosaic floors of onyx black and pearl white in every room of the palaces. The public baths were decorated with brilliant mosaics as well, formed into fields of stone flowers or numerical patterns. There were red and orange frescoes on the palace walls, some still with their gold-leaf edges. Ben Ya'ir and his kinsmen lived in the smallest palace with a view of the valley. As for the Northern Palace, the most elegant and awesome structure, so fantastic it would rival any wonder of the world, weapons and supplies were kept there. Shops had been set up in small stalls, with cobblers and butchers, for no man among the rebels would ever live in a place of wealth as the king once had, setting up residence upon this mountain to prove he owned the world.

The men who had gathered at Masada were dedicated to Zion, willing to make any sacrifice, defiant in all ways, unwilling to be any man's slave. As for Ben Ya'ir, it was said he was not afraid even of *Mal'ach ha-Mavet*. When the Angel of Death came for him, he intended to pluck out that fierce being's twelve wings and lay them upon the ground, bloody and strewn with feathers, as a gift to God.

My brother and I stood gazing at Eleazar ben Ya'ir's residence.

"It's an honor to follow him," my brother remarked.

"Does he live in a palace and I make my home in the field?" I teased.

My brother told me that a chamber had been readied for my father and that I was to join him there and care for him. Amram had been shocked by how fragile our father had become. "Has he been ill?" my brother asked, concerned.

"He would not rest until we found you." I wanted to spare him from the truth. Our father's old age had been hastened by the burden of the men he had killed, by the daughter he had turned away, by a desert so fierce it had brought him to his knees.

When Amram wanted to know more of our time wandering, I said only that we had survived. I didn't mention the man who'd been scarred by a lion or the woman whose ghost was haunting me. Instead I told him about the wild goat who must have been an angel, whose milk had saved us from starvation. We laughed to think of a goat as an angel, and I admitted that I missed my pet, for she had become my confidante and my friend. My brother reminded me that our word for angel is also the word for messenger. That was how you knew you had been visited by such a luminous being, by the message you received. Perhaps the goat had come to teach me how to survive in a land so harsh it seemed impossible to do so.

"And what of you?" I asked. "Have you received a message?"

My brother seemed vulnerable at that moment, more a boy than a cold-eyed warrior. He had always told me his secrets, but that time had passed and now he seemed relieved when he was called away to the garrison before he could answer. His friend Uri's mother came to bring me to my living space. "Don't expect much," she warned.

Because I expected nothing, I was pleased by what I received. Our room beside Herod's wall was far better than any shelter we'd known since we had run from the city. There was a roof of fabric and three walls of wood. A small round oven was built into the stone wall, and there was a tiny chamber in which I could sleep. If I stood on my toes I could see through a spacing in the wall and gaze out at the cliffs. My father was waiting for me when I arrived. He had already blessed this place.

"I told you to trust in God," he said. "You should not have been so weak."

I swallowed my words. I did not say *You were the one who wept in the desert, not I. You feared wild beasts and starvation while I went to catch birds and dared to face leopards.*

I set up our house with what the council had decreed each family should be granted—straw pallets to sleep upon, two oil lamps, woven blankets, stone cups and bowls. Uri's mother brought us our ration of dates and lentils and fruit, along with a ceramic pot and a jar of oil for cooking and to use to light the Sabbath lamp. She warned me that life here was hard. I nodded, pretending to listen, but I almost laughed. She was clean, her hair plaited, and I was a barbarian who had faced down a leopard. I thanked her for her many kindnesses.

AFTER MY first evening at the fortress, I often found my way back to the orchard where the almonds were in bloom. It was the month of *Adar,* the beginning of spring. I needed a quiet place which would offer me an escape from my father's displeasure. He glared at me, unhappy to share his residence with me, begrudging me the corner where I was to live, cursing my existence. I never dared to speak back. I knew three new moons had passed since I had last had my monthly bleeding. In the orchards, Egyptian honeybees were swarming and the air was mild and pink. We had come from a wasteland to a garden, from valleys of death to fields of plenty. I was so accustomed to blistering white light that it pained me to see the many shades of green and gold and pink. I had to squint and hold one hand over my eyes. I had grown used to the silence of the wilderness. Here there were nearly a thousand people, a jumble of humanity, for a city had burst forth in the clouds with no need of the rest of the world. The council printed their own coins in metal shops. Grapes were gathered for wine, hives were kept for the honeybees. There were looms set up in the plaza for the women, and in the evenings their voices burst forth as they carded wool. Pens for animals were made of fences woven from thorn trees. Dusty sheep called to each other; black goats and their kids had space to run. There was the scent of bread baking, meals cooking, the fresh green fragrance of herbs, of coriander and dill and dusky gray sage.

It was too much for me to take in after our time in the desert, a torrent of noise and scent engulfing me like a tide. I yearned for what I'd once had. A bird among the rocks. The dusty prints of a leopard. I myself barely spoke, and if I raised my eyes to someone, it was for but an instant. Some women glanced at me as I walked by, curious. A few waved, but I pulled my scarf closer. Some young girls darted past on their way to the baths. I felt regret rise inside me when I spied them. I wished I could throw off my scarf and run with them, chattering, hopeful. If only I could slip off my garments and plunge into the bath, perhaps I could be cleansed and forgiven and start anew, a girl again. Yet if I'd had to take back all that had happened, I would have refused. I yearned for everything I'd lost. I wished I could reclaim the goat who was my angel. I would tie a rope of bells around her neck and another around my feet so that we could find each other whenever storms arose. I would watch the dark wash across the sky as I listened for the sound of bells. I would not have to pretend to be anything other than what I had become.

I spotted the *auguratorium*, the bird observatory left behind by the Romans when they'd camped here. It was one of the many towers built along the huge wall that circled the entire outpost. The observatory was in the most favorable position, overlooking the northern hills, the air tempered by cool breezes. I'd seen such towers in Jerusalem, sacred edifices where bird bones were thrown to tell the future, from whose heights magicians might observe the movement of flocks that could predict what was to come.

The sages said that magic might be studied and learned but never practiced; it was forbidden, yet it could be found in the dark or hidden in towers such as this one. I climbed the wooden ladder. The air was even cooler here, the gleaming distance shimmering in waves. I gasped at the world before me, blinking in the bright light. There were hawks gliding through the sky, but I didn't know what their flight meant, not when they dipped closer to the cliff nor when they soared into the western horizon. I had no talent for magic of any kind.

I knelt down to see hundreds of bones on the floor, left behind by the Romans when they fled. The ground was speckled with white shards. I had no idea what they signified. Yet I was deeply affected to see the sharp little bones, so hollow the wind made a song of them. I felt I was being watched. I gazed up to see that a dove had lit on the wall. I was quiet and held out my hands. After all I'd done and all my sins, it came to me, unafraid.

IN THE MORNING a girl was sent to find me, perhaps one of those who'd run by me on the way to the baths, a girl too young and innocent to know what secrets there were between women and men, who thought what you observed in the daylight was all there was and had no knowledge of the night. She was polite and pretty, no older than thirteen, with little earrings of carnelian and gold in her ears. She said her name was Nahara, which she shyly explained meant light. She had brought me a pair of sandals. She laughed when I hesitated, distrusting a gift from a stranger. "You'll need these where you're about to go," she informed me.

My own sandals had been ruined by my long journey, the leather falling off in strips. I slipped on the new ones to find they fitted me perfectly. As we went along, Nahara informed me that she was bringing me to the position to which I'd been assigned. She asked for my name, a word I'd not spoken aloud for so long I had nearly forgotten its sound.

"My name is ugly," I assured her. "Unlike yours."

We walked together across the Western Plaza, which had been paved with huge stones brought across the sea from Greece. Nahara kept pace beside me. "I have to call you something," she insisted. She was a serious, quiet girl, but stubborn, set between an older sister and a younger brother, accustomed to making her own way.

There were those who believed if you knew the name of something you had access to its essence. Most parents would not reveal a male child's name after birth, not until he was circumcised eight days later, so he could gather his strength and not be as vulnerable to demons who might call to him. Nahara shrugged when I said every name was a secret known only to *Adonai*. She insisted I probably had a beautiful name, for I had the most beautiful hair she had ever seen. All the women in the settlement were talking about it, she told me. They said I had been burned in a fire and that was the cause of the flecks on my skin and my flame-colored hair.

"They should be careful I don't breathe on them," I warned. "I could be a dragon. They might be covered by sparks."

Nahara laughed, then confided that her mother had spied me in the *auguratorium* and thought I had a special talent. "That's why you'll work with us in the dovecotes. She chose you when she saw you in the tower."

My heart sank. There were so many places I would have preferred to be sent, nearly anywhere would have been an improvement: the olive groves, the bakers', even the goat barns. There were three *columbaria*, the Roman-style dovecotes, where I was to work. Two were built as oblongs, but the third was a circular tower with a platform on the top floor used for observation. The windows of all were covered by screens, so prying hawks couldn't enter. All three buildings were made of stone and covered with white plaster, raised from the ground so that snakes in search of eggs couldn't slither inside. Thousands of birds were kept, and each of the niches carved into the white walls housed a pair of doves, mated for life.

During the time when the Roman garrison occupied Masada, the shelves had been used as funerary chambers, to store the ashes of the dead, but now they once again housed nesting turtledoves. Whatever the Romans had corrupted during their time here after King Herod's fall, our rebels took back for their own usage. What they had used for death had been transformed into life in the beating hearts of the doves. We did not believe in turning flesh to ash but rather in honoring the bones of our forefathers returning the body to the earth, from whence it came in the days of creation. What had housed the dead during the Roman occupation was once more filled with song, the cooing *tirr tirr* I had learned to imitate in the wilderness so that the doves might come to me and consider me one of their own.

Among the abominations the Romans had committed was to use the synagogue for their stables. People said it had taken weeks to clean out the excrement and cleanse the area. Even now there was said to be the smell of horseflesh when the rains came, so incense was lit every morning. But no incense could disguise the rich, moist odor of the doves' leavings, which assaulted me when Nahara led me into the stone dovecote. Of the three, this was the largest, filled with the stench of the birds. Even worse was the noise. When we entered the murk through heavy wooden doors, the sound was overwhelming, for together the doves shared one voice. I stopped, shaken by the fluttering of wings, once again yearning for the silence I had known in the wilderness.

Nahara smiled when she saw my reaction, her face upturned. "They don't bite," she promised. "You'll become accustomed to them."

She picked up a bird that had fluttered to the floor, holding it gently. We were to care for them, feed them, collect their eggs. Most important, we were to gather their excrement, used to fertilize the fields. That was why such beautiful groves arose on this cliff, where the soil was little more than limestone covered with a thin dusting of earth, and why the air smelled like almonds. The doves' leavings turned the fields fertile; their waste was the secret to creating a garden in the wilderness.

There were three other women in the dovecote, all busy until our arrival. Now they turned to me. One would imagine such nasty business would have been the last sort of work anyone would have wanted, but these women seemed proud of what they did.

One, an older woman whose name was Revka, gazed at me disapprovingly, as though I had stumbled uninvited into her domain and she had already gauged me as unworthy. The others were Nahara's elder sister and mother, each more beautiful than the other. Aziza was sixteen, composed, with dusky olive skin. As she stood beside her mother, I could hardly tell them apart. But it was Shirah, the mother, who had chosen me.

Nahara whispered for me to step forward, reminding me of her mother's faith in me. I wondered if her choice had been made when she spied the dove who came to me without being called.

In this place of noise, Shirah was serene, a dark quiet engulfing her. I approached her, then stopped, flustered. Our glances met, and I felt something unexpected between us, a surge of heat. It seemed I was transparent in her eyes.

"I wonder how a lioness will manage in a dovecote. Can you put away your teeth and claws?"

The other women had gathered round, and they laughed at Shirah's comment. I felt vulnerable and exposed, even though the chamber was dim, with only thin streams of sunlight entering through the roof and screened windows.

Shirah had one long black braid down her back. She was extraordinarily beautiful, with high cheekbones and dark, nearly black eyes. The other women thought she was teasing me, having sensed my displeasure over handling birds. They didn't understand what she meant. But I did. She knew what was inside me.

"Hardly a lioness," I said contritely. "Only a poor wanderer."

"Aren't we all?" the older woman, Revka, replied. "You think you're so different from us? You're not too good to shovel the shit of these doves, are you?" she asked scornfully. "If you are, you can leave right now."

The women were gazing at my red hair. As Nahara had said, it was what people noticed first. Perhaps they believed that the tawny color was what Shirah referred to when she spoke of lions. They had no idea who I was or what I'd done. The birds fluttered around, unbidden, drawn to me. I kept my eyes downcast as I spoke. All I wished was to be left alone.

"I'll do whatever work you ask of me," I said.

Do unto me what you desire, whatever your will. I deserve nothing more than what has befallen me.

Shirah approached with a basket formed of palm leaves, beautifully constructed with a leaf-over-leaf pattern. Her eyes were huge and deep, ringed with kohl. She wore gold bracelets on her arms and amulets tied around her throat on red string, including two gold charms, which glinted in the half-light. Her daughters came and circled their arms around their mother's slim waist. Their love for her was evident, and I envied them. I wished I'd known what it was like to have a mother, someone who would stand beside you no matter what you'd done.

The birds were cooing. I felt a pulse in my throat, remembering how I had waited for my prey in the wilderness, how they had come to me and how I had destroyed them. Shirah handed me the basket. I wondered if it had been woven with palm leaves from Ein Gedi, if some woman had set down the crossing leaves pattern on the morning of her own death.

"Even a lioness has to work," Shirah told me.

THE WORK BEGAN right away. We were all wearing white, for vivid color was thought to disturb the doves and keep them from laying. Perhaps it had not been an accident when the Essene woman, Tamar, gave me my tunic, for it seemed as though she'd somehow known I would be chosen for the dovecote. Perhaps I wasn't as invisible as I had imagined.

There was no time to doubt myself or to complain. Aziza quickly taught me how to feed our charges millet and wheat and vetch, and how to chase the pairs from their niches when we needed to collect eggs or clean out their droppings. Whichever eggs we let remain in the nests would soon hatch, and the parents would care for the fledglings together. Aziza was eager to help me learn the ways of the dovecote. She resembled a deer, with slim legs and arms, and a thick braid of dark hair, like her mother's, glossy, black as night. But whereas Shirah's eyes were pitch, Aziza's were an unusual pale gray, like river water, filled with moving light. There was a tiny scar, much like a teardrop, barely noticeable, set beneath one eye.

Nahara came to gossip with her sister about me. Both sisters' eyes were shining. They enjoyed having someone new to tease, an occasion to break the monotony of their workday. "She wouldn't tell her name when I asked," Nahara informed Aziza.

The sisters stood with their hands on their hips, considering what to do with me. I was ashamed to be considered worthy of their interest.

"We have to call you something," Aziza insisted, wanting to befriend me.

The sisters were so close their words were like beads on the same strand of gold. Perhaps if I said my name aloud, I'd be rid of their prying. We were to work side by side, after all, and they needed to call to me.

"Yael," I managed, for it was a word that left a bitter taste in my mouth. It had always sounded like a curse, and it remained so on this day.

The sisters seemed satisfied, assuring me that mine was a beautiful name.

"Do you have anyone here with you?" They wanted to know more about me, so that we might be friends. I shrugged coldly, with only a gleam of response.

A lion, a ghost, a goat who is an angel, a hundred birds with broken necks.

"I was brought here by my brother. Amram, son of Yosef bar Elhanan."

To my surprise, their curiosity faded, and my words dropped like stones. I heard the echo of my brother's name. The silence that came back to me was something I understood, the realm of secrets best left untold.

Nahara was called to her mother. She seemed grateful to have an excuse to run out to the smallest of the dovecotes, even though the dovekeepers usually recoiled from working there, for the building was so compact only one person could stand within its walls. Beside me, Aziza quickly returned to her work, chasing the doves away, collecting their eggs. I could see through the mirror of her languid, gray eyes. She didn't have to say any more for me to understand how my brother's name had blazed for her. Once spoken, it refused to disappear.

IN THE DAYS that followed, I kept to myself during my hours at the dovecotes, attending to whatever tasks I was given. I was pleasant enough, but I spoke only when others spoke to me. I was their servant, nothing more. I wasn't one of them and didn't pretend to be. I had had a friend once, and I had betrayed her. I didn't need another.

The other women took their meal together at noon. I ate alone. I went into the orchard in the midday sun, taking along some dry cheese and flatbread. I neared the wall and peered out, gazing north, the direction we had come from, where we had left the bones. One day some of the women who worked in the fields came to sit beside me. They had tied up their hair and covered their heads with scarves to shade their complexions. Their hands, however, were brown from their work in a small pistachio grove, slick with nut oil. They had come here from Jerusalem, following their husbands, or fathers, or brothers. Now they acted like those fortunate ones who had found their way to the Garden of Paradise. I'd heard them singing as they worked. A few carried babies in woven slings tied to their backs or hips. The unmarried women asked me to meet them at the baths. I shook my head and said I was unable to do so. I wanted no one to notice my rounded form when I took off my cloak. As my excuse, I said I must remain at the dovecotes, for I had just begun there and wanted to please Shirah. When they heard this, the women grew suspicious.

"Fine," one said, rebuffed. "It's your choice if you prefer the Witch of Moab."

The field women who gathered around cautioned me, murmuring that Shirah had come across the desert from the far side of the Salt Sea. The salt had lifted her up, allowing her and her children to cross without drowning. Shirah, they assured me, could call the clouds to her the way she called the doves in the dovecote. After her arrival there had been downpours for weeks. Torrents fell until the world was green and people were weeping with joy. This was why their leader, Ben Ya'ir, had sent for her. Shirah was his kinswoman and cousin, but there was more to her arrival. Even a great man may sometimes call for a witch.

I found these women to be self-absorbed fools. What sort of witch would work in a dovecote, eat lentils for her meal, shovel out excrement, collect speckled eggs in a basket? She was a woman like any other. Still, when I went back to the dovecote, I noticed there was a curious intensity about Shirah; what was silent to others rang out clearly for her. Sometimes, at the end of the day, when she was locking the door, she would turn to gaze at me. In that instant I felt she knew everything about me. Even stranger, I had no desire to hide myself from her. I wanted to speak of the night when I cut myself for the twenty-first time, and the morning when I left to set out in search of a cure, and the evening when I returned to find that Ben Simon had already entered the World-to-Come. Perhaps that in itself was witchery, to make someone yearn to reveal herself.

*

ONE EVENING a young woman was waiting beside the largest dovecote. She was a servant, brought here from Jerusalem by her master's family, living alongside them as their cook and housemaid. I had seen her in the fields. Now she gestured to Shirah from the shadows, urging her to come away. Shirah spoke with her daughters, sending them home to see to their younger brother and begin the evening meal.

When Shirah left with the housemaid, I followed, curious. I removed my sandals and went barefoot, as I had when I'd stalked birds. I felt something wicked in my actions, yet continued on. Shirah and the housemaid did not stop until they reached the far end of the wall. There they slipped into a dark corner. We were not far from the place where large looms had been set up for women to work on in the evenings, after their daily chores had been completed. I paused behind a column where green-tinged shadows spread along the stones. I felt as I had when I had crouched in the wilderness, waiting for my prey. There was a beating of my pulse in my throat.

Shirah drew the image of an eye on the wall with a piece of charred wood. She took a needle from the hem of her tunic, and while she recited an incantation she pierced the eye with the needle. The low, rhythmic sound of her voice drifted to where I was hidden. Although I didn't understand the words, I guessed what she was doing. She was binding some man to be true, as I had done in the desert on the night when I drew the face of the lion in the dirt. Other men might stray, but this one would be bound to faithfulness as thread was bound to the stitches cast by a needle.

I shouldn't have lingered. I could have easily returned the way I'd come before anyone saw me, but I was caught up in the spell. The chanting entrapped me, the singsong of Shirah's voice winding itself around me as though it had the ability to bind me as well as the lover of the housemaid. Shirah turned to eye me as the scorpion glances at the mouse. I hurried away, yet still felt her gaze.

The following day I wore my scarf across my face when I went to work in the dovecote, hoping it would cause me to be invisible, much the way my father's cloak hid his true nature. Shirah ushered me inside, a smile playing at her lips. I would have sworn she saw through my veil. When the others went to take their noon meal, cooking lentils and peas in an outdoor kitchen, Shirah insisted she needed my help. There was an errand we must attend to. I had no choice but to go. Like the housemaid who had come to her, I was only a servant.

We went into the fields, carrying our baskets. The sun beat down upon us.

"What I did at the wall, I was asked to do," Shirah informed me as we passed beneath the lacy green shade of the almond trees. "It wasn't love the girl asked for, merely decency."

From where they sat over their lunch in the grove, the field women stared at us, whispering, save for one, the housemaid who was still gathering pistachios for her mistress. Pale petals were falling around us, half of them bitter.

"When the time comes and you want my help, I'll listen to you as well," Shirah said. "I'll do as you ask."

I blushed, confused. "Did I ask for anything?"

Shirah dumped the basket from the doves around the tallest almond tree, one that was abloom with a thousand flowers. It occurred to me that she could divine the truth even when it went unspoken.

"True enough," she replied. "You haven't."

We began the walk back to the dovecote, side by side, past the mulberry bushes with their jumbles of black berries, past the pistachio tree where the housemaid was at work, stripping the pods from the branches. I noticed the young woman did not raise her eyes to us, even though Shirah touched her shoulder in a silent greeting. "Not yet," she said to me.

IN THE HALLWAYS of the Western Palace atop the plateau, what had in the past served royalty now served us all. Wheat and grain were stored in what had once been elegant chambers. The tanners and bakers and metalworkers labored in a hall where the marble floors were as fine as any in Athens or Rome. To those who came from small villages, the glory of this place was astounding. Here, where there had been huge royal gatherings, we now worked in the service of the Almighty, not for our own greed. The rebels were pure in their concerns, yet the men were on edge, my father among them. He went to the synagogue built in to the western wall each morning, to pray and listen to the wise men talk about what the future would bring. I woke an hour before my father, to heat barley cakes in oil for his meal. I was his servant, his dog, and his chattel. His desires were my demands, his moods ruled my life.

The men met at the synagogue, worrying over the welfare of their leader, Eleazar ben Ya'ir, who had left our fortress several days earlier to rally support in desert towns throughout Judea. His followers were anxious for his return. In his absence, our peril was felt a hundred times over with only the unforgiving brim of the mountain there to protect us. When an old man at a public meeting demanded to know who would take Ben Ya'ir's place if he should fall in battle, all the rest fell quiet. No one wanted to think about Masada without a leader, a body without spirit. Without Eleazar ben Ya'ir we were lost, at each other's mercy, at one another's throats. His band of warriors included my brother, and I was especially worried, for those who have recently been reunited should not be parted.

That very day, as if to answer any doubters, Ben Ya'ir—our rescuer and our redeemer, the man who had saved our people when Jerusalem had fallen—returned. He came at dusk. People went to the walls to watch as he and his closest companions climbed the path to God's domain. There were those who believed he could speak with angels, that Raphael himself walked beside him, a gleaming sword raised to our enemies. We gazed over the cliffs that protected us and felt blessed to have such a noble leader.

Because of the winter's heavy rains, the world below us was green. The desert was covered in myrtle, a sign of good fortune. We women wove myrtle into our undergarments, so that we would carry the sweet scent of the desert with us when we walked. There was a sense of joy rising with the turning of the season, and the joy of my own secret that I carried within me. I caught sight of Amram and was relieved. I now wanted to see Ben Ya'ir for myself, the man who had led my brother and his friends to this remote and dangerous place. There was a crowd and people were jostling each other, all with the same goal, to see him and be comforted by his strength. I had to rise on my toes for a glimpse. People were willing to die for him; they would stand before him, denying arrows access to his flesh. Many bowed their heads in his presence, as they did before holy men and sages.

In Jerusalem he might have gone unnoticed in a crowd. He was not a man who stood out because of his appearance. He was not tall or handsome, merely broad-shouldered with a plain, straightforward expression. There were several scars marking him, and his arms were huge, capable of throwing an ax across the battlefield. He dominated all other men and had a fluid energy that made it impossible not to respond to him. He shone because others followed, because they adored him and deferred to him and trusted him. He was dark, but there was a light inside him, a brightness that was unexplainable. Even when he stood motionless our eyes went to him, and in that way he commanded us all.

The returning band of warriors had brought back donkeys loaded down with weapons—arrows and bows of many sizes, along with dozens of shields gathered from the defeated. Another band from the Roman garrison had fallen before them, and what had belonged to them was now ours. Some of the bronze armor would be melted down so that our fortress could have its coins—on one side vine leaves would be printed, on the other the words *For the Freedom of Zion.* Two men in chains tramped behind the donkeys, humiliated, their heads bloodied; their eyes flickered over the crowd. They were Roman soldiers conscripted by the legion from a land so far away no one had ever seen anyone as colorless as they, with milky white skin. Although they wore Roman helmets, their tunics were from the land of their birth and were woven into odd patterns of slate, blue, and red. It was sobering to see them before us; we always thought of ourselves as the victims of an unjust war, yet here were these two conscripts, in irons.

There were slaves among us, brought by those escaping Jerusalem, but they were treated as housekeepers and fieldworkers and often given their freedom after their years of service. They were not bloodied and in chains. Now people applauded the capture of our enemies, who stooped their heads, waiting, most likely, to be slaughtered. But soon enough the crowd forgot them. They were more interested in our hero, shouting out Eleazar ben Ya'ir's name as thirsty men call for water. I overheard some women say that Ben Ya'ir's eyes changed color; they were a cool gray, like the still water in a well, but occasionally his gaze turned to the clear green of a stream that falls into a pool. As a man, he was as complicated as the color of his eyes. He would stride away if you disagreed with him, but after some thought he would search you out and ask you to further explain your opinion. He was a man to whom arguments came naturally, but he was tender as well. When one of his men fell in battle and was too wounded to live, Ben Ya'ir did not send a warrior to execute the horrid deed of mercy. He completed the task himself, then spoke the prayers for the dead, an act of charity that can never be repaid. He was open in a way that made people respond to him on a deep, essential level; they revered him and feared his anger, yet loved him as well as they would a brother or a son.

On the day the slaves were brought to us, Ben Ya'ir had a fresh scar down his neck and chest. He wore his hair long and braided as our warriors did, but he always kept his shawl wrapped around him, ready to pray at all times. It was quite possible that what people whispered was true and he did indeed know more than other men, and was made even more fierce by the power of prophecy. He could divine the righteous from the wicked, and when he gazed upon his enemies, he could see beyond their garments and their flesh to look upon their spirits.

When the crowd moved toward him, excited, stamping their feet, I shrank away, afraid he might see me for who I was. The seething drive forward might easily crush those who didn't move quickly enough with the pulsing throng. Above us there came a flock of wild doves, but if that was a sign, I hadn't the ability to read the prophecy, and the doves quickly turned away, flying east and then north, toward Jerusalem. I saw Shirah watching them, and it seemed her face flushed with despair. I wondered if she had understood something I had failed to notice, and why she carried a branch of myrtle with her, as brides were said to do on their wedding nights.

Ben Ya'ir had the crowd enthralled. He told of the Romans that had been defeated in this most recent battle, soldiers dressed in helmets and mail, their shields nearly impenetrable when they huddled into a formation that resembled a turtle. Only the bravest warriors could combat them, entering into the fray with drawn daggers. Ben Ya'ir lauded his warriors for their courage, singling out my brother for praise. Amram lowered his head so that he would not appear prideful, but he was clearly honored by the recognition. I spied the silver disk of Solomon around his neck, still providing protection.

Ben Ya'ir went on to recount the treasures sacked from the Roman camp—a gold breastplate decorated with precious stones, gold signet rings, jars of wine, coins to be melted down. He proclaimed that our victory was due to our God, and that our hearts must be strong to honor Him.

"If this life seems difficult now, it will only become more so," Ben Ya'ir announced, his expression grim, the light fading from within him. But this sobering statement hadn't the power to stop the rising tide of triumph. I had never seen a crowd become one in this manner, one flesh, one spirit, swaying from side to side. The warriors in particular seemed under a spell; they were to a man entranced and absorbed, or so I believed until I happened to glance across the plaza. There was Amram, among his brethren, many who had been wounded in the battle they'd fought. I would have expected my brother to be intent on Ben Ya'ir's every word, enthralled by his beloved leader, as his brothers-in-arms were. Instead he was staring at a girl on the edge of the crowd.

It was Aziza, her eyes lowered, her sleek hair pulled back beneath her veil.

THAT NIGHT I went to the *mikvah*. It was a place of renewal and hope, what I felt now that my brother had returned. Oil lamps burned in the niches along the stone walls illuminating the darkened chamber. I'd hoped to be alone—although my condition did not announce itself, it was evident to one who might look closely. When I arrived the women from the field were there. If I turned to leave I would offend them, therefore I undressed in the dark, removing my tunic and scarves, hoping to conceal my rounded shape. I hid Ben Simon's dagger, which I always carried with me, beneath my folded garments, then quickly took the stairs and slipped into the water before anyone had time to study my form.

"You finally decided to be one of us," they teased. "Why so shy?"

I let them think I was mild in my temperament. I hung my head and said the specks on my skin had always embarrassed me. There was no harm in allowing them to see me as they wished to, a girl who chose to keep herself hidden out of timidity. I knew when to join in the teasing. I remembered how to smile, whether or not I meant it. Women were freer to speak in the bath; they shared secrets as they formed a circle in the water. The field women questioned me about my brother, which came as no surprise. Wherever Amram walked, women threw themselves at him. Many of the women in the bath found him handsome, but I had few answers for them. I said I rarely saw my brother, and they accepted my reserve. They set to discussing Shirah. If she had not been a distant cousin of Ben Ya'ir's, a young woman named Naomi whispered, surely she would have been cast into the desert. Shirah was a practitioner of *keshaphim,* initiated into the secrets of magic. Our people believed that any item with a sun and a moon upon it must be taken to the Salt Sea and thrown into the water, but several women claimed to have seen gold amulets with such figures worn at the witch's throat. It was rumored that in her kitchen there was a box kept locked with a key shaped like a serpent, Deraqon, another figure from Egypt that had been outlawed. Inside there was said to be a myriad of sins that would become your burden if you dared to open the lid and set them free; they would swarm around you, like wasps, stinging and biting, never leaving your side. One young woman claimed to have already been stung when she dared to call Shirah a witch.

I took note of a quiet woman with plaits of honey-colored hair who stayed at the edge of the group. She was the servant girl from the wall where the binding spell had been cast, the one whose arms were stained with the brown tint of pistachios. I knew that she recognized me as well, for she couldn't meet my glance. I hadn't realized just how young she was, not much more than a child. I felt a pang of sorrow for whatever she had lost on this mountain.

The other women kept on with their gossip. A witch was only a woman, they whispered, but the daughter Aziza was something even worse. She was one of the *sheydim*. Half human, half angel, a combination that formed a demon. The women in the bath vowed that Aziza's father was an angel sent to earth to teach sorcery to those evil women who yearned to know such secrets. Creatures like Aziza were born of these unions. It was difficult to measure who they were, for they could eat and drink as we could. They could have sexual relations and make men long for them; they could even die like mortals, but they were nothing like us. They could see the future in a cup of water and turn the pages of the Book of Life to view the names that were inscribed within. They flew from one end of the world to the other in the time it took for us to rise from our beds. They practiced patience, but they took what they wanted, entitled to all we had in this world; in that way they were the same as all messengers from heaven, a puzzlement to those of us who had no choice but to be bound by our human needs and desires.

I listened to such claims without comment or expression, but there was a shiver of unease along my spine. Everything I'd done since leaving Jerusalem was surely a sin in someone's eyes. If the women from the field knew I had called to a lion and brought him to me and had never once turned him away, even during the time of the month when I was a *niddah*, what would they have said of me? What might they have thought had they caught sight of me in the desert, waiting on the cliff, wanting him more than I wanted purity or obedience or duty?

I turned away when they spoke badly of Aziza. I had seen her shoveling out the nests in the dovecotes until her hands were bleeding. It was hardly suitable work for an angel, any more than it was a calling for a witch.

"Watch her," the women insisted. "She will never come to the baths. She won't remove her tunic or scarves when anyone can see her body. There's a reason for her modesty."

They were jealous, envious that wherever Aziza walked men gazed at her, that her hair was the color of night, that her smile was sweet, that she would not have thought to speak about them with rancor as they now defamed her. Perhaps they, too, had seen her blush at the mention of my brother's name. Several of the women clearly wanted my favor only because I was Amram's sister. The one called Naomi drifted up beside me, so close I could feel the heat of her body in the cool water. Jealousy burned like that. I knew this only too well.

"Be careful around the witch's daughter," Naomi warned me. Clearly, she believed I was a woman who wanted a friend. "And never try to catch her. The *sheydim* have wings."

Aziza's wings were black, she went on, like those of a raven, and like a raven, it was said, she sang to announce the arrival of the Angel of Death. She perched on Herod's wall each time our warriors went out, gazing over the landscape through silver-colored eyes.

"You're mistaken," I said humbly, not wishing to press the issue.

I knew that the Angel of Death was never announced. He came in silence and left in sorrow. He arrived when you imagined you were safe, as he had when we were following the path of blue flags through the desert, a cure for Ben Simon in hand.

Walking back to my chamber from the *mikvah*, my hair dripping wet, I felt cool and superior to those foolish women in the bath. But as I crossed the plaza, I saw a figure in the dark that seemed to resemble an angel, moving the way angels are said to do, in the corners of our sight.

For an instant I feared that Death was indeed near and the women in the bath had been right. I shivered to think his messenger had been let loose upon us. Or perhaps I had forgotten to lock the dovecote and the doves had escaped to conceal themselves in the branches of the olive trees, rustling the leaves. It was too dark to see clearly, so I stopped where I was, blinking back moonlight. I saw the glint of a girl's shape sifting through the night.

It was then I spied my brother beside a small pool where a hundred years earlier King Herod had kept fish, small, glimmering creatures said to be made of pure gold. When a hawk plucked up one of the king's treasured fish, he would sink to earth immediately, weighed down by greed. I saw a girl run to Amram, flying into his arms. There was no need of a spell to bind him, he was bound in the knots of his own desire without the use of the slightest bit of sorcery. He had walked into this net of love and tied the ropes himself, not because Aziza was an angel but rather because she was flesh and blood.

A SUDDEN cold wind surprised us all in this mild month. When it had gone, fruit fell from the trees and scattered across the stones. Some women vowed the remains of the figs dashed onto the ground formed the shape of the red hawks that circled above us, waiting to claim our fortress for their own. There was a hurry to take the scythes into the fields of emmer and wheat, and collect what could still be of use before the stalks turned brown. Our people said a prayer, led by the wise men and the members of the council. The highest of our priests, usually cloistered inside the synagogue, where he studied and gave advice, now came to stand upon the wall and lead the men in prayer. His name was Menachem ben Arrat, and he was known to be one of the five most learned men in Judea. People said he had heard God's voice on the mountaintop. The situation was dire, so he now revealed himself, for without the orchards we would have no sustenance and without the doves there would be no orchards. I had learned to appreciate the cooing of the birds, a call so beautiful King Solomon's great glory *Song of Songs* celebrated it as though it was the voice of one's beloved. *O my dove, that art in the clefts of the rock, in the secret places of the stairs, let me see thy countenance, let me hear thy voice, for sweet is thy voice; and thy countenance is comely.*

The council set forth a ruling on our behalf. The dovecotes were blessed and offerings were made for the flocks' good health. We burned balsam and myrrh in small silver holders, for the smoke would ensure that our charges would produce eggs easily. Because of the biting wind, the doves shivered on their perches and tucked their heads beneath their wings. We were given one of the Roman soldiers from the north to do the heaviest of our work, carrying baskets into the fields, laying down hay, and raking it up when it was used and dank. The other soldier had been exchanged for two white donkeys that traders from Edom brought to us and was already gone from the fortress. That was a slave's worth in this world. Ours wore metal cuffs on his feet that were unlocked when he came to us. He kept his eyes averted and did as he was told. He had twisted his fair hair into braids rather than allowing it to hang lank as it had when he first arrived, but despite this attempt to conceal how different he was, he still didn't look like us in any manner.

He seemed ashamed of his situation, yet when Revka motioned to him, he was quick to do what was demanded of him. He was tall, nearly a giant, well muscled, with long arms and legs. Inked on his strong forearm, there was a black tattooed image of a creature that looked like an ibex but with huge curled horns. The slave saw me staring and gazed back at me openly.

"Don't worry," Revka remarked when she noticed his rude demeanor. "We'll make every effort to tame him."

The slave threw her a dark look, then went back to work, cleaning out the nests. I quickly came to believe he knew more of our language than he let on. He shrugged and pretended he didn't understand, but I could see the truth in the way he looked up one day when I broke an egg and murmured a prayer for the spirit of the dove who might have been.

"Do you know what I'm saying?" I asked.

He glanced away. His strange blue eyes were cold to look at.

I noticed that he often scanned the plaza through the slats that covered the dovecote windows, which allowed air in but contained the birds. I thought he might be searching for the other slave.

"Your comrade has been sent away," I told him. "We will not see him again."

Although I wasn't certain, I thought he winced to hear this news. I pitied him, perhaps because he was now the only one of his kind. I thought of the leopard I had faced in the wilderness, how the beast had run from me when I leapt upon a stone and roared. How alone he had been as he darted into the thornbushes, as I'd been alone when he'd left me.

"Well, if you know what's good for you, you won't listen even if you're able to understand us," I cautioned our captive.

I kept watch and saw that he was clever; he had begun a new method of cleaning the dovecotes with a rake he had devised. The slave had found rusted nails on the floor and had used them to attach twigs to a twisted branch of the olive tree that had grown in through a space in the roof. Every time he realized I was studying him, he seemed abashed, cautious. He made me think of a Syrian bear I had seen once in Jerusalem, set in irons to perform tricks for his Roman owner. The bear had kept his eyes lowered, but once, when he could no longer restrain himself, he had bared his teeth, only to be slapped down. He had held his paws over his head, as though he were a man being beaten. Although others in the crowd laughed, I had recoiled and run away, my heart pounding.

"Do you have enough food?" I asked the slave at the end of one day.

I mimicked eating so he might understand. He shook his head, shrugged. I knew he slept in the fetid loft above the dovecote, where he was chained at night, that he was given grain and crackers as his ration and little more. I began to leave him piles of twigs, so that he might have a fire and warm himself when the nights were chill.

"Are you deaf?" I wondered aloud.

He looked up then. He was a stranger from a land covered with snow, something I had seen only once in my life, when I was a young girl and it fell in Jerusalem dusting the hills, sent by Shalgiel, the angel of snow. Some children had mistaken it for manna and eaten handfuls of it, freezing their lips.

The slave understood me. I was sure of it.

I knew what it was to yearn for a life so distant it seemed that it had never been anything more than a dream. Did he dream of snow and wild blue goats, or of his comrade, taken in chains across the Salt Sea?

I urged one of the doves out of its niche, held it until it quieted, then quickly broke its neck. I nearly laughed to see how startled the slave was. Perhaps watching me the way he did, he did not expect such an abrupt and deadly action. But I was not afraid of cruelty; I knew it was inside me, as it was inside the leopard who must catch his supper to survive. The slave was grateful enough when I handed the bird to him to cook for his dinner; he hid it away in the corner, where he might reach it when he was chained at night.

When Revka, always sour and ready to place blame, noticed a bird missing the following morning, I declared that I'd seen a hawk earlier that day. Such things happened often enough; a dove would arise through the narrow opening in the roof and be struck in midair. Then there would be feathers floating down, and if you narrowed your eyes, a thin rain of blood.

WHEN I WENT to the wall to look out at the far reaches beyond our settlement, I was often stunned by how set apart we were from the rest of the world. The wilderness appeared endless, the earth so distant it seemed impossible we might ever walk upon it again. If this was what it was to be an angel, to be Raphael or Michael or one of the *sheydim* who peered down upon mankind, then it was a lonely and terrible place to be. We were a city and a world unto ourselves, with more people arriving all the time. The desperate, the devout, the beaten, the lost. That was why there was so much gossip; it was difficult to keep secrets in such a crowded, unforgiving world. Families shared their lives, with only thin walls of rough fabric made of goat hair strung from ropes to separate us.

We heard what should have been private, lovemaking and arguments alike. We knew whose children wouldn't behave and were scolded and whose wife muttered curses as soon her husband left their chamber. The baths were always teeming, with talk as well as with bodies. Shops were filled with those desiring flour and oil. So many had traveled here from Jerusalem there was not enough for all; we were forced to share everything, to wait in lines for food and provisions doled out carefully from the dwindling storehouses, to toil far into the evening hours. I understood why the men went out raiding. I was only a woman, not privy to the knowledge of men at the synagogue or in the barracks, but even I understood what awaited if God failed to favor us. Although the fields were green now, it was impossible to know what storms might come, whether there would be clouds of locusts, how we might go hungry in the month of *Av*, when the world was burning once more.

For the time being, we were in the mild season. We could pick wild radishes and greens that grew between the rocks on the other side of the Snake Gate, appearing in places where it seemed impossible that anything could ever grow. Still, we knew that times of plenty didn't last. That was why Herod had stocked his storeroom with enough provisions to last a hundred years, a time we had entered and passed. The jars of oil and wine were emptying. We tapped on the sides, and when the clay echoed we knew there was nothing inside.

There were now so many of us that wood was rationed for our fires. I wondered what would happen if our crops failed and we were left with our wits and nothing more. One night when I went to fetch some kindling kept at our door, it was gone. My father said goats had eaten it, but the goats were locked in their pen. He said I was a fool who couldn't even count sticks. But I knew that one of our neighbors had stolen from us. That was what happened in lean times. The truth about people surfaced just as surely as tiny silver fish arose from the sand in the desert when there was flooding, miraculously appearing in the ravines amid the sudden rushing streams. It was said such fish could bury themselves in the sand for seven years, their flesh so dry it would seem to be nothing but dust. At the first hint of rain they would show their true selves, exactly as people did whenever they were given time enough and cause.

MY FATHER was happy to have nothing to do with me. He let me clean and cook for him but ignored me at all other times. I heard him offer his opinion to some men who asked after me, eyeing my red hair. "She's nothing," he said. "Only trouble."

My father sat outside our chamber on a bench he had built as the dark sifted down, his cloak draped around his shoulders. In the half-light he disappeared, quickly becoming the wall, the darkness, the night itself, as he had done when he lurked outside the Temple, practicing invisibility. I wondered if I alone could see him there against the stones, facing toward Jerusalem, yearning, as I did, for a life that had past. I had compassion for this man, despite all he had done. I alone was his partner in crime.

My father was not too proud to partake of the meals I prepared despite his contempt for me, slowly devouring a stew of lentils, beans, and barley. In the hours when he left our chamber I had the freedom to shut myself away. I could hear other women gathered in the plaza singing as they worked on the looms; their voices sounded sweet, much like the songs of birds. I had taught myself to spin and to weave, but I never joined in. Had I gone, someone might have questioned me and then known me for who I was, nothing but trouble, exactly as my father had declared, a ruined woman whose time was growing near. Soon, I would no longer be able to hide the truth.

No one came to call; even my brother was absent, taking what little time he had away from the garrison to slink off with Aziza. My single visitor was the ghost in my dreams. She alone came to me faithfully. In time I came to know her better than anyone. I slept with her each night, and in my dreams she wept. I did not believe in tears, my own or others', I thought they were shameful, a sign of weakness, but I had no choice but to lie silently beside her and listen as she cried. I was chained to her the way the slave from the north country was chained to the dovecote's stone wall.

One dark night it was Nahara rather than the ghost who came for me. It was the hour my father had roused me when we fled Jerusalem, but Nahara did not shout as he had. Instead she crept onto my pallet and placed her hand over my mouth. That was the way I was awakened, to make certain I didn't call out and rouse my father. For a moment I imagined I was in the desert and it was Ben Simon who wanted my silence, and I didn't resist. But the hand was too small, too polite. When I opened my eyes, Nahara was there, insisting I hurry. I reached for my tunic and followed her outside so that my father would not be disturbed by our whispering. There were always watchmen posted, but we found a dark corner.

"My mother wants you to follow me." Nahara had a sweet, nononsense nature. She clearly expected me to do as I was told. "She needs your help."

"Let your sister be the one to help," I recommended, anxious to return to my chamber. There were so many stars in the dusky night I could see them falling as I gazed upward into the darkness. They seemed so near, like the Salt Sea in the distance, when they were so far away.

"My sister doesn't have the nerve for what we're about to do." Nahara was so serious she might have been the elder sister. Unlike Aziza, she had dark eyes but hers were flecked with yellow, appearing half-shut, a subtle glance that suggested deep thoughts. "Aziza will never attend to a birth. She says she can't bear to see the blood."

"How is that possible? I've heard that your sister can do things no mortal woman can do," I ventured to test her. "Perhaps my brother would know more about that?"

Nahara smiled. If she seemed older than her years, well, so had I when I was her age. "I doubt it. What would a warrior know about women's ways?"

"I need my sleep," I objected, but Nahara tugged on my sleeve, refusing to give up.

"My mother says you have to come. She says she'll help a lioness in return for what you do tonight."

I felt fully awake when I heard this. Was the message a veiled threat or a promise? There was nothing waiting in my chamber other than a ghost, curled up and weeping. No one in my house but an assassin who berated me when I swept his floor. When Nahara told me we were in search of a black dog, I became curious and decided to accompany her. Nahara carried a pitcher; she handed me a length of rope. There were many black dogs in the settlement if that was what Shirah wanted. I found one right away and grabbed it. Simple enough. But when I brought the stray to Nahara, she laughed, covering her mouth so no one would hear.

"Is he not good enough?" I said, annoyed. I had a strong rope around the creature's neck, but Nahara crouched down to remove the noose. She was amused I had imagined our task would be so easy.

"That one." She pointed to a fierce she-dog who snarled at us from a distance. "Can you manage her?"

"One black dog is not a lion," I remarked.

I caught the she-dog as I had trapped wild birds in the desert. I sat beside her, paying no attention when she drew her lips over her teeth. I remained silent, for that was my gift and what I was best at. After a while I slipped the rope around her neck. The she-dog looked at me. As soon as she did, she belonged to me, as the birds had, as I had looked at Ben Simon and belonged to him.

Nahara came racing over, pleased with my accomplishment, her dark hair flying behind her. Yet we weren't finished with our task.

"Now you must take the ingredient we need," she instructed. "She may bite when you do."

Then I understood. The she-dog's teats were hanging; she'd recently had pups. It was her milk we were after.

"Why not you?" I countered. "You're small and fast. I'll keep her from biting you. Just go to her as you would approach a goat, but do so quickly."

Nahara shook her head. "I'm not a woman yet. It has to be you."

I kept the rope tightly hitched around the she-dog's neck and bade her to look at me. Without speaking I told her not to move. I instructed her with my touch and with my silence, and she behaved. Her body was warm and yielded to me; surely my touch was more gentle than her pups' sharp teeth. When I was done collecting her milk, I freed her, then followed Nahara along the oldest part of the wall. People said the stones here were made of the same limestone Herod had used for construction of the Temple in Jerusalem, his mark etched into a border around each one. I wondered if he had been certain that the stones with his mark would be everlasting, and if perhaps *Adonai* had made them fall simply to prove that a man was only a man, even if he was a king.

We crossed to an abandoned section of the palace, ruined by

fires in the years of the Romans but still useful if you wanted a place of privacy in this teeming world of ours.

"Why didn't you get Revka to help you tonight?" Surely she was more trusted than I. "Is she afraid of a dog's bite?" I mocked.

"She has the two little boys to care for, and this may take all night."

"Revka?" I was surprised. She was so bitter, barely speaking. "She's too old for little children."

"Her grandchildren. She takes care of them and they sleep beside her. You're all alone. No one will miss you."

I couldn't argue with that.

"My mother wanted you." Nahara looked at me with a respect that surprised me. "She told me you'd be able to catch the black dog, and you did. You should be flattered."

We entered through an iron gate, then together used our strength to push open an ancient door of carved acacia wood that brought us into a corridor leading to the oldest of the storerooms. These chambers had once been so filled with treasure there was said to still be gold dust between the stones. We went down a hundred steps that twisted underground, and true enough, there was a faint shimmer on the stairs. The air felt damp and cool, murky, the shadows a dim slate color. The hallway grew more narrow as we went on. At last, we were forced to walk single file. Nahara carried a lamp filled with olive oil. I had the pitcher of milk. We came to an empty room made of crumbling stone.

There was an echo as we went on, though we were barefoot. Someone was calling out, but the sound was muffled. I recognized the plaintive bursts of pain. Sia had cried in this manner when she fell ill, her hand covering her mouth so that she might hush her sobs, hiding her frailty from the rest of us.

When I peered through the long furrows of shadows cast on the wall, I half-believed there was a demon flung onto the ground, much like the one imprinted upon my brother's amulet, the female monster Solomon is said to have killed on the Temple floor. As we came near, I could make out the form of a woman rolling back and forth in agony. She was the young housemaid who had begged Shirah for a spell, the one who'd stayed on the edges of the bath the night when I was told Aziza belonged to the world of angels and demons. She had traveled to this place as a servant but had recently been cast out by the family who had rights to her when her situation became evident. Now she was no longer considered worthy to pick mulberries or pistachios, or to carry her mistress's baskets. She had been lurking near the storerooms, stealing food from the goat barns. Her current state of misery affected me deeply. I felt fainthearted at the sight of her as she tore at her abdomen, panting, riddled with pains.

Shirah was urging her to sit up, but the young woman refused. There was a child about to enter our world, one who had no father and no family. If it became known that the father of this child was a married man, this young woman's fate would be impossible to escape. The council might well recommend she be cast out onto the mountain. This birth must be a secret, and as I would soon understand, secrets were Shirah's greatest gift.

Shirah signaled to me, but I stood motionless, stung by panic as I had once been stung by a wasp. I, who'd been born of a dead woman, had no right to tend to anyone bringing forth life.

"Hurry," Shirah insisted. There was a second pitcher beside her. "Mix the milk with water."

I did so, then watched, caught up in a dream as Shirah and Nahara held the woman up and urged her to drink the mixture of she-dog's milk. The housemaid spat some of it on the ground and made a terrible sound, the cry of a woman who was drowning. She held on to her belly as the pain tore at her. Shirah and Nahara lifted her up and did their best to make her walk, but even this made no difference. The baby would not come.

Shirah now commanded the housemaid to crouch upon the birthing stool she had brought along, and to bear down. Still there was nothing. The housemaid was so young she seemed little more than a child at this moment. She cursed not the man who was the father but herself. I felt something rise in my chest and throat as I surveyed a birth that would not come to pass. I had Ben Simon's knife in my tunic, cold against my skin. I thought of the knife that had been used to take me from my mother, and her great echoing cries, and the silence of her last breath.

Shirah came to me and shook me. "Stop dreaming! Go to the dovecote and get me a basket of droppings."

It was broiling hot inside the storeroom, and Shirah was drenched. Her black hair streamed down her back. The kohl around her eyes was melting so that her eyes seemed to stare out from behind a veil. I thought I had never seen anyone as beautiful or as fierce. Her tunic had been flung open, and I was shocked to see a swirl of red tattoos on her shoulders, a practice that was forbidden to our people. Those who had been marked so were said to belong to the *kedeshah,* holy women who were loyal to religious groups with practices so secret and controversial they had been outlawed long before Jerusalem fell.

"Go on!" Shirah demanded. "If this woman had anyone else to turn to, do you think she'd be here? She has no one, only a man who wants nothing to do with her and a baby who refuses to leave her womb."

The faster I did as Shirah said, the faster I would be back in my own chamber, away from this mad scene. I went recklessly through the hallways, which seemed a series of dungeons, black as pitch, for I had no lamp. At last I reached the doorway that led me into the night. There was a pale moon, and the lemon-tinged light was nearly blinding after the dim air of the storehouse. Still, no one noticed as I ran to the dovecote, my footsteps silent on the granite stones. I unlocked the door, then made my way among the birds as they fluttered about, surprised to have been disturbed at such a late hour. I began to fill the basket, frantic, my blood racing.

It was then I saw the slave. His chain reached from the loft where he slept down to the floor. He had been awakened when the door to the dovecote was thrown open, ready to defend himself if our warriors had come to mutilate him, or murder him, or trade him to nomads. I had completely forgotten about him. I could hear my own panicked, raspy breathing. Tears that did not fall were burning behind my vision. Our eyes caught. We looked at each other much as two animals who had met at a pool might have, both thirsty and mistrustful, both perfectly capable of violence. After a moment, the slave nodded for me to continue what it was I'd come for. He sank down and lowered his eyes, so they seemed like slits. He pretended to be sleeping, his back against the stones. I was grateful and told him so. Whether or not he could speak our language did not matter. He gazed up, and I could tell he understood.

I finished my gathering, then locked the dovecote and ran back the way I had come. There were almond blossoms falling from the trees, and the ground looked white. I thought of snow, and of *manna*, and of Jerusalem. I thought of the slave crouched down among the doves. My breath hit against my bones.

Shirah was waiting for me, pacing the floor. She had piled her long, sleek hair atop her head and had thrown off her veils. With a fine-edged pen made from a hawk's feather, using blood rather than ink, she had written the name of our Lord on her arms, the letters reading upward, leading to heaven. She had concocted *pharmaka* from the precious leaves of the rue, an herb most women with child avoid, for it brings on cramping. Many refused to touch rue, for it burned the flesh. Often it was removed from the ground by tying it to a dog, which allowed the curse of pulling out the root to fall upon the animal. Some women used the herb when they wished to miscarry, but rue could also be depended upon when a full-term baby needed to be hurried along, both for his sake and for the mother-to-be.

Shirah gathered the dove droppings and set a fire using them as peat. She fanned the flame until there was a plume of smoke. The scent that emanated was bitter but also familiar. It seemed the doves had followed us to this place; we could hear their wings beating, fast as our breathing, fast as the birth must become if mother and child were to survive. After the laboring woman drank the bitter rue, retching as she did, Shirah had us take her by either arm. We forced her to stand above the fire. The air burned with heat, and we were all slick with sweat. I grabbed off my shawl, feeling I might suffocate. I could hardly see for all the ash and sparks. The world was made of salt and smoke, and there was no choice but to go forward.

We had entered into the deepest of places, the seat of the great goddess Ashtoreth, written of by the prophets, a goddess who was with us still, even though the wise men in the Temple had done all they could to destroy her. Neither could they defeat what many claimed was the female aspect of God, the Shechinah, all that was divine and radiant, the bride to *Adonai*'s groom. The Shechinah healed the ill, sat among the poor, embraced the wicked and the good alike.

The woman who was laboring sobbed in our grasp. As for me, I had stopped thinking and merely did as I was told. I didn't know how I had been drawn here, woken from my dreams, dragged from my chamber into this dim night. I of all people, a harbinger of the Angel of Death, known to *Mal'ach ha-Mavet* before I was known to humankind, a murderer of my own mother, now stood guard for the Queen of Heaven.

The housemaid pleaded with us not to keep her positioned over the fire. She said she was burning alive, that the sparks were entering her, entwining with her blood and bones. I asked to be allowed to move her, but Shirah insisted the smoke was needed to open her womb. "Kindness can be a curse," she said. She crouched beside the servant woman and began to chant.

Beshem eh'yeh asher eh'yeh tsey tsey tsey.

Shirah's voice was hoarse and hot, the intonations rising. She spoke the words repeatedly, until the chant wound around us and we could hear only its tone and its desperation.

Va'yees'sa va'ya'vo va'yett. In the name of I am what I am, the name of God, get out. You have journeyed and now you have arrived. Amen Amen Selah.

The woman had been wailing, but now the sound worsened. Jackals called to each other in this way, crying in the night. The poor servant woman was so far inside herself, at the deepest core, it seemed impossible she would ever surface again. I thought of my mother in her last moments, before the silence fell, how her voice might have called out against the brutality of her fate, how my father might have wept at the door as he cursed me.

The laboring woman spoke to those who were not there, praying to our God, *Adonai*, and to Abraxas, a god of the Egyptians, and to Ashtoreth. She made secret bargains, promising all she would be willing to sacrifice if only her torment would end, her life, her soul, her newborn child.

"Take them!" she cried out. "Take me as well!"

I was frightened that she would call the warriors to us with her wailing, or summon demons we could not repel, but Shirah said no, it was silence we needed to fear. Silence at a birth meant that the demons had won and that Lilith, the night creature from Babalonyia with long black hair and black wings who preys on other women, seducing their men and stealing their children, had prevailed.

Shirah wrote down the name of Obizoth, the demoness that strangles newborns, then burned the papyrus upon which she'd written that vile name. The smoke was scarlet, the color of blood.

We were the defenders and we were in battle. I felt I could have taken a demon by the throat, should it dare to appear before us. The desert had taught me that we must destroy so that we might live. We had piles of salt to throw upon any creatures of the night that might venture close by. I took a handful and rubbed it across my abdomen, for unborn children were especially vulnerable to demons.

We remained beside the fire, the sweat from our own bodies stinging our eyes. As the fire flamed red and then blue, Shirah recited her devotion to *Adonai* so that the angel Raphael would thwart any attempt to do harm to the baby when at last it emerged. The mother-to-be began to have contractions. When I looked, I could see movement inside her; a storm was passing through her body. I found I was reciting Shirah's incantation. I had learned the words and memorized them, for I, too, had come to believe this alone could keep us from harm.

Shirah had us move the woman away from the flames as soon as her liquid came in a rush. I realized that I was terrified the child might not follow, but Nahara, though she wasn't more than thirteen, had no fear of what was to happen.

"Finally he arrives," she said, overjoyed. She clapped her hands, then crouched down, ready. The baby came into her hands quickly, his sulky face twisted into a scowl. Nahara grinned, fearless, though blood was everywhere. I thought, *She is a woman and I am not. She is already everything and I am nothing at all.*

"What will happen to her now?" I asked Nahara, nodding to the new mother.

"She will return to the woman who is her mistress and say she found a baby in the cliffs."

"And will she be believed?" I wondered.

"My mother will escort her. They'll take her in. They'll believe what they must so that the man of the household can have a new son."

Shirah knelt and reached inside the woman, chanting as the afterbirth was coaxed from within. It would be buried in the orchard, where no one would discover it. What had once given this child life would bring good fortune to our crops.

The night had been a whirlwind. At last silence washed over us. We were slick and hot, too spent to cleanse ourselves. Now that the baby had been delivered and was bound in clean cloth, the mother grabbed for him and put him to her breast. I heard a sob and realized it came from my throat.

I understood the reason Shirah had wanted me here on this night. She had divined what was inside me. She came up beside me to whisper, so no one would overhear.

"Did you think you were the only lioness?" she asked now that our work was completed. "Did you think I wouldn't know?"

MY BROTHER led a raid soon afterward. It was an honor for him to do so, a mark of his bravery and his favor in the eyes of Ben Ya'ir. Yet those who loved him wished he were not so honored. We feared his was an errand that would lead him to the World-to-Come. In the dovecote, Aziza was overwrought. Her hair was tangled down her back, a mass of black. She refused meals and spent her evenings by the wall, gazing at the emptiness of the white fields of stones God had set before us. It was still possible to see the footprints of the warriors who had ventured to the valley below, but they faded, and the dust blew them away, and soon enough it seemed that they had never taken this path.

The skies were overcast, and there were fires in the distance, for nomads roamed and troops from the legion were not far off. The smoke swelled into the clouds, turning the world somber. Amram was gone for days. Soon Aziza took to her bed, refusing to come out even when the sun finally broke through the gloom. Not even her younger sister could convince her she must go about her life. She was in the grip of the terror that held fast to every woman who waited for a warrior.

My father and I also looked out over the cliffs, searching the horizon. Despite the distance between us, we were equal in our love for Amram. Perhaps because of our shared worry, we had begun to take our evening meal together. We did not speak, other than to mention the food, but we could finally be in the same chamber without one of us turning away. I tried not to think of how my father would react to my dishonor if he knew I carried Ben Simon's child, how his loathing of me would multiply, how he would humiliate me and cast me out, how I would prove him right. Nothing but trouble. I, who could drown someone from the inside out, who would seduce another's husband, as Lilith was said to do, was not worthy to sweep my father's floor. My father would shear the hair from my head and shred my clothes to mark me as a *zonah*, then he would tear his own clothes, as we do to mourn the dead.

I could only be silent if he did so, for silence was what I knew best.

IN THE FIELDS, the fruit trees had not borne as sweetly as they might have after the sudden cold spell. Herod's supplies were dwindling fast, the rations reduced. My father complained about the meals I made for him, and he had every right to do so. Our people began to go hungry. Amram and the other warriors had been sent into the valley to take what other settlements had in their storerooms and fields. Some might call this thievery or mayhem or murder, but it was the way we lived now. The rule of the desert was one I'd learned well, mere survival. My brother vowed that even a bandit could be pure in the eyes of the Almighty. He insisted that God's judgment depended on motive, and ours was to stay true to Israel. Surely God would look down upon us and send fortune our way.

Since the birth of the maidservant's child, Nahara had taken to confiding in me. One day, when we had spent hours working side by side, she admitted that, before my brother went down from our mountain to lead the raid, Aziza had gone to him with a powder of burned snakeskin. Their mother knew every manner of spell, and although Aziza had never showed an interest in such matters, for Amram's sake she had peered into the magic book her mother kept under lock and key.

When Aziza had embraced my brother at his leave-taking, she'd wound the snake's powder into his hair. As she held him near, he had no idea that within her embrace there was the white-green essence of a serpent that would bite his enemies and protect him from evil. My brother might not understand what lengths Aziza was willing to go to in order to save him, but I did. I would have done the same if I'd had access to such a potent spell. I would have burned the snake to ashes if it could have kept my beloved from harm.

When the warriors completed the raid, it was clear they had not been favored. The settlement they had attacked had been forewarned by the barking of dogs, and the battle had been fierce, with losses on both sides. Our men did not return to the fortress but instead went into the cliffs directly across from us, a pockmarked, shadowy place known to the beasts. We knew then that they were *tamé,* made unclean by their proximity to death, and that they must now purify themselves. The survivors needed to pray and fast for seven days before they could be welcomed back.

The families of those who had gone out waited mutely by the gate with the full knowledge that some of us would soon be in mourning. When at last the remaining warriors returned, I nearly fell faint when I heard people shouting Amram's name. I went to find my brother, grateful beyond measure that he'd been among those left to bury the dead. But being so close to *Mal'ach ha-Mavet* had burned him, the way steel is fired in an oven and made harder.

He had been forced to bury his friend Jonathan, the one who had studied to be a scholar, who'd had thoughts of becoming a priest but had picked up the dagger instead. On this day Amram wore Jonathan's prayer shawl, with its white and blue fringes. There were women whose sole work was to make the violet-blue dye used for prayer shawls, boiling shellfish that could only be found on a single shore of the Great Sea, adding salt and sand and stone until the color became the color of the heavens. Each knot in the garment was a sign of devotion. Amulets were attached to the threads, to bind demons and bring fortune to the devout. And yet Jonathan had been taken by death. His family sat concealed in a darkened room, tearing at their cloaks, refusing to speak to anyone, closing their shutters to ensure light would not enter their chambers.

My brother came to eat and drink with us, but he did not lift his eyes. There were streaks of dark blood on the shawl around his shoulders. My father was so happy to have his son returned to him, he didn't notice the difference that had been stamped upon Amram, his grim expression, his fixed gaze. He saw only a strong man who could lift a sword so heavy he could slay any rival, but I saw something entirely different. My brother had taken a step away from the living. He had walked too close to the World-to-Come when it claimed those around him. The demons had reached out to him and tainted him, clutching at his spirit, attempting to snatch him over to the other side, the side of despair and seething misery. The Angel of Death saw all with his thousand eyes; his touch was said to be tender should he choose for it to be so. If you allowed him to embrace you, you might sink into his arms and never rise again. I saw the way my brother gazed at the cliffs below. He was seeing what he believed had been written for him, the fate he had eluded when his friend took his place.

When my father remarked that Jonathan had died a warrior's death, as every man should, I saw Amram shudder and turn away.

We went to stand outside at the end of our meal, after our father had gone to pray and offer thanks for his son's safe return.

"It should have been me," my brother remarked, unable to escape the gloom of his bereavement.

Poor Aziza, I thought, her spell had not protected Amram as she had intended. Jonathan had stepped in front of my brother intentionally, taking the blow meant for Amram in the name of their love and friendship. I insisted this could not have been a mistake. God had a design for our lives, and Amram's return must have already been written, whether or not he thought he deserved it. My brother still wore the amulet I had given him. I reminded him that he was in God's favor, as Solomon had been. "We cannot know or understand God's plan," I said.

I took my brother's hand and placed it over my middle so that he could feel the life within me. It had quickened, and had formed itself fully, as a fish in a lake. My brother shot me a look. He was quick to guess I had been in the arms of a lion.

"He was meant to protect you," he said of Ben Simon, who had been his teacher, a man he had revered and put his faith in. "If this is anyone's burden, it's mine, for sending you to him."

"Can I question the Angel of Life any more than you can question the Angel of Death? This was meant to be."

My brother looked at me and understood: what I shared with him was not my burden but my joy.

PERHAPS it is possible to discover more in silence than in speech. Or perhaps it is only that those who are silent among us learn to listen. The Man from the North who was our slave had no choice but to be among our chattering all through the day. I pitied him, as I pitied all men in chains, but perhaps there was more that we held in common. We were both outcasts here, each in possession of a past no one could imagine. It was sometimes easier to be with a stranger from whom nothing was expected and to whom nothing was granted in return. I had become accustomed to this man. We all had. His hands were callused from work, but he never complained. He ate what little we gave to him. He lowered his eyes when we gossiped, although once or twice I had seen him smile. It was a strange sight, one I turned away from. For his expression made it seem he was not a slave, but a man. I knew it was an error to think of him that way.

Once, when he was carrying a heavy basket for me into the fields, some unruly children threw stones at him, laughing, until I chased them away. Still they shouted out, dubbing the slave Leviathan, the name of a huge sea monster, because of his great height and strong arms. Maybe that was where my compassion began, the kernel of it grown from the way in which he was reviled.

I turned to the children who teased him, warning that if they continued to do so they would bring demons into their midst. "Run!" I shouted, and the rude name-callers scattered like seeds, giggling and hurrying away.

The slave nodded to thank me in his halting manner, but I shook my head to stop him.

"I couldn't stand to hear their voices. That was all." I said this so he wouldn't dare to assume his comfort was my concern. "I sent them away for my sake, not yours."

I had often caught him staring at me as we worked side by side. Now I knotted my scarf more tightly. I had come to believe he could speak our language perfectly if he desired to do so. He seemed to be aware of all that was said, although when anyone asked him a question he shrugged and muttered something in his own rough vocabulary, pretending to be as ignorant of ours as the doves were. And then one day, not long after I had chased off the rude children, as we were working beneath some fig trees spreading out manure, he suddenly spoke to me.

"You hair is like fire," he said.

He spoke our language strangely, the words frozen, cautious, yet he clearly knew it well, and perhaps had learned it before he'd been captured. Conscripts in the Roman army walked beside soldiers from many lands and found ways to communicate. This pronouncement about my hair, however, was not what I expected. I laughed despite myself. "Be careful," I said. "You could get burned."

After a silence is broken, there is often a torrent of speech. The Man from the North now told me that where he came from many of the women had red hair. Before he was conscripted by the Roman Legion, he had never been beyond the borders of his village, which contained perhaps two hundred residents, most of them his own kinsmen. His land was so cold that snow and ice lasted much of the year, the sky dark even during the day. For a brief time of the year, his world would become green, not as the desert blooms in clutches, in a mild haze, but in a curtain of deep, shuddering green, with grass as tall as olive trees and forests so wide it would take a month to find your way across.

The hotter our world became, the more I yearned to hear of his. We sat shaded by the fig trees in the blazing heat, unaware that the sun struck the earth so brutally. I listened, refreshed, to hear that in his land there were lakes as blue as lapis where the fish were the size of men. Warriors tattooed themselves with black ink and fought as fiercely as wolves; in combat they held shields that were stronger than anything we had, a metal that could not be broken with lances or axes. Such men could go an entire moon without sleeping so that they might keep watch over their women and their flocks, the sheep with hair so long it touched the earth, the goats the color of snow with eyes that were yellow orbs. If an enemy came up behind a warrior from this northland, he would quickly be slain with a single strike upon his throat.

"If all this is true, then why are you a slave?"

It was an insult to make such a remark to a man who had once been a warrior and then a soldier for the legion and was now the lowly slave of women. He might have taken offense, but he merely shrugged.

"Why are you?" he said simply.

I laughed. "I'm not."

The Man from the North's expression made it clear he disagreed.

"I'm not," I insisted.

He gazed at me sadly. "You will be. I saw it in my own land."

The Romans had captured his country, then had offered a way out of starvation for those who'd been conquered. The Man from the North had stood with his brothers and chosen to live. He was taken across the Cold Sea and brought to Rome before being sent out with the legion for Judea. While in Rome, he had seen miraculous things, baths where there was hot and cold running water, houses in which women and boys could be had for a small price, shops that sold monstrous creatures—elephants and eels and huge fish with lances attached to their heads. He had been to the Colosseum with the throngs who pushed and shoved through the cobbled gateways, watching gladiators battle. He could not believe all he'd witnessed; those vivid visions seemed like dreams to him still.

I asked if it was true that the Romans set men to fight against beasts. A man was no different from an animal in the Romans' eyes, the slave told me, perhaps better sport because a man often called for his mother or his beloved in his last moments in the world, whereas an animal knew when to surrender.

I thought of Ben Simon and the mark on his face, and of the creature who had found him too bitter to eat. I asked the slave if he had seen men battle lions. He nodded, saying that gladiators feared lions more than any other creatures, even more so than the crocodiles who swam in huge tanks rolled into the center of the arena on logs, pulled by heavy ropes and chains by over a hundred men. Those water beasts could take a man in their mouths, dragging a victim into the deep to drown him, but it was possible to fight off a crocodile, to ram a knife into its eye and force a retreat. Some gladiators survived. But once a lion attacked, it would not back away. It would fight to the end, until there was a surrender and nothing was left but bones.

"Why do you ask about these beasts?" he wondered after I'd questioned him so thoroughly.

I shrugged, feigning no particular interest. "I dream about them sometimes."

"Keep them in your dreams," the Man from the North advised me, but I could tell from his gaze. He knew there was something more.

I TOOK TO listening to all of the slave's stories. Some were so far-fetched I barely believed him. He spoke about a creature called a stag, huge compared to the ibex that could be found in Judea. He could track one through the snow easily enough, even in a storm, for these deer rubbed their horns against trees and left their marks in this manner. In his world, the foxes turned white as snow was falling, then, when winter faded, changed back to red before your eyes. He vowed that the color of my hair was shared by all the most beautiful women in his land and, he added slyly, in mine. I laughed at some of what he told me, disbelieving that rivers could run silver, that the monsters in the ocean were so filled with water they spat into the air, that there were packs of wolves a hundred strong, calling to each other in the night with pure, cold voices.

Revka often watched us in the fields. Sometimes when we walked back to the dovecote with our empty baskets, she would shake her head, scowling. Despite her ill will, I wasn't about to stop listening to the Man from the North. When he spoke, I didn't think about the desert, or the past that beckoned to me, or the sins I had committed, only the land I would never know, the drifts of snow, the bands of men with black tattoos who lashed flat branches to their feet so they might walk through the snow as bears do, with ease.

The slave trusted me enough to recount the details of his capture, though he was taut with rage as he recalled that event. When the Roman garrison was sacked by our warriors, he and his kinsman had fallen to their knees, vowing that they had no allegiance to the Emperor and would never lift a hand against us. He couldn't raise his eyes when he spoke of this humiliation. Our people had allowed them to live because they made an oath against Rome and because they had been stolen from their homeland. Everyone else was slain, though some of the soldiers were little more than boys who pleaded for their lives and cowered at the sight of a knife.

That night the blood of the Romans who had been killed welled up into the clouds and turned into a rain. The blood rain followed our warriors into their tents, streaming down in rivers. Our men panicked and were about to run away, but Ben Ya'ir instructed them not to flee. He could do that to his warriors, the slave had seen it firsthand, make them yield beneath his gaze. He boldly informed them that a rain of blood was not a curse but a promise. It was the future they had to face, as all men must face death eventually. They could do so as cowards or as men of God, that was their choice.

Every man in his command stayed. The slave remarked that he knew then Ben Ya'ir was a man who would never give in, no matter the circumstances.

In the morning, when the dark lifted, the blood that had fallen from the sky had turned into flame trees. Because of this the men were shielded from the noonday sun, a clear blessing from *Adonai*. Our warriors fell to their knees in gratitude.

I blushed at the mention of the tree that I had so often stood beneath and dreamed of. I said the flame tree was a favorite of mine, and he nodded and said he wasn't surprised to hear so. On that day, however, even though he lay in irons, chained to his kinsman, a mere slave and nothing more, he knew the true meaning of what our leader claimed to be a miracle when he saw the flame trees. It was not God's grace they had seen, the slave assured me. He knew the omens of war and was aware of what red flowers blooming on this day meant. Our people would have to walk through fire.

Because he had witnessed the massacre, God would consider him guilty as well. He, too, would have to face fire. He gazed at my hair as he spoke. That was when I insisted it was time to return to the dovecote. We walked back the way we had come. A breeze shifted through the trees. That was as good a reason as any for me to cover my head. We had spoken too freely, and nothing good could come of it. I retreated into silence, but the Man from the North had one more thing to recount. He confided that he hadn't known what to feel when he was spared by our warriors. Should he be grateful or outraged? He'd been rescued from the Roman Legion, only to be taken in slavery. This humiliation was not what he had foreseen as the path of his life.

"What did you intend?"

"I intended to find a woman like you." He was speaking to me as if he weren't a slave and I was not a woman who carried another's life within her.

"You're confused," I demurred. "You think because I have red hair I'm like one of the women you knew in another world."

We had crossed the field and were approaching the largest of the dovecotes with emptied baskets in hand, the sky blue above us, the air fresh, and it seemed that we had indeed entered into the slave's country during the season when everything was green.

"You're taking forever," Revka called as she peered out the door, watching us yet again, even though she was not my kinswoman and my deeds were none of her concern. "Hurry up. There's work here. Did you ever hear of it?"

"I'm not confused, Yael," the Man from the North told me before we went back inside, where Revka might overhear. "I know who you are."

It took half the day for me to realize he'd said my name and even longer to admit that I hadn't cringed at the sound.

IN A WORLD of blood one expects to see red, but when I awoke to a stream of blood flowing from within me, staining the pallet I slept upon, I was stunned. I had carried my child for more than six months, assuming he was safe. But I had been dreaming of the ghost who slept beside me. She had been whispering in my ear all night, refusing to leave me be, weeping for all she had lost in the world, unable to let go of me still. I had wanted what had belonged to her, now she desired what was mine. Perhaps her words had wounded me and this was why I bled. In my dream we had been together on the cliff where we'd left her bones. Feathers were tumbling down from the sky, and all the birds I'd killed with my bare hands had come alive.

I was in desperate need of a remedy, something that would stop the bleeding and bind the child I carried to the world we walked through, not the World-to-Come. I went to my father's chamber in the darkness of early morning and took what few coins he had. I was not embarrassed to steal his silver. I would rather be a thief than a woman without a child.

As I hurried across the plaza in the dim light, I felt a wash of unforgiving heat, formed by the pain that blazed inside me. I asked a watchman where Shirah lived.

"What would you want with the witch?" he asked.

"We work in the dovecotes," I told him. He looked at me carefully, perhaps to judge if I was guilty of something and was now merely trying to determine the nature of my crime. Perhaps he had picked up the scent of my blood and knew I was unclean. "The doves are ailing and I'm not wise enough to know what the ailment might be," I insisted.

Though he seemed suspicious, he pointed me toward one of the palaces. I thought, of course, Shirah was one of Ben Ya'ir's kinswomen and therefore was meant for a palace even if some accused her of sorcery. There were those who whispered that life was not so different here than it had been in Jerusalem: those who ruled managed to live well, while those who followed hungered. But I discovered that Shirah resided in an outbuilding that had been a kitchen, used by servants in the time of the king. When I rapped on the door, it opened. We had no locks. The mountain was our lock, the serpent's path our key.

There was no one inside, but I went in and peered about. The floor of her chamber was patterned with mosaics that spread out like a fan. There was a wooden altar beside shelves set into the stone wall. These shelves were piled high with bowls and pitchers; there were jars of honey and wine, along with vials of herbs. The floor echoed as I went to open the door so that I might peer inside the small sleeping chamber. Aziza and Nahara were entwined on the same pallet. Their brother, Adir, a dark boy of no more than eleven, slept by the rear door. There was no sign of Shirah, only a square of straw covered by a woven blanket that had not been slept upon.

I turned to find her entering her house, light on her feet, as though she were a thief herself. She was breathless; perhaps she'd been running. Her head was covered by a shawl stamped with a pattern of gold leaves, and there were half a dozen chiming bracelets on her arms. She stopped when she saw me, then quickly regained her composure.

She had been out walking, she told me, slipping off her bracelets. "I couldn't sleep," she said. "Perhaps we're the same in that."

"Perhaps," I agreed.

I didn't ask what dark matter she'd been attending to. I had begun to lose my strength, and before I could say more, I slumped against the wall. When Shirah saw that I was staining, she chastised me for not speaking of the problem immediately. She had me sit at a table that was only a rough-hewn piece of wood set upon a trestle. She felt my belly and knew by mere touch when this child had begun and when he would enter the world. I showed her the coins I'd brought along and begged for a potion, but she waved the coins away. She told me a cure wasn't so easily found. Although she wanted no payment, she would try to help. She boiled the leaves of the madder root, a plant that is said to turn the bones of any animals who graze upon it red. She added berries of the bramble bush and gave me a tea that was scarlet and steaming. I drank it though it burned my lips. This mixture wasn't the cure, Shirah told me, but we could hope it would end the cramping.

"Is there anyone who wants your child to be unborn?" she asked. "Anyone who wishes you harm?"

I felt as though an arrow had pierced me. There was only one such person. As I had taken from Sia, she would take from me.

"A ghost," I said in a low tone.

"Is she here with you now?"

I looked up to see that my ghost had indeed followed and was standing at the door, watching me reproachfully.

I nodded.

"Well, she comes for a reason." Shirah studied me. Kohl ringed her eyes.

For a moment I felt I was drowning. "I took something that didn't belong to me," I admitted.

"I see." She continued to study me, reading my every expression. "Do you regret this?"

A simple enough question. But I couldn't give the answer she wanted. When I shook my head, Shirah sighed.

"If that's how you feel, then you'll have to accept that the one you stole from will take your child."

If Sia had lived, the baby I carried would have belonged to her if Ben Simon had claimed it as his own and married me. She would forever be his first wife and could have arranged to take over my life. Perhaps that was her intention now.

I leapt up, beside myself with worry. The knife I carried as a love token clattered to the floor. Shirah reached for it. I could feel heat rise into my face as she ran her finger over the blade. It was still sharp enough to bring forth a bead of her blood.

"Sit down," Shirah crooned. She cautioned me that if I was agitated I would only quicken the blood between my legs. "Don't help your rival with her revenge."

I did as I was told.

"When you're with a man who has a wife, you marry her as well. Surely you knew that at the time?"

I tilted my chin and gazed directly into Shirah's eyes. "I would not undo what I had with him."

"But that's exactly what is happening," she cautioned. "If you want the child, you must rid yourself of the ghost, and to do that you must possess regret. A ghost doesn't just go away. She's sewn herself to you. You're sharing the same skin, so she thinks this child belongs to her even though she's in the World-to-Come. There's only one way to be rid of her."

I listened closely, not knowing which I felt more, terror or gratitude.

"Do what I say and don't take it upon yourself to change anything. Cut a lock of your hair. Tie it in a knot. Go to the place where the new willows stand below this fortress and burn your hair on willow wood."

She returned to the vials of herbs and plucked three leaves from a jar, wrapping them in a piece of white linen, then handing me the folded scrap.

"Eat these when darkness falls. What you swallow is the taste of what you've done. Be prepared for that. Only you know how bitter it will be. But don't bother with any of it if you have no regret. If that's the case, pour your rival a cup of tea every morning, because there she'll be, with your child in her arms."

My eyes were burning. If I wasn't careful, I would weep Sia's tears once more. I said nothing.

Shirah leaned forward, lowering her voice. Her head scarf slipped down. Her hair was plaited in a sleek braid, then looped up gracefully, in the Egyptian fashion. "If you are ready for forgiveness, you will have to take up the angel Raphael's name three times. Then three times say *I should not have harmed you*. At the very last, say it backward three times to make sure what you've done disappears."

Shirah took up the assassin's knife. Before I could react, she reached to slash a long shock of my hair. It fell between us like a snake. I thought I heard it hiss as the merciless black vipers do.

"You have to give yourself over to her if you want to be free of her. Just know that what's done can be undone, but what's undone can never again be."

I SET OFF the next day. I asked the watchman at the gate if I could walk along the path of the serpent. There were some small willows which grew nearby, new, pliant trees whose branches I wished to use to fashion a basket. The watchman was young, and he failed to question me further, waving me on, even though women were not allowed to go beyond the gate. I went forward straightaway, down the plummeting path, before he thought better of it and called me back.

The air felt especially dry on this day. Little sparks sprang up from the chalky earth as I ventured forth. Winter had disappeared. Soon the land would burn and I would burn with it. I walked quickly on the downward pitch, the desert before me. Everything looked white in the haze. There was no difference between the earth and the sky. I spied the stand of willows Shirah had spoken of and veered from the path onto a ridge, then down into a hollow, where there was a canopy of shade and a pool of still, fetid water. I sat there sheltered by the trees and tried to catch my breath. My cramps had been stanched, but there was still the trickle of blood. A flutter of despair beat inside my chest.

I'd brought Ben Simon's knife with me, that odd killing token of his love. I thought that of all the people he had murdered, he'd done his best work with me. There was a part of me that was forever gone. I could hardly resist the lure of the cliffs and the desire to end my struggle. I did my best not to think of such cowardly actions. It was against the law to harm oneself, a sin so great there was no forgiveness and only a field of fire in the World-to-Come.

I set my thoughts on the pattern of the leaves of the willow as I looked for fallen branches, and on the smoothness of the bark as I inhaled its scent, so fresh and green. I gathered the kindling in the white scarf the Essenes had given me. I brushed away stray leaves. When I did, they looked like rain falling, or the tears on Ben Simon's face when he saw the two sister-brides in the desert.

I brought the firewood to a cave where I wouldn't be seen, slipping inside a crevice that split the rocks. Women were warned away from such places. There were wild beasts in among the rocks, and robbers, perhaps demons as well. The sky was glowing with fading light, and the cliffs were streaked pink and gold. I waited for nightfall. I breathed the way a leopard might, panting, still feeling heat between my legs where I bled. I felt alone, drawn deep inside my own silence.

When it came time and the sky was sifting into darkness, I made a fire between the cliffs, so the wisps of smoke wouldn't be noticed by the watchmen who patrolled the walls. I slipped off my garments and folded them. I had brought along pomegranate oil, which I poured into my hands and rubbed into my hair and skin. I then threw the knot of my shorn hair onto the pile of burning willow twigs. The sharp odor of a part of myself set aflame sent a shiver through me.

I crouched among the rocks and ate the herbs I'd been given, even though they made my tongue swell. It was blessed thistle, and the taste was indeed sharp, leaving a gritty film inside my mouth. I could barely swallow. When I had consumed the leaves, I felt a shadow reach a hand inside me.

For what seemed a long time, I sat back on my heels and waited for the spell to begin. I watched stars drop down from the sky. I glimpsed the bright arc of the new moon. It was *Rosh Chodesh*, the new month of *Nissan*. In the plaza this night was being celebrated, for this had been God's first commandment to Israel, that we should keep time by charting the new moon, for it meant the renewal of our people and was a reminder that there is light in the darkness. This was what it meant to be human, to know that time moved and all things changed.

I realized then that I needed to forgo silence, which had been my sword and my shield. That was the price I must pay. What protected me once, I now must cast away. It was my gift, but no more.

I began to pray. *Amen Amen Selah*. The spell wound around me as the dark spun into light. The stars dropped closer. I was afraid of what was about to happen once my true nature was revealed before the eyes of God. But what was to be was now beyond my will, in the hands of fate. I had eaten of the herbs, started the flame, said the prayer that opened my wounds and my heart, lifted my voice to the Almighty.

The fire's roar sounded like the voice of the ghost. I had called to her, pleading for her to come to me as she had once bathed with me and brushed the ashes from my hair. The fire was so bright I shielded my eyes, but it burned brighter still. Something inside me broke apart and splintered. I made a sound I didn't recognize as my own voice. I called out, pleading, and then my pleas were answered.

Sia was before me.

Her cloak was in tatters, her hair in knots, her arms were nothing more than bones. I could not bear to see the harm I'd done to her. I ran to the edge of the cliff to escape her. Stones shifted beneath my feet, and I could feel myself sliding. If I leapt I would fly to the desert floor below, a petal from a flame tree, a dove set free. But the ghost still would not let me be, even now. She would not release me to the death I wished for myself. She reached out, pulling me back from the edge. I fought her, but she refused to let go. When at last I had no choice, I wrapped my arms around her, my one and only friend. I gave myself to Sia.

When I begged for forgiveness, it was not her tears I cried but my own.

I fell asleep on the rocks, sprawled out on a dark ledge where the thorn trees grew. When I awoke it was almost morning. Sia had been in my dreams all through the night. She was with a lion in the desert, beneath a willow tree. She had taken him back from me, as she deserved to, but unlike me, she was not a thief. She left me what was mine. I felt the child move within me and wept with joy. I was not a demon or a leopard, only a woman with red hair. Now, as light split apart the sky, turning the desert pink, I slipped on my tunic. My body felt raw and bruised. I saw the marks I had made long ago on my leg, pale, like the arc of the moon. They seemed to belong to someone else, but I was the one who would have to carry the scars.

I knelt by the fire to make certain there were no burning embers left. That was when I spied the tracks of a lion. There were only a few such beasts left in the desert, but one had come here, answering my call. He had been there all the while, watching over me, before he left me at last.

I ATTEMPTED to speak to my father to make amends, but each time I approached, he turned away. He waved at me, his signal for a dog, for that was what I still was to him. He had become an even more miserable man here at the fortress than he'd been in Jerusalem. He, who had courted invisibility, had become what he desired to be; no one could see him now. Old men were invisible in this world of war, thought of as useless. My father was no longer vital. Ben Ya'ir needed young men who could fight in hand-to-hand combat wielding axes, not assassins who hid their sharpened knives inside their robes and stalked their enemies in the dark corners of the Temple courtyard. No one honored the great Yosef bar Elhanan for his ability to slink into the houses of his enemies, at one with the darkness of the night.

He'd been assigned to keep track of the weaponry. It was a lowly job, meant for young boys and old men. Replacing the tips of arrows was beneath him, but no one would listen to him, no one valued him. He began to fold in on himself, a tangle of envy. Now when he saw my brother return with the warriors, my father was jealous rather than proud. Amram had always been the one to shine in his eyes, but lately our father had begun to look upon him with distaste. Like the teacher whose student surpasses him, my father resented my brother his victories and his youth.

It was as though he no longer had children. We were only shadows on the wall, there to mock him and betray him.

ONE EVENING my father spied Aziza with my brother, secluded beside the fountain. Everyone knew she was the witch's daughter. She was not the wife my father wanted for his son. He turned in her direction and spat on the ground. *Shedah*, he hissed, as though he'd spied a serpent. He called my brother to him, and they argued with such ferocity I covered my ears.

My brother announced that he planned to wed Aziza despite my father's claims that he wouldn't hear of this match. Amram threatened to denounce my father, and my father made threats of his own. If Aziza's mother was to discover her daughter's impurity, perhaps she would see to her punishment herself, bind her in a spell of silence or cover her with boils, cut off all her hair or cast her beyond the gate. I was in a corner spinning yarn on my spindle, doing my best not to interfere, but my heart was hitting against my chest as my brother and father raged against each other. The air in the chamber was hot, charged. The more my father railed, the paler my brother appeared, turning to ice. Pale light is dangerous, reckless and cold. Amram put his hand on his knife. Perhaps he had forgotten it was our father before him. I whispered his name, hoping to wake him from his dark dream. My brother glanced at the knife he had plucked from his belt as though he were indeed a dreamer. Quickly, he let it go.

"Don't speak to me again," he admonished my father before he departed. "If you see me, walk by me in silence, as I'll walk by you."

In that instant, what little family I had was dismantled. That night my father refused his meal. He took to his bed, face to the wall. He had become older than his years, a man who had thrown away all he might have had, ruined by his own bitterness.

I felt pity rise within me.

"He'll be back," I assured him.

My father shook his head.

"I'm sure of it," I said, though the rift between them was deep. "Amram is your son and your student."

I followed my brother to the garrison. There I found him splitting wood. He was in a fury, grunting as he worked, like a man rending an enemy in two. But his enemy had given him life and was his father. This enemy had taught him the secrets of invisibility and had crossed the desert to find him.

"He's an old man," I reminded Amram.

Perhaps my heart went out to our broken father because he had been my partner in our terrible crime. "Mourning our mother has caused a poison inside him."

"When we go to Aziza's mother to ask for her blessing, will you stand by me, Yaya?" he asked.

He spoke to me so even though we both knew the girl who had been Yaya was no more. I nodded, then found the courage to ask if he would also stand by me, no matter where fate might lead me.

The boy he had been was gone as well, the one who had proudly announced he would become an assassin as we stood together in Jerusalem. All the same, he was still my brother.

"I found you in the wilderness," he reminded me. "Why would I abandon you now?"

SOON AFTER, I began to dream of my mother. All my life I had been dreaming of lions and of ghosts, but no more. I could feel my mother's presence. I longed to see her, to have a list of her virtues, to know if we were anything alike.

I went to my father early in the morning, before I lost my nerve, having awoken from a dream of my mother's voice, the one I'd heard as I entered this world. The assassin was outside the barracks, cleaning weapons, sitting on the stump of an old olive tree. Young men and boys who passed by had no idea he had been one of the fiercest men in Jerusalem, that he had possessed the ability to conceal himself and had murdered more men than there were leaves on the willow tree.

My father was hunched over, his hair white, the lines on his face deeply etched. I had never before asked a favor of him, but I wanted one now.

I asked him to tell me the color of my mother's hair.

"You haven't guessed why I can't look at you? Every time I look at you I see her in your place."

At last I understood why each time he gazed at me grief shone in his eyes. My mother's hair had been the same color as mine. Like her I was a flame tree. Despite everything, I still burned.

THE RAINY SEASON ended early. The harsh trail of the future was evident in the white-hot sky above us, a fire waiting to be ignited. Each day barrels swollen with water were brought up from the pools below, tied to the backs of donkeys, until at last our cisterns were full enough to last through the harsh summer months. The air seemed enraged already, the wind blowing across from the far side of the Salt Sea, sparked with heat.

We celebrated the Feast of Unleavened Bread, but this year was unlike any other, for we could no longer bring sacrifices to the Temple. We feasted when our prayers were complete, but we kept an eye on the desert as we rejoiced in our freedom. In the evenings I had begun to accompany Revka to the looms. Working there kept our minds on the task at hand. But we could not avoid the gossip of other women, and although we didn't join in, we couldn't help but overhear. Often the women at the looms spoke of our leader, who was our hero and our only hope. They praised him, and there were those among them who wished they were his wife. Even married women spoke of this, and hid their eyes so no one would see that, although they laughed, they were serious in their envy of the one to whom he was wed. I hadn't known Ben Ya'ir had a wife. Revka pointed her out. A quiet, dark woman in veils who kept herself apart. I'd seen her walking through the orchards without knowing who she was.

When I wondered what it would be like to be the wife of a great man like Eleazar ben Ya'ir, Revka laughed bitterly. "Take a good look the next time you spy her," she suggested. "See if she seems happy with her fate."

*

I THOUGHT OF how little we knew of our own fate when I went alone to the dovecote. There the Man from the North spoke to me of the threat that hung over us. He took my hand in his, which was reason enough to kill a slave, if you believed in slavery, or in murder, or in anything other than what I believed in now.

"If you think Rome won't come here, you're mistaken. They may have already begun their plans. They won't let a single fortress stand in Judea. They want to show the world they've won."

"Did they confide in you?" I teased. I took my hand from his. He looked like ice, but ice is known to burn. "Is that how you know so much? While you were carrying their weapons and saluting them, did the generals take you aside and tell you their plans?"

"I listened and I heard. That's what I do."

I had set to waving away the doves in order to gather their pale, speckled eggs.

The Man from the North came to stand beside me.

"I plan to leave before Rome comes here."

He spoke straightforwardly, as if we were equals. He was admitting a crime before the action was taken, confiding his intended escape. Had I believed in attending to rules, I would have had to report his remarks to the council.

"That's your plan? To walk home? How do you think you'll accomplish that? You don't know what it's like to be in the desert on your own. You were protected and fed by the legion. You wouldn't like what you found out there."

"What did you find?"

What was inside me, the part no one knew, that which had been bitten by the lion.

"Something that will be apparent to all soon enough." I had no sense of what caused me to talk in this intimate way.

"You think I don't see you, but I do," the Man from the North said.

Anyone would have expected his eyes to be cast down, but he was staring right at me. In the end, I was the one to look away.

THE MILD MONTH of *Iyar* had come to us. Nights were no longer black, as they had been. Instead, they turned a deep blue, like the threads of a prayer shawl. Light drifted through the oncoming dark, lengthening the evenings, keeping the dusk at bay. I spent many hours at the looms and had become a fine weaver. I dyed some of the wool myself, my arms tinted by the vats of color set out after the sheep had been sheared and the wool spun and cleaned. Saffron and sunflowers were used for yellow, green could be produced from stained lichen, red from madder root and from the peeled skin of the pomegranate, black from the mulberry tree.

I had begun a weaving that was not unlike the garment worn by the Man from the North. He had allowed me to take a piece of cloth from his tunic so I could study the unusual pattern. I kept it beneath my sleeping pallet, along with the last blue square that remained from the scarf my brother had given me. The token didn't mean anything. I simply appreciated the intricacy of the weaving. As I worked, other women gathered around to offer praise. I showed them how I fed the loom with different strands until the sequence emerged, the thread crisscrossing, forming squares. Blue like the sea, white like a star, red like a ruby.

The Man from the North had taking to calling me Odeum, our word for ruby. The others in the dovecote soon overheard and were quick to determine that he spoke our language. Once he'd been found out, he was at their mercy. There was no way for him to pretend he didn't understand their commands.

"Just like any man, he can talk when he wants to," the women cried. Aziza and Nahara took to calling me Ruby as well, just to tease me. When anyone wanted the Man from the North to do something, they would laugh and call out, "Let Ruby tell him. He's her slave."

The Man from the North flushed red when the women spoke of him, but I laughed along with them. I had begun to take my noon meal with the others, even though I ate little, only fig cakes and crackers, the most I could consume without becoming ill. I had come to enjoy the company of Shirah and her daughters. Revka was still difficult, but I yearned to win her favor, if only to make peace. I offered to walk with her across the plaza.

"For what reason?" she asked.

It seemed she trusted no one.

"So you'll stop being suspicious of me," I declared.

"That won't happen," she grumbled. Still she allowed me to carry her allotment of water and grain.

Her grandsons ran to meet us as we approached her chamber. When I spoke to them, they stared but did not reply. I had heard others whisper that neither boy possessed a voice.

"You have something to say about them?" Revka asked, glaring at me.

"There's not that much to say in this world," I offered. "Let's keep our mouths shut."

She laughed at my remark, softening toward me.

"When you have a son, you'll understand," she said. "You'll do anything for him."

It was said that a woman about to have a daughter was hungry all the time, but one who was to give birth to a son would not enjoy food until the instant he was born. Neither Revka nor I said more. She had let slip that she was aware of my condition, and I was now mindful that her grandsons had lost their voices under circumstances she didn't wish to speak of. I did not venture to ask if demons had been at work, as some people suggested. In return, she did not question me further.

I understood that to have a son was an honor. Yet it was said that at the moment when a mother first glimpsed a boy-child, she would also see the man he would become, the ax he would carry, the bow he would wield, the battles that awaited him. Even a witch could not undo her son's desire to be a man. I had spied Shirah in the doorway of the small dovecote far across the field, her black hair tumbling down, her voice mournful when she called for her son. Most often, Adir didn't answer. He spent his time at the garrison with the warriors. Shirah still tied knots in the boy's tunic to protect him. She threaded packets of salt and parsley to the fabric to keep away evil. But I had seen him in the alley removing those stitches one by one, casting the charms onto the ground.

WHEN I COULDN'T SLEEP, I sat on a small bench in my chamber spinning with a hand loom. I could do this work in the dark, the door cast open for a trickle of moonlight. The dye I'd used on this wool was *shani*, scarlet, a crimson color taken from boiling the husks of small insects. Red thread always served as protection and was noticed by the angels and by *Adonai*. As I worked, the thread was indeed like rubies in my hand.

I gazed out at the fountain in the plaza and saw a shadow. There was no longer any water running through; the rains were long gone and the night was silent. For a moment I thought it was Aziza, come to meet my brother. I rose to shut the door so that I might respect their privacy. It was only then I recognized the figure in the dark. Shirah was the one standing beside the fountain, like a woman desperate for water. I could hear her crying as though the world were about to end. I couldn't help wonder what on earth could make a witch ache so.

When she left, I fully opened the door to my chamber so that I might drink in the cooler air of the night. I thought about the brutal time I had always feared, the month of the lion, the red-center of *Av,* when we would yearn for anything cold. As it was said that the rue plant sparks bright red at midnight, its strength dispersed in the heat, I would burn more brightly in *Av*. I thought of the flame tree in Jerusalem and of the goat who had been my angel and of the trail of blue I had followed through the wilderness. I thought of the woman in the World-to-Come with whom I shared my name and how I owed her both my life and the color of my hair.

I stored away my spindle and slipped into the dark, my cloak clutched around me. I went to the *auguratorium,* where the bones of doves and eagles had been cast upon the ground to count the years in a man's life, or the number that his flock would grow to be, or the strength of his sons. Wise men had divined what was to come for warriors and kings from the flight of the swallows and from the collection of blue-white bones, but there was no one to decide my future, or even suggest where it might lead.

I took the curving stairs, worn down by the tide of years and by the footsteps of the sages. I wanted to see the earth below me, a world that was so beautiful and so cruel, the land my child would walk through. There were women working at the looms even at this late hour. If I turned west I could identify their voices, but if I turned east I heard only the wind. Inside its roar were the voices of lions, of men who walked through the dark, of women who had been lost.

There were seven hawks circling above me, echoing the seven sisters, stars that gather in the sky. I wore the white garments of a dovekeeper. Perhaps they thought I was ready to take flight and considered me a sacrifice. I climbed onto Herod's wall, balancing on the thick stone blocks edged with the mark of the king. I lifted my arms straight out. The wind went through me. It shook me to my core. There was nothing but emptiness before me, yet I was not alone.

Spring 71 C.E.

Part Two

Summer 71 C.E.

The Baker's Wife

There was only one language we understood,
one prayer we remembered, one path we
walked upon, so far from the throne of heaven
we could no longer hear your voice.

They say that women cannot know the ways of our God, but I have seen His truth with my own eyes. Our God knows all and sees all and has as much compassion for the sparrow as he does for the hawk that hunts it across the sky. Before Him, everything disappears in the wind. If you place a handful of grain on a rock and turn your back, it will fly away. If you leave a sparrow in a tower, it will not be there when you return. If you ask a hawk for mercy, your words will be rendered mute.

That is what happened in my life: I turned my back. I could no longer hear the voice of the sparrow. I asked for kindness from a creature who knew only cruelty. I didn't understand what the wind was capable of and how we must bow before it, grateful no matter where it may take us.

*

AS A girl I lived in a village north of Shiloh, where it was said the spring water could prevent miscarriages and bring children to barren women, such was the pleasure of God in this land. We settled in the Valley of the Cypresses, where the fields were green and there were five black goats in every shed. I married when I was a young woman, too inexperienced to know there was evil in the world. I was happy and I thought happiness lasted. On my door I kept an intricately decorated *mezuzah*, a symbol that brings happiness and luck. Each time I passed by I felt fortunate, assured that God would deliver us from evil. I uttered my thanks to *Adonai* without thought and with the foolhardy conviction that wickedness would never come near. At night my bed was filled with straw so soft that I fell asleep as soon as I closed my eyes. My house was made of stone with beams fashioned of local cypress cut in the woods nearby. My husband was kind and good-hearted, yet still I was granted more. When my daughter was born, she was so beautiful people stopped in the marketplace to congratulate me on my good fortune. I should have begun to worry then, for as fortune comes to you, so does it slip away.

AS THE YEARS drifted by, my dreams were rich with the scent of bread, for below our sleeping chamber my husband had his bread ovens, the kind we called a *tannur*, made of mounds of rounded clay. The pale smoky clay glowed with orange heat when the ovens were stoked before daybreak. Throughout the years the fire that burned below our rooms ensured our warmth. There was a millstone in our courtyard, and two donkeys to pull it, grinding the wheat we stored in a tall, wooden granary.

My husband had learned the art of baking from his father, as he had from his father before him. No baker's bread tasted the same as another's, that was what my husband told me, for a baker's life went into each loaf. Some baked with piety, some with prayers, some with the intent to create more than mere sustenance, raising their craft into an art, entranced by the beauty of the flame of the *tannur* and by the art of the *challah*.

My husband was all three, pious and filled with prayer but also intent on the mystery of the rising loaf, the miracle of the manner in which wheat and water became alive in his hands. The bread he baked was so delicious wayfarers often found us by following its yeasty odor through the village, guided by a map of rich fragrance sent into the air expressly for those driven by hunger. My husband left out a dough offering to honor *Adonai* every morning as he said the blessing. In return his blessings rose to God and we had all that we wanted in this world.

My husband had his secrets, as all bakers do. I was privileged to learn from him over the years simply by watching him work. He kneaded the dough longer than most, and the yeast he used to give the bread life was a secret recipe kept in cool stone jars, left to ferment for the best part of a year. He dusted the dough with cumin and coriander and salt before he slid the loaves into the oven on flat wooden boards. Perhaps most important, he made his mark on the dough, the letter *R* scrawled in honor of my name, Revka, for after so many years I was still his bride, the girl to whom he'd pledged his life.

When the days were without haze, we could see to where snow sometimes fell in the highlands. The vista I saw from my own house was the only one I ever wished to survey. I would never have believed I would come to live in a king's fortress where the wind engulfs us and claims us, making it clear we are nothing more than a moment in time. A hundred years earlier, Herod walked across the same plaza I must cross each morning on my way to the dovecote. Now there are poor men sleeping in his chambers, but these poor men draw breath while the king who murdered his own wife, Mariamne, and his sons, and anyone else who stood in his way, is nothing but dust. Warriors sharpen their knives in what had been the royal stable, a huge, cavernous place that once housed a hundred horses, each said to possess the ability to climb the serpent's path in the dark. Blindfolds were slipped over their eyes so they could not see how treacherous the ground they trod upon truly was. Had they been aware of the staggering heights, surely they would have panicked and tumbled into the abyss, one after the other, as if falling from the sky. The same holds true for us. If any among us who reside in this stronghold paused for a moment to tear the blindfold of faith from our eyes, we would see how perilous our perch was, how shattering a fall would be.

If we lost our faith, we would become like the clouds that swell across the western sky when the wind pushes them into the desert, promising rain but empty inside.

IN THE MORNING, I always had a moment to myself before my grandchildren arose. For me, it was the best time of the day. I watched the boys sleeping next to me, their faces serene. I imagined they were in their own beds at home, that their mother was outside the door readying their morning meal, that they hadn't lost their voices in the desert, stolen by a demon, grabbed from their throats and stored in a locked box in the World-to-Come.

I tied threads knotted into the wool of their garments for protection while they slept. This was permitted until they turned nine, then I would have to give them over to the will of *Adonai,* or so people said. I was grateful for the amulets Shirah offered me. I paid no attention to those who claimed she was a witch, whispering that her presence on this mountain would bring us to ruin. I had seen what was wicked in this world, and it wasn't the woman I worked beside. Inside my grandsons' tunics I bound small pouches which held salt to keep away Lilith, who steals the breath of children, a shell from the red sea as a gift for the angel called Michael, the root and seeds of the mandrake, which would chase away the terrors that came with dreams, for there were surely terrors for the three of us that remained of our family, as certainly there were for the fourth among us who survived, the man who no longer spoke to us, who lost himself when he lost his faith.

I leave Noah and Levi their morning meal before slipping into the predawn. Small pressed cakes of almonds and figs so they would know sweetness, dates that grew wild on the cliffs so they would taste the fruit of the desert, flatbread I fried in oil on a griddle, sprinkled with coriander and cumin and salt, so they would remember the taste of their grandfather's bread. On some mornings I took note of Shirah's son, Adir, racing along the path where mint grows wild. He's a charming boy, wild, with black hair and yellow-flecked, slanted eyes. He recently turned twelve, but I knew that inside his tunic were dozens of knots. It is written that one has to rely on *Adonai* without the use of magic, and so it should be. But our boys were valued highly. The mother of a boy was considered impure only for seven days after she gave birth, while she who delivered a girl was considered *teme'ah* for twice that time.

I understood why Shirah would do anything necessary to guard her only son.

I did not listen to what others said about her, but once, when she was ailing and I brought her soup made of turnip broth, I spied a hidden altar to the goddess. I had entered the chamber without waiting for a reply after rapping on her door. Shirah quickly closed the cabinet where the altar was concealed, but I saw the spark in a lamp lit before an offering of honey and oil that had been set out to honor alabaster *terafim*. One, the small, luminous figure of a woman, had her arms upraised. I recognized Ashtoreth, the mother and warrior, whose presence has long been outlawed. We were not to have idols, nor were we to give thanks to the goddess.

Those women who did made certain to close their altars so the lamps that burned were never revealed.

Shirah thanked me for the soup. We did not speak of matters some might claim to be sorcery, and I did not raise my eyes to her altar again. I had compassion for her, for I had often spied worry spreading across her striking, fine-boned face. Try as she might to keep him a child, Shirah's son was already straining to be a man. She called out cautions, but Adir hurried to the garrison, determined to be among the men he admired. When the wind is so strong that we women know we will choke on the rising dust if we fail to tie our scarves across our faces, boys will always ignore the elements and race through storm clouds, dreaming of glory. Even a witch can't stop her son from becoming a warrior. There is no spell great enough for that.

BEFORE YAEL CAME, I was the new woman in the dovecotes. I thought I would be sent to the baker, for my husband had taught me much about the mysteries of bread. But I was wearing my white mourning shawl when I arrived at the fortress, and perhaps the council members were reminded of doves as I stood before them, head bowed in defeat. The moment I entered through the carved wooden doors of the largest dovecote, a circular tower with flaps for light in the roof, I was certain a curse had befallen me. I couldn't understand why the original dovekeeper and her beautiful daughters took such pride in what they did. They assured me I had been honored, and they welcomed me with wreaths of flowers, which I quickly cast away. I thought that doves were filthy things, good for a stew or perhaps a few fresh eggs, nothing more. I had now sunk even lower than these simple creatures, for it was I who was commanded to collect their leavings into barrels. I was a slave to their waste and their filth, disgraced in the eyes of the Lord. Such was my station in life. Such was my fate.

I CRIED the first night after I worked in the dovecote, a woman my age who should have known better, embarrassed to find myself in tears, my back turned to my grandsons so they wouldn't know of my humiliation. We had arrived at the mountain only days before. Our feet were still aching, our skin sunburned, our silence thick in our throats. Everything seemed new and strange—the men in silver armor, the women toiling in the fields under almond trees. I should have given thanks for our salvation, instead I wept like a child in despair.

Although I tried to hide my sorrow, I could not. My grandsons' small hands patted my shoulders for comfort, and I felt the concern in their touch. They could not speak, and perhaps their affliction allowed them to divine what others ignored, the true nature of the world. They could catch a moth in the dark by taking note of the soft, fluttering rhythm of its wings. They could gauge whether the wind had traveled from the west or if it arose in the east simply by the sound. Perhaps these abilities were miracles.

Where there was one miracle, surely, there would be more.

I cried myself to sleep and awoke early after an unsettled night. My eyes were red and puffy. I expected the boys to still be asleep, but my younger grandson, Levi, who had just turned seven, was crouched beside me, waiting for me to wake, his gaze trained upon me. He took my hand and led me outside, my guide through the dim light. I felt that I was still in a dream, but the dust and the sound of goats in their pens were real enough. We were here inside this fortress, so far from everything we knew, the fields of poppies and thistle, the cypress groves, the blooms of pomegranates, whose bell-shaped, scarlet flowers would turn to fruit before our eyes.

Levi led me to the wall that overlooked the white cliffs which stretched on as far as we could see. We watched the doves fly. Let loose at this hour so they might stretch their wings, they turned the entire sky white. They rose and disappeared, then returned again, drawn back to their nests. They were devoted to their mates. Therefore, couples were never allowed to fly together; the loyalty of one brought it back to its partner time and time again, despite the lure of freedom.

I understood what my grandson was telling me in bringing me to see the beauty of their flight. It was an honor to work with creatures who lived in the sky, so close to *Adonai*. If it was my fate to do so, it was not a burden but a gift. I turned and kissed Levi's forehead and whispered a prayer of gratitude for all I still had.

THERE HAS BEEN talk about us ever since my son-in-law brought us here. People gazed at us trying to guess at the catastrophe in our family, convinced that even among the unfortunate, we deserved their pity because of my grandsons' inability to speak. They know nothing more, only that we were driven out of our home, as they were, and that we chose to come here. We could have gone north toward Nazareth or Galilee, where the air was said to always be cool, where we might have begun a new life, searching out a village where no one knew of our bad luck. But my son-in-law was no longer a man who could live that way, settled into the practical matters of daily life. He was not about to herd goats, or find us a house made of stone in a town where we would walk to the well and cook our meals and forget what we had been through. He wanted revenge, nothing less. At Masada he had found what he was searching for, the company of men willing to die for what they believed in.

I don't know how much time passed in the wilderness after God deserted us. *Blessed is He who spoke, and the world came into being.*

Just as creation began with words so, too, did our world come apart in silence. None among us spoke. The boys because they could not, my son-in-law because he would not, myself because there were no words worth speaking aloud. The world was broken, and there was only one road that remained, splayed open before us as if made of bones.

I understood that by making this mountain our destination, we were headed for a no-man's-land, a place from which there was no return. We had been banished from the world as we'd known it. We had seen too much and lost too much to walk into another town and unload the few belongings we still had and start anew.

Here my son-in-law is called the Man from the Valley; he needs no more of a name than that. He lives in the barracks, but even his own brethren fear him. He will go headfirst into any battle, unafraid and unyielding, with the grim expression of one who is determined to face down the Angel of Death. He wields an ax, the only weapon he needs. He eschews armor. *Take me down,* he goads the angel, *Mal'ach ha-Mavet. Take me if you can.*

Some people say the Man from the Valley sleeps with his ax, that he loves it the way another man might love a woman, or a father adore his child. He, who was once a scholar called Yoav, is now as brutal and merciless as the angel Gabriel is said to be, for Gabriel stands at the left hand of God, the side of the righteous. His sword is made of fire, and his eyes are fire as well. If he appears before you, you can sink to your knees and beg for mercy, but you will most certainly burn.

My son-in-law has not cut his hair since our time in the desert. He vows he never will again. He braids it into plaits that fall down his back. Already his hair has turned white, though he is a young man. Brambles and thorns are threaded through the strands as they are in the wool of sheep and goats, but he doesn't notice, for he lingers in the world of grief, not in ours. Thorns mean nothing to him. Brambles are all he expects from the world. Some children whisper that he can breathe fire, like Gabriel, who is said to possess the ability to destroy entire cities with a single breath. When they see this Man from the Valley, the children run from him. He has no friends, takes no woman to his bed, keeps no one's confidence. What happened has turned him into something that is like the wind—you cannot see him, but you know he is there, ready to do damage.

When I think of my son-in-law, I cannot help but recall the story of the rebel Jew some call Taxo. King Herod's men chased him into a cave in the time when our fortress was still a palace, but this man would not bow to the will of the king. He would not offer his sons to be conscripts and refused to pay his share of taxes. The king could not allow rebellion, for such things breed as swarms of insects do, erupting into stinging fury, the one becoming the many, gathering strength.

When Herod's soldiers were lowered from the tops of the cliffs on thick ropes, dressed for battle and ready to defeat him, the rebel cut the throats of his seven sons, one by one. He then slashed the throat of his wife before he followed, leaping into the ravine where he'd scattered his sons' bodies. He would not allow those he loved to be subjected to the torture and cruelty of the king. Instead he left this world alongside them, even though it is written that none of our people may harm himself. As Taxo cast himself upon the rocks, perhaps he imagined God would blame the rocks for his death and he would be forgiven in the World-to-Come.

Though our law states that no man may wound himself, Yoav has destroyed the father he had once been to his sons, and in doing so he has destroyed himself. My son-in-law never comes to see the boys, for when he lost himself, he lost them as well. Should he happen upon the children in the alleyways or the orchards, he walks on the way a blind man might. At first the boys ran to him and clutched at his legs, but it did no good. Yoav does not blink, or stammer, or even gaze upon them, not if they throw themselves at him, desperate for his attentions. All that is good in this world is concealed from the man who was my son-in-law. The glinting water in a cup is sinister in his eyes, the clear sky is an affront, and his children have become nothing more than reminders of how flesh can burn and be turned to dust.

People take his negligence as proof that something is wrong with the children. Why would their own father disown them, even though they are so beautiful, with golden hair and dark eyes, reminiscent of their mother's? There are those who whisper that the boys are possessed and this has caused their silence, but I understand that words aren't necessary. The doves have taught me that. It is possible to speak without words, to know another creature's wants and desires though there is only silence. That was my lesson to learn, my fate all along.

Each morning when I arrive, the doves know me; their song rises and falls with pleasure and acceptance. It is always there, a river of sound. Someone who isn't accustomed to such noise might cover her ears and run outside. Yael did exactly that on her first day with us, hiding her head in alarm. We laughed and teased her, calling out that if mere birds could frighten her so, she had best never face a fierce beast. And yet the doves go to her as if she could speak their language. Though she doesn't seem to care for them, they fly to her as if charmed. It's her silence that draws them in and comforts them.

As for me, I'm grateful for my work in the dovecotes. The more distracted I am, the more possible it is for me to go on for another day. The sun streams in, and I begin to feed my charges their grain. I chase the nesting ones away to search for eggs. Most flutter up, but if they refuse to leave their nests, I shake my apron at them. How is it that I can feel sorrow for the doves, so much so that when I take their speckled eggs and place them in a basket I often weep, and yet when I dream of the men I killed, I feel nothing at all.

BEFORE WE came here we believed that our village in the Valley of the Cypresses was heaven, or perhaps we imagined it was not unlike the heaven we would someday enter. We should have known it would be taken from us. Nothing in this world is lasting, only our faith lives on. One day soldiers from the legion arrived, six across, walking down roads my own father had helped to build. First the legionnaires came, trained in Rome, decorated with chain mail and helmets; then the fierce auxiliary troops arrived, many of them tribesmen, wearing leather tunics, carrying long broadswords and lances. They wanted any riches they could find. From that morning when they entered our village, our land belonged to them and our lives did, too. They killed a white cockerel on the steps of the synagogue. In our law, that is a sin. They were well aware of this doctrine. The bird's blood defiled us. This initial act of violence announced what the future would bring, if only the priests had bothered to read the signs left behind by the rooster's bones. A hundred of our people went to rally against the legion and demand an apology. These were men who paid taxes and had homes and families, reputable, honest men who were certain this day would end with an apology from Rome.

They could not have been more wrong.

We did not see beyond the cypresses that grew with fragrant twisted bark set within a wood that had been there for so long we thought it would last forevermore. Outrage howled from ruined villages nearby for those who could hear, but we turned a deaf ear to their misery. For those who breathed deeply, there was the stink of war, but it was also the season when the oleander's pink blooms sent out their fragrance and perfumed the air. Our land had been conquered many times, the sweet groves and fields drawing outsiders to us just as surely as the baker called to his customers with the rich scent of his loaves. But that was in the past; we wanted to believe that our lives were settled. My husband paid no attention to what was happening. In that he was indeed single-minded, as well as hardworking. The wise men and rabbis bowed to the legion, accepting taxes so high we could barely survive, but as long as there was wood for his ovens, my husband was happy. He cut the logs himself, and there was a pile as tall as a mountain in our yard. My husband asked only for a blessing from *Adonai* for what he was about to bring forth into this world each day, the mystery of the *challah*. He had white powder in the creases of his skin. Each time he kissed me he left a white mark, a baker's kiss. He assured me that, if we paid no attention to what was around us and did no harm, we would be safe. People always needed bread.

He left our home determined to bring the first round loaves to the synagogue as an offering, as he always did. He had vowed to avoid trouble, but on this day it found him. Our neighbors had collected in a beleaguered group on their way to plead their case so they would not lose their homes to the Romans. My husband was convinced to go with them. He had his tray of offerings, the loaves covered by a prayer shawl that had been so finely spun gold threads were braided among the purple fringes. He was ready to go to the rabbis, but when his neighbors scolded him and said all men must make a stand, he was compelled to make his mark with the others. The letter *R* fashioned into the crusts of the loaves he baked should have been enough of a mark for him, my name his inspiration and his shield. Instead, he joined those men who wanted more.

I KNEW something was wrong when I smelled smoke. There were loaves in the oven. I checked them, but they weren't yet burning. Why did he go on this day of all days? Why on this morning was he not single-minded when at all other times he saw nothing but his own bakery? The barley, the salt, the coriander, the cumin, these were the ingredients that made up his world. Until now the only difficulty that had plagued my husband was that rats slunk through the windows; like many bakers, he often had to lay down hemlock to turn them away from the flour bins. Now there was peril in every corner of our world. The demons had flung open the doors to our village. They had declared us to be victims as they stood on a dark ledge and rubbed their hands together gleefully. What you are given, they declared, we now take away.

As the hours passed, I began to pace back and forth in alarm. The baker had expected to return before the loaves in the slow-burning oven were brown. Does a man go off and disappear like that? He'd told me to remove the loaves when the sun was in the center of the sky if he hadn't yet returned. I didn't. What had he meant by that? Had he had some idea of the trouble to come? Noon came and went. I gazed out in alarm as I saw the shadows lengthening, the smoke drifting over courtyards and roofs.

I thought if I waited to remove the loaves, my husband would smell the bread and know it was burning and run back home. At worst he would be cross with me for not doing as I was instructed. But he still hadn't returned when the sun had begun to drop down in the direction of evening. By now the loaves were charred, the crusts black with soot.

I had one thought, and that was to find my husband. I could be single-minded, too, perhaps that was what had bound us together for so many years. I opened the door, frantic to begin a search for the Baker, ready to dart into the street though it was now teeming with our neighbors, many of them stained with their own blood and with the blood of their fathers.

As I was readying myself to leave, I found my son-in-law, Yoav, in my doorway. He wasn't a fighter then, not yet the warrior who would vow to never again cut his hair. Instead, he was a gentle man who longed to run from trouble. He had the panicked look of a scholar who is suddenly faced with the brutalities and the vile concerns of life. Like my husband, he had been dedicated to his work, concerned with his studies and with the will of *Adonai*. I had already wrapped my head scarf close to my skull, possessed with the intention to search for my husband, but my son-in-law stopped me. He warned I must prepare myself for what he had to say.

I raised my chin, ready to push past him, not willing to listen. What could stop me from going to my husband? What excuse could my son-in-law offer that might compel me to give up my search? My son-in-law, who was devout and would never touch a woman other than my daughter, his wife, placed his hand on my arm.

"There is a reason I tell you not to go out there," he murmured.

There could be only one reason. A world that had unraveled so completely that the man I'd spent a lifetime with had been lost. I could see the truth in my son-in-law's eyes when he began to speak. He confessed he had seen the husk that had been my husband in the center of our town, cast upon the plaza with dozens of our neighbors, broken like a branch in the wind. It was too late to retrieve the body. If I tried, I would only lose my life as well.

Despite his report, I tried to push past the place where my son-in-law had planted himself in my doorway. He was stronger than I imagined, or perhaps I was weakened by regret.

"Listen to me," Yoav insisted. He said it in a way that gave me no choice but to hear. "There is no other way for me to say this, and no time to reason with you. Your husband is already in the World-to-Come."

There was no map to lead the living there. I could not reach him. The Romans were already piling up bodies in the street. They had lit the fire which had alerted me to the misery of the day. Now I realized it was not bread I smelled on the waves of smoke pouring through town but the bitter odor of flesh.

Yoav was a young rabbi who was respected and learned; because of his rank he'd had to think twice before taking a baker's daughter as his bride. Most rabbis searched out other rabbis' daughters in marriage, for like congregated with like, as the birds in the sky gathered with their own kind. But of course Yoav had wanted my daughter. Zara was beautiful beyond measure. No wonder he had courted her, ignoring the more suitable girls who chased after him. My daughter's name meant beautiful morning, and she truly was brighter than anything in this world, her skin golden, her hair like wheat, her countenance made even more lovely because her black eyes were a reminder of night before morning broke through, a time when the world was a mystery and shadows were all we had.

I'd often wondered if perhaps Zara had been given to me by an angel. How else could a plain woman such as I be blessed with a daughter who resembled a queen? I took great pride in her, and for good reason.

I never once stopped to consider that what you are given can also be taken away.

WE HAD BEEN flattered when Yoav came to live in our house. My husband always cut a piece of the loaf offering for him every morning, the first of the bread baked that day. Now this learned young man we had so honored with our pride and respect had been turned pale, quaking with fear. As I leaned against him, sobbing, he was no different than any other frightened man, no better certainly, perhaps more terrified than many. He insisted I hurry and pack. I hesitated until he informed me that my daughter and her boys were already awaiting us.

Something compelled me to pack a few extra ingredients. You would think I would take up my finest robes or my marriage bracelets, those special, valued items I kept in the cabinet beside the bed, hidden where no thief could reach them. Instead I took what had belonged to the Baker: a wooden bowl, a clutch of heavy spoons, the white cloth he tied around his waist while he was at work, the garment he wore so that no evil would come upon us as long as he was dressed in his prayer shawl. At the last moment I collected several of the vials he kept beneath the stove: coriander and cumin and salt. A jar of the fermented dough which caused the loaves to rise.

I knew that the dead did not leave us so quickly, so I whispered to my husband as I packed. *Look at us now,* I said to the man I'd lived beside for so many years, as if he was beside me still. *Look what we've become.*

We were like rats, scurrying away before the flood of death overtook us. I grabbed the burned bread from the oven, scalding my hands. Blisters would rise on my fingers, but at least I made certain we had the last loaves of the Baker's bread to sustain us. Yoav took my arm to lead me away. I knew we dared not linger. But I believe my son-in-law was not the only one with me in the bakery that day. I am convinced there was an angel standing beside me, whispering *Take this, not that.*

At the last moment I reached for the small jar of the hemlock my husband used on vermin.

Perhaps the angel had given me what I needed most of all.

PEOPLE we had known our whole lives were swarming out of the village, some carrying all they owned. Chaos had overcome us, and our lives were like stones thrown in a game of chance, cast up into the air, only to fall and scatter upon the ground. Broken pottery littered the road, and many tossed away belongings they soon discovered were too heavy to bring on such a hurried, frantic journey. There were stray dogs barking and the echo of babies crying. Everywhere there were flames as people set their own homes on fire rather than allow the Romans to sack them after they'd been abandoned. People wanted to ensure that their enemies couldn't enjoy what they had labored a lifetime to possess. By the next day not a brick would remain, our world having been snatched away overnight. There were women in the street sobbing, but the wind had come up, the merciless wind from the sea that in time would bring us winter, and no one could hear these women's voices. No one could determine if they uttered oaths or prayers.

I followed at my son-in-law's heels, intent, as he was, on making certain that my daughter and her children were kept safe. I wept as we went on, certain I'd bring a curse upon us by not preparing my husband's body. I was meant to sit beside him all night and help him travel into the World-to-Come with lamentations and prayers. At any other time I would have remained with the husk that had once housed his spirit before the body that had contained him was left in the cave beside the bones of our people. I thought of our forefathers fleeing from Egypt, of their children who stumbled in the sand as they made their way out of bondage, of the waters that rose and then parted before them. Their agony had never been more real to me. I felt I might weep on their behalf.

I draped a white shawl over my own shoulders, already in mourning for a man who had baked my initial into every loaf of bread. I slipped on the color of the garments of the dead, as though I had passed from this world along with my husband. For a moment, I thought I should stay behind, give up my life at the hands of the Romans and allow my spirit to join with his. But I had a vision of my daughter and of her children, dearer than any treasure, and I knew what I must do. I prayed for my husband, but I left our village that evening. Like the rats, I fled what was tumbling down around us, forsaking the lives we had led that were now destroyed.

BY NIGHTFALL we were journeying toward the wilderness. It was the month of *Tishri,* when we celebrate *Rosh Hashanah,* the festival marking the time the Almighty begins to write down the names of those who belong in the Book of Life and will live for another year. I had no idea that we would still be wandering during *Yom Kippur,* the time to atone for our sins, and that the book would be closed on that day, then sealed. The names that had not been written on its pages were those who would not live into the next year.

We were prepared for a long journey. My son-in-law had brought along the two donkeys and the cart that had pulled sacks of emmer and wheat to the bakery and turned the millstone to grind flour. I carried the last five loaves of my husband's bread, tokens of what had brought us our good life. My daughter had packed jars of olives and oil and had brought along cheese wrapped in cloth and leather canisters of water. We ran, and the donkeys ran with us. Above us there were huge flocks of birds, all fleeing the billows of smoke issued by the many fires set in the village. We slept huddled together, in the open, unused to the cruel way of the wilderness, yearning for the scent of baking bread and the softness of our own beds. My son-in-law wore the long tunic of a scholar. He looked distraught when my daughter embraced him and told him we would be lost without him, perhaps frightened that the faith she had in him to lead us was misplaced. He was more at home with his scrolls and prayers than he was guiding us through the wilderness.

At night I dreamed of my husband. He was with me as the dead often are before they move on. They say those who have left us don't change who they are even in the World-to-Come. My husband was kneading bread, working hard, as if he was still in our world. He seemed the same, a kind and serious man intent on his baking, just as he'd always been, but he was using ingredients I didn't recognize. The dough was red, and the spices were ground from the petals of black flowers and from the sharp stingers of honeybees. I heard him speak then. He said, *Every loaf of bread feeds you in the way you need to be fed*. My husband had been a simple man and had used words only when necessary. Now, in my dreams, I felt certain he was telling me something I needed to hear. I awoke wishing he had said more.

In the morning, the flocks of birds fleeing over the hillsides were so enormous they blotted out the sun. I held my tongue, though I was certain this was a bad sign. The white cockerel who'd been murdered on the stairs of the synagogue was following us, that was what I believed, sending his messengers to pursue us. The birds passed us, their flight faster than we would ever be, and that told us something as well.

If we had paid attention, we would have understood there are some things in this world you cannot outrun.

THE DAYS PASSED, and before long we had eaten nearly all we had, the bread, the olives, the cheese. We began to ration our food. My son-in-law's plan was simple, the tactics of a logical man. We would wait out the Romans, then return to our village and start anew. I didn't say what I knew, that there'd be nothing to return to. We would have only blood and broken bricks. I saw that my son-in-law was intimidated by the wilderness before us and our place in it. The desert loomed, a harsh landscape even for those experienced in surviving its dangers. In all his hours of study, Yoav had never built a fire from twigs with the use of a flint, never hunted with a bow, never found water or made his way over limestone boulders and rocks so harsh they set our feet to bleeding. He was an important man in the village, but here he was nothing. Before long we were lost. Each thorn tree looked the same to us, ravaged, black. Each hillock led to yet another. Only the sky changed, flushing pink at twilight, and then sifting into a dove gray light before the darkness overcame us.

Yoav began to pray, hour after hour, as if that could prompt him as to what to do next. I had tried and failed to make bread in a griddle over our small fire. I could only make crackers that hadn't the strength to rise. I finally was able to cook bread on hot stones that I placed beneath burning kindling. The boys called the black, risen loaves ash bread; it was as bitter as it was satisfying. The goatskin bags of water were less heavy, drained by our thirst, and the rains hadn't yet come. Yoav promised that *Adonai* would lead us, and we had no choice but to accept his decree. Secretly, I wished we could find a guide among the tribesmen in their blue robes that we sometimes spied heading toward Moab. I would give them all I had if they could help us navigate a trail.

Though our village was gone, I still thought there was a world for us to return to.

I kept my eye on the heavens. There were more birds all the time. Each day their numbers increased. I tried to count them, but it was impossible, they were as numerous as the stars, and in the end I gave up. I still felt the Baker was with me, and that brought me comfort. I spoke to him under my breath, trying to amuse him with my descriptions of the many sorts of winds we encountered: the billowing kind, the howling sort, the soft, warm wind from the south, the stark, blue wind that arrived at nightfall and abruptly departed at daybreak, the violet wind of despair. I chattered to my husband whenever no one could overhear.

Then one day I awoke and he was gone. I felt his departure as surely as if I had seen his spirit rise. All at once, my aloneness settled deeply, a stone inside of me, hard and sharp. While I slept, my husband's spirit had been claimed by the World-to-Come. He was utterly gone. When I spoke of the hissing, rain-spattered wind that would come to us when winter arrived, he made no reply. When I described the sunstruck wind of the drifting dust funnels, I was speaking to no one but the dust itself. There were only black birds above us now, a bank of feathers and flesh that roiled across the sky like storm clouds. I waited till dark to weep, holding my grief inside, for there was no point in sharing my sorrow.

We had no choice but to go forward, as only emptiness was around us. The following day we did so. I had to leave that unmarked place, abandoning the last of my husband's essence. I carried my loss as my burden; it weighed me down and made me slow. I could not keep pace with the tired donkeys who bleakly made their way. The boys ran back to me and grabbed my hands and urged me on. Because of them I continued, but God must have known it had crossed my mind to stay behind. I wanted to lie down beside the rocks and dream of the Baker, to call for him to come back to me, even if it meant giving up this world. Perhaps that was the sin I committed. I forgot that even the worst of lives is a treasure.

WE WANDERED to a small oasis. There was a waterfall flowing from a cliff, pouring over the rocks to form a pool of fresh water. We felt blessed, overjoyed by our good fortune.

"I told you to have faith," my son-in-law chided. "God has done exactly as I said He would."

There were date palms and a jumble of fragrant jasmine. Reeds on fleshy stems grew along the banks of the pool. White flowers drifted in the green water, each forming the shape of a star. There was a cluster of wild mulberries where wasps and dragonflies gathered, their drone like music. The air was cool and sweet when the breeze stirred. I could have described that breeze to my husband if his spirit was still beside me, a wind so calm it inspired envy in all other winds in every corner of the world.

My son-in-law thought we could wait out the Romans here, in this mild place. We should have known that in such cruel times it was best not to be attached to a single location, even if there was water and the air was refreshing. Envy is envy, both for the wind and for men on earth. The better the place, the more others covet what you have. Be a pauper, a wanderer, a secret in the darkness of night. Once you possess something others do not, you are a target for the wicked. It would have been better if we'd made our camp in one of the caves beyond the oasis, or perhaps gone farther into the wilderness, following the trampled paths beaten down among the thornbushes by bands of wild camels. But my son-in-law feared the heart of the desert and intended for us to stay where we would be safe. I had a rush of fear, a premonition. I saw the speckled shadows beneath the palm tree form the shape of a viper; it slithered along the sand, stopping at my feet.

My daughter hushed me when I spoke of my fears, suggesting we move on. There were people who had entered the wilderness that spread out before us never to be seen again, she whispered. Wanderers who were abandoned or devoured by beasts, defeated by hunger and thirst, kidnapped, enslaved by the tribesmen who wore blue cloaks. Here we had everything we might ever need; to leave would be an ingratitude in God's eyes.

"Think of the children," Zara urged. "They're happy here."

When I looked at the boys, cheerfully shouting as they played together in the shade of the date palms, I put away my fears. We stayed where there would be water, the most precious element of all, even though hyenas came to drink in the twilight, drawn to water, as all beasts in the desert are. These fierce creatures stayed close, their eyes gleaming as they stalked the donkeys, another omen we ignored. At night these ungodly spotted animals made a wailing sound, for they desired what little we had, or perhaps they wished to convince us they were tame, like dogs, longing for our company, when what they really wanted was our flesh.

We saw few people during this time, only stray travelers who filled their water flasks, then moved on, too wise to make camp in such uncertain times. We were told that Zealots from Jerusalem had taken over several outposts nearer the Salt Sea, including Herod's fortress, that marvel of a palace perched on white cliffs, built by a king so cruel he murdered anyone who opposed him. One old man, a hermit with his feet bound in cloth and his tunic shredded by the wind, warned that, although the desert might appear vacant, it was teeming with life. What looked empty was full, much like water in a cup. What was most important was invisible to the eye.

THE BIRDS had remained with us, like a plague hovering in the sky. Even I, a simple woman, knew this foreshadowed evil. One day there were so many we hid in the tent where we slept, frightened by such extreme darkness in the middle of the day, a world blackened by ravens. When we went out the next morning, the road that led to the east was strewn with feathers. Birds had fallen from the sky, stricken by some unknown disaster. Zara and I were busy foraging for twigs to make a fire so we could take our noon meal. Before I could stop them, my grandsons had gathered feathers and begun to play with them, adorning themselves, pretending they'd been turned into ravens. My daughter and I exchanged a look. All at once we had realized it was *Yom Kippur,* the Day of Atonement, when we ask God to forgive our sins. In the wilderness every day was much like the next, and we had forgotten the divine aspect of the day until that very moment. We had not been meant to work or eat, only to beg for forgiveness.

It was said that in the Temple there was a scarlet rope hung at the altar; at the close of *Yom Kippur,* after fasting and sacrifice and many prayers, it would turn white when God forgave us our transgressions. Now we had ignored the most holy of days, and in doing so we had turned our backs on our God. The boys were dancing in the sand, covered with feathers, clucking to each other like birds. It was the sort of mistake that calls demons from their hiding places. I wondered if we had taken the wrong path in our journey and had heedlessly turned to the left, the side that gives rise to all evil.

My daughter's husband was furious when he saw the boys romping like savages. Compelled to make amends, he ran to pray, pacing into the desert, the wind hitting against him, leaving its mark like whips. He shouted through that ferocious wind that he would make things right and beg for forgiveness, he would pray for God's mercy, even if it took him all day and all night. But my daughter and I knew what we had done could not be righted. We had forgotten *Adonai*. We'd thought only of ourselves and our own trifling human needs. For that, we would suffer. Our sins would grow and swallow us whole.

I had named my daughter after morning's radiance, but *morning* has two meanings, and perhaps I called down a curse when I chose to call her so. Now I wondered if I had foretold what was written even though learned men insist no woman can foresee what will come to be. They can say what they like. I knew nothing good would come to pass in the desert on the *Yom Kippur* that we forgot. My daughter's husband could pray for forgiveness until his throat was dry. I could tell by the rising wind, the one without mercy, that there would be none.

THAT TERRIBLE DAY would still continue to overtake my every thought if the racket in the dovecotes did not distract me with a constant stream of sound. A clatter of noise mirrors silence, for one is alone in both situations. I often noticed Shirah watching me as I worked. I wondered what she made of me. I was not afraid to get my hands dirty, and did not overstep my bounds. When she had her eye on me in the dim air, I bowed my head to hide what resided within me. There was a single stream of sunlight that poured in the roof, and I avoided walking through it, afraid the brightness would reveal the truth of my mourning. But one day, not long after my arrival, Shirah suddenly took my hand in hers. I was startled by her action, and before I could think to pull away, she gazed into my rough palm. Her touch was like water, cool upon my skin. Afterward, I could tell that she knew. I had a murderer's hand. It burned at night, in the dark. Other women looked at the moon as it rose to see their fate reflected, but I peered into the palm of my hand to see what was written and what I had done.

As I did not wish others to speak of me, I turned away from the gossip concerning Shirah. If she was indeed a witch, I had no fear of her, for when she clasped my hand in hers, she took a portion of my burden upon her.

"Being human means losing everything we love best in the world," she murmured as she released me. "But would you ask to be anything else?"

I WAS SILENT at the time, but afterward I wondered if I would indeed have preferred to be a snake rather than a woman, if I would have chosen to live my life beneath a rock, striking at dusk, devouring my sustenance, ravenous and alone in my cold skin. Did a snake love her children? Did she weep beneath her rock, yearning for arms with which to embrace them, for a voice with which to tell them stories, a heart that could be rended in two? Often I couldn't sleep when I thought about such matters. These were the times when I saw Shirah walking at night. Perhaps she knew the answers to my questions, but I never asked, just as I never questioned where she was going or where she had been. If she had a box of sins kept under lock and key, as some people vowed, that was not my business. Once you have broken God's laws, you are aware that He alone can judge us. You know that no man can understand what a woman may be driven to do.

WHEN YAEL first came to us, I was convinced she was a foolish, selfish girl who thought too well of herself to clean up after the doves or carry heavy baskets of dung into the fields. I would have never imagined she would come to live in my house, if one can rightly call a single chamber with a curtain as a divider from neighbors a proper home. And yet I myself had been guilty of those very same notions upon my arrival, bitter that I had been sent to work in the dovecotes. I'd held on to the position of my old life with an arrogance to which I had no right. I'd wept, convinced I'd been relegated to the lowliest position on the mountain, until my grandson showed me the truth of the doves. Now I understand the pride Shirah and her daughters show, a devotion which had puzzled me when I first walked through the carved wooden doors, a scarf tied over my face, afraid to draw a single breath because of the stench of the rich loam.

Without the doves, this fortress would have already fallen. The leavings scattered in the orchard have turned our world green and lush, nourishing the roots of the dates and olives, feeding the almond trees, causing them to burst into blooms of pink and white clouds. Without the doves, we would have starved long ago. It was outlawed to kill one, for without the Temple there could no longer be sacrifices; a man who took one out of greed risked being *karet*, turned out from God's view, for such a deed was considered a crime against us all.

Each time I cut open a piece of fruit, I was grateful to the pale, pliant creatures we cared for. Whenever one was ailing, I brought it home to nurse it to health. I kept such birds in a wooden shelf beside my bed. I listened as they cooed, finding comfort in their song.

These were the only nights when I didn't dream.

I BEGAN to change my mind about Yael, daughter of the famed assassin Yosef bar Elhanan, the murderer who people whispered had once possessed the ability to walk through walls and disappear in front of men's eyes, sister of one of our young warriors. I noticed she could work her own brand of magic. All she had to do was reach out her hand, and the doves would come to her. She needn't cluck her tongue or offer grain, tricks I used to call them to me. I was surprised by her abilities, struck by jealousy. I was always the first to unlock the door in the mornings, the one to feed the doves and nurse them back to health. It was I who threw stones when hawks came to light on our roof, ready to slip through the thatching and destroy the nests we tended so carefully, or to strike when we let the doves fly in the early morning, assured of their loyalty and their return.

Yet it was Yael they went to, not me. She stood in the dark and they flitted around her.

"Why do they prefer her?" I asked Shirah, for she had been among the doves for the longest time. I suppose envy shone in my eyes.

"She speaks their language."

"Really? Of birds? What language is that?"

Shirah smiled in response. "You of all people should know."

Then I understood. It was the language of silence.

I HAD GUESSED what Yael was hiding beneath her tunic and scarves, although she would not speak of it, and for good reason, even though we were far from the laws of Jerusalem, where women in her condition were called before a council of wise men and elders, then cast out to fend for themselves. Women who committed adultery and conceived were forced to drink bitter water and dust from the Temple floor, which some believed made the children within them fall away. This was the *sotah* ceremony, where their innocence or guilt would be proven by God when they were forced to drink His name written upon a piece of parchment and dissolved in a cup of water. People whispered that evil repelled God's grace.

Should the wicked attempt to take His name into their bodies, they would fall to dust.

But perhaps on this mountain, with so much danger before us, there was little time to search out sin and little reason to do so. Did my neighbors not wonder what sins of their own had brought them to this place, why our people must suffer so, why God's ways were so mysterious, why He had forsaken us on this mountain?

The constant howling of the wind drove some people mad; many among us cursed the fortress and were brought lower than they'd ever imagined. There were women who wept during the windstorms until tears streaked their faces with lines of salt. Did they not ask why they had been forced so far from Jerusalem and everything they had known and loved? In their darkest hours, as they huddled with their children in the dwindling light, their shawls their only protection from the sandstorms, they clearly wondered what we were fighting for.

I never asked that question. I gazed out at the land beyond the serpent's path and thought of the many forms a beast could take. There were those who revealed themselves at noon, squarely setting their feet upon the earth, and those who sifted inside your dreams. There were those who came from Rome, the beasts I despised more than any others, their claws beginning to show as they crossed the Great Sea, for salt repels demons. When I thought of such wickedness, I could not sleep. To protect myself I chanted the incantation Shirah instructed me to recite when I tossed and turned at night. *I ban and make an oath against destroyers and demons and plagues and afflictions and terrors and nightmares.*

Still I lay awake, unable to close my eyes.

There were occasions when I spied my son-in-law climbing the path, set apart from the other warriors as they returned from missions meant to protect us or when they attempted to locate the provisions we needed from the world outside our walls. I did not wish to think about the mournful deeds they had committed, the blood that had been drawn, the lives taken.

The Man from the Valley who would not walk beside his brethren no longer had a resemblance to the scholar he'd once been. He was never without the ax for which he'd traded his most precious chalice, carrying the weapon so near his torso that it seemed a part of him, threaded to him with invisible red silk. His hair that had turned white overnight was so long that people said God was able to grab him away from danger. This was the reason he still lived, though he placed himself in peril time and time again. He was known to be furious in a skirmish, willing to forge into battle with little thought to his own life. I understood why he did this, for I knew what he was fighting for; in that he was no different than I. Anguish such as ours is fed on bones and blood. We had no more choice than the wind does as to where we must go and where we belonged. I was grateful for this quiet time on the mountain. Here, at last, my grandsons were safe, able to rest without danger while the doves at my bedside hushed them to sleep. As for me, sleep was a country I no longer visited, despite my incantation. When I did, I wished only for my waking life, the hours when I didn't see the nightmare images of all that had happened and all I had become.

THERE WERE MANY who were leaving cities and villages when we fled. They were mostly good people, but there were also those who veered to the left of the road, the side of the wicked. Before the Baker slid the last loaves in the oven on the huge wooden breadboard he always used, before I knew he wasn't coming back, before black feathers fell onto the road, it had already been written that we would meet those who were evil and that they would come upon us late in the day, when the sky flared blue and the air was scented with jasmine.

They came for the donkeys, which they spied from the cliff. They came for the cool water that glittered in their eyes. But they stayed when they saw Zara tending to the fire. They saw her brightness, so beautiful it appeared that morning was breaking before them, and their intent changed. They forgot the donkeys and the pool of water and the Tenth Legion, the Roman regiment they had deserted, fearing punishment from their superiors, the canes of the generals broken upon their backs in exchange for misdeeds and grudges.

They were already beyond the line that divides us from the creatures of darkness. They crossed the worn path left by the pack of hyenas who had been stalking us, crying in the night, trying to gain our favor with their sorrowful yelps, hoping for scraps before they came to devour us. Four Roman soldiers who had lived without water or food or hope ventured down the hillside, their chain-mail armor weighing upon their frames, men once but no more. It was easy for them to become beasts; one step and their humanity was an illusion. Beneath the armor there was only teeth and claws, hunger and thirst. It was the Sabbath, and Yoav was gone into the desert to pray, his prayer shawl thrown over his shoulders. The wind was rising, so he didn't hear any of what happened to us. He was committed to God and to the sound of his own voice. Ever since *Yom Kippur* he had been absent all day and into the evening, praying for our deliverance. When the first star appeared in the sky, we would light the Sabbath lamp with the last of our olive oil, and he would return to us. That was the sorrow of it. He saw the light but never expected the darkness.

I spied the soldiers as you might spy a demon, a shadow in the corner, melting across the ground. I didn't wait to think further. I sent the boys running. It was as though a key had unlocked the future and for one brief instant I saw through to the other side.

"Go quickly and don't venture forth," I told my grandsons. "Not until I come for you. Even if the night falls, even if the sun is eaten by the moon, no matter what you hear, even if someone calls you by name. Don't answer. Don't talk." I looked into their eyes as I instructed them. "Above all else: Stay hidden."

I sent them to the ledge behind the waterfall where they sometimes played. The children were small enough to slip inside a crevice that had been formed where the rocks met. The water was a curtain as it rushed past. I thought if anything went wrong the boys wouldn't be able to see through the water and God would protect them.

But water is clear, like an open window, and their eyes were open as well.

THE MEN fell upon Zara at the fire. I heard her voice the way you hear a bell, it rings and sounds above all other noises. I ran to her, and one of the intruders threw me to the side, for to him I was no more than a dried locust, good for nothing other than a raven's dinner. I could taste blood brimming in my mouth. I charged at them, screaming, but they were four, and brutally strong, and I was a woman and unused to fighting. While two of them held Zara, tearing at her garments, the other two made quick business of me. The world grew dark when they took a rock to my head. I could feel the heat of my own blood washing across my forehead. Everything was black as night inside of me. To my shame I didn't see what my grandsons saw, I only understood when I saw the broken shell Zara had become. But the boys observed it all: how the soldiers took turns with their mother, how she tried to fend them off, how when they were finished they tortured her with fire and with burning rocks and sharp sticks for no reason other than the sake of their own wickedness.

When I came out of the darkness and awoke again to this world, it was too late. The beasts were going through the meager possessions that were stored in our tent. I went to Zara even though

I knew that we had entered the realm of demons and that each demon who walks the earth has the strength of a thousand men and that I was only a woman, made old in these few hours, an ancient, worthless thing. I dragged myself through the sand.

One moment we had all the time in the world stretching out in front of us, and in the next instant my beloved daughter was dying in my arms. She was whispering for me to finish it and let her go to the World-to-Come. She pleaded with me as her blood washed over us, the blood I had labored to bring forth into this world. It was not enough for them to use her for their pleasure and then leave us be. It was not enough for them to take all that we owned—the donkeys, the water, the tent, the provisions—and abandon us to the hyenas who were already circling. They were the angels of destruction, I saw that clearly, though they appeared to be Roman soldiers. They had come to us from the dark side of the world, where no light can penetrate. Zara's skin was blackened where they had held burning sticks and rocks against her. They had put the rocks inside her just to hear her scream. I snatched those rocks away, but it did no good. She was already speaking to those in the World-to-Come, already broken. Now I saw that she had been split in two with an ax, and all that was contained inside her body had spilled into the earth.

In that moment, as I crouched beside her, I turned into something that was not a woman.

The beasts had tossed their weapons and armor and brass helmets onto the ground. I took up a knife they'd cast aside, slick with blood. I did as Zara asked, though it was a crime against God and against our laws. I whispered in her ear that she would be free now and that she should close her eyes. Then I did what no mother should ever have to do. I took the knife and cut her throat. I did it the way a sacrifice is made, for even a beast of burden is sent from life in this way, with compassion, in a single swift slash, completed without pain. As I did so, I leaned over and placed my mouth on my daughter's bruised lips. Her last breath entered me, and I held her spirit inside me as I had before she was born.

The evil ones took what they wanted. They laughed when they saw me lying beside Zara. When I went after them, roaring, wielding the knife, one of the soldiers grabbed it from me and held it to my throat. I was grateful when he did so. This was what I wanted. I asked him to kill me. "Go ahead," I said. "My death will be your gift to me."

If he couldn't completely understand my language, he most surely knew the meaning of the words. I could no longer endure the agonies of this earth we walked upon. But the one who was their leader told his cohort to wait. The soldiers were hungry from their wickedness. Like animals, they wanted more. They commanded me to cook for them over the fire where they had killed my daughter. The smoke carried the scent of the perfume she wore, a mixture of cinnamon and ginger oil, a cloud of fragrance arising from the ashes.

An idea began to form inside me.

"Will you deny us?" the leader said. He had a smile on his treacherous face, as though asking a favor from a neighbor. "Surely you can cook."

I was no longer a woman, but I was still a baker's wife. I thought of what my husband had said to me in my dream. At last I understand his meaning. I told the beasts I could do more than simply cook a meal. I could bake bread, enough for them to carry into the desert to make certain their hunger would be satisfied for many days to come. I would feed them in the way they deserved to be fed.

"You had better not be lying," the one who wanted to kill me remarked.

I took out the griddle and my husband's wooden spoons. I tied his white apron around my waist.

"What do I look like?" I said to them. "This is my life's calling."

I must have looked like a beaten-down old woman, but one who knew the mysteries of bread, for they urged me to continue with their meal. They dozed in the sun. The scorched scent of death didn't bother them, as it never bothered the hyenas, who stalked their prey from the hills, or the jackals, who lived in ruins, feeding off the bones of the slain. While the beasts were subdued, their drowsy eyes closed, I baked beetles into the loaves and filled them with curses. I found the coriander dashed onto the ground as they had pawed through our belongings and took some for seasoning so they would not suspect that what they ate was anything more than bread. At last I spied the vial of the ingredient the angel in my kitchen had bid me to take. Not a grain had spilled. I mixed it with the water and the last of the flour, added a portion of yeast from the cool earthenware jar, then set the mixture under a swath of fabric to help the dough rise in the dark.

Before the loaves were ready, the beasts awoke. They had more damage to do in the world. They were running from service to their Emperor, anxious to flee, but I was slow, tending to my portion of vengeance and despair.

"We can't wait," they told me. "Hurry," they shouted.

I had no choice but to cook the bread directly over the fire before it was finished rising. I expected it to be thick and flat, like crackers, the way griddle bread is, or be dusted black, as ash bread becomes, but it rose into perfect loaves. I knew then that the angel that had been beside me in my kitchen was beside me still, helping to form the dough.

The dark pulse of grief was in my throat. I was thankful I wasn't asked to speak, only to serve. I could hear the ravens above us. I thought of the feathers on the road and of the many signs the angel had given me and how I had failed to pay attention. That would never happen again. I cut the loaves with the bloody knife, burning my fingers as I then tore the bread into pieces, and I served it to the beasts who looked like men. They were wearing the insignia of the legion, though they were traitors to their own kind, and were therefore still decorated with the sign of the wild boar. I thought how fitting that pigs should eat this bread. I smiled as though I were a woman who hadn't witnessed all I had seen on this day, a mother whose daughter's body hadn't been kicked into a ravine where the jasmine grew.

I was the other thing now, the thing I'd become.

They wolfed down what I had baked, eating more bread than any men I'd seen before. Their violence and the days of stalking others had caused them great hunger. I served them again and again, as if they were my masters. In their eyes I appeared to be a woman and their servant, nothing more. Then, stomachs full, they went to fill their flasks as well as two large barrels from the pool so that they might take enough water for their journey. They stood so near the waterfall I grew dizzy, fearing they might spy my hidden grandsons and murder them for sport should the children dare to call out. I did not know that the angel had permitted me one last favor. He had taken the boys' voices so they couldn't give themselves away. When they opened their mouths to scream and sob, not a sound came out.

By then the beasts were crouched by the pool, their faces in the water like dogs, suddenly possessed by an unquenchable thirst. I breathed in my grim success, knowing this was a sign that the poison had claimed them. They could not stop their desire for water even though they clutched at their bellies, which were overly full, nearly ready to burst. I watched cold-eyed as they drank themselves to death. That was what happened to the rats in my husband's bakery. We often found them drowned in a bucket after they took the bait, dying from the terrible thirst the hemlock brought on.

One of the men came to me on all fours, begging for mercy. He choked out that he had a wife and children waiting for him. He claimed to be a good man in the life he'd led before, but his words, like all things in the desert, were carried away by the rising wind. In truth, I was someone who no longer listened to such entreaties. I had no pity inside me, only my daughter's last breath.

BY THE TIME night fell and my son-in-law returned from his prayers, I had slain all four beasts, slitting their throats for good measure, not out of mercy but to make certain I had accomplished the deed. I had washed my daughter's body with clean water and wound her in the white linen shawl she had worn at her wedding. She'd brought the shawl with her on our journey, the single treasure she'd taken from home, whereas I had reached for poison. The choice you make about such matters reveals who you are deep inside. She was a good wife, while I was a creature who would do anything to protect what was mine. I gathered stones to place over her body so the jackals would not come for what was left of her. If the stones were heavy, I failed to notice. They were red and chalky and stained my hands. Perhaps that is how I became marked for the rest of my life and why, if anyone looked too closely, my hands would doubtless give my true nature away.

I must have appeared to be a demon myself. As soon as my son-in-law saw me, he sank to his knees. When he took in all that had come to pass in his absence, he beat on the earth; he wept and cursed and tore at his cloak. I wondered if he would run into the desert like a madman, forsaking us. This could not happen, even if he wished for a crude release from his agony. I refused to allow my daughter's death to be the death of her children. I needed my son-in-law to help us get away. I took hold of his prayer shawl, though I should not have touched even the hem. This time I was the one to tell him what to do. I said to be quick about it, for time had shifted to become sand beneath our feet. I knew we must leave this place before anyone searched for the beasts at the pool.

While Yoav packed all that we had left onto the donkeys, I went to the waterfall, for that was where my treasure was stored. The boys stared at me with their dark, gleaming eyes, but they would not come out. I clapped my hands and called to them, but there was no response.

The sound of the falling water was deafening. I crept behind the waterfall, my feet slipping on the cool, wet stones. I was too large to fit into the crevice where they huddled against the damp rocks silvered with mica. They were only six and eight years old, and yet they had seen what no grown man on earth should see. I held out my hand and begged them to come to me. I told them that I carried their mother's spirit inside me, and that we would take her with us wherever we went. We had to make haste. Their mother would want us to do so. After a while the boys grasped for me and followed me out from behind the water. They did not speak a word as we left that terrible place, or later when we made a hurried camp under the stars far from that waterfall. They have not spoken since.

WE HAD ENTERED the territory of silence, slipping inside of it the way shadows fold across the earth with the lengthening day. The wind was the only thing we heard unless we met travelers on the road who told stories of Herod's palace and of the men from Jerusalem who followed the way of the curved knife, Zealots who now ruled the king's fortress. Yoav listened to these stories of rebels, absorbed, his grave profile turned away from us. We made circles in the wilderness to keep our distance from the Roman garrison. With no destination, and no knowledge of the wilderness, we stumbled upon the road to the Salt Sea. As we journeyed, my son-in-law changed before my eyes. The world began to slip away from him, and it seemed that he already walked beside the angel

Gabriel. That which we saw to be the earth below our feet, he saw as fire. At night he went off into the thornbushes, and I could hear him sobbing and my heart broke in two alongside his. But in daylight he was hardened, his eyes narrowed, his skin burned by the sun. He consumed only green herbs, and if none were to be had, he ate nothing at all. When we came to a nomads' settlement, he traded the silver chalice he used for the wine blessing.

The old man in the settlement of goat-hair tents and unclothed children could not believe the good fortune of his trade. He was only too ready to give up his ax in return for pure silver. It was a heavy weapon, made for a woodsman rather than a warrior, much stronger than the one that had split my dear Zara in two. As we went on, I could hear Yoav practicing with it in the early-morning hours, when the sky was still black, turning to the ax as he had once turned to his prayers and his scrolls. He slept beside it, as he had once slept beside his wife.

My premonition that Yoav would run into the wilderness and forsake us in his grief had been correct, only not in the manner I had envisioned. He was with us, yet he had been summoned to another place entirely, the kingdom of vengeance. This was when his hair turned white overnight and grew long and tangled. His body became lean and strong. We heard little from him, except when he practiced the art of destruction, throwing his ax with such force that he grunted and groaned, like a man in his death throes. His own children, those sweet silent boys, shied from him. I realized that he looked like the madmen we sometimes spied in the desert, warriors, hermits, prophets, priests; men who saw only their own path and no one else's.

MY FIRST SIGHT of the fortress took my breath away. A mirage emerged from the stone, a miracle appearing beneath the midday sun. We paused in the valley, spellbound. It was the season of the winds, the time when the *Ruach Kadim,* the hot and furious wind that arose from Edom, brought us clouds of dust. My grandsons were wrapped in capes, staying close to each other for comfort. Perhaps they spoke to each other through their dreams, for they seemed to communicate and could clearly understand each other without the use of language. They refused to be separated and slept beneath the same blanket, just as they ate from the one plate and drank from a single cup. I thought the sheer cliffs leading to Masada would frighten them and they would hesitate. I expected that their father would have to tie ropes around their waists to help them navigate the cliffs, but the younger one, Levi, was the first to start up the spiraling snake path, scrambling like a goat, and Noah applauded his brother's sure-footed bravery and was quick to follow.

I then had the vision that the boys would never have a father again, and that this perilous climb would be the last time we would be with the Yoav we had known before this other man, the one who would not be separated from his ax, took his place completely. The sun struck against the earth as it had when the beasts in the oasis had fallen upon us, emboldened, without mercy. My grandsons were climbing up, the clouds of dust rising behind them, carried by the wind in little whirls that disappeared before our eyes. I placed my hand on my son-in-law's arm before he began his ascent. Yoav turned to me, but his eyes were hooded. He was like the hawk, seeing only what he must to survive. All he wanted was revenge, but I gave him more. I told him I had bent to take Zara's last breath. *Neshamah,* our word for soul, means breath, and so she was with us still.

A sob escaped from my son-in-law when he heard this. He shook his head and turned from me. "I can never hear her name again," he insisted. "Don't speak it in my presence."

I had come to realize the depth of his love for her. Everything else about him had changed, but in this he was constant. He was the only one who could understand what it meant to lose Zara. Because of our mourning, we were bound together despite the silence and the wind and the man he had become. I signaled for him to lean down, and he did so. I then did the second most terrible thing a mother could do, in some ways worse than burying her beneath the stones. I breathed my daughter's last breath into his mouth. I gave her to him so that her spirit would belong to him and he could carry her with him, so that he could still be a man with a soul, even though he had lost everything else.

MY ONLY CONCERN was for my grandchildren. They were my world, my present and my future. I vowed to pay attention to our daily life, nothing more. Once we came to this fortress, we moved into our small chamber, built in to the king's wall, a mere curtain dividing our residence from that of another family. At night we could hear our neighbors, the children laughing, the parents arguing or making love. In our room, there was only silence. That was the way our life was now. We no longer needed language; there weren't words for what we had witnessed. The boys watched me with their dark, night-flecked eyes. I insisted we were safe and made every attempt to show them this was so. I put a thread across the threshold so no one could pass without my knowledge. I slept with a knife beneath my pallet. I turned each day into a ritual of sameness hoping the children would be comforted by the small tasks and duties of everyday life. In their presence I was calm and patient, the practical grandmother they could depend upon at all times and in all things, but my smile went slack whenever I was alone. Each morning I went to the dovecotes. Each evening I returned to cook dinner. But each night I wept.

*

MONTHS PASSED this way. We became accustomed to the dry air of the mountain and the scent of salt carried from the sea below. We began to know other people in the settlement, all of whom had come to this fortress when there was nowhere else for them in Zion. We were all in God's hands, and in that way we were brothers and sisters, no matter where we had come from. There were warriors and assassins, rebels who had committed crimes and those who insisted crimes were committed upon them. There were learned men and tanners, potters and goatherds, simple men and those who could read Aramaic and Hebrew, as well as Latin and Greek. There were those who had been cast out of Jerusalem and those who'd run from the burning of Jericho, as well as refugees from small villages like my own.

Many of the women wanted to befriend me and asked me to join in the group that met at the looms in the evenings to discuss the day's events. They meant well, but I kept my distance. I could not tolerate their chirping good humor any more than I could abide their faith. Though I pretended otherwise, the past had not melted away. It was all I had, and I clung to it and savored it, for my daughter was in that land of grief. My sorrow filled me, leaving little room for anything else. I was squinting out at the world from behind the barricade I'd placed between myself and all others just as surely as there was a curtain draping down to separate our chamber from our neighbors' home. I understood that fate could not be eluded forever; it came on leathery wings, swooping through the darkness like the bats in the orchards.

We heard rumors of Roman scouts who had set up a camp not far from our fortress. Our warriors went to confront them, but there were too many of the enemy, and in the end our men had to slink away and wait for the Romans to break camp. Our enemies left little behind but the bones of pigs and piles of their own waste. But they also had left behind a tower of rocks. Those rocks were terrifying, for they marked the place as one to which they intended to return.

Still I was determined that, for the sake of my grandsons, our lives should continue without event for as long as possible. I was resolved that we should keep to ourselves. No friends, no enemies, only the three of us. I did my best to prevent any disruptions. Then one night there was a knock at our door. I felt a lump in my throat. I had known all along that at any moment the world might barge in upon us. No door could prevent every intrusion. No barrier was strong enough to keep out the movement of time. The chaff beaten from the wheat rises into the air and is carried by the wind to another place, whether to a green field or a stretch of barren land was dependent on God's will.

I prayed for the rapping to stop, but there it was again. My grandsons were stirring. Their hearing was so attuned they had heard the knocking the moment it fell upon the door. I held a finger to my lips as I went forward.

I feared what was to come and stood there shivering, like a tame bird who shies from the opened door of the cage. I wanted our small, quiet existence to remain constant, for every day to shine as a mirror image of the one before. I reached for my knife. Our chamber had once been used as a storehouse. Mice often came here, searching for grain. Now they scurried off, dodging my footsteps as I ventured to see who might visit at such a late hour. I peered through a hole between the stones.

Yael was there in the dark. No soldiers, no beasts, just a woman with long red hair. She had a basket of belongings with her, so little she might have owned nothing.

I considered sending her away, that was my inclination, but I could see she was desperate. I relented and let her come in. She sat on the pallet where I slept. I didn't ask what was wrong; I didn't have to. Her face was ashen, except for a dark blue ribbon of a bruise on her cheek where someone had recently struck her. I had compassion for the silence she carried and found myself drawn to her, as the doves were.

She was uncomplaining, only murmuring that she was sorry to disturb me. She and her father had argued. I'd seen him in the plaza, and he seemed a cold and selfish man, one who thought himself superior to those around him. I'd seen such men look down upon my husband because he was a baker, the same ones who thought Yoav was too good to live under our roof. I set a place for Yael to sleep, gathering a blanket I had woven and died hyssop blue in memory of my daughter, who had loved the color of that flower. Yael had come here in search of shelter though I had been cold to her, remote since the day she arrived in the dovecote. She was my daughter's age. She was alive when Zara was not, and I had held that against her, pecking at her, resentful. I winced to think of what I'd done. Still, she had seen something in me that had brought her here. She knew that I understood the language of silence. I would no more ask Yael to surrender her past than I would offer to tell her what I myself had done.

IN THE MORNING, we walked to the dovecotes together as though our days had always begun this way. The bruise on her face where her father had lashed out had already begun to fade under the balm I used to treat it, a poultice made of honey and figs. We did not discuss her father's cruelty, or the fact that the child within her would soon arrive, a reality she could not hide despite the shawls she wore to cover herself. Instead we spoke of the heat and of the failure of the almond crop. The pink blossoms had burned this season in the last days of *Tammuz*, as if someone had set them on fire, singeing the edges of the petals with a powdery, black film. Much of the fruit of the trees had never formed, puckering instead into ruined bunches that exploded into ash when plucked. There was gloom everywhere, and worry. The initial mantle of freedom we'd experienced on arriving at the fortress diminished as crops began to fail. We were so isolated from the rest of mankind I could not help but think of the angels, how removed they were from us; so far away that, even when they attempted to catch us as we faltered, they were too distant to truly understand our sorrow.

"I always dreaded *Av,*" Yael said of the month we were about to enter. "But not this year."

She sounded fierce, ready to fight the blaze of the season. *Av* was the month when her child would enter the world. I'd assumed she would be weakened now that she'd been cast out of her father's house, but that was not the case. Her strength seemed renewed. She stared down those who gazed at her with curiosity, exactly as I'd done when people whispered about my grandsons' inability to speak. In that we were alike, branded by what we had done but prideful when it came to our children, even when God had deserted us.

Usually I was the first to arrive to care for the doves, but on this day we had tarried while I introduced Yael to my grandchildren. Shirah and her daughters were already at work; they stared when we entered together, as puzzled by our new alliance as they were by the mark on Yael's face. I had done nothing but complain about Yael since her arrival, true enough. But a woman can change her mind.

"I needed help with my grandsons," I said, indicating that our being together was a simple matter, despite the bruise which clearly signified more had transpired. "I'm too old to play games."

That was that, no need for further explanation. A good thing, since none would be forthcoming. Women were hurt every day and kept the cause to themselves. Yael threw me a grateful look and quickly set to work. I took note of the slave's expression when he spied the injury upon her face. Had he owned his freedom, I imagined he might have been seized with the need to go in search of whoever had harmed her. I signaled for him to pay attention to his duties. He did so, but all the rest of the day he was attentive to Yael's every move. It was odd to see him behaving as though his loyalty tied him to a woman who carried another man's child.

"Leave her be," I told him when no one would overhear. He couldn't seem to take his eyes off her. "She has troubles enough, she doesn't need yours."

"What makes you think I have troubles?" he asked in the hesitant way he spoke our language.

I paused and took him in as he worked with the rake he had invented to gather dung, a warrior the doves no longer feared. I had thought of him as an oddity because of his fair coloring and his great height, which forced him to crouch down in the dovecote. Now I saw that he was indeed handsome, broad-shouldered, with appealing features and huge, rough hands that were surprisingly tender when he cared for the doves.

"You're not a man?" I said, implying that every man in this world had troubles of his own.

"I was," he said. "Once."

I wasn't so old that I didn't understand his meaning. Despite the bonds of slavery, he would become so again.

EACH DAY we could hear our warriors preparing for raids. Our storerooms were low on supplies, our stomachs empty. Summer was always a time when our lives were lean, but this year was worse than others. At the evening meal I ate half of what was on my plate—a few chickpeas, some pressed dates—to ensure that the boys and Yael could have more. We had each been given one of the *ostraca*, a bit of stone with our name or initial carved upon it, and that mark would grant us only so much food and water and firewood each week. It was a troubling time for everyone. The heat of the summer was fully upon us, the billowing air so dry that we wore scarves over our mouths to cool our breath. The water in the cisterns had already reached a low mark, and we were just entering the month of fire.

Yael and I did not speak of our arrangement, but she continued to stay in our small chamber. My grandsons were shy with her at first, but one day she called them to her. Although the boys were hesitant, they gathered near when Yael pointed out a scorpion in a shadowy corner. When she was a little girl, she told them, she would watch such creatures in the hall where she slept but was always careful not to touch them. She warned Levi and Noah, they, too, must never disturb a scorpion, staying a respectful distance away, appreciating not only the deadly sting of such a creature but its cunning silence.

My dark-eyed grandsons watched, mesmerized, visibly delighted as Yael caught the fearsome intruder in a jar. She nimbly pinched him up between her fingers. I wondered what else she had done that had called for such bravery, or if, like mine, her courage sprang from sorrow. The less you had to lose, the easier it was to pick up the knife, the sword, the scorpion. When she carried the deadly creature out to the terraced gardens nearby, the boys followed at her heels, thrilled by her daring. Seeing them so lighthearted and filled with interest made my throat tighten, and I felt I might lose my voice as well. Marked by grins and deep concentration, the boys appeared no different than any other children; no one would have taken them for two boys who had lost the power of speech in the web of a demon. They were fascinated, crouching on their knees in a patch of Syrian radishes to watch openmouthed as Yael allowed the scorpion to go free in a shady nook among a cluster of onions.

"The world is many things to many creatures," she told the children as we all surveyed the walled garden, what was surely a forest for a small creature that had been torn from its home. The scorpion had scuttled out of sight. "We are considered giants by some and ants to be stepped upon by others."

PEOPLE were whispering about Yael, wondering who the father of her child might be and speculating about the night the assassin Bar Elhanan had cast out his own daughter. My grandsons, however, had already grown to adore her. Although I kept my distance, I became accustomed to her as well. If people spoke poorly of her in my presence, I glared at them, and that was the end of it. Though I preferred to keep to myself, there was a way in which I was comforted to have Yael in my home, to hear her breathe easily in her sleep, as my own daughter might have done had she still been with us.

Admittedly, I was grateful for help with the household chores. Even in her state, so big with the child that was to come, Yael was far from lazy. She cooked our meals, crouching over the fire pit to fry our food on a grill which fitted over the ring of stones. She went to the storehouses to collect our daily allotment of beans and grains, and made certain there was firewood, all to repay me for taking her in. But the stories she told were the only repayment we needed. The boys' eyes brightened when they listened to her at bedtime, mesmerized. In all of the scorpion's exploits, silence was an asset and a gift, not a flaw but a virtue. The scorpion could do what others could not: he could see in the dark, hear a fly buzzing on the far side of the mountain, sense danger while the rest of the world slept.

"Did your mother tell you these stories?" I asked one evening when Yael and I went to the plaza. We had taken to working at the looms on a regular basis. We kept ourselves removed from the other women, but it was a pleasure to weave and our garments were tattered; we had need of shawls and cloaks. When we busied ourselves in this manner, it was possible to forget the dust that rose in clouds all around us and to distance ourselves from our hunger. If we had nothing else, then at least we had the sheep's wool and the work of spinning and weaving.

"I had no mother." Yael kept her eyes downcast.

We reached the looms, where we settled, bringing forth our lengths of carded, dyed wool. Yael was working on a pattern everyone praised. Even those gossips who whispered about her were impressed. There were intricate threads of color forming a line of continuous blocks of multihued squares. I noticed it was the same pattern as the cloth the slave wore.

"Every human has a mother," I insisted as we worked.

"Are you sure I'm human?" Yael said, her chin tilted, teasing me.

I had never seen a woman with hair so red, or one with so little fear that she was willing to grasp a scorpion between her fingers. Others might whisper she was possessed by a demon and swear she was unlike other daughters and wives. But I had seen her on the night when her father cast her out, when she huddled in a corner like any other beaten woman. And I had taken note of the expression on her face when she stood beside the Man from the North.

She was human.

WHEN THEY thought they were alone, I heard what I should not have pass between them. Yael was fortunate that I was accustomed to silence, and therefore held my tongue. A gossip would have been unforgiving, making quick use of the intimate encounter I'd stumbled upon. A hawk had been circling the largest dovecote for several days, intent on taking our doves for his dinner. We set out sticks tied together with rope that looked like a child's toy; when the breeze stirred, the sticks whirled and frightened the hawks away. But one hawk was fearless; he wouldn't be chased off. He looked underfed and seemed intent on having his supper. Hunger struck everyone in the desert at the same time.

When the hawk lit on the window ledge, Yael found some grain and reached out to him. I was stunned to see the creature eat from her hand, as if he were a dove himself. I was not the only one to take notice. The Man from the North had come up beside her. I overheard him say that in his country hunters trained hawks to strike down prey and bring back partridges and doves. Their sharp yellow beaks were wound with strands of leather, clamped halfway closed so they couldn't devour their kills; they had to learn to wait patiently when they brought back their prey, hungering until the hunter tossed them a bit of meat.

It usually took months to gain a hawk's trust. The slave was astounded by how easily Yael had called this one to her. He said she must possess magic. He sank to his knees and bowed his head, only half in jest, declaring she had bewitched him as well. Yael laughed at his remarks—I remembered because I had not heard her do so before. It was a lovely, surprising sound. She said that women with red hair had the ability to tame wild creatures. Since the slave had come from a country where many of the women looked so, he should have known this to be true. He got to his feet, though he had to shift his tall body just to be near her.

It was then I overheard him say, "You're not like them, Yael. You're not like anyone."

I wasn't certain if he meant his words to be a compliment or an insult, but then he took her hand and kissed it, at her wrist, the place where what someone needs and what she desires cross each other to become one.

YAEL WAS NOT my daughter, but she lived in my home, and that prompted me to be concerned. I knew that a woman at the end of her term might look for solace in curious places. Being with child could cause confusion, and kindness in a cruel world might coax Yael into forgetting that the Man from the North was not one of us. On the blanket where she lay at night, she tossed and turned, uncomfortable in the heat. In the mornings she brooded, her eyes filled with sleep. I wondered if she dreamed of her baby to come, as I had long ago, if she had already seen her child's face and had perhaps chosen a name, though it was best not to do so. Naming the unborn alerted demons a child was about to come into the world. Hand over a child's name and that newborn might be more easily called into the darkness. I had done so, tempting fate. Perhaps the night demons had followed my daughter ever since I called her Morning.

WE DIDN'T complain about our work at this brutal time of the year, for the dovecote was cool, its plaster walls giving some relief. We were sheltered from the season's unforgiving fever. Below us the valley sizzled in a pink haze. The world beyond our gates glared with light, and we wore our head scarves pulled down to shade our eyes. There was not a single green shoot to be seen; even the fierce leaves of the thornbushes had shriveled as if made of parchment. We could hear the jackals crying at night, and we shivered at the sound. Huge flocks of birds flew above us, abandoning our barren land, searching for water and sustenance in far-off places, flying to the mountains in the north or east to Moab where the fields were said always to be green.

Each day the Man from the North set out a line of grain on the window ledge for the hawk. When he spoke in his language of unearthly grunts, the creature seemed to understand, a glint in his yellow eyes. The bird had a red head, and because of this the slave called him Odeum, ruby, which was also his name for Yael. Yael grinned when he did so, knowing he was provoking her. She teased right back and said only a fool would keep a hawk so near to a dovecote. Eventually we would arrive to find that the hawk had slaughtered all of our charges. She had fed the bird of prey a few grains out of pity, but the slave had gone much too far, making a pet of a wild thing. Could he not understand his mistake? Here was a creature no one could ever trust.

"You're wrong about him," I heard the Man from the North say. "He's at your beck and call."

"A hawk is always a hawk," I informed them both, unable to hold my tongue any longer.

After I made my remark they were quick to fall silent and return to the tasks at hand. How could they argue with me? They knew my statement to be true. You cannot change a hawk's nature any more than you can teach a dove to kill. And yet later in the day, when I saw the slave and Yael bringing baskets of dung into the fields to feed the ravished, heat-struck earth, the hawk glided above them as though he were a dog, tame and subservient. I thought perhaps I had been wrong, too quick to judge the essence of a being by its appearance, still not fully understanding that, in the world God has given us, all things must change.

FOR NOW the one constant was that the days fell heavily, all with the same hypnotic, unrelenting heat. Heat waves rose up in shimmering curtains of light. There were lines of exhausted, baffled women at the storehouses, each waiting for her family's share of water and food. I felt immobilized inside the month of *Av* the way I had once lingered inside my dreams as I slowly awoke to the yeasty odor of baking in my old life, on those precious mornings when the countryside was green and the scent of the cypress drifted in the air. I had been caught up in time then, as I was once again, but one tableau was a treasure chest, the other a cage.

We had so little here on the mountain, but at least we were safe. In the world outside ours, the violence against our people had only grown worse. There were rumors that the dead were heaped upon the main roads throughout Judea, that the Jordan River was so rife with bodies you could walk across on dead men's backs as if they were stepping-stones. News came to us that another Essene settlement had been decimated. I'd heard of their people, those who called themselves the Children of Light and who had occupied the settlement known as Sechacha. One day a small, impoverished troupe appeared in our valley. We saw dust rising as they approached. Their white linen garments glinted brightly as they crossed over the rocks. Our warriors went down the serpent's path to meet these visitors and bring them to us. It was well known that the Essenes abhorred warfare, and we were a fortress. Still, like the rest of us, when they had no options and no place else to go, they came to this mountain.

There were seven men and three women, along with four children. The men carried their belongings in packs tied onto their backs with thick ropes of woven flax. The women followed behind, simply dressed, barefoot, unadorned. It was the women who toted the goatskin containers of water and cheese and led a flock of scrawny goats tied together with leather strands forming a *ribqâh*, so that from a distance the animals appeared to be one creature with five heads. There were also two black donkeys laden with tall ceramic vases; inside were the rolled parchment scrolls of the Essenes' teachings. The men were learned, holy in their aspect, especially one elderly man, who was perhaps the most ancient I had ever seen. They had been traveling ever since the Romans destroyed their settlement, living in caves, leaving behind their writings whenever possible to ensure their beliefs would not be lost should they be the next to be slaughtered.

When the visitors entered through the Snake Gate, a crowd had already gathered. The survivors appeared dazed, alarmed by the fortified conditions of Masada. They gazed with grim faces at the parapets our warriors had readied, the piles of armor, the spears with sharpened bronze tips kept beside the synagogue so that wise men could bless them. The Essenes had stumbled into a province made for war and war alone, where weapons were stocked in the manner that other villages might store oil and wine, where every stone had been rounded with a chisel, ready to be used as a weapon should the battle come to us.

We gazed at each other in the presence of these gentle people, made aware that blood and vengeance coursed through us as if we were barbarians. It was war that roused us from our dreams in the morning and sang us to an unquiet sleep at night. Some among us cast our eyes downward, stunned by what we'd become. Others glared at a group they considered fools, unwilling to fight for Zion.

The oldest of the Essene men, whose people called him Abba as a term of respect, was carried by his followers. He was weak in his body but strong in spirit. His people lifted him high upon their shoulders so he could call out to us.

"We all belong to our Lord. All that is now and ever shall be originates with God. Before things come to be, He has ordered their design. His glorious plan fulfills our destiny, a destiny it is impossible to change. We have come because we were meant to be here though we are as different from you as night from day."

I didn't know if our people would accept Abba's proclamation, or if shame and fury would make that impossible. There was a tension, shown in a great and echoing silence; then Yael ran up to one of the women in the group and embraced her. Their joy at seeing each other broke through the silence. We learned this was her friend Tamar, who had once had four sons and now had only one—the others, along with her husband, had been slain in the raid upon her settlement by the legion. Now all this Essene woman had left was a boy of ten, one named Yehuda, whom she clung to as if he alone held her to this earth she walked upon.

Ben Ya'ir himself allowed the Essenes to stay. He came to speak with their leader, this learned man who was both father and priest, who wore pure white linen and was barefoot, whose face was unlined even though he was so very old. They sat together beneath an olive tree, speaking for hours. They then sat with Menachem ben Arrat, our great priest. At the end of that time the word went out—no one was to trouble the group of outsiders, no matter how different they might appear. Their customs were their own, allowed within our walls while they stayed among us.

All fourteen of the Essenes wished to live together in one abode, as was their practice, for what belonged to one belonged to all. They were granted a small stone barn on the far side of the orchard that had in the past been used to shelter goats ready to bring forth new kids. They would eat their meals together, sharing what little they had beneath the same tree where their leader and ours had spoken and come to terms. They bathed with cold water before each meal and offered their prayers fervently before any food passed their lips. Three times a day—at dawn, and noon, and again after the first three stars appeared—we could see the men at their prayers, facing toward Jerusalem. The six men who were faithful students of Abba set up long tables fashioned from planks of hardwood in order to roll out their scrolls, the documents stored in the ceramic vases that had been carried through the wilderness on the backs of their lumbering donkeys. They made their marks with an ink drawn from walnut oil and the gum of the turpentine tree.

Yael and I brought them olives and cheese and an allotment of wheat. Nahara came with us, bringing flasks of water and oil that her mother sent. A young Essene man, often at Abba's side and clearly his favorite, came to help Nahara carry the water. In order for him to do so, Nahara needed to place the flasks upon the ground, for the young man could not risk taking them from her hand; all she had touched might be considered *tamé*.

He murmured a prayer as he carried away the flasks, for among his people he had the power of blessing even though he was no more than seventeen.

The Essene women were grateful when presented with our gifts, yet the reflection of the slain shone in their eyes. Nahara stood aside with the young Essene man; she was too young and pure to hear of brutalities served upon the Essenes. But Yael and I sat with the women as they told us in matter-of-fact voices how their children had been murdered. They didn't cry out or swoon with grief, for they believed their children would rise again at the End of Days. At that time mothers would once again embrace their sons and daughters, and husbands and wives would again be one.

Tamar was quieter than the other women, her face pinched with sorrow, achingly pallid. When we went to leave, she placed a hand on Yael's arm, drawing her near. "I won't lose this one," I heard her say. Her boy, Yehuda, was sprawled in the grass, looking upward as the first stars began to appear in the darkening sky. The Essene men had gathered in the field, and we could hear them chanting in deep, luminous tones. It was so hot that every movement of the air was like a plume of flame, every star a lantern in the night. "Promise you'll help me, as I once helped you," Tamar whispered. Everything about the Essene woman seemed bruised; even her tone was an incantation which sprang from her affliction. She nodded at Yael's swollen middle. The baby would come any day now. "I knew when you wanted a fever charm it was a man you wanted to save. I could see it written upon you."

Yael glanced at me. I quickly looked away so it wouldn't seem that I'd overheard their conversation. When I saw Yael embrace her friend, I knew her promise had been given. As we walked back I didn't ask why she would grant the fervent wish of this woman who belonged to a group so different from us, who clearly looked down on our ways. I didn't question which man's life she had tried to protect, or why she had been willing to cross the desert on his behalf no matter the sacrifice. I merely added these bits of information to my list, ready to offer them up should Yael and I ever disagree and I needed to prove that she was, indeed, human.

WHEN THE MONTH of *Av* was upon us in all its force, and the moon was as red as the sun, Abba sent the young Essene man to the dovecotes to work among us to thank us for the rations we brought to them. Because his people were so strict, and men were not allowed to touch women outside their own families, this young man, named Malachi ben Aaron, often worked in the small dovecote alone. Yet soon enough he was befriended by Nahara, and before long these two were engaged in long conversations. Malachi ben Aaron was only a few years older than Nahara herself. He was strongest among his kinsmen, and extremely well spoken. Because of this he was granted great respect, and he seemed to regard himself as a man of honor. We who worked beside Nahara still thought of her as a child; perhaps it was merely that we wished to see her as such. We were surprised to see that two who had so little in common often sat together on the wall during the noon break. Malachi spoke and Nahara listened, rapt, as if every tale he told was an illumination. Some of his words wafted toward us. He spoke of the End of Days and how his people were preparing, confessing their sins, following the path of light, offering their life on earth to *Adonai*. They would not fight the Romans because this world we walked through was not the end for them; they would arise after death and shine in God's favor.

Since my arrival at the mountain, I had known Nahara to be a serious girl, older than her years in ways of learning and responsibility. Her mother had taught her to read Aramaic and Hebrew. As he instructed her, Malachi was surely impressed with her—for good reason; not only was she bright but she was lovely and pure. Before long they both began arriving earlier at the small dovecote so their discussions could begin as soon as Malachi had finished his morning prayers. They whispered in the breaking light, and those whispers became a bridge between them.

Like others of his household, Malachi wore only white, his hair braided. He eschewed sandals and went barefoot in the dust, for his people believed they must walk into heaven barefoot and wait there in the mist for the world to be resurrected after the End of Days. Malachi was quiet, a hard worker, a scholar who was not afraid to get his hands dirty. He had been sent to the dovecote because Abba believed that hard work and praise to God went hand in hand. Though Malachi was young, he wrote upon the parchment scrolls with his elders, and it was said that his letters were so beautifully wrought that the angels came to observe them as they formed; he was so righteous, the walnut oil ink he used turned to blood and appeared red upon the page. It had already been decided that Malachi would take Abba's place when the time came, and the two often sat with their heads together, deep in conversation and prayer.

Despite Malachi's virtues, after only a short time Shirah began to seem displeased with our new helper. Though he was often sent to the far dovecote, where there was room only for one, Shirah had discovered that Nahara could be found working beside him in that small space. We could not help but wonder if their shoulders brushed or their hands touched. When he prayed at noontime, making a holy place beside the twisted olive tree, kissing the strands of his prayer shawl and then offering his kiss to God, did he pray to clear his head of earthly thoughts and desires? Shirah watched him closely, eyes narrowed, a dark cast over her face.

One noontime while Nahara went home to fetch our meal of lentils and olives, Shirah sent Malachi away. The rest of us stepped back to watch; in many ways these were Shirah's dovecotes; she had been here the longest, and we deferred to her in everything.

"You can leave right now," she told the Essene. "There's no reason for you to stay through this day."

Three perfect doves had been chosen to be brought to the synagogue for the priest's dinner, and I was plucking out their feathers. I bowed my head, but I listened to the conversation.

"Is my effort not good enough?" Malachi asked, bewildered. Among his people he was not challenged, and now a woman was dismissing him. He raised his eyes to hers, a flicker of mistrust in his stare.

"There's nothing wrong with your work," I heard Shirah respond. "You're just not needed here."

Shirah must have taken note of my expression, for I was confused as well. Malachi had lightened our workload, and I saw no need to have humiliated him by sending him away. The Essenes had sent us their best man, but not in Shirah's opinion. When we were alone, she confided, "If she was your daughter, you would do the same." She feared the attraction between the Essene and Nahara, and I understood why she would not want him for her daughter. Malachi was too pious to see anything but God and himself, that much was true; the woman he chose would not walk beside him but would follow behind, head bowed.

When Nahara returned with our meal, she was astonished to find Malachi gone, her face flushing as she gazed around for signs of him. She glared at her mother with bitterness, and I heard her say to Aziza, "She sent him away to spite me."

"I'm sure she has her reasons," Aziza responded, which was true enough.

"She's cruel," Nahara remarked, her voice sharp. "That's the reason. She is devoted to what she wants. You of all people should know that. You're wise to keep your secrets."

Aziza lowered her eyes. "She's our mother."

Nahara was grim. "One who doesn't care about our happiness, as you well know."

I thought Nahara was mistaken about her mother's intent. Malachi was not suitable for her; he was known to pray until the first brightening of the star-strewn night. Aziza seemed to agree.

"Look at the way they live," she told her sister when Nahara complained to her. It made sense that a mother would did not want the fate of an Essene woman for her child, one of service and poverty and sacrifice.

But although Malachi had been sent from the dovecote, his presence lingered. There were times when those around you can see your fate but you yourself are blind, stumbling toward a coil of mistakes. This was such a time for Shirah's young daughter. We could all see her future if she chose one path rather than another, but she could not see it herself. She sulked out, slipping past the heavy wooden door though her work was not completed. Shirah went after her, but it was too late. In an instant Nahara was nowhere to be seen. It was as though she'd been snatched from the earth and all that remained was her shadow. Perhaps she had already followed Malachi to the stone goat barn of the Essenes, removing her sandals to walk barefoot among the women. She had been an obedient girl, but now her duty seemed to lie beyond her mother's domain. I stood in the doorway beside Shirah. At this moment she hardly seemed a fierce practitioner of *keshaphim*, only a mother who could easily be broken by a child's heedless actions.

"She'll be back," I offered hopefully.

Shirah stared into the empty plaza. She shook her head. She'd seen love a thousand times before. She had fashioned charms to induce it and amulets to sever its ties; she had recited spells to bind lovers together and others to break them apart. She was sufficiently practiced in love's ways to recognize its web, even in the dim light of the dovecote.

"Unfortunately, you're wrong," she said to me, her soft voice breaking with regret. "She's already gone. And if he knew who she truly was he would never want her."

I could feel a sudden chill in the blistering air. I thought this was what we had wanted, for there had been daily gatherings so that we might all pray for rain. Now a light rain had begun, unexpected fortune at this arid time of year. But the rain was strange, falling in bleak bands of white from the slate-colored sky. I licked my lips and realized it was laden with salt. It was a rain from the Salt Sea, a strange occurrence that sometimes took place when the wind arose and carried a cloud of dust. The furious, hot blasts had also picked up water and salt, and dumped those elements upon us. It was a bad omen, for what appeared to be rain was only seawater. A salt rain could poison orchards and contaminate cisterns. Men with wounds would weep in pain tonight; women would be unable to light fires and cook their families' evening meals. The goatherds would find the fresh milk we called *halab* turned to salty curds in the milking pails.

It would have been better to have no rain at all than to have this.

Shirah had begun to recite a spell as we ducked back inside to elude the downpour. She stunned us all when she grabbed one of the doves. She took up the knife we used for our meals. As though possessed, she made a gash across the dove's throat, then turned the bird so that its blood dripped onto the stone floor. The murder of a dove was a crime punishable by law. Certainly none were to be taken for the darker uses of *keshaphim*.

Aziza turned away when she understood what her mother intended, to come between Nahara and the Essene she had chosen. The Man from the North averted his eyes as well, so that he would not witness a deed that seemed far too intimate for him to behold. As for Yael, she alone stood rapt, drawn to the feathers falling, the blood on the floor. I noticed she was quick to murmur the words of the chant along with Shirah, as though she hoped her voice might give strength to the spell.

As they chanted, the rain from the Salt Sea splashed over the doorway and washed away the blood. In time I came to believe this was what dissolved the spell, turning it worthless before it was begun. Aziza and the slave tried to quiet the doves, who were flapping toward the ceiling, frightened by the rain pelting like stones rattling above us, and even more disturbed by the sudden murder of one of their own kind. I spied Shirah's grave expression as she tried to sweep away the salt, to no avail. My heart went out to her. Even the witch people so feared, one who knew magic better than most learned men, could not stop a girl who was utterly determined to have her way.

I hurried home to see to my grandsons, stepping widely to avoid the shifting piles of salt that had gathered on the mountain from this wicked rain. Across the field, I spied Nahara walking with the Essene boy. Their women had presented her with one of their fine white shawls, now draped over her hair. Seeing her beside Malachi, sheltered by a length of the purest linen on earth, I knew before Nahara herself did.

She had become one of them.

AS THE RED MOON of *Av* pulsed, a new life ripened, pushing out the water inside Yael with the heat of his imminent arrival. She was kneeling at the fire where we cooked our meals when her skirts were suddenly drenched. I saw terror flare in her eyes. I hastily sent my grandchildren to Shirah, so she would know Yael's time had come. Her son, Adir, could watch over the younger boys while we gathered to welcome the newborn child.

Yael and I began to make our way to the storerooms, stopping when she needed to yield and draw a breath. Her father had not once called for her during the last days of her pregnancy, when she'd been confined to our chamber, too heavy and uncomfortable to move. But her brother had visited. He had murmured an apology for disturbing our household, then had gone to kneel beside Yael, still in his silver armor, so that he shimmered in the half-light. I had heard them speaking of Jerusalem, occasionally bursting into laughter as they remembered the house in which they'd grown up, the flame tree that had stood in the marketplace. He came frequently after that, growing comfortable in our household, allowing my grandsons to climb over him and play at being warriors. Yael often teased her brother about Aziza, calling him a lamb who followed blindly after his beloved.

"Does she feed you hay?" Yael asked, and laughed. "Does she lock you in a pen at night?"

"Are you trying to anger me, Yaya?" Amram said with a grin, using her childhood name.

Yael brought out a scrap of blue, the bit of scarf he had given her that still remained. She waved the token to remind him that she kept it for luck, tucked beneath her sleeping mat. I'd seen it there myself. She failed to mention, however, that the swatch of cloth from the slave's garment was hidden there as well.

During Amram's visits, they didn't discuss the baby to come, but the warrior once brought a rattle he had carved, with plum pits inside that clacked together when the toy was shaken. Yael was pleased, relieved that her brother had accepted her situation, whoever the father of her child might be.

"I blame myself," I overheard him say to Yael one day. I imagined then that the father had been a comrade to him. "Never give something precious into the hands of another."

"What I am about to bring into the world is precious," Yael assured him. "So if you are to blame, then you are the one to whom I offer my gratitude."

NOW THAT the time for the baby's arrival had come, we walked through the evening light to the abandoned storeroom where we would meet Shirah. My arms were looped around Yael for support, allowing her to lean against me when the pains burst upon her. We paused on the stairs, where she doubled over, gasping, astonished by the force of the child within her.

"This is what he'll do to you for the rest of his life, so be prepared," I warned.

Yael tried to smile, but her pangs were too strong to allow it. She began to ramble in a low voice about a lion she had lost in the desert, a man she had loved, the price she must pay for her sins. I did my best to hush her. Her face was flushed with discomfort and heat. "I gave him back," she murmured. "Isn't that enough?"

I had no idea if she was speaking about the man or the beast or the child who was about to come. She seemed in the grip of a delirium. I was relieved to see Shirah hurrying across the field. She had called for Nahara, who had agreed to accompany her despite their falling-out. Nahara was barefoot, the white shawl of gauzy linen draped over her head. Her hair was braided in a single plait, in the fashion of the Essenes. Nahara and Shirah did not speak as they walked side by side, their faces dark and serious, their differences obvious in the distance they kept between them. When they reached us on the steps, Shirah quickly felt Yael's middle. She nodded, satisfied, then urged us inside, where we could build a fire and boil a pail of water, making certain to drive out any demons who might have fallen into our cisterns.

Before she would agree to go any farther, Yael gestured to Shirah, her upturned face a tangle of emotion. I heard her whisper. "If there's a choice, make sure to take the child. Let me go."

"Yes, yes," Shirah agreed. She threw me a look to let me know this was the time to agree to anything. We helped Yael into the storerooms, then down a long hall, pausing when the pangs became overwhelming, continuing again each time they eased.

"This is where the demon rolled on the floor," Yael murmured warily.

"She was a housemaid, not a demon, and her child is large and healthy," Shirah said to assure her that all was well.

Soon enough the fire was lit and the water boiled, all done quickly and in silence. Nahara and Shirah worked together as if their intimacy had not been severed. I noticed that Nahara was praying while Yael began to labor and that she glanced, disapproving, at the figure of Ashtoreth that Shirah had placed on a stone shelf so there could be an offering made of the blood of childbirth.

The baby was nearly ready before we were; it seemed he couldn't wait to enter our world. Yael sobbed and asked us to make a single vow: we would make certain she would see his face. She spoke as though she were on her deathbed and would have only a single opportunity to witness the life she was about to bring forth. She continued to plead, insisting she would be willing to walk into the World-to-Come if she could but once see her child, unlike her own mother, who had given birth with closed, unseeing eyes.

"Nonsense. You'll see him every morning and night," Shirah promised, advising the mother-to-be to attend to the task at hand.

"I want to know the color of his hair, and if his eyes are dark or light," Yael went on.

"Yes, yes," we all were quick to agree, for the air had shifted; it was dense and thick. The time had come. Blood brimmed where Yael had bitten down on her lips, and her face was ashen.

There was a birthing stool to crouch upon, but Yael could not focus on it, nor would she do as she was told. She begged Shirah to raise the child as her own if need be, making certain he would not be turned out the way motherless infants sometimes were in times of strife, left in the wilderness for the jackals. Shirah managed to calm the panicked creature with a torrent of promises. Nahara brought water to soothe her fevered forehead and lips.

Once begun, it was a surprisingly easy birth. Yael now bore down when she was commanded to do so; she was fierce, all the more so when Shirah urged her on. "A woman who wails, labors well. It's only silence we must fear. So go on, roar," Shirah instructed.

Yael did so. She was indeed well spoken in fury, and it seemed this wordless rage was her true language. She pushed with all her might, her face straining and flushing. Once, twice, and then the baby's head appeared. Yael was exhausted and said she could do no more. Shirah and Nahara set to work with oil and hot water and entreaties. At last, the mother-to-be gathered her strength and bore down a third time. The child entered this world, falling into Nahara's hands as though he wished to be no woman's burden. He was a large, handsome, dark-skinned boy. We quickly wrapped him in linen and placed him in his mother's arms.

I went to take in some fresh air after the child had safely arrived, exhausted by the labor I had witnessed and by the sheer emotion of the night. I had been thinking of my own child, that beautiful girl I had lost, how it seemed only moments had passed from the first breath she had drawn to her last. To my surprise I found the Man from the North on the steps. Like a ghost he'd unclasped his manacles, then slipped from the dovecote to climb over the living hedge of thorns that kept the goats and sheep secure in their dusty pastures. If anyone had seen him, he would have been killed, taken for an escapee and a threat to us all. He shrank into the shadows as I drew near. When he recognized me, he instantly approached to ask after Yael.

"You really are a fool," I said, "to come here and pace as if you were the father."

"I'm no one's father," he said regretfully. He gazed at me, his face transformed by worry. "I'm not here for that. I've come because of her."

"Double the fool," I said, "since she's not your wife."

Despite my words, I was moved by his determination. I assured him that Yael was well and already mending. Still, he pleaded to see her, unsettled until the sight of her face could convince him that she was safe and well. He swore she had called to him, insisting that her voice had brought him here. He'd heard its fevered pitch and the agony she'd been burdened with, even though she'd been in a dungeon of a chamber, surrounded by stone, and he'd been locked in the dovecote. He was so sincere I led him inside, urging him to be quiet. No man was to see the workings of a birth, but he was a slave, and hardly a man. I had taken pity on him, unusual for me. Perhaps we had grown close as we worked side by side in the dovecote. Perhaps it was the manner in which his eyes shone when he spoke of the child's arrival.

As we ventured forward, I could hear his steady breathing behind me. We stopped at the threshold to the chamber. From here we could view the flickering lamp Shirah had lit before the figure of the outlawed Ashtoreth, Queen of Heaven, giver of life.

The baby was in his mother's arms. The Man from the North nodded, relieved to see for himself that Yael had indeed journeyed into childbirth and passed through unharmed. She appeared to be entranced by the infant in her arms, her eyes vivid and glimmering, her complexion glowing with sweat. When she laughed, enchanted by the child's expression, I saw the slave grin as well, proudly, as if the boy was indeed his.

The Man from the North gripped my arm and gave me thanks, then left us to our business. Nahara was pouring boiling water on the stones to cleanse them. She seemed an outsider already, unwilling to speak with us, present only for the time she was needed, and now ready to retreat. She kept her eyes lowered. She was on her hands and knees, scrubbing at the blood. When I offered help, she smiled lightly.

"God's help is everything I need," she murmured, devout and beautiful and pure, but no longer the girl she had been.

Shirah was crouched beside Yael. Their heads were close together. When Nahara gazed up, I saw her take note of this. Shirah had slipped off one of the gold amulets she wore for protection. She presented it to Yael, promising it would bring good fortune and keep her safe from harm. One side of the disk honored our true king, *Ehyeh Asher Ehyeh*, *I am who I am*, the nameless One with a thousand names. *Ha-nora ha-gibbor*, the mighty One, the hero.

On the other side, Hebrew letters were mixed with Greek. *Chayei ʽolam le-ʽolam. Eternal life, forever.*

These golden amulets had come from Egypt, for there was the form of the moon and the sun stamped upon the one she granted Yael, signifying the power of the Queen of Heaven. Our people were not allowed such images, but Yael strung the amulet around her throat, pleased. It was a gift from one mother to another, accepted with gratitude. The women kissed each other to celebrate the new life. A son cannot be named until he is circumcised, and so Yael simply called him boy as she held him to her breast, the word as loving as any name might be.

Nahara gathered the afterbirth in a cloth. She would bury it in the orchard, as was our custom, beneath the drooping trees, allowing the essence of this new life to refresh the blighted earth. She stopped beside me, her white tunic splashed with blood. She had always seemed older than her years, now she seemed a full-grown woman. She coolly assessed the amulet her mother had fastened at Yael's throat.

"That's a gift for a daughter," she said to me of the necklace, her tone cold. "She's letting me know she's not saving it for me." There was a good measure of hurt in her voice along with her scorn.

Nahara was unadorned, as Essene women were, her feet bare upon the cold, flat stones. The bracelets and charms she'd once worn had been given away. I'd seen children playing with them in the dusty garden beside the stone house, as though they were toys.

"Would you have taken such a gift if she'd offered it?" I ventured to ask, for Nahara had been the one to turn her back on her mother's ways.

Nahara shrugged, knowing I was right. You cannot give a gift to someone who is bound to deny it. Nahara now spent her days caring for the Essenes' goats, idly feeding them weeds as though she had been a goatherd all her life. I had spied her with the pious women, dabbing water on her head before a meal, swaying in prayer, eyes closed in the ecstasy of the Almighty's grace. We who worked in the dovecotes did not discuss what was evident: she would not be returning to us.

"What would you do with gold?" I went on, for I'd heard that the people she'd aligned herself with believed possessions were worthless, meant for this world alone. "I thought what belonged to one Essene belonged to all."

Tonight Nahara been an equal partner to Shirah in bringing forth Yael's child, yet she seemed consumed by a child's jealousy as she gazed at Yael. "That shouldn't include sharing one's mother," she remarked in a hurt tone, so that anyone might think she'd been the one who had been cast away when she alone had made her choice on the day of the salt rain.

EIGHT DAYS LATER, I went with Yael when she brought her son to the synagogue to ask for the ritual every boy child must endure for his faith in our God. From the time of Abraham it had been this way, and so it continued, with many believing our male children were considered *tamim*, perfected, by this ritual. It was said that Domah, the angel of the grave, cannot burn or harass any man who has been circumcised when he enters the World-to-Come; the suffering in the here and now is said to prevent suffering for all eternity.

We stepped inside the doors of the synagogue but were allowed no farther. It was not for the elders to perform the ritual. The child's father must make this covenant between his son and God, and if there was no father, that was not their concern. Yael clutched the baby to her, frightened that no man would stand up for her child because of the circumstances of his birth and that perhaps she, like Moses' wife, Zipporah, would have to complete the deed. I knew Yael carried a knife, but she shied away from the very idea of cutting her own son, vowing that her hand would be made unsteady by her devotion and her love.

At last her brother arrived, apologetic, his prayer shawl around his shoulders. Amram was clearly uncomfortable with the unfamiliar task of caretaking. I wondered how he would manage the covenant when he flinched even as Yael fitted the newborn into his arms. The baby caught the warrior's glance and held it with his unblinking ember-colored eyes. There was a red mark on the left side of his face, one we were all hoping would fade. "I didn't think he'd look like this," Amram blurted.

"He looks like a baby," I remarked matter-of-factly. There was no reason for this child to be viewed as one of the *mamzerim,* a bastard with no rights, not even the right of circumcision, although he would certainly be seen as what our people call a *shetuki,* a silent one, any child who does not know his father.

Amram laughed. "That he does." He nodded to Yael approvingly. "He looks strong."

I did not notice anyone else's presence until Yael took a step back.

The old assassin was there in the shadows. He'd been there all along, a cold eye set on the baby.

"He'll complete the ritual," Amram said of their father.

Yael clutched her baby closer, uncertain, stunned that her father had agreed to participate. The last contact she'd had with him was when they'd quarreled bitterly over her condition, and he'd struck her, driving her from their home.

"Do you think I don't remember how to use a knife?" the assassin asked when he saw her hesitation.

Yael raised her glance to him. "Oh no. I'm sure you do."

Clearly that was her fear.

"Am I not your father?" the assassin said.

Yael gazed at him, unsure.

"Is that child not my grandson?"

Yael's brother quietly urged her to have faith. It was he who had persuaded his father to come to the synagogue, and the two, who had turned away from one another, had made amends because of the birth of this boy. "This child belongs to us, and we to him, never more than on this day. He is not a burden, for he has brought us together."

Only male relatives were allowed to be present at the ceremony when the child would be named. He was ready for the covenant, he had enough life and breath to shield him so that Lilith and her demons could not call to him as easily as they might have in the hours following his birth. Until this day he'd still had one foot in their world and the other in ours; now he was rooted, fed by his mother's milk. This ritual would set the path for his entire life to come.

The assassin kept his head bowed as he waited for Yael's decision, a sign of respect he had never offered to his daughter in the past.

"Take him," Yael said. "But even when I'm not watching, God will be there."

We waited nervously beside the western wall. Yael's face was white. She refused to sit on a nearby bench and paced instead. When the baby cried out, she took hold of my arm.

"A cry is a good thing," I reminded her, echoing Shirah's words. "It's silence we need to fear."

Amram himself looked ashen when he at last carried the baby back to his mother. Yael's worried expression broke into a grin when she saw her brother's face, his usual swagger replaced by the weight of his immense responsibility to the newborn.

"You look worse than he does," she teased.

"I think it was more painful for me," Amram agreed.

Yael opened the child's blankets. The cut was perfect, leaving only a slight flush of blood. The baby was already dozing in his mother's arms, exhausted by his own cries and by the sudden flash of pain he'd known, as well as by the wine that he'd been fed to dull that pain. The old assassin was standing in the threshold. Yael, still unsure in her father's presence, at last nodded her gratitude, but Yosef bar Elhanan had already disappeared, as if he had never been present. I gazed into the plaza. There wasn't even a shadow to be seen.

"Did he speak of the child?" Yael asked her brother, curious despite herself.

"He blessed him," Amram said. "Let that be enough."

WE KEPT the wound clean, applying a balm of balsam and honey that would bring about healing more quickly. But there was more to be done to announce this child's arrival in our world, later, and in secret.

We brought the baby into the field on a night when the moon was waning. Shirah was waiting for us. We three stood where the afterbirth had been buried to commit to a naming ceremony of our own. It was a starry night, but we avoided the light and gathered in the shadows so as not to be spied by the guards and questioned. Shirah had broken an eggshell into halves, onto which she had written the holy name of God as many times as could fit in tiny black letters, the ink drawn from crushed mulberries.

Ehyeh Asher Ehyeh.

We lit a small fire of green wood. Yael placed the baby in the grass. He whimpered, then dozed. She removed her head scarf and her robe to stand before God as she had been on the day her mother died, the day she was born, in this very same month of *Av.* Shirah began to chant words of protection under a screen of smoke.

Redeem this child and save him from all afflictions. Allow him to become a man and sing glorious songs of praise to our Lord and king, the mighty God who created us. Amen Amen Selah, may God keep you from all evil and may He allow you to dwell in Jerusalem and in all holiness.

When the hymn was completed, Shirah buried the eggshells beneath the tree. The moonlight was yellow as it swept across the field. Already the afterbirth had disappeared, feeding the earth, giving gratitude to the Almighty. Yael took up her shawl and her tunic. She reached for her child and named him beneath the open sky, as he had been named earlier that morning by the men at the synagogue. She called him Arieh, the word for lion, even though he slept through our rejoicing as though he were a lamb.

WHEN OUR WARRIORS next went into the desert, it was not to fight but to hunt, trying as best they could to satisfy our hunger. When the Romans returned to the place they had once marked with rocks, our men were forced to retreat, their foray cut short. They had no choice but to outrun the enemy, who had returned to spy on us. For their troubles, our warriors brought back partridges that were more bones than flesh and a stray baby ibex, left behind by the herd. It was *Tishri,* the time of the growing season, and we should have been rejoicing. Instead a silence swept over the mountain, a sense of foreboding.

In the dovecotes, we all felt Nahara's absence. Aziza especially pined for her sister. She often went to the field near the Essenes' camp, where she sat cross-legged in the grass for many hours, but Nahara never came to greet her. When Aziza followed the goats her sister cared for, Nahara was quick to lead them away. Hurt by her sister's refusals, Aziza began to fashion arrows to fill her time and keep her hands busy. We had all been asked to help with the weaponry, and many women gathered in the evenings to shape stones for slingshots. All the same, Aziza hid her work from Shirah.

"She wouldn't think it proper for me," she confided.

As it turned out, Aziza had a light touch. The arrowheads she crafted were thin, beautifully made. Each was bound to a wooden shaft with linen twine. Shirah's elder daughter was surprisingly well suited to such work, for metal was to her what cloth and thread were in the hands of other women. I saw in her what I had spied in the Baker each morning of his life, the love of fashioning something out of ingredients that would be nothing without a human touch, be it salt or wheat or iron that was transformed.

The Man from the North revealed that, in the country where he'd been born, each warrior's arrows were decorated with the sign of his tribe, in his case a stag, the creature he had told us about but one we hardly believed in, for he said this deer's shoulders were as tall as a man, its antlers spreading farther than the span of a vulture's wings. From the time he was a boy, he assured us, every arrow he'd carried had been engraved with the image of that miraculous creature. "Tie feathers to the end of the shaft," the slave told Aziza as she constructed her weapons. "That is how to make them fly."

Because Amram was thought of as a phoenix, rising from every battle to fight again, Aziza crafted arrows that might be worthy of him, adorning each with hawk feathers dyed in a bath of madder root. Soon her hands were red; I overheard Yael teasing her, suggesting she was so consumed with passion that heat was rising from her skin in waves of scarlet.

When it came time to test Aziza's handiwork, she sent Adir to the garrison for a bow. Adir returned soon enough, laughing, joking and making rude remarks, suggesting that his sister had best not touch the bow or she might shoot herself accidentally. Aziza grinned and sent him away with a push.

I sat with Yael, who had her baby resting in a sling made of finely spun wool. Arieh was a quiet boy, with dark, liquid eyes, as calm as the sheep he'd appeared to resemble on the evening of his naming. Though only weeks old, he slept through the night, clutching the square of blue fabric Yael let him hold to settle him. He still had the red birthmark on his cheek, but it had been treated with a salve mixed from wheat, honey, and aloe, and had begun to fade. We imagined that his thick black cap of hair was a sign of his virility, marveling over the size of his hands and feet, and his small, manly penis, suggesting he would likely be able to lift a donkey above his head by his tenth year.

"Perhaps we should let Arieh test the arrows if he is already a warrior," we teased, for we had no man among us.

Aziza handed the bow to the Man from the North, even though it was a crime to place a weapon in the hands of a slave. He took up the bow, grateful for the trust. Each of Aziza's arrows made its mark when the slave turned to his target—a knob on the stump of the ancient olive behind the dovecote. He stood in the threshold so no one else would take notice. When we called out praises, he bowed. He noticed the intent expression on Aziza's face, her gaze fixed on the bow in his hands.

"Let me teach you," he suggested. "Then you can see for yourself the worth of what you've crafted. These arrowheads are among the finest I've ever used."

Aziza backed away, shaking her head, her eyes masked. Still, there was something resembling desire etched across her face.

Women were not to touch weapons, such was our law, but we had already broken the law by handing the bow over to a slave. We who had already sinned did not question or condemn. We stared back at those who whispered about Yael and her baby until they were the ones forced to lower their eyes.

"Try what you've made," I urged, if only for our amusement.

"Fine." Aziza nodded. "But only to please you."

The slave showed her what she must do, and she listened carefully. She held the bow with ease, a broad smile bursting upon her face. Her very first arrow hit the mark. I could see the surprise on the slave's face.

"You have a warrior inside you!" he remarked.

"Pure luck." Aziza dropped the bow and went to gather the fallen arrows, admiring her handiwork, making certain each feather was in place. "The phoenix always prevails," she said. "Whoever Amram strikes will fall before him."

Shirah had remained inside the dovecote. Now she came to the doorway. Her expression was trancelike, difficult to read. She had changed since Nahara's departure, becoming more wary and withdrawn. Some people whispered she had the ability to see through our world into the next. If this was indeed true, then for Shirah the future was not a distant place. We, who had no idea what was to be, sat in the courtyard enjoying ourselves, applauding as Aziza hit the target again and again, her agility and grace a revelation to us all.

As for Shirah, she only watched, the way one might keep a wary eye on a swarm of bees already in flight, when it was too late to wave them away or return them to the hive. When the damage had already been done.

BEFORE LONG the new year was upon us, a time for celebration. But we entered into the holiday of *Rosh Hashanah* frugally and without joy. Our tables were set with simple things, gourds and leeks, a few thin partridges, lentil salads, yogurt cheese. Yael brought some of this meager feast to her friend Tamar. The Essene woman was grateful, and in return her son, Yehuda, a dreamy boy who was often climbing trees in the orchard when he should have been at his studies, surprised my grandsons with the gift of a carved spinning top. The children were delighted with their present; they were happy enough with so little. They didn't notice how Yehuda stared at them, curious once he'd discovered they didn't possess the power of speech. Noah and Levi seemed to accept their plight, however. They made the best of things, ignoring the stares that greeted them in the plaza from the curious who tried to guess what had caused them to become mute. The boys enjoyed the new baby in the house, spending hours entertaining Arieh with his rattle, or with gourds made into flutes, and now with the clever little top Yehuda had fashioned.

Arieh seemed drawn to my grandsons' sweet silence, his eyes following them around our chamber. We catered to our little lion, who threw back his head to laugh when my grandsons made shadows dance on the wall. Already when they played a hiding game with him, ducking behind a length of fabric, he called out for them with a shout, chortling and cooing until my grandsons silently reappeared, so still they might have indeed been shadows rather than flesh-and-blood boys.

This new year was especially bitter for me. Every piece of fruit I cut in half possessed a flavor I couldn't abide. What was sweet, I had grown to despise. I ate bitter greens, and was accustomed to the taste of salt on my tongue. I went to the synagogue and stood with the women in the back. Men must not be distracted by women, but what of women who were distracted by their own thoughts? I recited the prayers I knew by heart, but my voice was hesitant, listless.

I had grown so pale that Yael asked if I had fallen ill. I said no, but I could no longer bring myself to go to the dovecotes in the morning. Instead I chose to remain on my pallet, my face to the wall. I saw shadows as my grandsons passed in and out of the threshold. I saw all that had happened in the desert every time I closed my eyes.

A year had passed since my daughter's life had been taken. On the Day of Atonement, I went to the synagogue to say the prayers of lamentation, but my loss was like an arrow piercing through me, and these rituals were not enough to dull the pain. Melancholy was around me like a shroud, my sorrow sewn to me with the black thread demons are said to use. When I went back into the plaza, people avoided me. They could see the darkness I carried. Even my grandsons shrank from me, preferring to sit beside Yael and hear her stories. There was only one individual who might understand me, one who'd walked the same path and stood beneath the same sky.

Surely, Yoav was somewhere in a darkened corner, aching as I did.

IT WAS EVENING when I went to the barracks. I had not left my chamber for several days, other than to pray in the synagogue. If you do not leave your bed, you become unused to walking. If you do not forgive yourself, you cannot forgive anyone else. I had disposed of the beasts at the oasis, but they had disposed of me as well. The woman I had been, she who had awoken to the scent of bread baking, who swept the steps each morning with complete certainty that the new day would be like any other, had vanished. I was a shell, a beetle, a shock of flesh stitched through with demon thread.

The warriors were at prayer on this evening. I noticed an enormous pile of rocks had been chiseled into smooth, hard balls, to be used in a catapult should we be attacked. These rocks were piled high where before there had been lengths of wood. Now the wood was used up, and there was little enough of it to be found on the surrounding cliffs, only a few stray sunstruck bushes with bleached, scaly bark that smoldered rather than burned when tossed upon a fire. It was the planting season, but the air smelled like an oven in which bread had burned for days. No one worked the fields; protection from the elements and from our enemies occupied us all. I wondered what my husband would have thought of a world that was too hot for bread, too brutal for human kindness.

I waited beneath the remnants of a mulberry tree not far from the barracks. The leaves rustled in the dark. The sound echoed like a rattle, or perhaps it was more like a snakeskin shaken in the wind. I sat on the stump of a tree whose bounty had once fed a king. Soon the young warriors returned from their prayers. They took up their work even on this holiest of days. I spied the great assassin of Jerusalem, Bar Elhanan, cleaning the flat bronze blades of spears with rags and sand as though he were a slave himself. He had come to my home several times, only mumbling a greeting to me but lighting up when he saw Arieh, whom he sat upon his knee. I glimpsed Yael's brother as well, out in the field where he vied with his friends in a contest to see whose eye and aim were best and who among them could shoot an arrow through one of the narrow windows set into stone, made for pouring hot oil and boiling water onto enemies should they be foolish enough to try to breach the wall.

I waited so long I began to hear the echoes of owls in the caves. The warriors retreated to the barracks. As the assassin crossed the plaza, I saw the age in his step, the heaviness of his burden, for he carried all the cruelty he'd been party to on his shoulders. I had resented his desire to come to my chamber because he had taken to visiting his grandson, but in that moment I felt I could not judge his actions in this world, not after all I'd done.

The moon was in the center of the sky watching over me, lonely, cold. Still I stayed. At last my son-in-law came through the plaza, his ax in hand, his expression brooding. He was still a young man, though his hair was white. His arms were bare beneath his prayer shawl. I saw that he had wrapped several thin lengths of sharp-edged bronze around his muscled forearms; the fierce, bloodied twists were meant to turn every move he made into excruciating self-punishment. Such abuse was not allowed; it was the mourning practice of nomads and barbarians. Still, he had done as he pleased, breaking our laws. There were bands of bloody scars where he had cut directly into his flesh with a knife, a row of injuries set above his dark blue veins. The self-inflicted marks were the blue of the hyssop when it bloomed, my daughter's favorite flower. Around them arose bruises that were the gorged color of plums, her favorite fruit.

When I called his name, Yoav narrowed his eyes as though I had uttered a curse. But I gestured to him, and he recognized me and approached. He stood beneath the dry leaves of the mulberry tree, half-dressed in his silver armor. I wondered if he slept in it, if he dreamed of battles and blood or of my daughter's beautiful face.

"It's the day of sorrow," I reminded him, thinking we might pray together or light a lamp in memory of Zara.

He snorted. I thought of the blindfolded horses of the king, set upon a path they could not see. Some must have protested; they must have reared up, furious to be sightless in the brutal grasp of the serpent that led up the mountainside.

"Every day is that," said the Man from the Valley, who was still my son-in-law even though I had no daughter. "What should I pray for?"

He seemed both ashamed and furious; there was scorn in his voice at the mention of prayer. Of course he knew the day. He had counted every moment since he'd found her beneath the heavy rocks I'd placed over her so that she might be protected from any other creatures of prey.

"You have two sons," I reminded him. "They have your wife's dark eyes."

Yoav stunned me with a roar of grief. I drew back, uncertain of who was before me, this Man from the Valley who confided in no one and slept with his back to the wall, ax in hand, ready to fight while he was dreaming. "I told you not to speak of her," he admonished me.

"Or of the boys?"

He faced me, defiant. "This world is nothing to me. Why would you think I care about such things?"

"I came to you because you carry her with you," I said, reminding him that I had offered him her last breath. He had taken it and now she belonged to him. In exchange for this great gift, he needed to respect me still, no matter how bitter he had become. He nodded, recognizing the bond between us and the sacrifice I'd made. He restrained his temper and listened to reason. The man who was still my son-in-law came to sit beside me under the black mulberry tree. He had never asked how I'd managed to kill those beasts, how I'd lured them to their deaths with bread. Perhaps he resented me, for I had performed the deed of vengeance he was likely ashamed not to have committed himself. But back then he was a man who knew only prayer, while I had already become a torrent of fury.

"There must be something here for you still," I insisted, trying to speak to the man he'd been, not this violent warrior intent on torturing himself. "The air you breathe, the water you drink, waking each day to see the sun. There must be something you still want from this world." There was so little that remained of him, but when I looked down into the dust, his shadow seemed the same.

Yoav laughed and shook his head. "You're asking what I want?"

For a moment I saw the scholar who had come to the Baker to ask for our daughter's hand, the young bridegroom so overwhelmed on his marriage day that even after the legal contract, the *ketubah*, had been drawn up and agreed upon, he seemed stunned to realize that Zara was indeed his. When he caught sight of the beauty of his bride, he was speechless, and his friends teased him, vowing he'd been mesmerized.

"Their voices," he said.

We could hear the warriors who had gone in to their evening meal, breaking their fast, the raucous conversation of young men, some too young to know the horrors they would encounter when they ventured into the desert to defend us. Most of those young warriors looked away when they saw the Man from the Valley, with his scars and his bands of metal, easily convinced they would never become like him, a death-giver maddened by war.

"Can you give me that?" Yoav asked. "I want my boys to speak like any others. Can your God do that?"

It was my wish as well, one I had prayed for to no avail. We were so alike it was painful, two people who had drowned in the same pool. We observed the night and the stars above us in silence. I could not promise him that God's grace would prevail.

Yoav shrugged when I had no answer. "Exactly," he said. "Come back to me when they can speak. When the innocent aren't burdened by a curse, then find me. Until that time, I have no faith. If there ever was a God, He has forsaken us and is no more."

We sat together with that terrible and reckless thought. The chill light of the falling moon filtered down.

"I'll fight until there is no one left for me to go up against. Then I'll lie down knowing I had no God."

When I left that place, Yoav was still there, beneath the sun-bleached boughs of the ancient tree. All the while we'd made our way to this mountain, he'd possessed the unrelenting brooding of a man stalked by sorrow. Now he was searching for death, wanting to confront it and be done with this world. I knew what he dreamed about, and it was not my daughter. Such a dream would have broken him in a thousand ways. A vision of Zara would have been endlessly more painful than the sharp strands he strung around himself in self-punishment.

I did not look back as I made my way from the garrison, or pay attention to the owls who glided across the sky at this hour. I had an errand and didn't dare delay. I made a vow to get this man the one thing in the world he still wanted, the sound of his children's voices, a reason to believe.

I WENT to the synagogue to beg for an amulet that might cure my grandsons. I humbled myself, my eyes on the ground, my voice pleading. But the great man, Menachem ben Arrat, only shook his head. He reminded me that he had the fate of our people to pray over and therefore could not be concerned with the troubles of two small boys. He dismissed me as if their plight was meaningless, as perhaps it was for him, and had me escorted out.

Despite the priest's denial, one of the scholars gave me an amulet in which there was a rolled prayer for forgiveness. I buried it beside the temple, as was the custom, but as I wiped the dirt from my hands, I wasn't convinced that a scholar's charm was strong enough for my needs. I was already headed in another direction.

Evening was falling, and the women were at work on the looms set up in the plaza. The men were coming to prayer, called by the blast of the ram's horn which was sounded from the ramparts on the wall, passing me by as I went to the opposite end of the fortress. I neared the barracks, where I spied Aziza acting as a willing audience for her brother while he practiced with a bow, showing off all he'd learned. Adir had become the pet of some of the younger warriors. Although he was a decent student, he had no idea that his sister was the one who had revealed herself to be an expert marksman. We had not told him because such things were forbidden; Adir might not understand if he learned we had ignored the law. Any weapon touched by a woman, even by accident, must be cleansed with both water and prayer so that her essence would not linger, diverting the warrior who might use it next, for even the faintest touch could bring lust to that man's heart. Perhaps that meant a woman who was well trained in arms would be the superior warrior, her attention never wavering from her task. Aziza's shoulders and face were sunburned from her hours of practice behind the dovecote under the guidance of the slave, her lean body finely muscled from the effort of working the bow. Still she applauded her brother as his arrows rose, then fell with a clatter upon the stones.

*

I WENT on across the Western Plaza in search of Shirah, relieved to think I might find her alone. When I came to her door, however, there was no answer. I peered inside to see that the chamber was dim. A scrim of smoke lingered, for incense had been burned before the altar. On the table there was a jar of eye paint made of crushed lapis stone, a palette for mixing paints and rouge that was made of a flat, opalescent white shell, brought from the Red Sea. A small ceramic vial of oil scented with lilies was opened, as though someone had left with great urgency. Lilies were associated with the Shechinah, what some called the Dwelling. It was the feminine aspect of God, that which was hidden and touched only by the truest of believers in a veil of knowledge and ecstasy. It was God's compassion, and those who died in the Shechinah's embrace were said to be favored by the angels.

I myself had heard only whispers of such things; still, I recognized the odor of the divine, extremely female in its essence, a mixture of purity and defilement, sweet and sour drawn in one breath. I slipped out of Shirah's chamber, for the scent led me on, through the plaza. I crossed toward the western wall. I peered over to the palace beneath me. At this hour, under the darkening sky, the ruined Northern Palace yoked to the cliffs was surrounded by a haze of lilac light. The fragrance of perfume was faint, yet it was stronger than the bitter odor of the barren valley below us.

The shops were closed, the tannery and winery shuttered, the bakery dark. Several strong men worked in the bakery, feeding the huge ovens first with cut wood, and, now that we were running out of logs, planks torn from the floors of the inner chambers of the palace were used to feed the flames. I had avoided these ovens ever since I'd walked past one morning to see the men at work, bare-chested, covered by their white aprons, sweltering in the heat the ovens cast. I was fainthearted at the sight of the bakers. For a moment I imagined I saw my husband among them.

Before I swooned, I realized it was someone else entirely, someone who didn't resemble my husband at all. The man working at the bakery waved at me when he noticed me staring. I hurried away. Ever since that time, I had cooked my own flatbread, flavored with the last of my husband's coriander. I did not wish to come to this place and stand in line with the other women, waiting for the fresh loaves, or be reminded of the scent of my own household in the Valley of the Cypresses.

Now, in the dark, I saw a shadow cross the bakery floor. A rat.

I went on to search for Shirah, coming to the entranceway that led into the earth. I continued, though I was made dizzy by the way the path careened down hundreds of tilted steps, many crumbling in decay. Members of the king's court had glided down these stairs, and not long after, Roman soldiers had patrolled here before our warriors overtook them to claim this fortress as their own. I went so deeply into the earth I seemed to be entering another world entirely, one that was dark and damp despite the arid landscape up above.

Although we'd had no rain for several months and the world around us was parched and aching, I heard water. At first the promise of water was like a dream, as it had been when we'd come to the oasis. I felt stunned by the lilting sound of its echo, by the very idea, as though I'd long forgotten what water was like, how it could be so cold and sweet, with white petals floating on the surface, how it could easily drown someone, taking the unsuspecting bather into the circle of its pale, unrelenting arms.

I continued on, drawn to the unexpected promise of water as rats are drawn to grain in the bakery, my hand set against the cool stone wall to help me keep my balance on the twisting stairs. The steps became smaller as I ventured down, each more tiny than the one before. I had to turn sideways so as not to fall. At last I realized where I was. I'd come to the largest cistern, a well so enormous fifty men could stand across it shoulder to shoulder and still have room to stretch. In winter this well filled from Herod's aqueducts to become a lake used to supply our baths and water vats. Now, however, the level was dangerously low. There was only a small, concentrated green pool collected in the center of the well, rimmed by sharp rocks. A single lamp had been set upon a stone, and the melting oil floated like liquid amber. I squinted through what was shadow and flickering light in equal measure. I felt so strong a chill I might have drifted into the land of ice the Man from the North so often spoke of, a place where a warrior could freeze through to his bones in moments.

There was the glitter of flesh in the water and the roiling movements of sexual frenzy. I shivered and thought of monsters, for who but crocodiles would slip into the water to take their pleasure? But surely monsters did not embrace each other with such passion, nor kiss one another on the mouth, nor wear the flesh of men and women. The two in the water were both dark, their darkness joining as they became one. When they pulled apart from each other, I could only observe the man's back and broad shoulders, but I could see that the woman wore a gold amulet around her throat and that her eyes, so dark in the water, were streaked with the powder of the lapis stone, a shade some people vowed was the color of heaven.

I stood against the wall and tried not to draw breath. I had stumbled into something it was best to leave be. Now I stumbled even farther as I edged toward the stairs in an attempt to flee. A rock fell and splashed into the water. The ripples went out in a shimmering circle as the falling rock was devoured by the pool. The woman in the cistern drew her beloved to her. As she did, I saw her throat and breasts. She was marked by henna-colored tattoos, a practice our people were not allowed, unless a woman was a *kedeshah,* one who was anointed, willing to offer her body as a sacrifice and as a blessing to her priests.

The swimmer turned and glared in my direction, seeing through the shadows. We caught each other's glance, as a gazelle might gaze into the eyes of a hunter, although which was the prey and which the hunter I could not say. Quickly, I backed deeper into the corner. My grandsons had taught me the language of silence. I didn't need words to tell me that the Witch of Moab was just like any other woman. She embraced her lover closely, her arms cast around him protectively to ensure I wouldn't see his face. It didn't matter. I knew who he was from the way the light fell across his back, as though it had been drawn to the light inside of him, that which shone and made men follow him as if they had no other choice.

I wished I could erase what I had seen. I had only wanted to ask Shirah's favor, and I'd discovered far more than I'd bargained for. I took the stairs as quickly as I could. Though I was no longer young, I fled as a young woman would have. It crossed my mind to run all the way home, but our eyes had met; there was no hiding from one another after our encounter. If you do not face something, it will follow you anyway. If I had learned anything from my time in the desert it was that once you ran, you could never stop.

I waited at her door, anxious as to what would happen next. Enemies had been formed for far less reason than knowledge such as mine, and a woman who practiced *keshaphim* was not an easy enemy to face. I knew too much, yet I knew nothing. Perhaps that made me the more dangerous of the two of us at this moment. If I had any gift at all, it was my ability to see shadows. I spied one now crossing the plaza; if I half-closed my eyes, I saw a raven, one who wished to fly but who was trapped, earthbound.

Her long black hair was hanging down her back, wet and loose, the scent of lilies clinging to her. We stood in the half-light cast by the moon. I noticed that even a witch could blush, especially one who'd been discovered in the depths of a well. A flicker passed across Shirah's dark face, not shame exactly but surrender.

"What is it you want from me?" she asked, resigned.

I thought of the doves, how they never met your gaze and always cast their glance downward. Unlike these shy creatures, Shirah was staring at me, eyes blazing, convinced, it seemed, that I might use my newfound knowledge against her.

"What you do is your business," I assured her. "I won't even remember tonight."

I had come for a favor, and that was what I asked for. I bowed my head and took in the scent of lilies as I pleaded for the only thing my son-in-law wanted in this world. My grandsons' voices returned to them.

"What makes you think I can do the work of God?"

Shirah was fearless even now when I knew enough to destroy her reputation and her life. Women who committed adultery were often cast out, their hair was shorn to the skull, their possessions confiscated, their children torn from them. Wasn't her bravery proof enough of her strength? She was the reason the council left Yael alone. They had approached once, with questions concerning Arieh's birth. Shirah had closed the door to the dovecote and she sang a prayer until they went away. If she could bring children into the world, fighting Lilith when she tried to claim them, then surely she could help two small boys find their voices. To convince her I would have to open my own silence. I did so, bowing my head as I told my story, keeping in mind the image of the Man from the Valley wrapped in thin strips of metal and marked by his own blood. As I spoke the past was drawn around us the way dark gathers at the corners of the world. There was the jasmine that grew beside the pool and the burn marks on my daughter's skin. There rose the angel who'd whispered to me in the bakery, the demon who'd sifted inside me when I took up the soldier's knife against my own dearest flesh and blood, the ghost of my husband, who'd assured me that every loaf of bread fed us in the way we needed to be fed.

Shirah sank back, her face ashen. Now only she and God knew the manner in which I'd killed the beasts who had fallen upon us, the delight I'd taken in watching them drink themselves to death, the terrible pleasure there had been in cutting their throats. I threw off my cloak, the better for her to see me and know what I had become. I was not a baker's wife or a grandmother or a woman who cared for doves, feeding the ailing birds spoonfuls of barley water, tending to them through the night. I was a murderess. I held the lamp to my palm to let Shirah see exactly what was before her. The mark of death.

I was spent and exhausted. Words had done that to me, twisted my heart as they poured out, clattered like stones onto the cobbled ground. Perhaps my grandsons were lucky to be mute, protected against the stories of their own lives. Shirah drew me close, and in her embrace it seemed that I was the child who had seen too much, peering through the waterfall at the horror of what a beast could do to a human being and what a human being could then become.

"For every evil there is a cure," Shirah said softly. "Any mother would defend her daughter. It would be a sin not to do so, a crime beyond any that are written. What you did, you did for love."

Against my fevered skin, her flesh was delightfully cool. She confided in me that water was her element and had been since she was a child, that was why I had found her in the cistern. Her mother had brought her to a river, and she found she could swim without ever having been taught to do so. What was dangerous to one person was a mercy to another. My son-in-law's wish was not an impossible task, she assured me, but the price was patience. Wait and have faith, she urged. Catch a demon and you will break the spell. Offer an angel gratitude and he might return the voices he'd taken to stop the children from crying out when they were hidden behind the waterfall. I was to pray every night to Beree, the angel of rain. This angel was silent, as my grandchildren were, so I should not expect an answer, at least not right away.

"I know what it is your son-in-law desires," Shirah now said. "But what of you?"

"His wish is mine," I assured her.

"No." She was not convinced. When she gazed at me, I felt my throat tighten, perhaps to hold back the truth. "There's something more."

Shirah raised my hand to her mouth. Before I could think to pull away, she kissed the center of my palm. In that instant I let go of the truth, that which I'd kept from her and from God and from myself. I broke into a shuddering sob. The soldiers had been beasts and it had been a pleasure to kill them, but they had been men as well. They had walked on the earth and under the sky. The one who had pleaded with me was the one who had stayed with me, for he had begged for something I now longed for as well.

I wished to be forgiven.

"It was always so in the eyes of God," Shirah told me.

She let her robe slip from her shoulders so that I could take in the full measure of the forbidden red tattoos on her skin that I had spied in the cistern. I knew what they represented: loyalty to the goddess, a life given in service, a woman's deepest sacrifice, scorned by our own people.

"Should I judge myself?" she ventured to ask. "Or should I leave that to the Almighty, who forgives us all for being what He made us?"

Beneath the mulberry tree I had nearly been moved to renounce my faith alongside my son-in-law. Who was there to look down upon my trials and my transgressions? Who could heal a wound that might never be closed? Shirah had tasted my sorrow and had trusted me enough to reveal herself to me in return. If she could, and if God would allow it, my son-in-law would be granted his heart's desire.

Perhaps then I could forgive myself.

I PRACTICED patience throughout the month of *Tishri*, for this virtue did not come easily to me. In truth, patience had never served me well in the past. If I'd had patience, my grandsons would have been beside the pool of green water when the renegades came to us, waiting like sheep to be slaughtered. If I'd had patience, my daughter's murderers would still be walking this earth. I thought of my husband and how he had waited for the dough to rise, never rushing the loaves into the oven. He'd known the exact moment to take the linen cloths from the rising loaves, when to slide the wooden board into the red-hot oven. It was as if he was the *challah* as well as its maker, and therefore understood its mystery from the inside out.

I began to study the slave. He, too, was a deeply patient man. He waited without complaint every evening, settled upon the stones of the dovecote until Yael's return the following day, as calm as the doves who waited for our return. But I took note of the heat in his pale eyes; he couldn't hide that. Even his patience would last only so long.

It was a difficult season, and the heat had not dissipated. Sleep did not come easy to me, although the others beneath my roof slept well, including Arieh, who was more than two months old, a healthy, quiet little boy. There came an evening when I was tidying our chamber, setting new straw into our sleeping pallets, when I looked out to see movement beside our door. I noticed a shadow, as I had at the oasis when the darkness of the soldiers crossed the sand. That was my talent. I could observe what was only half there: the beasts on the ridgetop, the rat in the corner, the woman meeting her lover, the vial of poison behind the spice jars, the lanky form of a man lingering outside our chamber. I thought it was a spirit who had risen to walk among us, having left his slumbering body behind. But, no, he was flesh and blood.

*

WHEN I recognized him, I understood that the Man from the North was not as patient as I had imagined. Perhaps this was true for all men. I now remembered there had indeed been days when the Baker cursed the ovens for being slow, when he pulled the loaves from the racks before they were fully cooled. Even the most patient among us has a breaking point. On this evening when I saw the figure slinking along the wall, I knew such a time had come for the slave. He wore a head scarf to disguise himself, but anyone could tell he wasn't one of us. His fair hair shimmered. You would think a man from the world of ice would hold little feeling, but that wasn't the case. How hot ice could be, how impatient, ready to melt.

The Man from the North was fortunate that I alone spied him. Anyone else would have set upon him immediately, and even if he was quick to surrender, whoever might have chosen to murder him would have been within his legal rights. I waved him away, clapping my hands, as I would to chase off rats. He slipped back against the wall, falling into the dark, disappearing, as a dream might. But unlike a dream, he left his mark. When I went to the wall in the half-light and ran my hand over the stones, I found them hot to the touch in the place where he had waited, cast by the impatience that was evident in any man in love.

The following morning, as Yael and I walked through the field, she kept her eye on the dovecote where the shadow who had stalked her was kept. My walk was slower than hers, and I saw her impatience when she bade me to hurry.

"The doves can't wait?" I asked.

She flushed and began to fuss with the baby she carried at her hip. "Dear heart," she said, masking her eyes, rubbing the soft skin under Arieh's chin.

"Is there a reason you're so impatient?" I pressed her.

She looked up at me, hesitant. I could feel her lie forming before it was declared. "No hurry," she answered, but her gaze said otherwise.

That was when I knew she was the one who had left the slave's chains unlocked.

She was treating him like a man.

I said I had a stone caught in my sandal. I stopped to slip it out, stating that I could not walk with a stone any more than a slave could become one of us. I glanced at Yael and saw she was flustered, angered by my remarks.

"Do you think he's less than we are? Is he nothing more than a stone?"

It was said that angels came to human beings for comfort. How lonely they must be, locked in the silence of their world. But a human burned in the embrace of the angels, his body set aflame, and the kindness of such creatures could become a curse. Here on this mountain, Yael's indiscretion would be considered treachery.

"If they find him roaming, they'll kill him," I warned. "If you unlock him, you unlock his death. Do you think he'll be happy to do our bidding once his chains are off? He'll want more, like any other man."

Yael softly admitted that the Man from the North had spoken of his plans to escape. He knew of others who had done so. Several of his fellow conscripts had deserted the legion before they'd crossed the Great Sea, still more had disappeared after reaching Jerusalem. I was silent, wondering if he might have known the beasts who had attacked us, perhaps had considered them friends.

When the Man from the North made his impassioned speeches about freedom, I suspected he was trying to convince Yael to flee as well. He insisted the Romans would soon enough be upon us—and it was true we more often spied scouts in the region. Before long we would be the slaves, the Man from the North had vowed. But perhaps he had forgotten that, when Yael left the dovecote, she was not alone. She had told me she would never return to the desert, where there were bones left beneath the piles of rocks, glinting in white heat, the remains of the man she had loved.

I knew about the lion who had bitten her and possessed her. She'd rambled about him when we paused on the steps so that she might draw breath on the night she labored to bring forth her child. Although she never spoke of it again, I knew she was not about to bring another lion into the desert. If the Man from the North was planning to escape, he would have to do so alone.

I made no further comment when I saw them working together. I turned away when she brought him a blanket and a goatskin bag of water. She was not my daughter, though I had allowed her to use the Baker's possessions, the vials of coriander and cumin, the wooden spoons, the apron he had tied around his waist. I had wept over these things before and would again, whether or not Yael ruined what was left of her life ministering to the slave. She should have treated him as a mere stone in her sandal. Instead, she saw him as a man.

When they went into what was left of the orchards, those trees that had not been hewn for firewood and still bore fruit, the hawk followed, dedicated, not veering away from the mountaintop. I watched their shadows stretch across the field, then disappear as a cloud passed overhead. I felt sure this was the sign of disaster to come. Perhaps I no longer believed in kindness and mistrusted it. I had come to consider compassion a knife in the hands of the angels of disaster.

ONE SABBATH EVENING, the council announced they would no longer bring conscripts or slaves to the fortress after a battle but would instead slay them along with their owners. Several Roman conscripts had been captured and now worked with the donkeys who carried up barrels of water. There was little enough food for the residents, we hadn't a surplus to feed more. What was a slave but a stone? people murmured. Exactly as I had said. I watched

Yael carefully after that proclamation; she frowned and gazed at the council in alarm as the slaves among us were denounced.

"It's a sin to keep people so," she said to me with a naked flash of emotion as we left the plaza.

"I suppose you won't listen to my advice," I muttered.

She laughed and linked her arm through mine. "I'll listen," she assured me.

"And then you'll do as you please," I remarked.

We laughed together, then I fell silent, for I realized how much I feared for her in this wicked world. Although she was not my daughter, I fretted as if she were.

THE NEXT MORNING I saw that Yael had brought the Man from the North a bow and several arrows, one for each of the seven sisters that gather as stars in the sky. She had hidden them under her cloak, but I recognized the shape of the weapon from its shadow when she stored it beneath a pile of straw. The bow was one her brother had carried. When he found it gone, he would question his friends in the barracks and never once remember he had not seen it since his sister's most recent visit. This was the shade I had spied in the field as the hawk drifted above them. She was willing to do too much for this man who was nothing on this mountain and should have been nothing to her as well.

"Don't tell me when it will happen," I overheard her say as she stood beside him. "I'll arrive one morning and you'll be gone."

The Man from the North was aware that he had a rival, but unlike most suitors, he wasn't jealous. Rather, he doted upon his competition, our little lion. He might have resented Arieh his mother's joys and arms, instead he was happy to help amuse the child, lifting him up to see the hawk above us. He whistled in a way that brought the bird swooping, which made the baby throw back his head and laugh. The slave often listed the names of things in his own rough language, trying to teach Arieh how he might say *dove* and *hawk* and *mother* and *snow,* as though convinced the child might someday live in the slave's cold land and speak as he did.

"You're wasting your time," I warned when he clasped Arieh in his arms, then tossed him in the air until the child melted with laughter.

Then one day he told the child his name. We worked in such close quarters that we all overheard. It was Wynn, a rough word that stuck in the throat. Shirah and Aziza exchanged a look, surprised that the slave would reveal himself. He had addressed Arieh in the manner in which a man might speak to his son. I knew then that the time of his leaving had come. A slave never speaks his name aloud; once he was captured, it was not to be uttered until he walked into the world beyond. His name was to be a word known only to his kinsmen who awaited him and to whatever God he revered.

Only a free man would take such a risk.

In the evenings I waited, holding the baby, while Yael ducked back inside the dovecote and unlocked his chains. It was a simple lock; the key was hung on a hook hammered into the dovecote wall. And yet it took some time before Yael emerged, smoothing down her hair. No one else would have spied her shadow, or known how it drew her back to this man, but shadows were my gift. Because she was not my daughter, I stood with the baby and sulked and said nothing.

This was the time of year when night came earlier, washing across the sky to flood the corners of the horizon. Each night when Yael left the slave, her expression was dark.

She erupted one evening when an edict went out that rations would be halved and there would no longer be clean water for animals or slaves. "No one should be treated this way."

"Would it have been better if they'd killed him?" I asked.

"When men act like beasts, they become so," she countered.

I couldn't deny this, so I let it be. "This is the world we live in," I murmured, and she took my hand, as if she were indeed my daughter.

YAEL WASN'T ALONE in her unhappiness. We all felt the constraints of the mountain, the lack of food, the petty jealousies. Many of the sheep and goats that we valued for their milk were being butchered out of need. People were going hungry. Cucumbers on the vine shriveled in the last bursts of heat, turning to ash, as the fruit was said to do in the blighted city of Sodom.

The council allowed a group of travelers to camp in the far field, beyond the Essenes' goat house. They were nomads who dyed their hands blue and spoke in their own tongue, but they brought with them livestock to share with us, although we would have nothing to do with the swine they kept. They, too, had been driven off by the Romans. Some of their women, the ones who had been violated by soldiers, cut deep gashes into the palms of their hands and soles of their feet to allow the sorrow to rise out of their bodies.

When they left to return to the wilderness, their flocks in need of grasslands, we found a baby who had come from a union a Roman soldier had forced upon one of their women. The baby had been suffocated, then placed beneath an almond tree, knees to his chest, his small arms folded, as though asleep and in peace, rescued from the harshness of the world. Yael stood beside me and wept. She had seen two child-brides from this tribe buried in this way in the wilderness. She said they had held hands so they might walk together into whatever world awaited them.

There were many among us who wished we could flee and find our way back to cities and towns. But there was nothing to return to. Our houses were burned, our towns destroyed. I wondered if Yael wished she could escape and make her away across the desert, over the Great Sea, to the world where snow was an everyday occurrence rather than a miracle.

I could see my grandsons playing near the wall much like shadows sifting across the gathering dark. My throat closed up as it often did when I gazed upon them. I thought of the baby, smothered, then carefully and lovingly laid to rest. Yael put her arm through mine, for we spent every evening together. The first star had appeared above us, the one they say is Ashtoreth's lantern, which burns so brightly it allows her to cross the sky when all others are trapped in the dark.

THE SENTRIES caught him one night in the month of *Cheshvan* when the air was glazed with cold. It was the beginning of the rainy season, the time of the year when we lived beneath the sign of the scorpion, which brought disorder and gloom, the time of the floods. Yet the sky hung over us like an empty bowl, throwing down darkness but nothing more. There had been no rain, and we all knew this was a sign that our people were not in God's favor.

The guards fell upon him as he crossed the field where the trees lifted their boughs upward, desperate in their thirst. He was near the portion of the wall that circled past our chamber, the place where he'd left his mark of heat upon the stones on the night I'd spied him waiting, perhaps with patience, most certainly with desire.

We did not speak of it, but we all knew that if he'd been heading to the Snake Gate to make his escape, he would not have come in this direction. There was only one reason why he was apprehended in the garden of onions where the scorpion resided, and that reason was Yael. Perhaps he had convinced himself that, if he spoke to her once more, and if the words were strong enough, they might pierce through her resolve and she might be willing to leave us.

We didn't know he had been captured until morning. There was a sharp breeze that carried the scent of myrrh, and also of fragrant cypress, reminding me of the valley where I had once lived. We usually had rain in this month, but so far none had fallen, though the priests were praying for such an occurrence three times a day. People were reminded of the stories of the great drought, when a sage named Honi called down the rains and saved our people. The situation warranted a miracle and the voice of someone who might be heard when calling out to God.

Upon discovering the news of the slave's imprisonment, Yael leaned against the wall of the dovecote for support, so that it seemed she'd been struck and could go no farther. The baby was tied to her, and he stirred in his sleep and made a whimpering noise. Yael quickly stroked his dark hair to settle him. What might a baby dream of? Milk and love, the language of a mother's care, the voice of a man who was born in snow? It is the sort of sleep we can never have again. Our rest is formed by our waking life and our waking life is formed by our sorrows.

No one told us where the slave was, but when we spied the hawk circling a tower, we knew where they'd taken him. They would have killed him, but it wasn't worth the effort. If they left him be, locked up and forgotten, he would die on his own. I saw Shirah's eyes flit over to Yael, who now forced herself to show no expression. No outsider would guess she felt more than the rest of us, unless they noticed she'd grown so pale that the freckled marks on her skin stood out like a scrim of blood.

We kept to ourselves that day, mourning the slave's absence, on edge and waiting for worse news to come. I, for one, had not expected to miss him as strongly as I did. He was such a big man and had taken up so much space that the dovecote seemed quite empty without him. The birds were unsettled; there were few eggs to be found, and the ones we discovered in the straw had dark spots speckling the blue-gray shells, a bad omen. We ate our noon meal together in the garden behind the dovecote in silence, taking small bites of cold barley cakes with olive oil as we waited for what was to come next. It seemed a stone had been dropped into water, and every circle that fanned out moved the tide of our destiny along the course of some inevitable destination. Today was not like the day that had come before; by tomorrow we would be carried even further from the everyday world we'd grown accustomed to.

When the guards came to question us, as we knew they would, we said we were stunned by the slave's disappearance. We had no idea that he had puzzled out the trick of unlocking his chains or that he'd learned to work the bolt on the door. Shirah found a thin twist of steel which she quickly bent to resemble a key. She handed it to the guards, suggesting perhaps this was the way the slave had escaped. Her glance went to Yael, whom she strove to protect against inquiry. Again, Yael's face was blank.

We went on, saying more, clucking like chickens, insisting that we'd thought men from the north were steady and dumb, unable to plan an escape. "But see how clever he was," Shirah said to the guards, shaking her head, "to make a key out of nothing."

"He'll starve to death soon enough," one of the guards told us, perhaps believing that was news we wished to hear.

Shirah asked if one among us could speak with their prisoner, saying he had devised a rake that was helpful and we wanted to learn his methods so that we might make use of the tool ourselves. Yael glanced at her with gratitude, aware this dispensation was the single way food and water could be brought to the tower. There was only one person who might allow such a meeting, our leader, Ben Ya'ir.

"Tell him our wish," Shirah said without hesitancy. "He will be generous to us."

But Ben Ya'ir had gone into the wilderness with his warriors, leaving no second in command other than the elders, and they would surely not listen to Shirah's pleas or even allow her to come within their doors.

We were told there was but one person who might convince the authorities that the Man from the North deserved a visitor—Ben Ya'ir's wife, Channa, the dark woman who lived in the lower section of the Western Palace, a villa in which the frescoes had been created by master painters from Rome. She held some of her husband's authority when it came to domestic matters, hearing complaints about living space or work allotments among the women. She was revered even though she set herself apart from all others. For days at a time she refused to open her door; her ration of food was brought to her, then left outside her gate, her water set beside her garden in buckets and goatskin flasks. She ventured out at night and was sometimes seen in the Western Plaza, flowing scarves wrapped around her that resembled a shroud, her sharp face set in mourning, although she had lost no one. She was a mystery and a shadow, but shadows were what I understood most of all.

When we stated our plea, the guard asked who among us would visit Ben Ya'ir's wife. I could feel the others' hesitation, and even Shirah turned away, wary of such an encounter. I found myself offering to go. I was the eldest, and because of this it was my duty. But there was more. I was the diviner of shadows who had learned not to show what was inside. I could pretend to be a baker's widow, a simple woman, and held a talent of disguise that would help with this task. The other women looked upon me, grateful for my offer, each with her own reasons for not wanting to go to the palace.

As I was to leave, on impulse, I decided to bring Arieh with me. I had a premonition. I thought I heard a voice say his name. Perhaps the angel who had stood with me in the bakery was beside me again. Perhaps he who had instructed me to take up the vial of poison now murmured that this child might be the key to unlock a prison door.

"Who could deny a smile to Arieh?" I said to Yael. "What harm can it do?"

Ben Ya'ir's wife might take an interest in the welfare of the dovecotes if she took an interest in the baby. If so, she might allow us to visit a man who was nothing more than a stone, but who all the same had entrusted us with his name.

WHEN I RAPPED upon the palace door, the great man's wife was quick to call *Go away*. I set to knocking once more. I'd often needed to call upon customers who had forgotten to pay the Baker; I did not give up easily when told to leave. The door of this grand house was made of red cypress, which I took to be a good omen. Our town in the Valley of the Cypresses was said to have been blessed by the angel Michael; perhaps the wood used for this door had come from our forest and had therefore been blessed as well. My mother's great-grandmother might have walked beneath this very tree's branches before King Herod's builders cut it to the ground.

Arieh squirmed in my arms. A wind was blowing and all at once I had a chill. Perhaps I'd made a mistake to bring the baby, for he was usually so good-natured and calm. Now, in the light of the dwindling day, he fussed as never before. I wondered how a woman could ever know if it was an angel who urged her on, or if one of Lilith's demons was whispering in her ear.

Though I fretted and worried that I had made a mistake, I knocked yet again. There were no shadows because of the clouds rushing past; perhaps that was what led me astray. I could read shadows far better than I could read flesh and blood.

Eleazar ben Ya'ir's wife opened the door a crack to peer out. She was thin and dark with a restless expression. "I have no time for you," she told me.

She would have gone on with her excuses and perhaps managed to send me away, but her eye caught on the baby in my arms. He grinned at her, the flame mark on his cheek hardly noticeable in the dim light of the doorway. It looked like the imprint of a kiss.

"Who's this who's come to call?" Ben Ya'ir's wife asked, her interest piqued.

"This is a child whose mother needs your favor," I replied.

Channa was aloof again. "I have no favor to grant. My husband is the one you want, not me."

When she breathed in, I heard a rasping sound. I wondered if her labored intake of air was the reason she often locked herself away and was so rarely seen among other women. She turned and coughed, bringing up blood, which she hid from me in her scarf. But I had caught sight of the shadow of the stain. It was clear that she had a breathing disease, the sort that forced a person to forsake the open air. Each breath was trapped inside the cage of her ribs and could not be released. It lay there, rattling, like dry leaves caught in a net.

"Perhaps I have a favor to grant you," I said.

My husband had often convinced customers to buy more loaves than they initially thought were needed. *You will never go hungry,* he told them. *Your table will be the envy of all.* Possibly there was a bargain to be struck. In the bakery this was always so, why not at the palace door?

Ben Ya'ir's thin, dark wife eyed me, suspicious. Her lips were bright with blood. "No one can help me."

I assured her that someone could. I would offer her proof that for every ailment there was indeed a cure. When I turned to leave, Channa called for me to bring the baby if I were to return. My prediction was correct. He was the key that would open a doorway so the Man from the North could escape his plight.

I WENT DIRECTLY to Shirah's chamber and sat at her table. We shared a tea made of the dried root of the hyssop. The boiled water was tinted sky blue. There was a plate of dried fruit, raisins and figs. My grandsons were in the courtyard with Shirah's son, Adir, along with the Essene boy, Yehuda, Tamar's son, who had become their great friend, though he'd been commanded by his people to stay away and pay more attention to his studies. All were taking turns with the spinning top, so we had our privacy.

"Did she speak to you?" Shirah tried to be offhand about the matter, but her gaze was sharp. "She locks her door to most."

I wondered how it was possible that others did not see the truth as I did. Did they not take note of the unusual color of Aziza's eyes? The shade was not unlike the Salt Sea, changing with her mood, now gray, now green, now dark as stone. Only one other person had such eyes. At the mention of Ben Ya'ir's wife, Shirah was struck with grief. When I spoke of Channa's illness, however, she did not seem surprised.

"While the hyssop flowers, she can go out only at night, when the flower closes and the scent evaporates," Shirah informed me. "She keeps the same hours as the rats."

Shirah took a sip of her tea, made of the bloom that caused Ben Ya'ir's wife such difficulty. She seemed to thoroughly enjoy its sharp flavor.

"I didn't realize you knew her."

Shirah laughed grimly. "I've never met her."

I thought this over, how it could be possible for Shirah not to know this woman, yet still be acquainted with the most intimate details of her life. In our world a man who was married could lie with an unmarried woman and no one would think him the worse for doing so; he might be required to pay her family for her shame. But a woman who gave herself to such a man had no legal rights. Even her bones would be sentenced to lie alone if she was convicted of any wrongdoing; they would be cast out and unburied so that she would forever be unable to find rest among her own kind.

"Channa has the power to open the prison gate," I reminded Shirah. "She might be willing to do so in exchange for a cure."

"Then we pay the jailer," Shirah said moodily. "Is that what you want of me?"

"Is that what she is?" When Eleazar ben Ya'ir's wife had peered out from behind her door, she had seemed like a prisoner rather than a jailer to me. "I pity her."

"Don't be fooled," Shirah admonished me. "Is what we see on this earth all there is? You understand there is a shadow world. Can you not spy a demon in the corner even though you cannot see her or feel her breath upon your skin?"

Shirah was convinced to find a remedy, for there was no other recourse. She went to the shelf where she stored herbs. There were brown sheaves wrapped in cord and containers of powders, thistle and garlic, wormwood and cinnamon. When she returned she held out a leather pouch of crushed myrrh. Her instructions were simple: I was not to let the fire flame too brightly or to add other ingredients to the mix when I presented it to our leader's wife. Cures such as this were strong and therefore dangerous. Death could occur if care wasn't taken.

"If she breathes in sparks, she may never breathe again," Shirah remarked as she closed the cord of the bag. There was a certain delight in her tone.

I reached for Shirah's hand in order to gaze into her palm. I was not educated in such matters, yet there was one sign I knew quite well. The brand I carried, the one that signified a murderer, a mark that had twisted into my flesh on the day I'd become the thing I was now. I was relieved to find that Shirah's hand was clear of such an abomination.

"Did you think you'd see her blood on my hands?" Shirah demanded, drawing away. She laughed, well aware of what I had been searching for. "If I'd wanted to accomplish that, I could have done so when I was a girl."

This was unexpected. "You knew her then?"

"I didn't know her then any more than I do now." Shirah led me to the door. "If you want her to accept this cure," she murmured, handing me the precious herb, "don't tell her where you found it. If she had my life and I hers, she would have done exactly as you imagined of me. If you want to look at someone's hand for the mark of death, search hers." Shirah nodded at Arieh now, dozing in my arms. "Bring him to Yael before you return to the palace."

"Why wake him? I'll carry him with me."

Shirah gazed at me. She could see inside me, and she knew there was more to my reasoning. I admitted that Channa had asked me to return with him. "Who could not be charmed by him?" I said, for our lion brightened all of our lives.

Shirah was troubled. Usually she appeared to be a girl, no older than Aziza, but at this instant she seemed her true age, a woman who had crossed the desert not once but twice, who had brought three children into the world and been marked with forbidden tattoos when she was little more than a girl herself.

"Bring him if you must. But whatever you do," Shirah warned, and in this she was very clear, "do not let her hold him."

I RETURNED to the palace and stood at the fine-grained door. This time, Channa unhooked the lock before I rapped on the wood, already waiting, curious, eyes glinting. Her breath was rasping, and she clutched at her chest, in the grip of her ailment. Still she warmed at the sight of the sleeping child and was quick to invite me in.

I stepped over the threshold of our leader's house, humbled. I was relieved that Ben Ya'ir was in the desert with his men so that I did not have to bow before his greatness or risk that in his wisdom he might see me for the murderess I was.

I followed my hostess past the frescoes, highly praised by all who saw them, and for good reason. They were painted upon plaster in glorious tones of orange and red and gold. Although faded, they were clearly the work of a master. The seven sisters that the Greeks believed moved through the sky in a burst of stars had been set upon the wall, lifelike in their human guise, along with the moon, the most beautiful woman of all, in a dress of silver with strands of gold leaf running through her garment; so present it seemed real thread had been stitched through the painted fabric. Lamps lit the darkened hallway, and there was the scent of pure olive oil burning. The chamber we entered was well appointed, furnished with tables and benches left by the king's household. I thought of our straw mats, our coarse cloth blankets, our dirt floors.

I asked my hostess to fetch a dish and some kindling. When she did so, I brought forth the myrrh Shirah had given me. Arieh was still dozing, so I laid him upon a small woven rug. Then I lighted the kindling with my flint. When the fire caught I told Channa what she must do. She would lean her head over the smoke and I would cover her in fabric so none could escape. She was to breathe deeply and keep the smoke inside her for as long as she could without taking another breath.

Channa recoiled, afraid she would choke to death on the fumes. She feared me, perhaps sensing the crimes I had committed. But I wasn't there to do harm. I lifted Arieh back into my arms, and I hid the brand of my sin, slipping my hand inside the sleeping baby's tunic, hoping I would not taint him merely by my touch.

"Breathe in and the way will be clear," I promised.

Ben Ya'ir's wife looked at me reproachfully, then did as I said. Though she didn't trust me, she was desperate for air, willing to take the chance that the cure might be worse than the disease. She leaned forward, and I covered her head with a beautiful woven shawl. I sat watching as her shuddering gasps eased during the time she breathed in smoke. When the myrrh had burned to ash, I removed the fabric from her head. Channa drew a deep intake of air without any rasping. Her color had turned from sallow to rosy. The scent of myrrh clung to everything, a bitter fragrance in its purest form. We studied each other while the baby woke and happily began to play with a twig that had fallen from the kindling pile.

"I'll talk to the guards about a visit," Channa said thoughtfully. I.had the impression, however, that her thoughts were truly on other matters. "I'll do what I can for your slave."

She led me back down the hall, past the orange light and the seven sisters on the wall. When I left she asked me for a promise to bring her more of the herb, so she would have access to the medicine should another attack begin. I said I would try my best to locate what she needed.

"I think you know where to find it," she remarked.

She smiled grimly, clearly aware that I was not the one who possessed the knowledge regarding such remedies.

"Tell the witch I'm grateful," she said.

YAEL WAS ALLOWED to visit the Man from the North, bringing a basket of food and a goatskin of water. She was instructed to speak to him through the door, but she had a glimpse of him when they unlocked the cell to shove the provisions inside. She saw that they had cut off his beard and his hair and had left whip marks on him with their ropes and chains.

"Go back to the palace," Yael insisted after returning from this terrible visit. Her face was swollen with fury. "Talk to Ben Ya'ir's wife again. Convince her to insist that the guards allow another visit. They'll kill him soon enough. The least I can do is bring food and water, and see if I might heal his wounds."

I said I'd have more luck with Ben Ya'ir's wife if I took the baby with me.

Yael was cautious. In this way she was far wiser than I. "Why would she care about a baby whose name she doesn't even know?"

"She's lonely, friendless. There's nothing to worry about. She's taken a liking to him. Who can blame her?"

Yael accepted the compliment. She ran her hand over Arieh's black hair and held him close. She could hardly bear to let him go, even for a few hours.

"It's hard to say no to a face like his," I reminded her.

"For an hour," she said. "No more."

The following day Yael watched over my grandsons while I went to Shirah for more of the breathing cure. Shirah and Aziza had already begun to cook their evening meal, but Shirah rose and went to her collection of herbs. This time she gave me both myrrh and frankincense—burned together they would be twice the remedy. Perhaps if the cure lasted longer, Channa would not ask for more. It was best to keep our distance from this woman, Shirah murmured. The wife of a man in power could become hungry for power of her own.

"Did she say anything about me?" Shirah asked.

I thought it best not to reveal the bitterness inside the truth. "Nothing. She only sent her gratitude."

Shirah laughed, but her dark eyes revealed her worry. "Her gratitude is a curse. Remember that."

I WENT DIRECTLY to Eleazar ben Ya'ir's house. From where I stood, I could hear the men at work in the fields even though the light was fading into pink bands that struck the white, dusty earth, turning it red. The men had brought buckets of water from the cisterns, attempting to save the crop of wheat, for still there had been no rain. The bees in the hives were usually swarming at this time of year; they dove through the air searching for blossoms, white narcissus and pink cyclamen. But this season they found none. Channa let me in when I arrived and quickly took the cure from me. I told her that she must never add to the mixture, and that the flame must be kept constant; too much heat would take away the strength of the cure. In return, she promised she would speak to the guards. Then she hesitated.

"Is the slave the child's father?" she wanted to know.

"This child has no father," I said.

She motioned for me to turn the child into her arms, but I held tightly to the baby as I stood inside the hallway that was intricately patterned with black and white tiles. Voices echoed here. Annoyed, Channa motioned to me again. I knew what she wanted. I thought of Shirah's warning, but I understood what it was like to long for a child. How could Channa bewitch us or harm us? She was a slight, weak woman who lived under a cloud of illness. I didn't think it would hurt to please her for a moment. I placed Arieh in her arms. Instantly, she was overcome by his charm. "Perhaps he needs a father," she said with yearning.

I quickly took him from her, shifting him back into my arms. "He has a mother," I informed her. "He needs nothing more."

Channa smiled then. "Everyone needs more."

THOUGH WE ALL joined in to gather what little food we might spare, it was decided that Yael should be the one to continue to visit the Man from the North.

"He was always your slave," Aziza decreed.

Yael looked up, hurt. "No man should be so."

The next time she went to the tower they unlocked the door and allowed her to sit beside him. She was flooded with anger, appalled at the crude, filthy conditions of his incarceration. She would not say any more other than that when he leaned his head into her lap, and she stroked him where they had shorn his hair in such a cruel fashion, there were still beads of blood along his scalp. She brought a poultice of aloe and honey, the same remedy she had used for Arieh's mark, and if the salve did not ease his pain, at least it brought him the knowledge that someone had wished to do so.

Channa had kept her part of the bargain, she was honest enough in that. I hoped the slave's well-being was worth the price that was being paid, for every time in this month of the scorpion when Yael went to see the slave I brought the baby to Ben Ya'ir's house and let Channa hold him in her arms. I was wary and careful. I never once let him out of my sight. Each time I reminded Ben Ya'ir's wife that this child had a mother.

I told myself she was listening to me, but in truth, she hadn't heard a word.

OUR WORLD was punished by thirst. At this time of year, in the month of *Kislev*, we expected a greening of the land, fields that were seeded and watered, melons and gourds already growing on the vines, figs pollinated by Egyptian wasps. This season was different. There would be no cumin or coriander or leeks or anise. The fruit trees were bare and black.

Though the days were bleak and we wore our cloaks, there was no sign of the much needed rain. It was time to scatter seeds for the spring, then plow the fields to bury them, the donkeys pulling metal blades across the earth. The men ordinarily cut down the barley, which would then be tied into sheaves and spread in the field so that the livestock could walk over the stalks to thresh them. But without rain, what good would this do? To winnow the barley, the wind was needed to blow the chaff off the grain, and the air now was lifeless and dull. Seed must be set down during times of rain so it would be trapped in the earth rather than dry up and shrivel before it could take root.

The men from the synagogue called for public atonement and fasting in the hope that their sacrifice might cause the rain to fall. We were summoned to the plaza to pray for forgiveness. The women stayed in the back, so we could care for the children and the animals if need be. The men gathered together, forsaking their duties and chores, a sea of prayer beneath the unrelenting sky. The high priest, Menachem ben Arrat, usually cloistered inside the synagogue, where he studied and gave advice, now came to stand upon the wall and lead the men in prayer. But as learned as he was, he could not make it rain, not even when he buried twelve lead jars with ceramic stoppers beneath the synagogue walls to keep demons from escaping into our midst.

It was decided that our people would fast until God sent relief to us. The drought became a hammer, and our people's thirst was a nail beneath that hammer. Some of the older men were so weakened by hunger by the second day of the fast that they fell to their knees, but they continued to pray even then, their shawls around their shoulders, chanting to a heaven that would not answer their prayers but gave them only dust in return.

The fast was called off after three days. Nothing had changed. We had no choice but to wait for God to see our plight. The leaves of the grapevines curled up. The olives grew white then dropped from the trees, clattering onto the stones. People began to whisper about the water the Essenes used for their rituals. Guards were posted near the goat house to see what rites performed there might call for water. So as not to bring attention to themselves, our guests asked for no more. Instead they took to reusing their water until the drops they laid upon their heads to purify themselves were as black as the feathers of ravens.

When Yael thought no one noticed, she pilfered some of the water we were to use for the doves. Some she gave to the slave, the rest I helped her carry to the stone house to place in her friend Tamar's hands. We brought some withered fruit and olives as well. Nahara approached us shyly. Shirah's younger daughter appeared to have become a grown woman, serious, dressed in white, her hands hardened by work. She asked after her sister but said nothing of her mother. I noticed that she glanced at the gold amulet Yael wore at her throat, then just as quickly looked away.

In return for the gifts of sustenance we had brought, Tamar gave us a length of the pure white linen their women had woven. We covered our table at the Sabbath with the fabric when we lit our lamp and said the Sabbath prayers. Once we had arranged the linen on our table, we could almost believe our poor chamber was a home like any other.

ONE EVENING as I made my way to the looms, I saw Ben Ya'ir walking in the orchard through a white mirage of billowing dust. He had returned from his journeys into the desert, his warriors bringing back nothing but wild birds they had trapped with nets, as young girls might have. Our provisions were lower than they'd ever been, our people distraught. I could see the weight our leader carried on his shoulders from his posture, the fate of us all resting upon his words and deeds.

Where another might have seen only darkness, I noticed the shadow of Ben Ya'ir's wife, watching. I had begun to know her from my visits with Arieh, when we sat together exclaiming over his charms. She made the baby laugh with a show of silly faces while she bounced him on her knee. I had come to understand that Channa had a wall around her meant to keep others out. Yet every now and then, I saw the curl of a smile upon her lips. When she spoke Eleazar ben Ya'ir's name, her face transformed, and I could imagine her as the girl she had been. Her love for her husband was evident, though she seemed as far away from him as the rest of us.

I realized that, as he walked, Ben Ya'ir was gazing in the direction of Shirah's house. He was drawn there as the hawks were drawn to the dovecotes. It seemed he had called to her, for Shirah stepped into the liquid heat of the evening. She wore no veil, and she lifted up her hair as though to cool herself. When Ben Ya'ir went to her, he placed his hand upon her throat, for she clearly belonged to him. They stood in deepest confidence, heads together.

If I could see what was between them, surely Channa could as well. I turned to her, but in the instant I had looked away, she'd vanished from the plaza. She ran so fast that her shadow was left behind. I followed it as the shade chased after its mistress, slinking over the cobblestones. At last I spied our leader's wife winding her way back to her chambers, the palace where Herod's son had lived once, a son the king had murdered when it suited him to do so, when he placed his needs before all others, as men in power often do.

As she reached a hillock, I saw Channa glance back at Shirah's house. Her eyes were bitter and black. She held one hand at her chest, for once again she could not breathe. Yet she remained there, though it was the season when she was known to lock herself away, for the hyssop was blooming—it was the single flower that could survive a season without water. In that instant, as her shadow fastened itself to her flesh, I realized that Channa was the sort of woman who was willing to do anything to keep her husband.

It came to me that, of all the spells known on earth, a child was the one ingredient that could bind a man to a woman in ways only the angels could understand.

WHEN I NEXT went to see Ben Ya'ir's wife, I did not bring Arieh. I had rethought our bargain and realized my error. Channa's face registered disappointment. Her eyes flashed as they had when I'd seen her on the hillock without her shadow.

"He was cranky," I told her. "A tooth is coming in."

If anything this news made her even more eager to see him. "Poor thing," she whispered. "If only I could hold him, I could soothe his pain."

I felt a chill when I saw her expression. I wondered if the pact I'd made with her had given too much away in order to help the

Man from the North. The next time I went I told her Arieh was too heavy for me to carry, he was growing so fast, and I could not bring him with me again. She said nothing. Not even good-bye. She showed me to the door and closed it behind me. I heard the lock clack shut.

Not long after, I saw her prowling along the wall near our chamber. It was dark, but I recognized her. I was surprised to see her there, she who kept to herself and usually avoided the plaza. But such things are known to happen; what is sweet draws out what is sour, as the good, in all their innocence, beckon the wicked. They say that Lilith has thirteen demons to assist her when she wishes to steal a baby. One of them is the Night herself, cloaked in starry black, able to vanish in an instant in the breaking light of day, yet still lingering without a shadow outside the door.

AT LAST Shirah fashioned the charm for my grandsons. I had been patient, and my patience was rewarded. Now that the time had come, I was anxious, for this was my last hope. Beyond that hope lay a cliff, and then nothing more than the unforgiving air. The charm was an incantation bowl, a beautiful, delicate piece of pottery, the making of which had been taught to Shirah by an ancient Babylonian woman. Upon the dried clay the names of God in Aramaic and in Hebrew had been written. In the center of the bowl there was the black image of a snake-headed demon with wings, shackled with ropes constructed from the letters of God's name.

This amulet shall gather voices and bind demons and set angels free to do what they must. In praise of God. Amen Amen Selah.

She had written these words inside a circle of angels, their wings pitch black, the feathers of ravens.

To protect and to heal, to return what belongs to the children, to reverse the effect and render the demon without a voice and without power.

"Place this under the bed and wait. Have patience still," she instructed me. "One ingredient is missing. Because of that this bowl is powerless. I myself cannot say what is missing, but when it appears, you'll know. Be quick to add it into the bowl and your son-in-law will have his wish."

I was nothing but a baker's wife, a mother without a daughter, a fool who had placed a baby in an envious woman's hands. How could I possibly recognize the most important ingredient of all?

"You'll know because it will come on the day I am in irons," Shirah told me.

THE MEN who practiced magic took to the plaza one dusty day. It was the end of winter and the drought continued. Our people seemed cursed. The priest and the rabbis had failed, and now the *minim* who practiced outside the laws of the Temple claimed that by casting arrows they could divine the cause of the drought. People believed them because there was little else to believe. They were parched, beaten down, desperate for water. Surely someone was to blame for our anguish. The crowd gathered around those practitioners who claimed to have access to God's truth. The men circled near, and behind them came the women, and then the children with sticks and stones in their hands. There was a line of fury on the ground, slithering forth. Someone would be blamed, we all felt that. Our people wanted more than a demon. They wanted flesh and blood, someone to turn against, someone on earth.

Many have said that the angel of rain comes to women in their dreams. It is Beree who causes them to cry when they feel they have nothing left inside, no soul, no tears. Perhaps this is why Shirah did not appear at the dovecote on this day. Beree had visited her before and now he had returned to whisper that she should prepare herself. The morning came and went, still Shirah remained in her chamber. She plaited her hair, drew on her black cloak and her veils, slipped on her amulets. Barefoot, she did not eat or drink or speak all that day. She sat at her table readying herself for the vision that had appeared to her when she first came to the fortress. She had seen herself in chains, in a season when the rain refused to fall.

The arrows thrown by the *minim* pointed directly to what had once been the kitchen of the king. The house of the Witch of Moab. She was waiting for the diviners at her threshold, her cloak held close. Exactly as she had predicted, she was shackled and led away.

I knew this was the day when the incantation bowl would be complete, for Shirah had vowed the missing ingredient could be added only when she was in chains. I could not attend to the spell, however. I fled the dovecote with Yael and Aziza when we heard news of Shirah's captivity. Together we rushed to the plaza. There was a crush of people, and the flare of overheated rage striped the air. People wanted a reason which might explain why God had turned against us, why the leaves on the trees were singed, why the olives were white and unripened, why we had only thirst until we were gasping, like fish upon the shore. They believed they now gazed upon that reason.

Watching the crowd engulf her mother, Aziza had to be restrained to guard that she wouldn't rush to Shirah's side and perhaps be held to blame as well. Yael grasped one of her arms, and I the other. She was stronger than I would have ever imagined, but Yael managed to calm her.

"Have faith," she urged, whispering to Aziza so no one could overhear and accuse them of plotting. The gold talisman glinted at Yael's throat, and her face was serene despite the chaos.

They say a witch's enemies must hold her in the air and separate her from earth if they wish to undercut her power, but when the *minim* tried this, Shirah laughed at them. The men lowered her and backed away, confused. They had no idea that water, not earth, was her element.

"There is no one but *Adonai*," Shirah declared to those who had accused her of bringing God's wrath down upon us. Her voice carried. We who had come from the dovecote faced her and were convinced she was speaking directly to us. Children in the crowd quieted. Several women Shirah had helped in their time of need glanced away, embarrassed not to offer their assistance in return. People whispered that Menachem ben Arrat, the high priest, had come to his doorway but had feared the witch's powers so that he came no farther and neither condemned her nor joined in the fray. Beside me Aziza shivered, but there was a proud cast to her eyes.

Eleazar ben Ya'ir appeared out of the crowd, on his way from the barracks, at first puzzled by the scene before him, then understanding when he saw Shirah in chains. He commanded she be allowed to go free. When the men who held her hesitated, he shouted, "Are you made to attack one of our own? A woman of my own family? We have real enemies who would like nothing better than to have us murder one another."

There was a moment when it seemed the crowd would not comply with his command. That moment passed, and at last one of the elders went forward with the key, but the threat of chaos had been there, hanging in the air, the instant when our people might have turned against their leader. An angry mob was not easily controlled, and a serpent sent by rioters offered a bite for which there was no healing.

This fortress would have fallen in the fever of that dishonorable instant had it not ended as coal fire is quenched by water. Our enemies would have had no further need to destroy us had the mob not backed away, for we would have destroyed ourselves. There had been several sightings of Roman soldiers nearby in the past weeks. The legion knew we were here, and they knew how well defended we were in our protected site. But they had no idea that we could so easily turn on one another, and that Ben Ya'ir's will was all that held us together, keeping us one.

I saw the great man's wife watching from where she stood beside the hyssop. It was Channa who had directed the *minim* to the witch. If she was disturbed to see that her husband now acted as Shirah's protector, she didn't let on. Her face was dark and impassive. Perhaps she had expected as much. Her breathing, usually so ragged, was perfectly even, and there was a flush of health in her face. I imagined she was gazing at the one who had cured her, but she was looking past Shirah, past her husband, to the child in Yael's arms. I felt a chill along my spine.

Now that she had been freed, the shackles loosened, Shirah grabbed for a stick and formed a circle in the dust.

"You wanted me here," I overheard her say to Ben Ya'ir. "Was it not for this, cousin?"

She stood within the circle, then reached inside her cloak to bring forth ashes, which she sprinkled on her head, chanting as she did so in a low, even tone. The crowd strained to hear and were frightened by a language they didn't understand. Many among them believed she was bringing a curse upon us and hung back, drawing their children near to protect them from evil.

It began all at once, before we understood what was happening. The sky paled and turned incandescent. Rains begin in different ways, but this was a torrent that had no equal. One moment the earth was dust, and the next lakes were forming. The world became wet and luminous, brimming with sheets of water. I had never before noticed that rain contained every color within itself, green as the fields, blue as heaven, white as a lamb, yellow as my daughter's hair.

Men sank to their knees, raising the fringes of their prayer shawls to their lips and then to the heavens to offer praise to God and to the mystery of life. We could hear the goats and the sheep in their pens. Before our eyes the living fence of thorns that held back the livestock gave forth buds, and then, as if commanded by the Almighty, those buds unfurled to become leaves.

People whispered this was the reason the Witch of Moab had been able to walk across the Salt Sea without drowning. She, who had slipped down a thousand steps into the cistern to bathe in the dark, was our salvation. I blessed her for this as I raced through the blasts of wind, hurrying to our chamber for the incantation bowl she had cast. I was only a simple woman, but I recognized the missing ingredient exactly as Shirah had assured me I would.

I brought the bowl outside and held it above my head, chanting to the Almighty, singing His praises though the wind was in my face, its roar filling my ears. The bowl overflowed, and my heart did as well. I could hear my grandsons calling to each other as I stood there dripping with rain, as joyful as I'd ever been. Their voices had been caught inside the waterfall all this time, stored in a vessel by the angel who had protected them from evil. Now those voices had been released, drawn toward the prayers in the bowl as the angel Beree rained down upon us. Later, I would bring them before their father, and although the children would shrink from his fierce form, when I urged them to speak a greeting, I would see the Man from the Valley weeping in gratitude. Perhaps his faith would be restored by this gift, as mine was.

I heard the voice of God all around me, but I was unafraid. I should have trembled before the Almighty and hid myself from sight. I should have taken a knife to my own flesh to cut away the mark of my past deeds. But now I understood that, although words were God's first creation, silence was closer to His divine spirit, and that prayers given in silence were infinitely greater than the thousands of words men might offer up to heaven.

I listened to the wind that had risen in the desert to follow us here.

I heard what it had to say.

Winter 71 C.E.

Part Three

Spring 72 C.E.

The Warrior's Beloved

You are my armor and my sword, my faith and my treasure, everything I'm fighting for.

My sister, you are like the dove, so beautiful and so distant, the child I saw born into this world as I crouched beside our mother. You are the reason I refuse to witness another birth. The cord of life was wrapped around your neck, and when I looked into your eyes I saw the World-to-Come, a place so distant and vast no one alive should ever view its reaches. You were gasping, turning blue, a fragile creature drawn into our fragile world. I was only a child myself, unwanted, brought into the marriage between our mother and your father in the land of Moab, where the women wore blue veils and no one knew what our mother had been, or what she would become, though they feared her all the same.

Because our mother was a foreigner, none of the women we lived beside came to help when the time for you came upon her. They arrived at other times, when their own needs drove them to appear in the dark, searching for curses or cures. They brought delicacies of lamb and herbs and olives in beautiful pottery dishes, clay bowls decorated with dark red designs. These women came to beg for our mother's magic when they needed it. She was kind enough to offer the barren among them love apples, the yellow fruit of the mandrake that ripens with the wheat, so that they might conceive. She gave them a healing poultice made from figs for rashes and boils and, in the most sorrowful cases, brought them her knowledge of *tzari*, the ancient Syrian cure used for leprosy, the illness wherein the flesh is consumed by demons and falls away from the bone. Yet when she was the one in need, the women of the camp hid themselves from view, terrified that our mother might bring another witch into the world, and that her power would double. Then, despite their aversion to her and their bloated grudging jealousy, they would all be forced to drop to their knees before her.

I was the only one to witness the occasion of your birth, and if the truth be told I, too, wished to run into the daylight, afraid less of witchery than of blood. There were pools of it, and the gushing heat of it terrified me. This liquid was alive, pulsing with the power of creation. I was too young, too innocent to be of help. But our mother cried out *Save her*, her words like stars, brilliant and stinging.

I did what I could. I unwound the cord. But that was not enough, so I breathed into your mouth and drew out the liquid that was drowning you. I tasted blood and salt, everything life is made of, and spat it upon the ground. It is a miracle when you know what you must do without any instruction, and that is what happened to me at the hour of your birth. This mysterious knowledge was granted to me by God in the time of my desperation, and for that I will always be grateful. I took your death and your life into myself. In that moment we became one being, sisters claimed by the same force. Because of this I will always look after you. Even if you try to break away, you will find you cannot leave me.

These days you turn from me in the fields where the almonds will soon flower. You insist you belong elsewhere, but I will not abandon you. I see you dressed in white linen, in the rocky field, tending to six black goats, your head bowed, your feet bare, and I weep to see you taken from me in your fervor and your desire for a man who can never know you as I do. Perhaps you do not wish for him to know you. You keep your back to me and will not speak, not even when I knock on the rough wooden door of the goat shed where you live beside the people you've chosen as your own. They are paupers whose only desire is to praise the Almighty with prayers for peace, even though outside the confines of our fortress the world snarls with war. You will not sit at our table, for our practices are not as strict as those you now revere, and our ways are unclean in your eyes.

I sent a dove to you, one that was pure white, a favorite of our mother's, thinking this creature would fill you with remorse and you would follow him, but the bird returned to the dovecote with my message unread. Inside the tube I had attached to the bird's leg I wrote your name and mine intertwined, as our fate intertwined at the moment of your birth. I cannot imagine whom I could ever love more in this world we walk through.

When I see you at the wall, at prayer with the Essene women at the hour when day becomes night, you don't glance at me, though my breath is inside you and yours is a part of me. No matter how you refuse me, our spirits combine to form a single thread. Even if you never speak to me, or raise your eyes to me, even if you are ashamed of me and of our past.

You are mine and mine alone.

YOUR FATHER was a wealthy man, and he knew what he wanted. Had this not been so, had he not traveled to Jerusalem from the far shore of the Salt Sea, our mother and I would have perished, cast out on the day I was born. I had no sister to comfort me as you did on the day of your arrival in this world, only the taste of my own blood in my mouth.

The man who was to be your father had come such a great distance to trade the riches he had amassed, piles of black myrrh and balsam, spices in heaps of ocher and red, baskets of frankincense grown from the white star flower of Edom, salt from the sea, limestone from the cliffs. Perhaps an angel stopped him on the street and whispered in his ear, suggesting that he turn his head. He wore a long scarf and the blue robes of his people, which were dyed with the root of the ginger plant. Although he was far from young, his eyesight was sharper than a falcon's and he took note of my mother's great beauty. Among the men he rode with, he was known for seeing what others could not. That may be why he spied us in a cart meant for sheep brought to the butcher as we were driven into the wilderness. The Angel of Death was waiting for us—*Mal'ach ha-Mavet*, who has a thousand glinting eyes—but he was defeated when your father followed us.

Your father gave the driver a handful of coins that he himself deemed worthless. He was a man who believed what mattered came from the earth, not from the treasuries of a temple or the workshops of men. He took us with him that very day, destined for the east, the ancient land across the Salt Sea, where the mountain is made of iron and mounds of black asphalt float along the shore, setting themselves on fire when the heat rises. Your father's people collected nets full of asphalt to sell at a high price to the legion so that the soldiers might forge paved roads in Alexandria and Rome.

Our mother confided that when she saw the black sea she didn't know if we'd been rescued or forsaken by this fierce, silent man whose arms were ringed with blue tattoos and who marked his own face with scars he had cut with a thin knife to commemorate his many battles. She feared he was bringing her to Gehennom, the valley of hell. In fact we journeyed from Judea to Moab, a kingdom that had been ruined and deserted more than once but that was now in full flower. Many of the tribesmen of this land refused to stay in one place but instead called every corner of their country home. This was the land Ruth had come from when she followed Naomi into Judea, though her people had cursed ours. From her line our great King David was born, a gift to his people and to the world. The land here was green, the earth rain-spattered even when other countries were aflame with heat, the vistas lush with fields of grass. There were acacias in bloom, the tree God asked be made into the Ark of the Covenant so that its strong and fragrant wood might house His word to mankind. Myrtle bushes grew tall in Moab, and there were spills of wild cassis. The bursts of yellow iris made it appear as though sunlight had spilled across the land as a blessing.

Your father and his kinsmen lived in the hills, made wealthy not only by the sale of asphalt but by the treasures they seized from caravans that traveled the King's Highway from Damascus to Egypt. Stolen goods some might say, but in the eyes of the tribesmen, these treasures were a simple payment, taken as their just due, for their homeland was the route connecting two nations. A robber is a king in his own land, that is what your father believed, the lord of his own mountain. Every man in this region was said to be born with a knife in his hand, a horse already chosen for him, and a prayer to offer to his God.

My mother was still bleeding from my birth when they stopped to make camp the first evening. All the same she wrapped me in cloth and laid me in a hollow, so that your father could make her his wife that night. To celebrate their marriage, he gave her a pair of earrings set with rubies. Anyone in Jerusalem would have known why she was marked by tattoos, a swirl of henna-red inkings upon her flesh. From the time she was a child, she had been trained to be a *kedeshah* in Egypt, a woman meant for the holy use of the priests, as her mother before her had been. But such things had become secret and outlawed. Our mother had been sent out of Alexandria, to be raised by her kinsmen in Jerusalem. She never managed to return to the city where her mother longed to see her again, waiting by her gate for her only daughter's return.

Our grandmother whom we never knew gave our mother two gold amulets for protection. On one was written *Chayei 'olam le-'olam—Eternal life, forever*—the gold imprinted with images of the sun and the moon. On the other the words *I have placed the eternal always before me* were inscribed; on the back of the medallion a fish had been engraved, to ensure that the wearer would always be near water, the most precious element, the giver of life.

Although our mother was sent to Jerusalem for her safety, she was repudiated for her sins there, accused of seducing a man who was married. It was claimed she had been wed both to him and to a demon. When the case was brought before the priests by the man's family, my mother refused to admit any wrongdoing. The *sotah* ceremony was held, in which God's name is written on papyrus, then slipped into a tumbler, where it is erased into the water and mixed with the dust of the Temple floor, to be consumed by the suspected adulteress. My mother drank God's name and did not falter; still, those who opposed her considered her to be in league with the demons. She could deny her sin, but I was the evidence, held up by my heels before three judges. Perhaps when they examined me they were looking for proof that she had indeed slept with a demon, searching for horns or wings, to see if I was a *shedah,* the child of a watcher, an angel who had been called to earth by my mother's beauty, or if I had simply been born of the flesh.

The tribesman from Moab who was to become your father did not care about such matters. Judgments made by our councils were meaningless to him. Our God was not his God. Our mother's sin was not his interest. He knew what he wanted. He was simple in that way, yet he was complicated as well. As for me, I was little more than a mouse caught in a snare, a creature he allowed our mother to keep as a pet when they set off the next morning and she refused to leave me behind. The world was still dark on the day they left Judea, as the sea was, but before them the horizon was radiant, like a pearl. Our mother told me that, after they passed by the black mounds of burning asphalt in the Salt Sea, she was grateful we had not fallen into the fires of hell. She felt her heart lift at the sight of the mountains, which are green even when the rest of the world is dying of thirst. The lilies that grow there are red, and she still wears their perfume; a ceramic vial of their scent was one of the few belongings she took with us when we came to this fortress.

Perhaps when she wears the scent of the lilies she remembers the morning when we were given another life.

OUR PEOPLE believe that the world is split in two. On the side of goodness are the *malachim*, the thousand angels of light. On the side of evil there are *mazzikim*, demons who are uncountable and unknowable, uncontrolled even by the Almighty's wishes. Your father was both combined. We made camp in the mountains, above the pass that overlooked the King's Road from Damascus. Your father did not think twice before he swooped down with his men upon a caravan to take what he wanted, but he was shy with children and kind to our mother. Though he was a warrior, he could become flustered in the presence of our mother and hardly knew what to say to her. His eyes burned when he gazed at her, and he often sent everyone from our tent so he could be with her, even in daylight hours. He had other wives who lived in a far valley, women whose names we never heard spoken aloud. Perhaps he loved them, too. Surely he could not look at them in the way he gazed at our mother. She was his favorite. Because of this, we were safe with him.

Then on a night I can hardly remember, before you were born, bandits came into our tent, nomads who had no law and no gods.

They came as thieves, but when they saw our mother, their purpose changed. She was so beautiful with her long black hair, still so young, and there were those who said she possessed the ability to hypnotize a man with one look, as she could heal the sick with a single word of prayer. She told me that, as they held her down, one of the intruders swept me up, though I was yet a little child, thinking he would have me as well, tearing off my tunic. I don't remember the screams she vowed I cried, furious wails that recalled the shrill cries of a mouse when it is caught and struggling in a trap, but my throat hurt anew when she told me the story of that night. She disclosed this account only once, when we left Moab to travel to Masada. I tried to remember every word she said. I knew she would not tell me again.

Just as I knew that night was the reason for my fate and for who I had become.

YOUR FATHER, alerted by his kinsman that there were intruders, returned before he was expected, his blue scarf over his dark, scarred face. He was like a whirlwind. Our mother held me close, hidden in her robes, while your father killed each of the thieves. The crude, keening sounds he made were terrible, like the wind when it falls upon you. It was said people could hear him far to the south, where there was a city rising out of red rock, its great temple and carved columns a wonder to be seen. Many among us swore that he possessed the cry of a *mazzik*, a demon from another world.

After the struggle was over, your father was the only man left alive in our tent. My mother confided that outsiders often whispered that the blood of your father's people runs blue, and indeed they were a tribe so fearsome even the Romans avoided them. But I remember that he knelt beside our mother with great tenderness, even though he was slick with blood. When he did so, he seemed like one of the thousand who watch over our world, an angel who had rescued us from the wilderness.

After that night our mother cursed what it meant to be a woman. Her life had been molded by all she could not do and all she never would be. But there was a gift she had as well, one no man would ever understand. Her mother had given her a book of spells, magical recipes that would offer her protection while they were apart. She carried that manuscript with her, the most precious of her belongings, along with the gold amulets she wore around her throat, preferring them to all other jewels she might be offered. No protection against evil was stronger.

But what was magic on that night? My mother had tried to bind the vile intruders by reciting an incantation, but we'd had need of another sort of protection, one made of iron, a man, a sword, a rescuer. Our mother offered thanks to the Queen of Heaven for our salvation. Still, her blood was hot and she was unsatisfied. She wished she had been the one to wield the knife so that she might have slain the robbers instead of merely standing mutely by to watch your father do so.

It was on that night that our mother decided to change who I was. She took me with her when everyone else was asleep. Even the horses were dreaming, quick, powerful steeds, left to stand in place without need of a rope, loyal to their riders until the day they could no longer run. Most people of Moab rode camels, but your father's people owned the most beautiful and fierce horses, who were granted water only every third day so that they might have the great attribute of camels and be inured to thirst, their fortitude surpassing that of any of our enemies' horses. Our mother chanted the song of protection, then she began the naming rites to Ashtoreth. When you change your name, you change your fate as well. The person you had been vanishes, and not even the angels can find you. We stood on the Iron Mountain, beneath the red moon. There was no afterbirth to mark this occasion, no sacrifice to give back to the earth. Instead our mother buried her own monthly blood. Then she cut my arm and let three drops fall into the earth as an offering to the Queen of Heaven.

My arm burned, and I might have wept, but my heart was full when our mother proudly said I was not to be like anyone else. From that time forward only my mother and God would know of my past life. My name had been Rebekah, but that name disappeared on the night of our blood. I never heard it spoken again. As for your father, he allowed our mother her wish, as he had allowed her to take me with them through the wilderness.

From then on, I was a boy.

SHE CALLED ME Aziza, a name of your father's people. It can mean one who is beloved, but it also means one who is mighty and fierce. There are those who believe the name is an ancient word for archer, one who is never without a weapon, never at anyone's mercy. That was what our mother wished for me. The people who lived on the Iron Mountain worshiped a great goddess among their gods; they saw the strength in their own women as well. Now when I witness my sister working in the field with the Essene people, adhering to their strict ways, crooning to the goats that she herds, a servant calmly waiting for the End of Days as if she was nothing more than a passive and beautiful ewe herself, I think that flesh and grass are one and the same, so fleeting, changing before our eyes. My sister was made in the country where the sky gleamed silver and the men were fierce. Had her own father spied her walking in the dust behind the Essene men, her head lowered, he would have been ashamed. But no matter how you might bow before others, my sister, the bond between us will last all eternity, until we meet again in a place where nothing can separate us, as it was on the night you were born, in your father's tent, with my breath inside you and my life the thread that kept you in this world.

ೂ

ALL THE WHILE you were growing up, I was your brother. You followed me as the dove follows the fields of grain. I dressed in blue robes, my hair caught up, then tightly braided in the fashion of young boys. Your father taught me to ride a horse, how to use a slingshot and a spear. I was a natural warrior, made for iron. It was my element from the start. Rather than frighten me, it brought me comfort. Metal was cold and heavy and reliable. It did as I asked. In return I was dedicated; there was never a day when I did not speak my gratitude to the sword I carried and the horse I rode.

Evil spirits have an aversion to metal, and there are those who whisper that the name of iron when invoking it before the Almighty is *Barzel*, what some believe is a combination of letters taken from the names of the matriarchs of Jacob's family, Leah, Rachel, Bilhah, and Zilpah. Weapons are kept from women, but such a naming suggests that perhaps men fear our talents in war as well as our desire for peace. I was watched after by the grace of the foremothers of our tribe, Rachel and Leah, but I did not walk the same path they had traveled. I never learned what it meant to be a wife. I never worked a loom. I did not go with the girls to welcome births, and for that I was especially thankful. Your birth was enough for me.

I preferred to be your father's son, waiting with the horses in silence while the men made their attacks. I held on to the reins as the warriors crept down on foot along the narrow pass to attack caravans traveling west toward Egypt, the carts and fearless horses laden with goods from the east. I helped carry piles of frankincense, strands of lapis and coral and jade, baskets of cardamom and cassia, purses filled with bars and coins of gold. I saw more blood on the ground than any of the girls witnessed at the birthings. I knew things they could not begin to understand: how it felt to ride through the hot night with a spear upon my back. How we swooped across the Iron Mountain, one creature, with one heart, hollering war cries, slick with sweat, darting beneath the moon. On these occasions it was possible to imagine that I had wings and was free as any bird of prey, fierce as any man.

My secret became my daily life. Our mother made certain that I bathed alone. When my breasts began to show, she bound them with a swathe of linen. That binding made me stand up straight, my full height, so that I might have been cast of iron rather than flesh. I could hit harder than the boys. I was faster, as well, and more nimble with a sword. In time your father grew proud of me, almost as if I was his own, as if our lie was the truth. At night our mother taught me to read and write. I learned Greek and Aramaic and Hebrew. There were girls who teased me and pursued me, as they did all the boys they admired. One kissed me during these games, and I laughed, thinking her a fool. I was above such matters. And yet I was confused, for when my friend Nouri pulled me away so we could flee from the girls, my blood raced. When he grabbed me, his fingers upon my arm stung, as though he'd burned me without meaning to.

I went to our mother and wept, like any other silly girl, as I told her what had happened. I fought the urge to be close to Nouri, but he drew me to him, as steel calls to steel. Our mother said it was time for me to understand I could never be like those heedless sheep who chased after boys. She told me she had seen my fate. Love would be my undoing. She whispered that she didn't tell me this out of cruelty, but out of concern. She had thrown down stones on the day of my birth, and my fortune had appeared on the ground before her, a warning she now shared with me, as her mother had once shared the divination of her future with her. I was not to look at boys or think of them as anything but brothers. On the day that I did so, my fate and my undoing would claim me. There were tears in our mother's eyes as she instructed me. I knew she wanted what was best for me and did not doubt her.

Not yet.

It was easy to give her my promise on that day. She embraced me and called me *daughter*, a dangerous slip of who I had been and was no more.

I AVOIDED Nouri after that, though he was clearly hurt that I had abandoned him. I didn't think about his handsome features, the way his face broke into a sudden smile. He wasn't as good a rider as I anyway; he would never have kept up with me. I was the best among the boys of my age, fearless. When I unbound my breasts to bathe, I felt the wings above my shoulders, twining through the bone, the secret of my gifts, a legacy from the one who was my father, whoever and whatever he might be. I half-believed he might be an angel, for there were such luminous divine creatures, winged, gliding messengers from God, who were said to become entranced with women on earth and visited them in the night, joining themselves to human flesh.

I rode with the cry of your people in my throat as I chased down rabbits and the shy hyrax who burrow in the rocks and prowl the thickets. I practiced my skill to impress your father, killing my first ibex when I was ten. He said nothing when the ibex stumbled and fell, but I could see what he felt in his expression as I helped to butcher the animal. It was *Adar*, the time when ibex calves are in the grasslands, but I had killed a huge male. Your father touched my forehead in a blessing for my skill. From a man of such silence, this was high praise.

I was glad to be a boy in this world of men and to be granted a great honor when your father allowed me to ride beside him. I burst into each day, my black hair braided, my cloak the indigo blue of your father's people. But our brother had been born, and as he grew everything changed. It was Adir our father looked upon with pride. Perhaps he really had forgotten who I was for all those many years, and only now recalled it was a girl child my mother had refused to leave behind on the first night of their marriage, before we reached the land of Moab and changed who I was meant to be.

IN THE RAINY SEASON, when there were no caravans, the men journeyed back to other villages, other wives. Your father and his kinsmen never stayed in one place but instead rolled down their tents and set off across the land, leaving their families on the Iron Mountain, visiting other wives and children far from our camp. They rode so far their shadows could hardly be seen by humankind. We stayed behind with the goats and the white-fleeced sheep. There were hundreds in the flock, all adding to your father's wealth, and they needed tending. The acacia trees were abloom with yellow flowers, and the fields of grass were so tall we could disappear and never be seen when we ran across the meadow. At night the bats flew together in one dark cloud, dropping down to the trees to drink the juice of the figs. The air was mild, and the rain turned the air the same shade of blue as the cloaks your people wore.

Our mother did not complain that we stayed behind on the Iron Mountain when your father went off. She had other attachments. When our mother was cast out of Jerusalem, I was not her only pet. She had also brought along two doves, and she was devoted to them. They perched inside a wooden cage and were fed grain and dates. When they drank water, they lifted up their heads as though praising God. Our mother sent them out one at a time, slipping messages into bronze tubes attached to their legs. The doves lifted into the western sky as she tossed them upward, vanishing in a blink. They always returned to her. In time their children and grandchildren did so as well, following the same mysterious route.

Our mother would wait for their return as dusk fell across the mountains in blue bands. She said the color of the sky reminded her of water, and of the land where she had been a child, before she was sent to Jerusalem. She yearned for the city of Alexandria, a place where the rivers were filled with miraculous creatures and monsters alike, where her mother had sung her to sleep with the same songs she offered us now. Throughout the years we were in Moab, she remained solitary. Perhaps she was thinking of the city of her birth. Perhaps that was why I often saw her weeping.

When one of the doves reappeared, our mother would become utterly absorbed. If you called to her, she would not hear your voice. If a bee lit upon her hand, she wouldn't take notice. Unlike your father, who was satisfied, I understood that our mother yearned for something more. Still I couldn't quite fathom her expression, not while I stood there barefoot, dressed as a boy. Only now do I understand. She was a woman in love.

Throughout the years we lived with your father, she was sending messages to another man, the one who was my father. Once I found a missive he sent back to her, written on a tiny scrap of parchment, smaller than a thumbnail. I knew then that an angel was not involved in the matter of my birth, for angels come to us in dreams and visions, not upon parchment. Our mother thought she had folded the note into her book of spells, but instead the message had dropped into my path. Perhaps the angels did indeed set it there, so I would know the truth about my origins, or perhaps a demon plucked it from between the pages. *My true wife* had been written. My mother had taught me the language of scholars, and because I could read Hebrew, I knew of her betrayal of your father, the man who taught me everything I knew, how to ride and how to hunt and how to be loyal to those I loved.

I tossed the parchment into the bonfire that night. As I did, it flew up like a wasp to sting me. There is a mark, beneath my left eye, that remains from that time. Because of this I can never forget what I found. Sometimes people imagine I am crying, they believe they've spied a tear, but they're wrong. I spent the first part of my life without tears, as any boy would. The mark beneath my eye is made of fire. It's the single element that can overwhelm iron.

WE STAYED until the summer when I turned fourteen. I knew that I bled even though the boys I ran with did not, but that did not change who I was, the fiercest among them, the rider with wings, Aziza, who carried both compassion and power within. I merely had to keep my blood secret, as I was to keep my body from view. The women here were not considered *niddah* when they bled, so I was not committing any true sin when I keep my secret and stayed among people during that time of the month. On hunting trips I insisted I was a restless sleeper and needed to make camp alone. When the others relieved themselves, I joked that I was a camel and could hold my water for days, waiting until I could sneak off on my own.

By then your father had given Adir a fine horse, the one I'd trained upon, no longer mine. Now I rode an old white stallion whose time had passed and who would never again win a race no matter how I might kick at him. Your father's people were moving south, to Petra, giving up their traveling ways. The city that had arisen from the red rocks, taken from the edge of the deep, nearly endless ravine, had begun to call them to its great beauty and the settled life they might have there. There was a pool reputed to be larger than any lake and terraced gardens that were incomparable. It was said that every wanderer came home to this place, and that even these wild men who longed for freedom, who had spent their lives in pursuit of open grasslands, could not ignore the voice of Petra. And there was another reason—the Romans might attack our camp, despite their pledge of peace and their fear of the legendary courage of the tribesmen. There was a rumor that, should any blood be spilled upon the iron cliffs of Moab, a dozen men would spring from the blood of the first. Perhaps the men were tired from their shifting homes, their many wives, and were eager for a single residence and a life of ease.

My mother pleaded with your father to let us remain in the mountains when he and his brothers and uncles answered the call to Petra. We could camp with those who were stationed to guard against the legion, should the Romans change their peace with the tribesmen into war. She said her spirit could not be contained in a city, even one so glorious. She told her husband she had become accustomed to this tent and to these stars, but I knew that wasn't the truth. There was something more. Something your father had not seen, though he had the keen sight of a falcon. Something only a woman would notice. In that way, I was still female enough.

On the day the women began to pack up the camp, pulling down the tents, gathering their kettles and their rugs, a dove arrived. I saw it float down among us as if it were a part of the sky that had wrenched away to plummet to earth. There was a violet chill in the air, and I gazed up in alarm, unsettled by the dove's arrival. I had the sense that everything was about to change and that the past was already smoldering into ash. Our mother had asked to stay behind, but your father had refused her request. He wanted her with him. He told her to take all of the belongings that mattered to her, for she might never come to the Iron Mountain again.

Our mother went up to the mountaintop with the bird in a basket, so that she could be alone to read the words that had been sent to her. I don't know what the message was, but when she returned to camp her expression was set.

We packed up, and it seemed we would be leaving for Petra in the morning, but my mother did not wait for the sun to rise. She woke me the instant your father set off with his brothers to ensure that the route to the city would be safe for the women and children who followed. As soon as he was gone, we readied Adir's fast horse. We had my father's great racehorse as well, for he had taken one of the mares, leaving his own steed behind for my mother, a mark of his devotion to her. The horse was called Leba, a name which meant heart. He was an animal so loyal he would never have gone with us had he not known me so well, but I had often fed and watered him. I'd always wished he would be mine someday, though I knew your father would never give Leba to me. Adir was the true son.

We took only the doves in their wooden cage and a single woven satchel of our belongings, along with a leather bag of water, and another bag of yogurt and cheese. I saw my mother reach for the book of spells from her mother and the ironwood box in which she kept the journal. She wore the gold amulets that had been given to her in Alexandria when fate seemed unlikely to bring her to Moab, and the earrings your father gave to her on their wedding day. She left behind all of the rest, masses of jewels your father had presented to her. There were jade necklaces, turquoise and gold bracelets, silver and lapis beads, gold rings set with precious gems none of us had seen before, some of which, rare opals, moved, incandescent, containing both water and fire within the stones. She laid out the jewels tenderly and with gratitude on the pallet where they had slept, but she showed no regret. Your father was the man who had rescued us but not the man she loved.

OUR MOTHER'S FACE was transformed all the while we rode west, as though she was young again. I had spent my entire life beside her; now she had become wholly unknown in a way I couldn't define.

It was true that you and our brother did not want to go. Adir sulked and fussed, and you called out for your father. You might have gotten us killed with your cries, but we rode so quickly that the wind took your voice up to heaven. We left the horses at the shore of the Salt Sea, so they might return to their rightful owner.

We weren't thieves. Your father's horse turned and raced back the way we had come. Adir's horse followed. In a flash they were gone. Only their hoof marks in the sand remained, and even that disappeared as we stood watching, for it now seemed that our lives in the tents had been a dream. If we ran back the way we had come, surely we would find nothing on the mountain where we'd lived for so long, not even ashes.

The only mark of that time was the scar beneath my eye.

PEOPLE SAY that our mother walked across the water and that Lilith's thirteen demons held the hem of her dress, but in fact we met a man with a flat boat. A simple, greedy man who wanted a high fee to take us across the water. He looked at my mother with his black eyes, happy to have her as his price. Instead, my mother traded the first jewelry your father had given her, the earrings she always wore. They were rubies from India, captured from a caravan of men who spoke a language no one had ever heard before. The rubies reminded me of your father, how pure they were, how elemental, so brilliant and red they seemed hot to the touch. I turned away, unable to watch this exchange. I had seen your father's blood shed on many occasions. Despite the Romans' rumors and stories, it had never been blue.

Before we left we gathered figs, along with a bundle of branches from the acacia trees. There was a storm rising, and the sea was filled with black lumps. They looked like stones set out to block our way. Our mother said not to worry. She swore that the water would heal and protect us; she had seen this as her own destiny. The boat rocked, and the man who rowed it uttered curses and fought with the sea. Still my mother was serene. Salt water splashed in our faces and threatened to blind us, but halfway across the sea turned calm, blue and then gray and then finally silver and still. The mountains of Judea were reflected in the water, floating before us. The vision made it appear that we had already reached our destination, though it was still a far journey. I caught the scent of fire and metal. My elements. My double life.

When we reached the other side of the Salt Sea, the boatman left us. In the silence around us, I felt I could hear the beating heart of the world, *lev ha-olam*, the center of creation in the distance of Jerusalem. We camped where we had been left, exhausted from our travels. At night, after you and Adir had fallen asleep on the damp sand, our mother motioned for me to follow. We made a fire from the acacia wood we had gathered on the other shore, the last acacia I would ever see that had taken root in Moab. My mother released her pet doves. Once they had disappeared, she added their cage to the fire and let it burn in a blur of flame.

Here in this emptiness, I could not stop thinking of the Iron Mountain and my life there, how I had imagined I was flying when I rode through the night with the troop of fearless raiders, how we had claimed everything we had come upon. I was fourteen, but I had killed several men. Afterward, I had burned the flowers of the acacia in tribute to each, as was the custom. Your father often brought back branches that were hung with hundreds of blooms for our mother. Although she thanked him, she wasn't partial to those beautiful boughs. She didn't appreciate the sweet nature of the flowers and how the bees were attracted to them. Those winged creatures understood the true essence of the acacia, the reason we burned it in honor of a soul. When acacia blooms are set aflame, they rise upward, in tribute to our God, who had made them.

The only thing that grew on this side of the Salt Sea was the Jericho balsam, a tree people say arose from the underworld that contains a flame inside an inedible fruit. Our mother took three of these fruits and cast them into the fire, and the flame turned yellow, like gold. She then told me to remove all of my garments. Because I dared not disobey, I did as she said.

I took off my leggings and tunic and then my cloak, along with the head scarf that was dyed the blue color of your father's people. Our mother burned it all. The fabric sent inky sparks into the sky. She unplaited my hair and combed out the knots with her fingers. I didn't complain, though it hurt. I said nothing and choked back tears. I had been told that at the beginning, when we first arrived, your father's people had whispered that he had brought back a witch from Jerusalem and that our mother possessed the power to entrance him. It was best not to look her in the eye, the women of our camp said, or to go against her. Now I wondered if perhaps they'd been right. I feared my own mother on this night. I stood there naked on the salt, my feet burning as she chanted in a language I did not understand, mud from the Salt Sea covering her arms and throat and face so that she appeared to be a demon herself. I felt unmasked, my breasts unbound, my hair so long it reached past my waist in a black sheet.

Our mother carried her small woven bag of belongings. When she reached inside, I dreaded what might be revealed. Perhaps a snake or a scorpion, or a knife meant to mark me a sacrifice, as Abraham had been commanded to bring up his only son, Isaac, before God. It took a moment for me to understand what she intended even after she revealed what she had brought with her from Moab. It was a skirt and a cloak made of silk that your father had given to her, a treasure from India, spun by butterflies. I dressed, slipping on the unfamiliar garments, along with a pair of fine leather sandals. It was dark that night, which was a good thing. I would not have been able to look at myself. I had become a stranger in my own skin. I still felt the wings above my shoulder blades, yet they seemed bound in a way they never had when there was a sheet of linen wound around me, concealing them.

Our mother and I said prayers together, those that are recited when a child is born and a human soul has entered into our world. It was the night when I became a woman, though I kept my name.

Aziza, the compassionate, the powerful. Aziza, the woman who knew what it was to be a man.

In the morning a messenger arrived from Masada. He had been made aware of exactly where we would be waiting. He gave us fresh water and food, then told us he was meant to lead us to safety. He looked at me in a way no man had before.

It was the first time in my life that I understood who I was to the rest of the world.

I made certain to lower my eyes.

EVEN NOW I am drawn to the ways of my old life. I spend as little time as possible inside the dovecotes. Doves do not interest me, no women's work does. I cannot weave or sew without pricking my fingers. When I cook, I burn the flatbread. My stew is tasteless no matter what ingredients I might add to the pot. There is not enough salt or cumin in the world to make my attempts palatable. I am clumsy at tasks my sister could complete with ease when she was a mere eight years old.

I often find myself beside the barracks, pulled there especially on the evenings that mark the new month, *Rosh Chodesh*, when the women gather to celebrate, for it is not with them I belong but here, alongside the warriors. When I find arrowheads, I hold them in the palm of my hand, talismans from my past. The blades fit perfectly in my grasp. Their cold, flat weight is what I yearn for. Metal alone can reach the center of who I am.

I have been in this fortress for so long, but I still dreamed of that other time, though I told no one, not even Amram, to whom I have pledged myself, despite my mother's warnings. Some things are meant to be kept secret, I learned that young, and I have kept our secret well. My mother may be flooded with doubts, but she has no proof that I have disobeyed. She's piled salt outside our threshold, so that I might leave footprints, but I leap over, leaving no trace. She's tied a strand of her hair across the doorway, but I merely crawl beneath it. I can outwit her at some things; all the same, I think of her prophecy every time I meet Amram. I am his, yet I know I have disgraced myself in keeping the truth from my own mother, the one who gave me life not once but three times.

From the start my sister was my accomplice. We had been here for nearly a year, working beside our mother in the dovecotes, when Amram first arrived. We spent days devoted to toil. The three dovecotes were like a family of goats—the father, built as a tower, then came mother and child, square and squat, small and then smaller yet again. They were my world then, as I avoided our neighbors and kept away from other women, afraid they would somehow see through to the differences between us.

When Amram arrived from Jerusalem at the beginning of the summer in the year the Temple fell, he was merely one more young man running from his enemies, convicted by his bloodline as well as by his actions, an assassin who could be seen as a murderer or a hero depending on who you were and where fate had placed you. I happened to be there, crossing the plaza. I was nearly sixteen, but still I kept to myself. I did not take note of any man until I saw Amram climb the serpent's path. He did so easily, as though the rugged cliffs were little more than a field. What was steep and difficult for others was for Amram no different than air to the lark. It was clear he could conquer whatever came before him, man or beast, even the land itself.

Watching him, I was almost ashamed of how handsome I found him. He was the warrior I wished I had become, fluid and lean, sure of himself. I envied him and wanted to possess him and all that he had. I remembered the way the dusk fell on the other side of the Salt Sea in waves of deep blue on the day my mother warned me of the prophecy that I should avoid love at all costs. But I was born to disobey her. I knew this when I found I could not look away from

Amram. I tried and failed, though I was iron and stronger than most in such matters. Aziza, the powerful, was somehow undone. Was there some angel or demon who remembered what my name had once been and now called me Rebekah from the reaches of heaven? I stood there like any other woman at the Snake Gate alongside all the rest who gathered there, charmed and seduced by Amram even before he reached us.

Perhaps the moment might have passed and I would have turned away and resumed my duties, if only he hadn't seen me as well, if we hadn't been transformed by a single glance that passed between us. I realized I had been caught from the moment I'd given in to my impulse to stand upon the wall to cheer him on. My intention was otherwise. Merely to view the sort of man I might have been in my second life. Instead, I became a woman in that instant. I gazed through the shimmering heat, watching his fate and mine twine together as he climbed the serpent path.

I WAS CURIOUS, drawn to him. When the rains came, I stood beside the armory, dripping wet, hoping to catch a glimpse of this man at the barracks. I circled the wall, in search of signs marking where he had walked: an arrowhead, a footprint, a strand of hair. When the dust rose I thought of him, when I gazed into the sky I was reminded of him, when I fetched water, ate my dinner, worked among the doves, all of it, no matter how trivial, brought him to mind. I would not have pursued him, but one day he stood in my path as my sister and I hurried to the dovecote. I raised a hand to shield my eyes so I could take him in and so that I might hide the mark beneath my eye. In that instant I was claimed yet again. He grinned, convinced he knew me, and I grinned back, knowing he did not.

Our mother was waiting for us. Had she been beside us, I would have been made to turn away. Perhaps everything that followed would have been different, but as fate would have it, she wasn't there, and for that I was immensely thankful. Nahara threw me a look when I told her to go on, but she did as I asked.

"You come this way every day," Amram remarked once my sister had gone.

"How would you know?" I spoke to him as I had once spoken to Nouri, as though I were an equal, not one who would bow before him.

"Because I watch you."

I felt the way I had when I was in the mountains, myself once more.

"Not as often as I watch you," I said, my grin widening.

Because I'd grown up among boys, I didn't have the guile of a woman. Amram laughed, surprised by my honesty. I suppose when I first kissed him, holding nothing back, I did so as a man would, unwound by ardor. If he was surprised by that, he was not displeased.

THE WOMEN in the fields gossiped about us. I heard their words, but such comments were nothing to me, wasp stings, grains of sand in my shoe. I let the sparks of their rude jealousy fall to the ground. None among them had the courage to seek out my mother and risk her anger with stories of my misbehavior.

We began to meet in the dark, beside the fountain in the Western Plaza. Whenever I was with Amram, my sister vowed I was beside her. She was my shield, my key to freedom, the little dove who carried the words I wrote for her to say when she went to tell Amram the hour when we could safely meet. I had rescued my sister once, now she repaid me. She often crossed the plaza with me in the evenings. We held hands and whispered like children, but when we neared the fountain, there came a point when she masked her eyes and I went on alone. If she did not witness our meeting, she would not be forced to tell an outright lie when she assured our mother she had not spied me with any man.

We found places to be alone, storerooms, gardens, the field late at night. Once again, as it had been when I gave my sister life, someone's breath belonged to me and mine to them. Amram swore he would keep our secret from my mother, and he was a man of his word. There were those who vowed that in Jerusalem he had been the most daring of the assassins, able to transform himself. His father, that great and fearsome assassin Bar Elhanan, was said to possess the ability to vanish while in plain sight. Perhaps he had shared this trick of invisibility, for Amram was able to slink past my mother, his presence little more than a cloud. We grew so brave we dared to meet in the cellar below our chamber, for there was a set of secret stairs in the floor of the old kitchen, and yet another that entered the cellar from the plaza. We slipped off our cloaks beneath the floor my mother stood upon. Perhaps I did so to spite my mother, to claim my life for myself and disprove her prophecy that love would only bring me anguish.

In our secret cellar, I tried my best to spy Amram in the dark scrim of shadows before he could see me. I could make out field mice in search of grain, and the drowsy forms of bats hanging from the ceiling, but Amram tricked me every time, grasping me before I knew he was there, sliding his hand over my mouth so I wouldn't cry out. I could have eluded his grasp easily and raised a knife to his throat before he blinked, but I told myself this was the game we played, hiding our true natures. Though he did not see me for who I was, though I should have known better, I never denied him anything. And yet I was dissatisfied.

He did not see through my veils, and I did not reveal my deepest self to him. Perhaps it was only to defy my mother, but by the time Revka arrived to work alongside us in the dovecotes, I had promised myself to him. Not long after his sister, Yael, came to work alongside us, I was his.

*

PERHAPS SOME secrets are impossible to keep, for it seemed my sins were written upon me. I was unwed, yet I knew what brides knew, how men groaned with passion, how they sometimes wept with all they felt, how their desire could bind them as tightly as the clothes I wore in this life—shawls and veils and cloaks—tying me to who I had become. Men eyed me rudely at the market when I stood in line for our rations of wheat and millet. They watched as I carried baskets of dung into the field and made suggestions I ignored. I was not like a ewe, there to take on the burden of their desires. I shouted to them that they should run home to their wives or their mothers. The very idea that I would bow to any man who chose to speak to me in such a manner made me a warrior once more. I let the shawl slip from my hair and shoulders, allowing my arms to shine bare in the sunlight. That was when the other women first began to whisper that I was one of the *sheydim,* a creature no one could control. In that they were correct. I did as I pleased, even though my mother had forbidden me to do so, even though it was a sin.

I began to wonder if there wasn't some merit in the field women's stories about me, if perhaps what set me apart from all others wasn't the life I'd led before I'd come here but was instead cast from the truth of who my father might be. Though he was not an angel or an incubus but a man who wrote upon parchment, I puzzled over his identity more often as time went on. I thought it odd that the messenger had known precisely where to meet us on the shore of the Salt Sea and that he had bowed his head to my mother, as though she were the wife of an important man. I wondered why, of all the places we might have gone in this world, we had come to this fortress and not another.

My mother would tell me nothing. She refused to divulge where she had sent the doves when she'd stood upon the Iron Mountain.

She denied having ever received messages in return, though the words that had been sent to her had burned me and I still carried their scar. All she would say was that she had been a girl who had followed the path the Almighty had set out for her.

"Would I ever be so coarse and full of myself as to ask God why He set me upon one path and not another?"

When she said this, her face was young and innocent. For once she, who was always so fierce, appeared vulnerable. My mother had taught me much. Because of her I could read more languages than most learned men, yet I knew little about her or about myself. Ever since Moab, our secrets had resembled a spider's web, one strand holding up the next. The words we did not say became the only things that mattered. We moved like spiders, circling one another, suspicious, waiting for whatever was to come next.

"Do I not have a path as well?" I asked, emboldened when she told me she had not questioned the direction in which God had led her.

She gazed at me thoughtfully. "One you must avoid at all costs."

That remark alone was enough to convince me I must find my own way.

AS OUR secrets forced us further apart, I kept to myself. Following my mother's lead, I confided nothing. I stayed in our chamber when she went to assist women in their labor, or ministered to those afflicted by fevers, taking her pitcher and bowl and a soap made of fat and ashes, insisting that the ill wash their hands to purify themselves. I did not accompany her when she went at night to the synagogue, where she would dig in the dirt to bury amulets in holy places for the protection of those who came to her in need. When my mother asked me to venture beyond the gate with her, to gather rue and marjoram and the yellow apples of the mandrake used for *pharmaka*, I had little choice but to obey. But even when I tried to honor her wishes, I was of no use to her. My hands weren't nimble. I tore at the leaves, and the fruit split apart in my hands. I hadn't the touch for sorcery. I owned none of the skills a woman must possess.

It was little wonder Yael took my place. My mother had chosen her to join us the moment she walked through the gate, as Yael followed behind her father, her head bowed, her red hair tangled with salt. Perhaps my mother was moved by her plight, which she divined as soon as she saw the sway in Yael's walk and the manner in which she covered her middle so carefully with her shawl. My mother had also been alone while she carried her first child into this world.

When Yael spoke her brother's name in the dovecote, I'd felt my blood race, fearful that my hidden life could be read in my expression. Here was Yaya, the sister Amram had spoken of so often, his childhood protector and friend. I should have pulled her aside to beg for stories of his boyhood, but I remained distant. I had no reason to put any faith in her or to trust her with my secrets. When she spied me with Amram at our meeting place, I waited for her betrayal, expecting her to reveal the truth to my mother, with whom she shared so many confidences. But she never spoke of it. Instead she took me aside to whisper that her brother was a fine man. Who I loved was not her concern.

Still, despite her kindness to me, she had become my rival. On the brutal day when my mother was taken to the plaza in chains, accused of witchery, Yael was the one who went to her, not I. She rushed to my mother, wearing one of the gold amulets from within our family, a gift that had always been presented by a mother to her daughter. I could see them through the sheets of rain, their arms entwined. I turned away and said nothing, swallowing the bitterness of my own jealousy.

I couldn't help wonder what else my mother had seen on the day I was born, if there had been an omen that had caused her to cast me aside, preferring a stranger to her own daughter.

THROUGHOUT the beautiful and mild month of *Adar*, Yael came to our chamber in the old palace kitchen in the evenings. She learned the spells my mother had been taught in Alexandria, along with Greek and Hebrew letters. They sat at the table, heads together, voices low so as not to wake Arieh, now nearly eight months old, who napped on the pallet where my sister had once spent her nights. I wasn't offended when they didn't think to include me. I had no interest in such matters. *Keshaphim* was nothing more than women's work in my eyes, with its recipes and its herbal remedies, no different than cleaning up after the doves, or spinning wool, or keeping the pots simmering on the stove. I had used it to protect Amram once, when he led his first raid from this mountain. But afterward I had felt unclean and had gone to the *mikvah* to purify myself.

And yet, as I watched them at their studies, I thought how much easier it would be if only I could do as my mother asked, if I could be the one to sit beside her, if it had not already been written that I was bound to disobey.

WHEN NAHARA left us, I was convinced she would return. I was the rebel and she the good daughter, my dear and trusted sister. In time I was certain that the Essenes' strict ways would grate upon her. Then she would remember she belonged to me.

But the season changed, the wheat grew tall, and still there was no word. There was Yael, in Nahara's place at the table. There was Arieh, cooing, playing with his toes or with his rattle on her bed. My sister dropped her eyes when we passed each other, as though we had not crossed the Salt Sea together and slept in each other's arms. She seemed not to hear when I called to her in the plaza. I thought she would come to me in her own time, but I was wrong. I should have realized that a ewe does not run through the open gate when her entire world consists of the pen in which she lives. Once such a creature has memorized the fence of thorns, she will not cross that marker, not even after it's torn down, for it still rules the boundaries of her vision and her life.

When I spied Nahara in the field, tending to the black goats, urging them on with a bent stick, following the men of the tribe, her eyes trained on Malachi, I wondered if my mother had been mistaken in her prophecy when she said that love would bring about my undoing.

Perhaps she had seen my sister's fate instead.

ON THE DAY of the Feast of Unleavened Bread, when we celebrate our people's release from slavery, the *kadim* arose out of Edom. No good could come of this, for once the wind began, it was said to last for weeks. There was no way to escape its brutal heat or hide from its fury. For weeks the birds would not rise into the sky, their wings beaten back by the force of the gusts and by the will of our God, reminding us that we must bow before Him and offer thanks for our life on earth. Confusion would reign when men tried to speak to one another, and women's intentions would be misunderstood.

In the dovecote, the birds were agitated and refused to lay. My mother drew the sign of the four winds on the earthen floor, then burned incense, a small pile of myrrh that caused the doves to quiet, though they still trembled. Yael took the birds onto her lap, and they were comforted, but the moment she went out the door, they began to worry and call.

When the Feast of Unleavened Bread was over and the bakers

were once again at work at the ovens, using what little grain they had for their loaves, the wind was still with us, just as fierce. Petals rained down from the almond trees in a blinding hail. Lines formed at the storehouses, where our neighbors waited for their share of food. People had to shout in order to be heard; in the end they often walked away from each other, shaking their heads. The *kadim* had brought a whirlwind; there was dust and grit where we slept and where we ate and in the seams of our garments.

Fortunately there was a single hour when the wind eased and brought a stillness for which we were all grateful. It came to us when the blue light of evening began to fall. The color of the horizon was so wondrous even the blind vowed they could see it. It was *beyn ha'arbayim,* a time that is neither day nor night, when the veil of illusion is thinner and we can see things in the lilac-tinged light that cannot be spied at any other hour. It was the time when demons or angels could appear, when the *sheydim* had first come into existence.

One evening Yael did not come to our chamber alone for her visit with my mother. She brought her Essene friend to us during the hour when the *kadim* wind grew quiet. Tamar's white robe appeared blue as it fell around her. The women approached us, eyes downcast. I shivered in the light and the wind. As for my mother, her face was haggard. She had seen a scorpion in a corner that morning. Ever since, she had been waiting for disaster to come to our door.

"Don't blame Tamar for what she's about to tell you," Yael advised my mother, her voice filling with concern. Her hair shone scarlet in the fading light. "She came to me, as she now does to you, to offer the truth, not to cause you any hurt."

Tamar's boy, Yehuda, had become a friend to my brother. We had thought perhaps she had come in search of him, as was often the case. But Tamar wasn't there for her son. It was my mother she wanted, yet oddly she came no closer. We were standing on one side of the doorway with Yael, who had joined us, while Tamar remained on the other side, as if to cross the threshold might bring a curse upon her.

It was a bad omen, to stand divided, yet no one moved.

"Once the Sabbath has come, there is no way to go backward to another day," Tamar remarked, her eyes downcast. She was a gentle woman, one who had suffered greatly, and it clearly pained her to say more. Yael urged her to go on, so at last she told us. "They went to Abba for his blessing."

My mother let out a sob upon hearing the news. She knew the Sabbath was often spoken of as a bride, for it was the seventh day of creation, and most beautiful of all. The bride in question was my sister, who had only just become a woman. She had married without my mother's knowledge or permission.

"There was nothing you could have done," Yael offered. "They were wed this morning."

Tamar was murmuring an apology for the manner in which her people had disrespected us. Because we had no man of our family, Abba had given his approval with the grace of God. My mother was no longer listening. She had rushed to the cabinet where she stored talismans and herbs, desperate for a spell that would set things right. The oil of the lily, that holy, precious scent, spilled upon the altar as she did so. For an instant it seemed that we had returned to the fields of Moab, and it was summer, and every flower was red. I saw that my mother was crying. That alone was terrifying. I could not recall seeing her weep before, not even on the night when the robbers came to our tent, when she changed my name and thereby changed my fate.

I wished I were still a boy, gone to raid caravans alongside the men, sent with the warriors to search for provisions, leaving heartbreak such as this for the women to deal with. I stood there mutely, unable to cope with my mother's grief. It was Yael who went to embrace her. Anyone might have imagined she was the daughter and I was no more than a guest, too awkward to do any more than watch as my mother mourned my sister's rash decision.

"It's done," Yael soothed. "She belongs to them."

My mother shook her head, indignant. Her black hair spilled down her back.

"You know as well as I do. What's done can be undone."

My mother hurriedly left our chamber. I clasped Yael's arm when she went to follow. For once, I would be my mother's daughter.

"Nahara is my sister," I said coldly. "This doesn't concern you."

Yael gazed at me, surprised, then backed away. "Of course."

I chased my mother across the plaza, my heart hitting against my chest. I heard the clatter of her footfalls on the stones. She was quick, but I caught up with her at the edge of the orchard. Our breath rasped as we stood there. The wind had returned. It shook branches and threw up dust devils. The time of the blue light was over and darkness began to spiral down. My mother was not surprised to see me. She knew my sister belonged to me.

"She'll come back to us," I said.

My mother shook her head. "Her father sent this as a punishment to me. This is how he seeks his vengeance."

I didn't believe that the man who had taught me all I knew would be so cruel.

"He wouldn't do such a thing," I ventured, my bitterness at how we had betrayed him rising with the gusts of the *Ruach Kadim*. "Unlike you, his love was true."

My mother glared. She wound her cloak more closely around herself. "If it's not a man who is responsible, then it is God's will. If that is so, we cannot unwrite what is meant to be. So pray that it was her father's curse."

Beyond the field, there was a lamp burning on the Essenes' rough-hewn table, illuminating the ragtag group that had gathered for their shared evening meal. Instead of the scrolls that were usually rolled out for the men to work upon, we spied a marriage feast of dates and wine, curds and sycamore figs. A tent had been set over the table as protection against the whirling dust.

My mother's gaze was fixed on the leader of the Essene people.

"We'll see if this is God's hand at work or simply the greed of men," she told me. "If they knew who her father was, they wouldn't even consider her to be of our faith."

She made her way toward Abba, the holy man who could no longer walk. Even nonbelievers bowed down to him to honor his great age and his favor from the Almighty, but my mother was not there to offer her respect. I noticed she had something in her hand, clutched tightly in her fist. The Essene men had taken note as well, and they stood blocking my mother, to prevent her from causing Abba any harm. I thought of how she had gone alone to the Iron Mountain, waiting for the doves. I understood why the women in Moab had been too frightened to look at her. As I had been on the shore of the Salt Sea, I found I was afraid of her as well.

"*Elohim* will protect me," Abba assured his followers.

"Will he?" My mother raised her eyes to Abba. Her head was uncovered and she seemed dangerous. "All I want is my daughter."

It was not a weapon my mother possessed but a handful of salt. And yet perhaps it was more fatal than a dagger, for it contained a curse she meant to set upon these people, a way to enclose evil so it could do her no harm.

The men shielded their eyes, lest they become entranced and transformed before her into monsters or goats. They murmured prayers, calling down God's mercy. My mother paid no heed. She invoked the angels of heaven and the spirits of wrath, pleading with the Creator of the universe to bring affliction upon her enemies. I thought of the way the robbers Nahara's father had murdered had fallen among us, like branches from the acacia tree, their blood like sap, so thick it took days for my mother to wash it away. As she did so she had cursed each one, the same curses she was uttering now.

The wind was shredding the garments the Essene women had strung on a wash line; it shook the marriage tent. As my mother raised her arms, the *kadim* seemed drawn to her. She called to the four directions of the universe. When she threw down her handful of salt, it rose like a pillar of smoke, there to do her bidding.

The sky turned black and we could not see a single star in the firmament, and it seemed that my mother had managed to close the curtain of heaven, hiding the Throne of Glory. I saw a look of wonderment and fear cross Abba's face. He had realized that my mother was a learned woman, not a ewe in the field, there to be commanded. She would not be defeated by a fence of thorns or the indignation of a righteous man.

The Essenes were immobilized, as a mouse stands motionless before a black viper. One of their women, an old grandmother, thought to run for a pail of dirty wash water to pour over the salt my mother had cast at Abba's feet. But there wasn't enough water to wash it all away, and what remained settled in a pattern that resembled a snake, turning black as it filtered into the sand.

Abba, who could barely walk, now stood away from his chair. He recognized signs, but he read them to his own advantage. He believed that his people had been chosen by God and that peace was the only true way to honor the Almighty. The end of our world was upon us, and what had been written could not be unwritten or undone.

"You cannot fight what is meant to be with weapons or with curses." As he spoke, his followers circled around for protection.

"I want her now," my mother told him. "You cannot take what belongs to another."

"She's not your daughter," Abba told my mother. "She's the daughter of God."

"Is that what you think?" my mother said.

Malachi came out of the house that had once been a goat barn, where his people dwelled together, eating from the same dishes, pouring water over their heads before each meal, living a life of prayer and of giving glory to God.

Abba gestured to him as he approached. "She belongs to this man."

The boy my mother had sent away from the dovecote had heard the rising conflict and turmoil in the field and had left his marriage bed. There he stood. The bridegroom.

My mother faced him, chanting the curses from the book of spells her mother had bequeathed to her, the book that had come from Alexandria, and had traveled to the Iron Mountain and across the Salt Sea. If what had come to pass could be undone, it would unwind at this moment. The wind shifted in the direction of this settlement, throwing up leaves and rattling branches. The bridegroom knew what my mother was trying to do, attempting to unstitch fate.

"She's already my wife," he told her.

"We'll see if she's your wife or my daughter."

No one dared interfere as my mother stalked past Malachi. Her cloak grazed him, and he flinched, fearful of the sin of touching a woman other than his wife. When I followed, I kept my eyes lowered even though Malachi beseeched me for help.

Nahara did her best to hold the door shut, but she was no match for us. At last she backed away. For an instant, as the door fell open, I imagined that my mother and I had become like the robbers in Moab, attempting to claim what belonged to another. I had a burning in my throat; every breath flared like fire. It was much like when I drew the hot liquid from my sister's mouth on the day she was born so that she might take her first breath. Perhaps my mistake was to spit the watery blood on the floor rather than swallow the essence of her soul. Perhaps she had never belonged to me, and I had unwound us from each other at that moment.

My sister wore her simple white robe. Her hair, usually braided and covered by a shawl, was unplaited and loose, black as my mother's hair, as long as mine. I had saved her, only to have her marry Malachi and live in this goat house. But wherever she went, however distant, she would be my sister.

"Come with us now," our mother pleaded. "Before you belong to him."

"Before?" Nahara raised her chin defiantly.

The room was hot, the scent of sweat and of sex lingering. There was blood on the pallet where the women of this sect had unrolled a sheet of white linen to capture the proof of my sister's purity.

"If he knew your father was not of our people, he wouldn't want you," I said.

"But she won't tell him." Nahara nodded at my mother. "It's too late. He's had me and I belong to him." Nahara seemed overcome with her power to hurt us. Her hands were on her hips, as if she were the queen of this stench-filled goat house. "If you want to save someone, save her."

She nodded at me, my sister whom I loved like no other, who had now become my betrayer. I thought of how tenderly I had cared for her when we lived in the tent on the Iron Mountain. Whenever our mother was called to her husband, I had sung my sister to sleep. She'd always slept well, her thumb in her mouth, drowsing as soon as I began the first phrases of a song which told her that the stars were above her, watching over her. I promised to take tamarisk leaves and use them as a broom to sweep the night away so that morning could come again.

"You're blind to all she does," Nahara now said of me. She faced my mother without any attempt at respect. "She has been with Amram a hundred times and you haven't seen a thing. Open your eyes now."

My mother turned to me.

"What did you expect?" my sister went on. "A whore learns her business from the one who knows it best of all."

When our mother reached out, I imagined she would grab

Nahara and force her to leave with us. Instead, she slapped her. Our mother, who had never done anything but embrace us, had been driven to this.

I heard Nahara's sharp intake of air. She raised her hand to her reddened cheek, but she didn't cry. She smiled, more composed than before, more certain of what she wanted, her father's daughter in this if nothing more, fierce and single-minded.

"You may try to silence me, but you don't deny it," she said to the one who had brought her to life.

Outside the desert wind had risen once more; the door of the goat house was thrown open with such force that the wood split apart. It was too late, just as Yael had warned. The wind would be with us for days, forcing us to cover our heads, to eat grit with our food, to listen to its wailing far into the night. I, who knew only iron, felt tears burning my eyes. Though she stood before me, my sister was no longer mine.

Our mother bowed her head, disgraced. I thought of the way she had labored to bring my sister into this world, for I had been her witness on that day.

Save her, she had commanded.

Never once *Save me.*

ON THE NIGHT that we left the Essenes, my mother tore at her cloak, as women did when they entered into mourning. There are those who say that our word for grave, *kever,* is also used to describe where a child dwells inside a mother, for life and death are entwined. The child my mother had labored to bring into this world was gone to her now. She would not tell the truth of who Nahara's true people were, for Nahara would then be a dishonored woman. Instead, she gave her up. We did not speak of my sister again, although my mother chanted for her for seven days, as one chants for the souls of the dead, for that is how long the spirit lingers near the body, unable to part with its earthly form.

From that time on we lived side by side in our chamber, but as time passed, we rarely spoke. It was only the two of us, for my brother had moved to a tent near the barracks, to better serve the warriors but also to avoid the silence between my mother and me. A deep pool of distrust had come between us, a drowning place. Anyone with sense would stay away from such bitterness, and Adir was a practical boy.

I took to working in the smallest dovecote, set apart from the others. I couldn't make amends. I had lied to my mother and deceived her. I had been with a man before marriage. What had been done could not be undone, for even in the hands of a witch, a ruined woman could not once more be pure.

AND YET, when I lay down to sleep, I was someone other than the woman I'd become. I often dreamed I was riding through the acacia trees. I thought of my old friend Nouri, and how I had betrayed him, pretending to be something I wasn't, a creature cast from sinew and muscle rather than a woman of flesh and blood. I had pretended no such thing with Amram, but perhaps I kept from him what was most important. I never told him my given name. Because of this he didn't know me and he never could, no matter how many times he might possess me, or how I might try to offer my love in return.

Because of this, even when I was beside him, I was alone.

He was not the one for me, for he would never accept the hidden part of me. He called me his sheep, his dove, his darling girl, but I was none of those things. I began to avoid our meeting place. He who had known me as a husband would, waited beside the fountain, burning for me. But I watched from the shadows, as angels watch our kind from their lonely distance. I longed for what I dreamed about, the freedom I'd once had. In my dreams I asked the father of my sister if he had seen the person I was at my core. He gazed at me sadly and did not answer, for he had lost us all and could not follow or respond, not even in a dream.

I began to slip into an old tunic that had belonged to my brother. It was brown, dyed with walnut shells, soft from wear. Immediately, I felt comfortable. I braided my hair, then pinned it with a brass clasp beneath a head scarf, so that I might wander through the fortress, a nameless boy who was most grateful to be ignored.

For the first time since we had come here, I was myself.

AT THE DOVECOTE we worried about the Man from the North in his confinement. We had moved through the month of *Iyar* and were nearing summer, the month of *Sivan*, when the heat rose up from the center of the earth and fell down from the heavens. The Man from the North was nothing to us, a prisoner in a tower, a man who barely spoke our language, who was made of ice and was never meant to be among us. But more than six months had passed. Another man would have starved to death, but another man would not have had Yael and the rest of us to see to his needs. Perhaps we had forgotten he was a slave. His quiet restraint had caused us to befriend him, for he was not like other men to us. We feared neither his strength nor his judgment. In many ways he had surprised us, never more so than when he spoke his given name before he was arrested. The others were stunned by the intimacy of this admission, but I understood why he might have revealed such a private detail. Know a man's name and he belonged to you. In return, no matter how you might deny it, you were his as well.

The first time Wynn spied me taking up the bow, in the month before his arrest, he knew I was more of a boy than a woman. He was a strong warrior, and he recognized the same in me. I should have been more cautious, but I was so accustomed to handling weapons, I couldn't hide my joy or my skill. I knew from the Man from the North's expression that he saw in me a brother, someone he might have hunted beside in another world and time.

"Good work," he said to me, after I had tested the arrows I'd fashioned for Amram. The women had returned to the dovecote. I was gathering the arrows, pulling each from the target of the olive tree.

"Yes, they're pretty," I said politely.

He laughed then. He had a strange way with our words; they seemed cold when he spoke them, more to the point. "Pretty? I meant your aim. How many men have you slain?"

I lowered my eyes so he wouldn't notice the gleam of the truth. "Do you think I attack my victims while I'm at the loom in the evenings?"

He took my hand and examined my calluses. "Those aren't from the loom."

He instructed me in his people's method of weaponry as he might have taught a younger brother. Slaves do not betray one another, and although I was not in irons, I was a slave to the truth of who I'd been born. This man named Wynn was a fine teacher, patient, more than willing to share his secrets of warfare. When I wound feathers to the shafts of the arrows, binding them to the wood as his people did, they flew with greater speed. I spent hours behind the dovecote at practice. Once I felled one of our own doves, a bird so far away anyone might have taken it for a wisp of a cloud.

Wynn educated me in the art of the bow, how to take a breath before I pulled back the string, then to wait an extra heartbeat before letting go. Adding that extra beat proved to be a miracle; it gave the arrow life and breath and speed. He spoke about a creature like a deer in his country that was faster than the wind, faster than the leopards in the desert, so quick only the birds could keep pace with it. That was what we wished for our weapons: the feathers fashioned the arrows into birds that would stir the air. The extra instant before the shot was taken accounted for the way a bird dips, containing the power of its wings, before it lifts upward to race across the sky.

WHEN MY FINGERTIPS bled from my practice, I told Amram that I had pierced them on the looms. Unlike the slave, he believed me. He was blind to who I was. It was as though I were the one who possessed the cloak of invisibility his father was said to have worn in the courtyards of the Temple when he struck his enemies. Amram asked me to weave a cloak for him in his favorite shade of blue as a token of my love. I agreed, though I knew this was a gift I would never give to him. I did not know how to work the loom.

My arms grew stronger after my many hours with the bow, as muscled as a warrior's, but I insisted my strength was honed from lifting the baskets that we carried into the field. For weeks afterward, Amram came to help me carry the baskets, imagining that the work was too heavy a burden for me. Behind his back Wynn grinned, and I grinned in return, for some secrets bring you closer in their sharing, just as others break you apart.

I DIDN'T WISH to know what was between Yael and the slave, though I could tell he burned for her. Once Yael had told me that whom I loved was my business, now I gave her the respect she deserved. All the same, I saw the way he watched her and knew she had left his irons unlocked.

"Have you asked her how many men she's slain?" I asked Wynn one day. The words had slipped out in jest, but he stared after Yael, wounded.

"One certainly," he said.

I should have seen then he would be a fool on her account and try to convince her to flee with him. He was the sort of open man who could not hide himself, even if it meant he would be locked in irons.

It was Yael who brought him his meager provisions during the time he was locked away. She told us she could barely hear him speak. He was so weakened he could not rise from his pallet, a rough thing made from the chaff of the wheat. The cell was fetid, made the more filthy with his own waste. Still Wynn did not complain or curse his captors, but instead he spoke of the land of ice where he had been born. It was as though he were seeing it before his eyes. The heat dissipated as he spoke of his country, and he shivered as though he walked in snow. His people believed that a man would return home upon leaving this life. In the next world he would walk beneath the great yew trees of his homeland and once again be reunited with those who had gone before him.

One day he insisted he could see a stag outside the window. It was the animal that was so difficult to hunt, for it flew across the grass as the birds fly above us.

"What a beautiful creature," he whispered.

Yael wept when she told us this, for there were no stags in our country, and no window in his cell.

It was a dark time. We had come to realize that our lives were here, so removed from the rest of the world we might as well have been in the World-to-Come. We would soon celebrate *Shavuot*, the Festival of Weeks, in remembrance of the day Moses was given the Torah. In the past our people would make a pilgrimage to the Temple in Jerusalem with sacrifices of *bikkurim*, the first fruits brought forth after seven weeks of working the fields, sacrificing the seven species of the harvest: wheat, barley, grapes, figs, pomegranates, olives, dates.

Such was our tradition and our law, but there was no Temple to journey to, and we had little to celebrate and no place where we might offer a sacrifice. Our orchards were failing, despite the rain my mother had called down. There was so little grain that many of the storage jars were only half full. People wondered if demons had been at work. Indeed, now when it rained the sky hailed down upon us so strongly the rain itself might have been made of stone.

Although it was said that Masada could never fall, and that God had made this mountain for the purpose of our rebellion, allowing us to continue to give glory to Him, I wondered how long we could endure a siege should the Romans come. The storerooms of the king would not sustain us forever. Herod's oil and wine and lentils had fed us, and we had depended upon them, but they were no more. There was a large oil press, but the olives on the trees were few and the oil produced was meted out in small jars. Now the rats ruled the storerooms. It was rumored they had been brought here by the Romans, purposely left behind in case our people ever took back this fortress, so that they might bring us disease, devouring what little we had left.

WORD HAD gone out that the Roman garrison had captured another Zealot stronghold in the desert. The fortress of Machaerus, east of the Salt Sea on the border of Moab, had fallen to the Tenth Legion, led by Lucilius Bassus, a general some people said was impossible to defeat. An oracle had declared that favor would always be his, and so it seemed to be. But although Machaerus's very name meant sword, perhaps its inevitable defeat had been caused at the hands of its own people. There was a bloody history in that place, and it was rumored that a great teacher named John had been imprisoned and beheaded there when he refused to renounce his teachings.

It was also reported that when rebels at Machaerus arrived at their fortress, they wanted to destroy all that had belonged to cruel Herod and his sons. In their zealousness, they chopped down an enormous rue that had grown there for hundreds of years, a plant taller than any fig tree, a talisman said to hold the secret to our people's freedom and success. With that one impulsive action, they had destroyed their chances at victory. Rue can save you or ruin you, it can bring luck or agony. Several warriors were said to be so haunted by their deed that they had tried to plant another herb in the same spot, but the roots always withered and refused to take.

When the Romans encircled them, one of their most beloved warriors had been trapped. He had been tortured in the open for all to see in ways too horrible for most decent men to imagine. His friends and loved ones were forced to watch as Romans cut off pieces of his flesh and filled him with burning thorn plants still alight, unwrapping his blistering skin from his soul. His fellow warriors pleaded for his freedom and the promise of their own safety, willing to surrender in exchange for the life of their brother. The bargain was made, and the rebels came down from their mountain. Their safety was assured but never granted. It came as no surprise to our people to hear that Lucilius Bassus was a liar. When our warriors thought of demons, they imagined his name. Each and every man at Machaerus was slain, their blood turning the ground black.

The Romans piled the pyres high with bodies—not only the dead were cast onto the flames but also the weak and the sick, those not worthy of being slaves. The sound of their cries echoed throughout Judea. Some women in our fields vowed there had been a rain of stones on that day, and when the last of the figs had been dashed to the ground, there had been ants inside the sticky fruit, destroying it from the inside.

There was a prayer meeting at the synagogue, and the men who gathered were stricken by the horror of the news. That evening we heard not only prayers but arguments. How could we avoid the fate of Machaerus? We could hear Ben Ya'ir's low, steady voice. We knew it was he because when he spoke all others fell silent.

"We'll never let our women and children die on pyres," he told his warriors.

There was no choice for us, he cautioned, no retreat. It was apparent that our strength emerged from his courage; all the same, when I went into the fields I saw that the figs had indeed fallen; in what should have been the greenest time of the year, that golden fruit lay blackened on the ground.

❧

YAEL WORRIED not only for Wynn but for her child as well. Arieh had served as the key with which to open the barred door in the tower. He had been presented to our leader's wife for her amusement in exchange for permission to bring provisions to the slave. But some keys can be used for many locks and should never be lent or given away. Our leader's wife had taken a dangerous liking to Arieh, and a new prison had sprung forth, one made from her arms and from the net of her desires.

I had spied this dark woman alone in the evenings, walking beside the wall that surrounded us, as though she were a shadow in search of the substance that would bring her to life. Perhaps the child was such a cure for the ailment our leader's wife carried within her, her barrenness and her despair.

Ben Ya'ir's wife had begun to withhold Arieh when Revka came for him at the end of the day, insisting on keeping the baby through the night, rocking him as though he were her own. She threatened that, if she could not keep Arieh with her, she could no longer offer the slave her protection. Why should the barbarian live and she have nothing for her efforts? She went so far as to go to the priest to choose an auspicious day for Wynn's death.

Yael herself went to the small palace when she heard of this. She bowed her head to Channa, but told her in no uncertain terms this was to be Arieh's last visit in exchange for the life of the slave. When she returned to retrieve the child that evening, the door was bolted. A guard was stationed outside, there at Channa's bidding.

He was a friend of Amram's, Uri, who had brought Yael to the fortress, a good-natured young man who was liked by all. Yet he denied her entry.

"We do as we're told," he said apologetically. "She speaks with her husband's voice as well as her own. You understand. I have no choice in the matter."

Yael took to lurking around the palace, much as beggars roam the markets, hands outstretched. On nights when Revka kept vigil beside Yael, it was the older woman who wept, blaming herself for what had come to pass, for it was she who had fashioned the agreement with Channa. My mother had warned that nothing good could come from a bargain with Ben Ya'ir's wife. She was dangerous, my mother said. More so than she appeared. I'd overheard Revka insisting that Channa's interest in the baby was only a lonely woman's attachment.

My mother had laughed coldly in response. "Then perhaps we should say a snake has an attachment to a dove when we speak of his hunger. Wait and see how much Channa is willing to devour."

Now Yael came to my mother, tearful, desperate for a spell that would help her regain her son. "There must be something you can do," she pleaded.

I was certain my mother would help her favorite. Instead, she shook her head sadly. "You shouldn't have let her touch him. Now she has him in her claws."

"Give me something to defeat the demon," Yael begged.

"She's not a demon, she's a woman," my mother said sadly. "In this case, that's worse."

I BEGAN to keep watch with the others. We had all come to despise Channa for the liberties she took, showing off the child, dressing him in a tunic she'd had woven for him. This woman, who had set herself apart for so long, whose servants toiled in her garden and kitchen while the rest of us went hungry, was now prideful, strutting through the plaza in the afternoons with the baby on her hip as though he were her own, chatting with the other women, who were quick to admire him, how handsome he was, how easily a smile came to him.

Revka's grandsons acted as spies on our behalf, tracking Ben Ya'ir's wife each day, reporting her activities to us. Noah and Levi had the ability to fade into the shadows, though their voices had come back strongly. People say that when you have lost something and it returns to you, it is doubly sweet, and so it was with Revka's grandsons. When they spoke, their words captivated a listener. It seemed the conversations that had been silenced for so long could now be released in honeyed tones, and what they described they did artfully, their reports appearing before us as though written in the air.

"She stops where the black viper lives on the rocks and makes an offering," they confided. "She feeds the baby from her fingers, filling him with figs and pomegranates and barley cakes as though he were a dove. She tells him he is so sweet the bees will follow him."

The older boy, Noah, looked much like his father, the Man from the Valley, the warrior who kept to himself, a fighter I was curious about. Amram had told me this man could not be turned away by bloodshed, plunging into the fray when anyone else would have retreated, and wisely so. He took risks only a madman would take on, courting the Angel of Death, calling out, daring *Mal'ach ha-Mavet* to appear before him as he wielded his rough-hewn ax, the only weapon he had need of. His brothers in battle admired him, they spoke of him with respect, even awe, but they did not wish to stand beside him. They knew that he who is without a fear of death is the most dangerous man of all.

What makes a dangerous woman, however, was not always so apparent, for what is unnoticeable to the human eye is often the most deadly attribute. What is hidden can destroy you. Demons appeared in the dark, when you least expected betrayal, when your eyes were closed. Because my mother refused to confront Channa, I wondered what this dark woman's power over her might be. I studied Channa, and still I saw a weak creature, but one who had woven a strong web.

"Our leader's wife whispers to Arieh that she alone protects him," Revka's grandsons told us. "She warns him against the women who wait at the wall. She tells him he must never listen to the one named Yael, that she will tell him lies and will beseech him to think he belongs to her."

Yael grew ashen upon hearing these slanderous words, the marks on her face standing out as though she'd been dashed with blood. Still she sent the boys to discover more. They crept through the garden beside the palace, making their way past the mint and marjoram and sage, slinking as close as they dared. The boys had spied Channa waiting for her husband at the door with the baby in her arms, as though Arieh was an offering.

"And what does her husband say to this?" Yael wanted to know when Revka's grandsons told of the situation, her voice sharp.

"He walks past her," Noah remarked. "He never looks at her."

When Yael heard this, she nodded, pleased. She was thin and agitated, yet doing her best to convince herself that the child would be returned to her. "What's done can be undone," she told us.

I didn't offer an opinion, but I had heard my mother say the very same thing upon my sister's marriage day, and Nahara was still bound to her husband. I was not certain that our lives were so similar to thread, able to be unspooled, then gathered up again.

ONE EVENING as I kept watch along with Revka and Yael, we saw the great man himself entering his chambers. My mother refused to come with us; she had offered a warning and had been ignored. I noticed she turned pale when Channa's name was mentioned. She was not among us when we recognized Ben Ya'ir's broad shoulders and his prayer shawl and how proudly he walked, much as a king might, though in fact he cared to own nothing on this earth and had cast away his possessions when he observed the greed of the wealthy in Jerusalem. His wife might sleep in the palace, but Eleazar ben Ya'ir remained outside under the stars or went to the barracks to spend his nights there so that his warriors would know he was no different than those he commanded.

We decided it would be best to go to him so that he might learn of Yael's plight. He was known to be fair; perhaps he would cast a judgment in favor of the true mother. But when the time came, the others were too nervous to face him, for the burden of our people was his. The weight of this fortress upon a single man was so heavy Revka and Yael feared they would seem like fools to plead for Arieh. How dare we engage our leader in such small troubles when Jerusalem had fallen and there were demons waiting for us all?

We were now the only fortress of rebels in Judea. All others had been conquered, and because we alone stood fast, Rome had become more interested in us. We were at first elated, prideful to show that we had not been vanquished and were firm in our resolve. But slowly we grew more fearful about the legion's response now that they realized we alone had managed to survive.

Even Revka, known for her sharp tongue, refused to approach our leader with worries over a single child, though he was our beloved Arieh. Ben Ya'ir was too great a man, with too many concerns. But I had no such fears. Eleazar ben Ya'ir was a warrior like any other. A man was only a man, and I had killed my share in my other life. I had seen that they all gave up their lives to God in the same manner.

I offered to be the one to go.

Yael was as surprised as she was grateful. "My brother sees your beauty, as do I," she said simply.

Lately I had come to believe that Amram looked only for a woman's beauty, nothing more. All that I was had been masked by my sheet of black hair, the woman I appeared to be. I said nothing to Yael, merely accepted her gratitude, then made my way alongside the palace walls in the falling dark. I was quiet; I knew how to stalk prey and how to fold myself into the shadows.

When I reached a window, I stood on a pile of kindling and hauled myself up to the ledge so I might peer through. There was very little furniture in the chamber; most of it had been broken apart and used for firewood. But the marble floor and the frescoes amazed me. For a moment I was in thrall, thinking of the royals who had once lived here, without fear or poverty. I understood why it was said that the Queen of Egypt had begged Rome to grant her this fortress to call her own. Then I observed Channa, and caution ran through me. She sat on a bench by the fire, whispering to the child, holding him close. The delight she took in him was so evident I was glad Yael was not there beside me to see.

Near the oven there sat a cradle carved of acacia, crafted by a master woodworker from Jerusalem. An amulet of protection was tied above the place where the child's head was to rest. The pallet itself was rich with a fine linen bedcovering, and there were bronze bells tied to the rockers, so that demons might be chased away by the sound. As for Arieh, he wore a purple tunic, as though he were the son of a king. It appeared that the child had no home other than this chamber, and that his every need had been seen to. At that moment I understood this woman had no intention of giving him back.

I thought of my sister's father, how he could become a whirlwind against his enemies, how I might be equally fearsome should I so desire. But I had to hide that part of me, as I did with Amram.

I could not climb through the window or reach for the knife set on the table so that I might take what I wanted. Instead, I knocked politely at the door.

I hadn't expected the great man himself to answer.

"I'm here for the child," I said softly, casting myself as a pretty woman and nothing more. I had burned half a dozen acacia branches in memory of the souls I had released. I had been covered with the blood of the ibex and felt its heat. Now I lowered my eyes. Still I had a glimpse of our leader, who gazed at me with such intensity I understood why Yael and Revka had been fearful of speaking to him directly.

"The child?" he said, confused by my presence and my request.

He seemed more powerful than most men, and I felt myself vanishing as I bowed my head. I forced myself to remember the person I had once been, the men I had killed, the nights that had belonged to me. I raised my eyes to his.

"His mother waits."

Ben Ya'ir turned to see Yael, alongside Revka and her grandsons, as they perched upon the wall. They were not unlike the shades that remain on earth when those who are unfairly put to death are unable to find rest.

"He has a mother?"

His surprise made me realize his wife had told him otherwise.

"Doesn't everyone?"

The great man's face twisted into a smile. I was relieved. Perhaps I smiled as well.

"And a father?" he asked.

"Not everyone has that," I was quick to say.

"Everyone has that," he assured me.

He told me to wait, then closed the door. I looked at the garden that was tended by slaves. There was a stone fountain from the time of the king, dry now, the rim cracked, the finials broken into pieces on the ground. A wealth of herbs and mint grew in neat rows, and the scent that rose up was green and sweet. I heard the sound of birds, though it was dark and no birds flew after twilight, only the silent owls that lived in the caves across the mountain. Still, they sang, an odd event at this hour.

I edged behind the fountain. There, below a trellis of cucumber vines with their deep green leaves, sat a wooden cage. Inside, two doves huddled close, cooing.

I felt the spark beneath my eye, as if the message I'd once found on the ground burned me still. My heart felt heavy, so much so that I doubted I would be able to run away, though I wished I could now do so. I wondered if this cage of doves contained the messengers to the Iron Mountain, and if this was why my mother had refused to come to this house and risk Channa's wrath.

Ben Ya'ir returned to the door, the baby in his arms. I could hear weeping echoing in the chamber behind him. I had made my way back through the garden, the scent of mint clinging to my garments, the sound of the doves a song I carried with me, one that had accompanied me from the far side of the Salt Sea, where the caged doves had eaten grain from my hand as they waited for my mother to set them free.

"Is this what you came for?" he asked, as he offered me the child.

When he spoke I understood why men would follow him even though they might die and never return, and why they would believe in him. Although I wanted to tell him I had stumbled upon the doves, I found I couldn't say another word in his presence. He gave the baby up into my arms. I should have thanked him, but I could not speak. He waited for me to do so for so long that the silence itself spoke of what was between us.

Before he turned back to his chamber, Eleazar ben Ya'ir put his hand to my forehead, gently, as he might welcome a daughter. In that moment I knew he was the man for whom my mother had made such sacrifices, the reason she had been cast out of Jerusalem, why she had waited on the Iron Mountain day after day, until the dove returned with the message to come to him at last.

WHEN I WENT to our chamber that night, I did not ask my mother to speak my father's name aloud. I saw her comb her long dark hair with a wooden comb made of acacia wood from the forests of Moab. I saw the tattoos on her flesh. She was the same, the woman who'd never wished to tell me who I was, who would not offer Yael help if it meant she would be forced to come before the enemy who had used me as evidence so that we might be set into the wilderness.

I gazed at my face as it was reflected in a bowl of water and saw my father's eyes staring back at me. Now, when people said his name, they were saying mine as well. I walked alone at night, dressed in Adir's tunic and mantle, seeking out those who spoke of my father, wanting to hear of his deeds in battle and his kindness to those in need. He insisted that all men were equal, whether they were servants or priests, and made certain all adhered to the law that stated we were not to collect the fruit from the four corners of our orchard, as God had commanded, to ensure that even the poorest among us could find mercy in their time of hunger.

I had the desire to speak to him, something I had been unable to do while I was in his presence. When I heard there was to be an archers' contest among the warriors, I went, like the boy I'd once been, a scarf across my face, the bow I'd used to test my arrows set upon my back. Perhaps I would see my father and he would know me for who I was, as I now knew him. I waited through the day, watching the men, their strong arms and backs wrenching as they drew their bows. They cried out in brotherhood and rivalry, blaming the wind when they missed their mark, praising the best among them when their aim was true.

When it came time for Amram to take his turn, I saw the obvious admiration his brothers-in-arms felt in his skill. I, too, wanted to praise him, but there was something more. I felt the sting of jealousy, a wasp in my heart. Ben Ya'ir was among the warriors who cheered on the young men, and he praised Amram heartily. I thought of how he had blessed me and wondered if he was the reason I'd been born to the sign of metal, why I wanted more than other girls did. Even now, as I spied the throng of young women on the sidelines, I knew I could never watch alongside them and not burn to be among the men.

I might have slunk back to the silence of our chamber, but in the pale hours of the declining day I saw the hawk above us, the one whose feathers I'd used in fashioning arrows for Amram. I thought of the splashes of red dye on my hands from the madder root when I'd crafted them so carefully. I had intended the arrows as a gift, yet I'd never presented them. I at last understood that I'd wanted those arrows for myself all along. I had designed them not in honor of the phoenix that signified my beloved but in memory of the red lily that grows in the fields of Moab, as a reminder of the person I had been.

I carried them now, hidden beneath my cloak.

I found myself at the archer's line, pushed there by a demon, or perhaps by my pride, an unknown boy allowed to compete, though clearly no one saw the competition within me. They didn't bother to watch as the first arrow hit its mark. Perhaps the second arrow convinced them to turn and stare. Perhaps it was the third. I was concentrating on one thing alone: the precise moment when I drew back on the bow, waiting, as Wynn had instructed, so that the arrow might dip and rise as birds do. I gave not a single thought to the girl I pretended to be. I heard the wind and no other voice. I thought of both my fathers, the one who had taught me all that I knew and the one I wished to learn from now.

When I narrowed my eyes, I saw my path before me, straight as iron.

My arrows sliced through those which were already in place, casting the other warriors' strikes to the ground. Those warriors were watching now. The red of the feathers were impossible to ignore, a field of lilies. By the time I was done, there was silence.

I saw Ben Ya'ir rise to his feet as the crowd let out a shout. My ears were ringing, as if a storm had settled upon me, a whirlwind from the far side of the Salt Sea. I murmured a whisper of gratitude to my sister's father, and to the men I'd ridden with, and to Nouri, whom I had always bested. I stood there for an instant, my happiness complete, wishing I could keep this vision before me always. But a vision is like a dream, it dissipates as soon as you attempt to hold on to it, and my vision rose up to be claimed by He who should never be forgotten. All at once I could hear the truth of the moment. My eyes and ears were mine once more. The crowd was calling for Adir, proclaiming him the hero of the day.

They thought I was my brother, convinced he was the master archer. They cheered on, but I turned away. The warriors and those in attendance continued to call Adir to them, so that they might honor him, but I hastened to make my way through the Western Plaza, quick to take the steps, leaping as though my life was at risk. The world was there before me, in the cliffs and the valley below, but this world no longer belonged to me. I had given it to my brother.

I found my way to an abandoned garden behind the Northern Palace, a walled-in area where women came to look for garlic and herbs that had been planted long ago and had been forgotten. There were larks there, pecking at the greens, but they all fluttered up when I came upon them, my breathing hot and ragged. I took off Adir's garments. They were nothing but a fool's disguise. There was rosemary growing where I stood, said to be the herb of remembrance, a gate to the past. My heart hit against my chest, and my limbs shook. I wrapped myself in my scarf as I wept for who I was.

The hawk had followed me. Perhaps he was the one Wynn had trained to come to the dovecote window, a fierce bird of prey who was willing to bow his head and take crumbs from Yael's hand. I scanned the sky. Watching him riding in the air above me reminded me what freedom was like. The past was with me whether or not I wanted it to be. I was myself despite how I might run from the truth.

Beneath my shawl, I still had the bow upon my back.

FROM OUR MOUNTAINTOP, residents often saw soldiers from the legion during the growing heat of *Sivan*. More and more *exploratores* were being sent to examine our mountain, gathering on the rocky floor below. They were reconnaissance soldiers whose only mission was to seek out enemies and report back to their generals. The Romans had long been aware that we were here, as they'd known about Machaerus and the other fortresses that were held by Zealots. We were far from Jerusalem, and so they had ignored us, but our fame had grown and stories about our glory had reached Roman ears. There had been more and more talk of our rebellion in the markets of towns throughout the region. *Shir tishbohot*, songs of praise, were offered for us, and those who celebrated us denounced Rome in whispers and then in louder tones. People said our mountain was invisible and that the *Sicarii* had used the Hebrew alphabet to call a curtain over us, a fabric constructed of air and vapor that separated heaven from earth. They said that the throne of our Lord could be seen from our towers. Any man who ruled here would rule the world.

Soldiers from the legion might come to survey us, but all they would see was how impossible it would be to mount an attack. Ben Ya'ir sent out word that, when the *exploratores* came, we should stay in our chambers so they could not count our number. Perhaps they would think we were stronger than we were, and possessed thousands of warriors, rather than a village left to old men and women and children each time our men went on raids. Let them look all they wanted. All they would see was the mountain where God's glory had sent us, a rock so impenetrable they could never bring us down. Some of our boys sent stones falling, skittering down as a warning, and they laughed as the soldiers scattered below.

I did not laugh to see the white tunics of the Tenth Legion or the banner of the wild boar. I felt a chill come over me. In truth our people were no match for Roman soldiers, who had been trained for one thing, to be a machine of death. Our warriors were best when they slunk about like wolves, striking enemies in the dark. The rebels' only hope of success was an attack that was unexpected, when thanks to God's grace, their quickness and ferocity might win out over might. Against well-armored, organized troops, who had so much experience of warfare, our people were woefully unprepared. Our fathers and brothers were freedom fighters, not trained soldiers. Unlike my sister's father, the men at Masada had not been warriors from the moment of their birth, each with a horse already chosen and a knife in his hand. They had been priests and bakers and scholars, their weapons knives and arrows and rocks, not bronze and iron. We were nothing against the relentless power of the Roman Empire.

WHEN OUR WARRIORS decided they would track a group of *exploratores* so they might discover how close the legion was to our mountain, Yael gave me a token to present to Amram, a slip of blue fabric, the color of heaven, and of God's glory, and of His throne.

Amram laughed and slipped the fabric close to his heart. "We won't be apart for long," he said, recognizing the charm. "My sister has seen to that."

He told me that the fabric would lead him to me no matter how far he might journey. He cupped his hands around my face and kissed me. In his arms I had a surge of fear, for what was between us was already over, despite the token. I went to the wall to watch him descend with the warriors. I had no idea that my brother planned to set forth with them until I found my mother there, beside herself with worry.

"He's nothing but a boy," she worried. She had looked ill of late, refusing her meals, keeping to herself. Now she was ashen. "Why would they do this? Why would he go?"

I was too guilt-ridden to answer. The warriors believed that Adir had been the archer at the contest and had therefore taken him on as their brother. That was why he now walked beside them, because of my red arrows. His fate was my burden, for I had caused them to look at him with esteem. My mother thought of Adir as her baby and was still tying amulets into his garments to protect him from evil. He tore such things from his tunic, laughing, saying our mother had no idea what it meant to be a man.

Adir was in his thirteenth year, but he was not ready. I had killed my first ibex when I was only ten, but I had been prepared for blood. I had ridden with men who were fearless. I had known to burn the acacia branches to honor the spirits of the dead. My brother thought being a man meant blindly following the path of the warriors, despite his lack of skill. He thought of great glory, not of pools of blood; surely he had not imagined the brutality he would witness when his comrades were cut down before him.

I prayed with my mother at our altar as she burned oil and chanted for Adir's safe return. I cursed myself as I did so, for I should have been the one to take his place. My mother wrote the names of God on her arms, and then on mine, so that we might be heard in heaven, even though women were not allowed this practice. It was only for the priests to make such entreaties to the Almighty, but my mother was not afraid to break the law. We sacrificed a dove and wrote upon its feathers with its own blood, binding any demon that might follow my brother into the valley. We chanted softly so none would overhear, for we did not dare to reveal what we did in our chamber any more than I dared to reveal the truth of my brother's leaving.

I proclaim the majesty of His splendor, to frighten all the spirits of the angels of destruction and those who strike suddenly and lead us astray. Destroy their evil hearts in the age of the rule of wickedness.

I spoke these words along with my mother, but I did not proclaim that I was the wickedness that had sent my brother into battle, and that I must be the one to make amends.

ON A CLEAR burning-hot morning, the nesting doves dropped to the ground without warning. We gathered them and held them close, trying to still their trembling bodies until they revived. Several died that day, for no apparent reason. Although we were hungry, we could not make them into a meal for ourselves or our warriors upon their safe return for the doves had died of some ailment.

Perhaps the hour when the doves fell marked the moment when Channa returned to the priest to choose a day for the slave to die. Certainly we all felt death close by; it passed as a shadow cast by clouds, and we grew cold. My mother took the doves to the altar in her chamber, she covered her head and whispered a prayer to keep away the Angel of Death, but the sacrifice was not enough. That same day a proclamation was posted. On the following afternoon, the guard would go to the tower and the world would be rid of the slave. We were not savages like the Romans, who crucified their enemies to cause the most pain a human could endure, stretching death out lengthwise, as a man might be stretched upon a wooden cross so he would linger in agony. Instead, the slave's throat would be slit, the kindest death, the one we gave to even the most lowly of beasts, so that his breath would leave him in a single rush.

When evening fell, Channa was waiting by the wall near Revka's chamber. She wore a cloak, but Revka's grandsons spied her instantly, as they were said to perceive demons. Our leader's wife had no fear, only the heat of her desire, which flamed hotter than the air around us. Arieh would soon be a year old; he was a quiet and dear child, already trying to walk. Channa had dared to come to Yael; she was heedless, as the desperate often are, more than willing to disobey her husband, who had warned her to stay away. But on this occasion Ben Ya'ir was among the warriors following the Romans and therefore could not judge her or punish her for her deeds. She was stronger than she'd once been, made so by my mother's cures, strong enough to cause damage. She carried a sprig of hyssop, as though taunting the flower that had once caused her so much misery.

Revka wept at the sight of her. "It's my doing. I called a demon upon us."

"No." Yael's face was masked, but she sounded sure of herself. "It's my punishment."

"You've done nothing," Revka insisted.

"One thief knows another," Yael murmured, resolved.

She packed up all of Arieh's belongings, then went to the wall, the baby in her arms.

"A bargain is a bargain," Channa said. "I'm not being too demanding, I merely want what I'm owed."

They were near the garden where Yael had released the scorpion. It failed to show itself on this night, but it was still there. The children had seen it, and they knew that which you cannot see can be more dangerous than that which is before you. We were fighting a battle just to keep ourselves fed; perhaps the scorpion went hungry as we did. As for Channa, she was a rich man's wife; despite her husband's insistence that we were all worthy of God's gifts, she took more than her share.

"You've done well in your care for him," she said approvingly to Yael when she noticed the flame-colored spot on the baby's cheek had all but disappeared. Yael had bathed the child in oils and rubbed a balm into his skin. "I'm sure we can agree as reasonable women." When Channa stroked his face lovingly, Arieh smiled up at her. "He's better off with me."

YAEL DID NOT lock herself away, as some women might have. She had no time for such indulgences. The slave had been allowed to live. The bargain had been kept; still, anyone who trusts a serpent deserves its bite. The wise see a creature for what it is, not what it says it may be.

After her chores in the dovecote were completed, Yael went out to collect firewood. She did so often enough that the sentries came to know her. The assassin's daughter with red hair. She went late in the day, when the sun was dropping down. In the dim light she found twigs that would serve as kindling, deadwood that would keep our fires hot. She didn't return until twilight washed across the pale sky. Sometimes she sat on the wall in the amber light, a basket of twigs beside her, the woven scarf on her hair slipping down, so that strands of her hair gleamed scarlet. She knew the guards watched, their glances lingering over her flesh. Because of this they allowed her to do as she pleased.

Each day she went farther down the mountain, finding paths few dared to take, except for the ibex, who had no fear of tumbling down the sheer cliffs. The head scarf she wore was woven in the pattern of the country in the north none among us would ever see, a land where the ice was as deep as a river, where a man could freeze in moments, where every warrior's arrows were marked with the sign of the stag.

When Yael asked for my help, I went with her willingly, though by then we had more wood piled at our doors than anyone else on the mountain.

"I'm surprised you didn't ask my mother," I said.

"Your mother would make them suspicious. The guards will trust you."

As we approached the sentries, Yael told me to pull my shawl away from my head so that I might allow the guards to see my long black hair. We were two young women gathering wood, cheerful, pretty. We waved a greeting. Every day, we made this journey. The guards never bothered to question us but only glanced at us, appraising our bare arms, which we allowed them to view and enjoy.

Yael said a prayer each time we passed a small cave. She whispered that a lion lived inside, but she swore he would watch over us. Sometimes she left him an offering of a dove, sometimes a few strands of her hair. She seemed convinced he was her guardian. All the same, I was relieved I had brought a blade with me, in case the creature she spoke of decided to turn on us.

The cool air of evening made it perfectly understandable when we began to bundle up beneath our cloaks. I wore an extra shawl, which made my appearance bulkier. My head scarf was tied tightly, nearly covering my face. One day Yael brought me a gray cloak. It belonged to her father, she said. I thought of her father's talent and how he had instructed Amram in the secrets of invisibility. I knew it was possible for a man to become a cloud or a mist in the eyes of his enemy; I had seen Amram himself do so when we wished to defy my mother and meet in secret.

As soon as I slipped on the assassin's cloak, the guards no longer noticed me. I disappeared before them, nothing worth looking at. They called out a greeting to Yael, whose shining red hair they so admired, but ignored me as I trudged behind, carrying a bundle of dry wood.

On the day it was to happen, I went to the tower at the hour Yael had chosen. After his meal, the guard posted there often fell asleep on his bench, his stomach swollen from his allotment of lentils and beans. In my pocket I had the key of twisted metal that my mother had fashioned to show how easy it would have been for the slave to escape the dovecote so the officials would not guess Yael had unlocked his chains. I kept the assassin's cloak over my head. No one questioned me as I went along the corridor, then took the stairs. At the end of the hall, the guard was dozing, as Yael had assured me he would be. I let myself into the slave's cell, stunned by the filth and stench that greeted me. The air was murky, yet I could see poor Wynn on his pallet of rags. He was so unclean no one would ever guess that the stubble of his shorn hair was pale as ice or that his skin had been the color of milk when he first came to us.

Despite the darkness, Wynn recognized me, rising to his feet to greet me.

"The warrior," he said fondly.

His voice was thin, melting in his throat. His body was no longer strong, weakened from a lack of air and food.

"I'm someone else today," I informed him.

"Who would that be?" He was thoroughly confused.

I grinned, then slipped off my cloak and stood before him. "I'm you."

NONE of the sentries took note when two women went through the gate, one barely noticeable, cloaked in gray. They were accustomed to us leaving the fortress at this hour, when the dark was drifting across the sky, when the curtain between the day and night splits open to angels and demons alike. They failed to notice that when Yael brought back kindling she returned alone, lingering at the wall to gaze over the mountains, where the hawk soared, circling back as though he might return, before he disappeared into the falling dark.

In the tower, I waited until I knew Wynn would be free, repeating the psalm of protection. *Shivitti Adonai l'negdi tamid. I have placed the Lord constantly before me.* I was glad to know it was the season when wild onions grew, when rabbits would be venturing out to eat new grass. Perhaps he would manage to survive in the wilderness so that he might find his way back to the country of the stag.

No guard came to the door I'd unlocked for his escape. I left unnoticed, wearing the tunic I'd brought along so that I might once again be a boy, easily thought to be among those who helped guard the tower.

THE WAR came closer in the shimmering month of *Tammuz*, when we tended the grapevines and the air itself smelled sweet. Great flocks of birds flew overhead, returning from the grasslands of the south, pelicans and storks, swifts and kestrels. There were flocks of people as well, crossing the desert before they could be captured, a tide rushing in advance of the Tenth Legion. Some of the wanderers came to us. When they pleaded for mercy, they were allowed to set their tents in our orchards, and the fruit that fell in all four corners was allowed to them, as commanded by our common law. The stragglers were not the only ones who were famished. Fallen fruit and flatbread were barely enough to feed our hunger. I went beyond the wall and caught songbirds in nets made of string. When I grew tired of hunting like a girl, I took my bow and shot pheasants to place upon our table.

No one said a word when they saw me walking in the plaza with a bow on my back; perhaps they believed the weapon was my brother's and that in his absence I was caring for what rightly belonged to him. Most likely they thought I only meant to clean the arrows I carried, for their tips were edged with blood.

Despite the fact that my mother had mourned my sister and now considered her among the dead, I brought pheasants to the Essenes whenever I could. Nahara was not dead to me. I often spied her among the modest, hardworking women. I thought of how she would follow me through the grass in our other life, how I would send her running home to our tent, swooping behind her like an owl, making her laugh. I thought of the years when we had slept on one pallet, often dreaming the same dream, so that even before our eyes were open we could chatter about our night visions. I had always yearned for her father to be my father so I might be her sister in every way. Now I was afraid she would run if I dared to speak to her and beg her to return.

After I presented the game birds, I went to sit beside Nahara on a wooden bench outside the goat house. Together we plucked the pheasants. Soon there was a circle of shimmering brown and green feathers at our feet.

"You can still hunt," my sister said pointedly. The Essenes did not believe a woman should touch a weapon, or take a life.

"When no one's watching." I grinned, hoping she would join in the joke of who I used to be. Instead she shook her head. My sister, whose dreams I had shared, whose breath was the same as mine, whose true father was a secret to her people, found my actions shameful.

"The Almighty watches."

I felt the stab of her judgment upon me. "I bowed to give my prayers to Him. He watches that as well."

"We're on the threshold of the end, yet you act as though the days will go on forever, one like the other." It was as though my sister had become my teacher and I had failed to learn my studies. Nahara was convinced we were walking through the End of Days and, like her Essene teachers, believed it was foolish to be consumed with the details of daily life. Those who refused to accept the truth that the world as we knew it would soon be no more would shortly be apprised otherwise.

The fabric of my sister's tunic and shawl was threadbare, for there had been no time to mend the weaving and, from what she said, no purpose in doing so. If it was the End of Days, then my sister's tunic would be her funeral garment. She confided that her people no longer slept. There was too much work to be completed on their scrolls, which revealed God's truth, and too little time to do so. Perhaps this was the reason she looked pale. She was so slim the bones below her throat seemed to be rising through the flesh. She said that her people often prayed throughout the night, waiting to see if the sun would rise again and if there would indeed be another morning.

We had blood upon us from readying the pheasants. The birds would be hung on a line so that the rest of their blood would be drained from their bodies before they were salted and cooked. Our people never consumed blood. It was one of God's strictest laws. Still our hands were stained with the pheasants' lifeblood. I took my sister's hand in mine. She had betrayed me to our mother; nevertheless, I could not abandon her.

"What do these people offer you?"

"Everything." Nahara withdrew her hand from mine, shaking her head, disappointed in me. "They offer a world of peace, Aziza."

She gazed toward the barracks and the stock of weapons stored there. Children had been set to work fashioning stones into round rocks that could be dropped upon our enemy with great force should they be foolhardy enough to attack us. Nahara turned back to me, her eyes damp. She had always been softhearted in times of killing. She would close her eyes when we came upon a rabbit in a snare. Our people did not eat rabbits, they were considered unclean, but Nahara's father's people had no such laws. *You do it,* she would say to me as the poor creature shivered in its trap.

I would take the rabbit and sever its throat, quickly, so that she didn't have to see. I would do whatever she asked.

"You can't think that's the answer," she said of the mounds of weaponry.

"What would your people have you do if we are attacked?" I wanted to know.

"Trust in Abba." Her hands were folded upon her lap. She looked calm and beautiful, older than her years. I thought she meant the leader of her people, then I realized she meant God. She, like the other Essenes, claimed a personal relationship with the Almighty. She spoke of Him as if she were indeed His child.

"And if that means we are to die? What then? Lie down and let Rome trample us?"

Nahara gazed at me with compassion, as though I were the younger sister, too simple to understand. "Then we rise again."

"Your father was a man of courage. Peace was something he fought to keep."

She smiled gently at my remark. I saw within her some of the girl she'd been before she left us.

"You don't fight for peace, sister," Nahara told me. "You embrace it."

"Not in the world of your father," I reminded her.

Nahara laughed outright, for this was undeniably true. "That was long ago. You were another person then. As was I."

"You cried for him when we left. We thought he'd hear you in Petra, that was how loudly you called to him."

"I was a child." Nahara shrugged her narrow shoulders. "My father was the only man I knew. Now"—she nodded to the long trestle table, where Malachi was at work on a text—"I belong to him." I had heard it said that Malachi wrote so beautifully the angels came to watch, for words were the first thing God created out of the silence and were still the most beautiful of all His creations.

"Then I will be happy for you," I said.

I walked away, leaving the pheasants with my sister, unable to tell her the truth. No matter what she did or whom she loved, I was the one who had given her life in this world, a world she was so eager and ready to leave, one in which there were acacia trees that called the bees to their blossoms, where there were endless fields of grass and cassis.

No matter what she said, she still belonged to me.

I WAS WALKING at night, as I had come to do so that I might relish my freedom as a boy, when I came upon the Essenes digging near the synagogue. The earth was rocky, white as the stars above. The hour was late, and there were clouds of bats in the sky, in search of the last of the sycamore fruit in the arid ravines below. The center of the hottest time would soon be upon us, and the air grew heavy with heat, thick as a curtain.

I crept closer, hiding behind a citron tree that no longer bore the *etrog* fruit. Though the tree was stunted and leafless, the bark still sent out a peculiar fragrance, sharp and sweet at the same time.

I saw that the men had hold of a large urn, formed of simple dun-colored ceramic, the kind in which they stored their scrolls. They buried it carefully, softly chanting, then were quick to replace the sanctified ground. Their chants brought them to a place of ecstasy, and they rocked back and forth, raising the strands of their knotted prayer shawls to the sky so that God might hear them take joy in their prayers.

I thought about the Essenes' strange deeds for the rest of the evening. The next night I went back to sift through the shadows. Again they were at work, secretly burying yet another urn.

In the morning I asked my mother what it might mean for pious men to disturb holy ground in such a secret and heedless manner. My mother had been ailing for days, listless and pale, leaving the business of the dovecote to me and Yael and Revka, able to eat little but soup and water. She'd made a tea of bitter vetch and cucumber, green in color, very strong, which she sipped through the day. She could not bear the rising heat and poured water over her head, braiding her wet hair so that it stayed damp against her scalp.

"They're burying their scrolls because they're leaving." She was quite sure of this, for she had studied the Essenes' ways when they first came to us. Their scrolls were everything to them, the documents of their faith. "They want to make certain their word remains should they perish, and they trust none among us to keep them safe. It's their way of packing up before they depart."

"We have to stop her," I cried, thinking only of my sister. The matter was urgent; we had to rescue her now. I would take a rope to bind her and a scarf to cover her mouth so she couldn't call out as she had when we ran away from her father. I would ask Yael for the cloak of invisibility, the one she'd used to lead the Man from the North away, so that I might cover my sister from head to toe. If Nahara's husband came to search for her, he would see only the dew in the grass.

My mother sadly shook her head when I suggested we take action. "It cannot be done. Do you think I didn't see her fate as well as yours?"

My mother's damp hair shone in the dark. Lately, she could not drink enough water and was parched throughout the day. She had taken to wearing a black shawl. Her hands and legs were swollen, and her skin was dull, yet still she was beautiful. Some men said the sky paled before her and that in the World-to-Come the angels would be hesitant to call her to their side for fear her beauty would blind them.

"The moment I met the Essene I knew he was the one who would tempt her with the path she must not travel. I saw her destruction as I saw yours. Why do you think I sent him from the dovecote?"

"I don't understand."

I felt a sort of fury inside me. All along my mother had told me that I was the one to be unwound by love, not Nahara. I had changed the direction of my life not once but twice, simply because she had told me to do so. I had done her bidding without question, without doubt. I thought of how we had burned my garments on the shore of the Salt Sea, how I had denied who I was, willing to do anything to please her. I had turned away from Amram. Unable to reveal my true nature, I now felt little for him.

"You told me I was the one who must stay away from love. Now you're saying it's also Nahara's fate? And what of Adir? Has that been written as well?"

My mother glanced away, but I grabbed her arm. She winced and turned back to me. I realized I was stronger. I was no longer afraid of her powers. I wasn't duty-bound to keep promises to a woman who had told me only lies.

"Tell me God's truth, not yours. Is this the fate of all your children?"

"It was me," my mother admitted. Her voice was hoarse; she seemed fragile and distracted. "It was my fate. Whomever I loved would be doomed." The air was murky inside our chamber, as though we were underwater. "I tried not to love you."

There were tears streaming down my mother's face as she said this, yet I had no pity. She had destroyed the person I might have been had she not interfered with my destiny. My entire life had been based on her lies.

"You succeeded," I said coldly.

"I wanted to protect you. From love and, also, from me."

I thought she might be crying, but I didn't care. "And did you try not to love Ben Ya'ir?" I remarked rudely.

"Oh, no," she said. "In that matter I had no choice." She lifted her eyes to me. For once she presented me with the truth. "I loved him too well."

*

THE GOAT HOUSE was empty when I arrived. The field there was little more than rocks; the grass had dried into shreds, worthless yellow tufts. Unlike the day of Nahara's marriage, when she'd held her body against the door to bar our way, the door now swung open easily. These people had not believed in locks, for the only key that mattered to them was the one Moses had used to unlock the many truths of *Adonai*.

They had so little to take with them, a few goats, the garments they wore, their writing utensils so that they might continue to praise God as the world around them broke apart. Inside, the floor had been swept. I wondered if the broom leaning against the wall had been in Nahara's hands. I took it in my own hands for that reason, but the wood was cold. There was not a crumb to be seen; even the rats that had lately come upon us would have little reason to search in the corners of this chamber or beneath the neat beds of straw. In the yard, the clothesline was still strung between two date trees, a thick rope made of goat hair I might have used to tie my sister, binding her to us had I been quick enough to save her a second time.

From the corner of my eye, I spied a boy behind the tree. Tamar's son, Yehuda, was weeping on the ground.

"She wouldn't let me go with her," he told me.

I saw he had been tied to one of the date palms. His mother had done what I had wished to do in order to keep Nahara here. Now Yehuda was forced to remain with us, where Tamar hoped he would be safe.

Abba had decided that his people could not be party to our war. It did not matter that they did not directly engage in battle. Their eyes must not witness our storehouse of weapons. They could not abide here willingly if they knew it was our intent to fight the legion should we be attacked. And so it had been decreed, a message sent from God above. They could no longer eat the fruit from our orchards or drink the water from our cisterns or approve of us in any way. If there were children of darkness and children of light, and if there raged a constant battle between the two, then they had drawn a line between us, even though their foremothers, Rachel and Sarah and Rebecca and Leah, were ours as well, even though we prayed to the same God, He who had no equal. We could not claim the same world.

I untied Yehuda and brought him to Revka's house. There were rope burns on his arms, for he had desperately tried to escape his bonds. I asked if Revka might tend to him in his grief. He was a dark-haired boy, with liquid eyes and a large, distinctive head, already straining to be a man, humiliated by his mother's decision to leave him behind. Revka's grandsons knew him well, and Yehuda seemed comforted to be with them, though his eyes still welled with tears.

I went on to the wall so that I might watch the treacherous path the Essenes had chosen. They were headed toward a cave perched on the mountain where the cliffs were all but impossible to navigate. Hyenas had lived there, and it would be filthy inside, rife with their leavings and scattered bones. A herd of ibex startled when the Essenes came upon them. The wild goats raced sideways in their effort to flee, rocks flung from under their hooves, a curtain of dust rising as boulders rolled into the valley below.

In the swirl of dust, I could have sworn I spied Domah, the angel of the grave, whose very name means silence, the one who visits the dead to ask for the soul's true name before the spirit can travel on. But when the air cleared, I saw only the Essenes in their white robes, barefoot despite the harshness of the land, ignoring the thornbushes that grew there and the scorpions that rested beneath the rocks. I thought I could see Nahara following the men, a shawl covering her head, her eyes gazing upward, as if she trusted the path completely and had no fear that she might fall.

But it was another woman, one whose name I'd never learned, not my sister at all.

ꝏ

ON THE FIRST DAY of the month of *Av,* Yael came to our table. It was the time of year that brought us little more than tears and salt. We were all wary in the month when both Temples had fallen, on the same date Moses is said to have broken the tablets given to him by God when he came upon his people worshiping an idol, the ninth of *Av,* the Day of Calamity, when evil is released upon us. If *ha-olam* is the world, and *le-olam* is forever, then the two are intertwined. Yet in the month of *Av* the world that was meant to last forever seemed a fragile thing. Stone disintegrated, death haunted us, cities fell.

We did not speak of the slave's disappearance. We still felt his presence, for the hawk had returned to perch on the sill of the dovecote waiting for the mistress who had so kindly fed him grain from her hand for some time afterward. But that kindness had bound him, and he was a wild thing. Yael chased him away. She did so again and again until he, too, vanished, flying north. On the day he disappeared, Yael left the door of the dovecote open, the way we do when someone dies, to let a spirit free.

Now that the slave was gone, Yael appealed for my mother's help because she believed it was possible to bring Arieh back to his rightful home without fear of reprisal. Yael had her veil over her hair, the fabric clasped at her throat. I noticed the glimmer of the gold amulet, my mother's precious gift to her, was gone.

"You continue to make bargains with dead women," my mother said mournfully. "Have you not learned from the first ghost?"

"Channa is not dead," I countered, confused.

I had seen her that very afternoon, walking in the plaza with Arieh in her arms, and she had been very much alive. People whispered that she had convinced her husband God had meant for her to have this child, even though she had been barren since their marriage day. She told Ben Ya'ir that the one who had borne him had come begging her to take him in. The boy had been a gift and a blessing from *Adonai*.

"She is dead to me," my mother remarked coldly.

"I will do anything to get him back," Yael vowed. "I thought it would be a small price, a few days apart. I had no idea what she intended."

My mother shook her head sadly. "If I go against her, I place my own child in danger. Is that what you expect of me in the name of our friendship?"

"I'm not afraid of her," I said.

My mother gazed at me, then quickly looked away. That was when I knew. I was not the child she wished to protect. I understood what should have been evident for some time. There had been signs that my mother was with child, but I had simply failed to notice what I didn't wish to see. Of course I knew who the father was. The man who still kept the doves he'd sent to her on the Iron Mountain. She still belonged to him.

"Did you think I was a witch and not a woman?" my mother ventured to ask.

Hurt beyond measure, I shrugged. "Another one for you to destroy with your love."

Yael flashed me a warning look, then went to kneel beside my mother, begging for her help. "I will never ask for anything more. I swear it."

"She's already given you a precious gift," I said, referring to the amulet. The charm's absence had gone unnoticed by my mother. I wondered what she would think if she found her gift had been forsaken.

Yael exposed her throat to reveal that the amulet was gone. When she admitted she had given the talisman to Wynn for his protection, I felt shame to have confronted her so.

"Forgive me." Yael bowed her head before my mother. "He

needed it more than I. If you help me now, I won't ask again," she vowed.

"But I'll come to you for something," my mother confessed. "Trust is worth more than gold, loyalty is the best protection. If I do this for you, when the time comes, will you grant me anything I ask?"

"Anything," Yael promised.

"Channa is not like the other woman who wanted your child," my mother warned. "That woman had a heart, though she was dust. This one has none. Believe me, she would see your child murdered before she returned him to you. And she'll put a curse on mine. Remember that when I come for what I want."

They took the knife Yael carried with her at all times, and they cut their flesh, then let the drops of blood fall into a cup of oil to be burned before the image of Ashtoreth at our altar. My mother then brought forth a bowl of *samtar,* the poultice that heals wounds caused by arrows. She coated her body as a warrior might before battle. She took a heap of ashes and another of salt, and the precious balm of Gilead, made from the gum of the turpentine tree. When Yael went to accompany her, my mother stopped her.

Yael was puzzled. "You may need me."

My mother shook her head. "Not you." She looked at me, then nodded. "You."

Though I no longer had any duty to this woman, the mother who had lied to me and betrayed me, there was a child's fate at stake. And there was something more, something I would not have admitted aloud.

Despite the many ways she had betrayed me, I yearned to be the one she chose.

I covered myself with *samtar,* as my mother had done, and then with oil. I braided my hair and allowed seven knots to be tied inside my cloak, the number said to repel evil when witchery was before you.

"Do you think she's a witch?" I wondered.

My mother laughed. "I know that she is."

IT WAS DUSK when we went, the hour when dark and light are difficult to measure and all things are possible. My mother intended to perform an exorcism. Raphael himself occasionally came to help in such proceedings, and there were rumors that it was he who was so radiant who once instructed an exorcist to burn the heart and liver of a fish to drive away demons. My mother had such ingredients with her now, the dried organs of a fish that had miraculously appeared in a *nachal* on our travels to this mountain, its sole purpose the exorcism of evil. I shivered when I realized this was what my mother meant to do, for it was a truly dangerous act. Once this world was opened, the exorcist herself could fall prey to evil spirits. There were stories of exorcists who never spoke again, who had lost their hearts as a result of their attempts, found with nothing remaining of them save for a pile of dry bones.

We went along the wall, past the garden. The scent of mint was in the air. We could hear the doves calling. My mother didn't hesitate when she heard them. A smile crossed her face as she went to kneel beside their cage. She opened the door and I thought she meant to stroke their feathers, as she'd often petted the doves she kept when we were in Moab. Instead, she shook the cage so they came tumbling out. She took one in each hand and raised them up. The moment she let go, they lifted into the sky.

"There's no use for them anymore," she murmured as we watched them vanish, as we had done years ago, in another life it seemed.

It came as no surprise when we saw that Yael had followed and was waiting by the wall. She wore a dark veil, as though to disguise herself, but we knew her immediately, and understood why she could not stay away. Perhaps her presence outside the palace would add to our strength.

We went to the door made of cypress wood. My mother leaned in close so she might whisper. I could feel the heat from her body and smell the oil she'd rubbed upon her throat and wrists. As the demon was chased out of the woman we were about to face, we must take the child. In that moment, and only then, would our enemy be powerless.

"She will try to terrify you with her claims, do not listen. She will heap misfortune on you, do not be afraid. There is a missing ingredient that she needs for her powers. It's something only we have."

I understood what that ingredient was. My father.

We had made certain to plait our braids tightly, close to our heads, so that the demon we were about to face would be unable to grab us by our hair. We had rubbed pomegranate oil on our arms and legs so that we might slip easily from its grasp. We chanted *Abra k'dabra. I will create something from the word. Amen Amen Selah.* For the word of our God was what would guide us and would protect us from evil. His song would be our only path, despite any sins we might have committed and any punishments we might deserve. What we believed in, and what we said aloud, we could create before His eyes and in His image.

My mother had streaked her eyelids with lapis and perfumed herself with myrtle and lilies. She lifted her shawl over her head, perhaps to appear modest in her rival's eyes. Channa would be all the more dumbfounded when she discovered who had come to call.

My mother rapped on the door, lightly, as she might have if she'd had a basket of vegetables to offer, greens, perhaps, or cloves of garlic. We heard a scuffling, but there was no answer. My mother knocked again, more strongly now.

No one came to the door, and there was no longer any sound from inside.

I stepped onto the woodpile and drew myself up. In a corner, I spied the empty cradle. There were only shadows. But the fire was lit. A pot had been set on a metal post to hang above the flame, and the meal within was still cooking. I could smell the lentils and stewing meat.

I took from my cloak the key fashioned from a slip of metal wire. It had worked in the locked door of the tower so that Wynn could be released, perhaps it would once again. My mother stepped away so I might try. It fitted the lock perfectly. The door opened with a click. We went into the chamber where the evening meal that had been set upon the fire would soon enough burn and turn black, for it was bubbling, past readiness. My mother cast the innards of the fish into this stew, and the smoke that arose was a pale green, the color of envy and of betrayal.

Through the haze of the smoke we found a lamp, and although the glow was dim, it worked well enough so that we might find our way. We went along the hall, down the corridor where the frescoes of the seven sisters had been painted by masters from Rome. Each of the sisters was more beautiful than the next, yet none was as beautiful as my mother, not even the silver moon. She drew me to her, and we stood together beneath swatches of ocher and amethyst and sea green. She nodded toward a doorway, urging me to listen. She had done this when we were children, so that we might ascertain the difference between the approaching hooves of her husband's great steed, Leba, and the sound of any other man's horse. When my sister's father was puzzled that we children had run out to greet him long before he arrived, we would tell him that Leba could speak to us, and that the language of horses was easy enough to divine.

Now, in the house of Ben Ya'ir, I heard what I thought was a beetle, the kind they say search for the dead. After a moment I realized it was the rhythmic rasp of someone's breath. I tapped at my throat, and my mother nodded. We had found the one we searched for.

We followed the sound, pausing when it became more muffled,

edging forward when it began again. The breath led us to a small chamber where oil and wine were stored, the tall jars among the last that had belonged to King Herod. The room was dark, but the lamp we carried cast enough light for us to make out the long furrows of shadows. One shadow was like a pool of water that bled toward us in the darkness. She had crouched behind the door, a raven in a dark tunic, hunched down as though she might evade us as easily as dusk fading into a field of blackened trees.

As if magicked, Arieh called out to us. Perhaps he knew his true mother waited nearby. The raven quickly reached to cover his mouth, but he cried out again. He had recognized us, and we took this to be an omen. God was watching over us.

"You have no right to be here," Channa said when she had little choice but to face us. She stood up, proudly, as though she had not been cowering in the dark with the beetles, a shadow huddled behind a door. "When I call the sentries, you'll be locked in the tower yourselves. Or perhaps I'll see you set out in the wilderness. That's where you belong. You were condemned, yet you think you can come into this house and treat it as your own."

Channa was eyeing my mother as one might a demon that had crept in through an open window. My mother gave her no answer. She did not argue or respond to these evil words. She stood in the doorway so that Channa could not make an escape. It was too late to hide or shriek. My mother had already begun the exorcism. She spread down two circles of ash, then motioned to me. We stepped inside the circles as she began the Song of the Afflicted. My mother's voice was lovely, pure and ethereal. At first Channa merely listened, falling under the spell. Perhaps she thought she was being praised, or she had convinced herself that my mother had come to pay tribute, to admit her wrongdoings and eat the salt she now threw toward her rival, as some were said to eat their sins. But our leader's wife's eyes opened wide as she heard the words my mother recited.

He that dwelleth in the secret place of the most High shall abide under the shadow of the Almighty. I will say of the Lord, He is my refuge and my fortress: my God; in Him will I trust. Surely He shall deliver thee from the snare of the fowler, and from the noisome pestilence. He shall cover thee with His feathers, and under His wings shalt thou trust: His truth shall be thy shield and buckler.

Perhaps the wings I had always imagined set upon my back had been placed there for my protection by the Almighty, for I felt sheltered, delivered from nets and traps. Whatever my mother said, I repeated with her. Whatever her sins, I forgave her.

Before us, Channa held the baby more tightly as she gazed at my mother in alarm. "You took what should have been mine. He was to give a child to me, not you! Thieves are murdered for their deeds, not forgiven. You can't place a curse on me."

My mother continued the song of the Almighty, praising Him and asking for His light.

Thou shalt not be afraid for the terror by night; nor for the arrow that flieth by day. Nor for the pestilence that walketh in darkness; nor for the destruction that wasteth at noonday. A thousand shall fall at thy side, and ten thousand at thy right hand; but it shall not come nigh thee. Only with thine eyes shalt thou behold and see the reward of the wicked.

I listened, enthralled. *Amen Amen Selah.* My voice rang out, echoing my mother's. Channa turned to me. When she looked into my eyes, she saw her husband in my gaze. I took a step backward when faced with her meanness of spirit.

"Stay in the circle," my mother warned.

Now Channa knew me for who I was. She crept closer, the better to see me. Here I was, the child she had set into the wilderness for the ravens to peck at and the jackals to feast upon.

"You should have been mine," she told me. She threw my mother a brutal look. Her breathing was so labored it was difficult to hear her, but we heard enough. "You are the destroyer and the sin before God's name."

Her voice was hoarse, wrenched from inside her. Her words pierced me as no weapon could; still I did as my mother advised and kept within the circle. I refused to hear the poison set upon me by her envy. I heard only my mother's song. I could see the words she uttered becoming visible in the air between us, incandescent, written by faith.

Because thou hast made the Lord, which is my refuge, even the most High, thy habitation; there shall no evil befall thee, neither shall any plague come nigh thy dwelling. For He shall give His angels charge over thee, to keep thee in all thy ways. They shall bear thee up in their hands, lest thou dash thy foot against a stone. Thou shalt tread upon the lion and adder: the young lion and the dragon shalt thou trample under thy feet.

Channa was beginning to reveal who she was and what wickedness she was willing to undertake. "Arieh belongs to me! A covenant was made with the mother, before God!"

She, who had sent us into the wilderness so that we might be taken into the arms of Death when my mother was thirteen years old and I only newly born, grabbed for a knife and held it at Arieh's throat. I started toward the child, but again, my mother grabbed my arm.

Not yet, she whispered.

Channa was clutching Arieh so tightly he let out a hurt little yowl. I was grateful that Yael was not present and could not see the demon revealing itself to us. The moment would soon be upon us when she had no power at all.

"You haven't taken enough from me that you need to take this child as well? I'll see him in the World-to-Come before I see him with you."

There was sweat upon my mother's brow. Her lips moved as she repeated the song. No wonder men were transfixed by her and angels came to speak to her. No wonder the rain did her bidding and even the daughter she had betrayed would do anything she asked.

My mother's black cloak fell open. It was the moment when we all became who we were in the eyes of *Adonai.* Channa was outraged to see that my mother was with child. Her breathing worsened, rasping, as though a hand was at her throat, keeping air from her as she had kept my father from us. A sound emanated from her that was without words, a wounded, bloody cry. It was the demon.

That was when I went forth on behalf of the stolen child, snatching him from her with such force that she stumbled, slipping in the place where my mother had piled the salt which would contain the evil within her. My mother had no fear in her expression as she watched her enemy falter.

Because he hath set his love upon me, therefore I will deliver him: I will set him on high, because he hath known my name.

"You witch," the wife of our leader cried.

He shall call upon me, and I will answer him: I will be with him in trouble; I will deliver him, and honor him. With long life will I satisfy him, and show him my salvation.

"Take him," Channa said of Arieh, all but broken before us. "Do whatever you want with him. But you can't have my husband."

I took the child and ran with him so that his true mother might rejoice over him in the palace yard. Later, we would make a feast to celebrate and sing his praises, but now there was only one voice as I heard my mother dismiss our enemy. For it was she, neither an angel nor a witch, but a woman who was no longer afraid to speak, who faced her rival and proclaimed, "I've had him all along."

ꕥ

TRADESMEN CAME to us from beyond the Salt Sea, bringing spices and incense, herbs and seeds. We were desperate for their wares, haggling over chicory and sorrel, trading silver coins and semiprecious stones for such condiments. One of the traders had with him a huge black dog, a mastiff from Asia. This creature went to the place where my brother often camped beside the barracks when he'd been an errand boy for the warriors, enthralled by their courage and their deeds. Now Adir was among the men, gone from us, yet something of his essence must have lingered here, for the huge, shaggy dog refused to be removed. He threw back his head and howled. The dog was an omen, that much was evident, good or bad I did not know.

I looped a rope around his large head so he would stop his howling, then led him to our chamber, where I tied him outside. The dog watched after me, yelping until I returned, offering water. When the tradesman to whom he belonged came for him, the black dog refused to go. He ran forward and bit his owner, then hid behind my legs, peering out, bowing his huge muzzle and head, whining.

"You've ruined my beast," the tradesman shouted. "He was fierce, now he's a sheep."

The tradesman came from the eastern side of the Salt Sea. I knew the tones in which he spoke, the accent of my first father. The voice of Moab was beautiful to hear, even though the tradesman cursed me. When I answered him in kind, suggesting that the dog had made his choice and had perhaps been mistreated, the traveler was stunned at my knowledge of his speech. He accepted a few coins in exchange for the creature.

I did not wish to have a dog, yet he often accompanied me to the wall in the evenings as I kept watch over the valley with the other women, waiting for the warriors to return. I called him Eran, which means watchful, for the name suited this enormous and quiet creature. When I clicked my tongue, as I had for my horse in another world and time, he followed me. He did not bark or growl, nor did he beg at our table. I felt he would bring us luck; perhaps his fate and my brother's were bound together. When my mother didn't insist we be rid of him, though she disliked dogs and thought them little better than jackals, and when she set out a bowl of bread and milk, my brother's favorite foods, I knew she agreed.

There came a night when Eran began to bark and would not be comforted no matter how I tried to silence him. Soon my mother awoke. We both had the same sense of dread and together went to the wall in the dark. There were other women there as well, many in tears, for they also had experienced omens. One had woken from a dream sent to her by the angel Gabriel, in which her dead father had ordered her to station herself beside the gate. Another had heard a bat, the sign of vigilance and of stealth, flirting through her chamber.

Near dawn we could make out the warriors returning; we saw the dust arise before we viewed their figures. When they began to climb the serpent's path, our hearts lifted, then dropped. I was relieved to see Amram, but the slight figure he carried over his shoulder was my brother. I recognized his tunic and his cloak.

Our men had followed the Romans. There had been a skirmish, and our warriors had bested the modest troop of *exploratores,* whom they had outnumbered, sending them into retreat. Several of the unprepared soldiers of the legion had been slain despite the protection of their mail armor and bronze helmets. The rebels had done well, but Adir had been felled by a spear, and his wound was deep; he was aflame with fever. His dark hair was snarled, and his eyes, with their yellow flares, so like his father's and Nahara's, were runny and pale.

We took him to our chamber, where my mother bathed his listless body. His fever had turned him cold, as if Shalgiel, the angel of snow, had embraced him and brought him low. My mother told me to quickly burn Adir's garments. We did this to protect ourselves from the demons who might spread disease, but we also burned the cloaks of the dead in this manner. Perhaps this was why I could not bring myself to do as I'd been told. Instead I washed my brother's tunic and cloak in a bucket, then hung them on the clothesline behind the empty goat house where the Essenes had lived.

Our people cleansed their hands before every meal, before every cup of wine, before we cut a loaf of bread in two. We did so for good reason. Demons could enter an individual who was unclean, and the fire of a demon manifested itself as a fever. My mother instructed me to wear a scarf across my face when I tended to my brother. We washed our hands with a soap made of lye and ashes until our skin was raw. Every morning my mother brewed a tea of bay leaf, rose oil, and hot pepper. Although my brother made a face after a sip of the brew, he did as he was told and drank. A poultice of *samtar*, combined with *reita*, the cure made from wheat, was packed inside his cleaned wound.

My mother burned oil at the altar of Ashtoreth. She found a single lily growing in an abandoned garden, the rare bulb planted there a hundred years earlier by the gardeners of the king so that the petals and stems could be burned in a green flame for the glory of God.

Redeem this child and save him from all afflictions.

My mother took two doves from their nest that were so beautiful they themselves knew of their own beauty and proudly preened before their kind. She sacrificed them to the Queen of Heaven, though our people were no longer to make sacrifices, even to *Adonai*, now that the Temple was destroyed. She wiped the blood from her hands carefully to make certain there wasn't a stain.

Allow him to become a man and sing glorious songs of praise to our Lord and king, our mighty God. Amen Amen Selah. May He keep you from all evil and allow you to dwell in Jerusalem in holiness and in peace.

Adir had been a boy who'd been eager for war; what he'd found was a grim surprise. He returned to us quiet and melancholy. Even after his fever passed, his leg remained affected by his wound. He could not stand steadily, and this especially brought him grief. The only one who could cheer him was the huge dog I commanded to stay at his side. Because of this, my mother insisted I wash the creature so that his filth might not bring demons to my brother in his current weakened state. I brought Eran into the plaza and threw handfuls of water at him, then covered him with lye soap while he stood there impassively, though he might easily have bolted from my grasp.

"Is this who took my place?"

Amram came behind me and surprised me with his embrace. I allowed his arms to encircle me, though I felt an odd reserve. As we stood together, the dog barked and growled.

"Stop," I told Eran, but he wouldn't be quieted, and this worried me, for he had never seemed so ferocious before. Whatever his reason, he did not like the man before him.

"My rival," Amram teased. "If he bites me, I'll have to bite him back."

I tied the dog to the stump of a date tree, then pulled Amram aside so we might have some privacy.

"You must tell the warriors my brother can't go out again."

Amram laughed. "All warriors must go when they're called upon. You know that. And he's one of us now." Amram then took from his tunic the blue square of fabric that was his token for luck. "At least you don't have to worry for me. When I leave again, I'll find my way back."

I wanted to command him, but I knew Amram wasn't a man who would do a woman's bidding. It was I who must make certain my brother remained safe. I made a vow to myself as I stood there in the plaza, though I said nothing to Amram. Adir would not be among them when the next raiding party went out. I would make sure of it.

When Amram set out to fight, another warrior would walk beside him.

I ASKED for her favor, and Yael did not deny me, for I was the one who had placed her son back in her arms. I had snatched him from the sinister woman who wished so desperately to be his mother she had convinced herself that she was. Yael waited for me in the plaza, where heat waves rose from the earth, the baby at her hip. Since Arieh had been returned to her, she refused to let him out of her sight for long. If she needed help and Revka and I were at work at the dovecote, she would occasionally leave him with her father, who had taken a liking to the child. He had made amends with Yael in the way he cherished her son. Perhaps he thought he had a second chance to forge another warrior. I'd overheard Revka ask why Yael allowed this man to be included in her son's life when he'd been so cruel to her. Yael said he was a changed man now, beaten down by the desert and by his age.

"When I see him with Arieh," Yael admitted, "I see the man he might have been had he not lost the one he loved most in this world."

Arieh's safety was assured while he was in the care of a grandfather who had been among the great *Sicarii* of Jerusalem, for the assassin's knife was still hidden within his cloak, even though he was now delegated to clean weapons. It was he I wanted to see, and I asked Yael to lead me to his chamber. The assassin had disapproved of me as unworthy of his son. Perhaps Yael imagined I wished to win him over. But a man such as he could not be easily convinced, and in fact I wanted no such thing.

"You remember Aziza," Yael said to her father.

Yosef bar Elhanan looked up, appraising me with a cool glance. I wondered how many men he had murdered, if the rush of blood had ever humbled him or made him seek forgiveness. He took the baby on his lap, then nodded. "The *shedah*," he said.

He meant to insult me, but I smiled prettily. Such things as smiles can be weapons as well.

Yael went to make tea, though she feared leaving me at her father's mercy.

"I'm used to such men," I assured her, for indeed I knew that among men words were not nearly as perilous as the ones women spoke.

The assassin ignored me and tended to the child with unexpected affection. I leaned forward so only Bar Elhanan would hear, for what I was about to say was far too intimate a request for anyone passing by to overhear.

"I want you to teach me to be invisible," I told him.

The old man had been jiggling Arieh on his knees, much to the baby's delight. I half-expected him to feign deafness when I informed him of what I wanted, but he was curious when I made my request and couldn't resist knowing more. He stared at me rudely, giving me no more respect then he would a common *zonah*.

"Why would I do this?" he asked.

"So I can protect your son and my own brother."

"My son is lost to me because of you."

I knew distance still remained between Bar Elhanan and his son, but I wasn't afraid to talk back to him and stand my ground. If I slunk away under the heat of his words, he would never respect me.

"If he's lost to you, it's because you're too lazy to go and find him."

The assassin chuckled and shook his head sadly. "True. I shut the door to him, and now I wonder why he doesn't walk through it."

I had hit upon his heart, for it turned out that he had one, so I dared to continue.

"I want to take my brother's place, for it should have been my place to begin with."

The assassin snorted a laugh. His weathered face showed only amusement. He seemed to believe I was there to entertain him with foolish tales. He would have begun to admonish me to keep to women's work had I not learned what my sister's father had taught me. You are only worthy of what you prove yourself to be. Before the assassin could dismiss me, I reached for the blade I carried. I leapt to stand behind him, placing the knife at his throat. Though it was forbidden to grab at me, Bar Elhanan had committed far worse sins. He ably grasped my arm and twisted it backward, nearly breaking it, all the while holding the baby on his knee. We were both breathing hard.

"For what cause did you come to murder me?" he demanded to know.

"That was not my purpose."

He let go, and I faced him once more. He gazed at me, confused.

"Are you a woman?" he said thoughtfully, impressed and puzzled by my quickness with a weapon.

"Most of the time," I answered.

Fortunately, he laughed. "I am nothing here," he told me. "But if you want to learn to clean spears and armor, then I'm your man."

"No. I want more," I said. "I want to be invisible."

By the time Yael had returned with the tea, her father had decided he would allow me to borrow his cloak. When we left, he suggested I visit him on the following day. I was interested in cleaning weaponry, he told Yael when she looked at him questioningly, and he had much to teach me.

ON THE DAY we were to leave we entered the month of *Elul*, a time of introspection before the holiest days come to us. I awoke in the dark while my brother, still healing, his leg bandaged, dozed on his pallet. I hurried to the goat house and dressed in his garments, burying my own beneath a pile of straw. I had been practicing weaponry daily with the old assassin, an uncompromising teacher. I was a puzzlement to him, but he was grateful that someone, even I, would ask to see his great skill. It bothered him not at all if I was harmed during our practice. His manner was remote, his methods cruel, but he had instructed me well.

The dog followed me while I retrieved my brother's tunic and cloak, waiting patiently. I thought perhaps he was at my side because he imagined I was Adir, or perhaps he assumed I was gathering a meal for him. Yet when I shooed him away, he insisted on traipsing along to the barracks. In the dark I dressed in armor, a sheet of silver scales. I wore my head scarf tied low on my forehead so that my face was obscured and I might appear to be my brother in the other warriors' eyes. Sure enough, a fellow named Uri came out and told me which spears to collect for the others. I did so willingly.

I had brought along only a small pack containing figs and pistachios and hard cheese, along with the gray cloak. The old assassin had taught me the tricks of invisibility, how to walk in shadow, how to step without making a sound, how to slip from the grasp of another's attack in a blur of fog. At the end of our time together, he had proclaimed me a worthy student, although he assured me I would not make a good wife for Amram.

"They can say you're a woman, but you're something else." The assassin was aging, but he was still clear-eyed, and his glance was piercing.

"A *shedah*?" I tried to make a joke of it.

He might have laughed, but he didn't. "A warrior," he said.

I bowed in gratitude, and left him there to clean other men's weapons.

*

THERE WERE SIXTY of us who left that day, a raiding party led by Ben Ya'ir himself. My heart raced to think that I was now to be one of my father's men, and that I was to follow him and perhaps bring some pride to him. I tied Eran to a post, but he shrank out of his rope and chased after me. Because he refused to leave my side, I used the huge dog as one might pack a donkey with belongings, enlisting a thick rope so I might tie spears onto either side of his body. Certainly, the beast was as strong as a donkey, and nearly as stubborn.

As we went through the gate, I was at the rear of the column. I could see the man who was my father in the lead and, behind him, Amram and his friends. I knew Amram even from a far distance, for he had attached the blue square to his armor. I could glimpse it as we made our way down the twisted path.

The heat was blistering, and the sky blazed white. I was unused to the armor I now wore, and the bulk of it made my gait awkward. The people of my sister's father had never worn anything that might have weighed them down. The lighter they were, the more fleet, able to dart in and out of battle; only their horses were protected by metal masks and chest pieces, for the tribesmen knew the value of such creatures. I longed for the horse that had been given to my brother, or the great warhorse Leba, who could always find his way home and had no need of a bridle. On horseback I would have been flying; now I trudged along.

The footpath was treacherous for the careless. Dust rose into our faces, and the rocks slid out beneath our feet. I stayed to myself, Eran at my side, and let the other warriors interpret my demeanor as shyness. As we went along, several men applauded me for my willingness to set forth so soon after my wound. They praised Eran as well, saying that a man whose dog was loyal to him was one you wanted beside you in battle. I dipped my head in gratitude, giving thanks in silence. Whoever gives his true self away does so with words.

We were setting forth in the direction of Ein Gedi. West of that place there was said to be a band of travelers who had settled among the local people and had in their possession gold and gemstones, oil and frankincense. On the mountain we were suffering from great poverty. When our walls fell down, we repaired them with mud and straw; when our lamps were without oil, we let them remain dark; when there was not enough wood, we used the waste of donkeys for our fires. We ate not stew or boiled meat but gruel, a thin mixture of barley flavored with the flesh of the few doves we had to spare for our meals. Our warriors had no choice but to take what they needed from villages and camps, so our people might live. It was no different than what I had done alongside Nahara's father. This was our country, and we were its kings, and those who entered were wise to understand they were at our mercy.

We walked until we were tired, sleeping in the open. The night was brisk, and I was glad for the dog's presence, for I lay beside him and he warmed me. I watched Amram from beneath the cover of my cloak and my armor, but I was careful not to reveal myself. I kept my head down so that he would not see the scar he thought was a teardrop. I used the tricks I'd perfected in Moab, going off alone to relieve myself, never shirking my duties, speaking rarely and, when I did, only in a dull voice. They all came to accept me as Adir.

As soon as I could, I went off to hunt. I shot a young ibex, and when the buck stumbled upon being struck by my arrow, I went to him and slit his throat so that his spirit might rise painlessly and with dignity. When I brought my kill back to camp, draped over my shoulders, Amram himself came to butcher the creature with me.

"You have good aim, little brother," he said to me.

My heart was hitting against my chest. I was both afraid that he would know me and perhaps more frightened that he would not. I swallowed my words and nodded simply in reply. My hands shook because of his nearness to me, and my deceit. I felt at that moment I was so clearly a woman that I was announcing myself with every breath I took. But I was not recognized. He clapped me on the shoulder heartily and still did not feel how hard my heart was beating.

I couldn't blame Amram for not recognizing me when I had taken such care to disguise myself. The old assassin had taught me that men never see what is right before their eyes. They look in corners and under rocks, but if you are standing in front of them, they will pass you by, believing you to be no more than an olive tree, a part of the landscape and nothing more. Bar Elhanan had learned this as he skulked through the courtyards of the Temple, searching out his enemies. Disappear into something, he instructed me. Become not what you are but what is around you. A stone, a shadow, one archer among many. Mice are unseen because they cloak themselves in the darkness so often that, when they do step out before you, they appear as shadows. A shadow is viewed with the mind, not the eye, he told me. That is how you convince those around you to see you as you wish to be seen.

I had taken to wearing the assassin's cloak in the evenings when I walked with the dog. There were rock hyrax living in burrows, and the hoof marks of ibex traveling through, in search of the waterfalls nearby, the place where it was said King David once made his camp. It was there *Moringa Peregrina*, the orchid with pink-white blooms that appeared every spring, could be found. David is said to have written over three hundred songs, one for every day of the year. There were no orchids where I wandered; only scrubby myrrh grew on the limestone cliffs. I plucked some out and tucked it beneath my cloak, as women often do for the value of its fresh scent, making certain to avoid the sharp stems.

The others left me to myself, accepting my reserved demeanor, while they prepared for the battle to come, testing their weapons, drinking what little wine they had brought along to sustain them. I was not the only one who was withdrawn. There was another warrior who remained on the edges of camp, refusing to eat from the ibex I had brought down, choosing to fast instead. I stumbled upon him when I went off to relieve myself far from the camp, as I did every night. This warrior recoiled from human contact; he needed no comfort, no cloak to warm him, no brothers-at-arms.

The dog did not growl when we came upon the one they called the Man from the Valley, who wound his flesh with metal. Though this went against our laws, no one dared to condemn him for his savage ways. His white braids belied his youth and were so long they trailed down his back. The other warriors said that in battle God was able to lift him out of danger, grabbing on to his hair to keep him from harm. That was why he was able to walk into a raging conflict and walk back out again, when any other man would have been slain. His flesh was covered with scars, many untended and unhealed. The metal dug into his muscular arms and left bands of blue and purple wounds.

He was kneeling beside a thornbush when I came upon him, chanting the mourning song for the dead, holding on to the sharp branches that pierced his skin to cause himself more pain. I had never seen a man so open in his agony. I felt that I could weep at the sight of him; instead I ran away.

I grabbed Eran by his neck, and together we fled far from that place, racing as if we were horses. The dust rose up, and the hyrax in their burrows hid from us. The tawny owls rose into the air above the cliffs; rattailed bats shuddered up from the jujube trees in a cloud of flesh and wings, forsaking the orange fruit on the branches.

The next day the man I'd stumbled upon was staring at me. I knew that no warrior wished to fight alongside him, for he cared not at all for his own life. He wielded his ax and no other weapon, but that ax was said to be blessed and could not miss its target. I gazed away from him, not wishing to reveal my true nature, or in any way to set a light to the fire of his fearsome rage, said to be so violent and unquenchable his brethren whispered that he fought at the right hand of Gabriel, the fiercest of all angels.

That evening we prepared for the night raid. I'd been made dizzy with the heat and the weight of my own subterfuge, along with the heavy, silver-scaled armor. We stood in line for our share of water under the harshness of the fading sun. When I asked for a portion for my dog, the fellow in charge of our rations shook his head.

"He'll have to drink the dirt," I was told. "There's not enough to give the beast his share."

I went away, troubled. I shared the provisions I'd brought with my dog and had thrown him the bones of the ibex. Nahara's father had taught me that you feed your horse before you feed yourself, but I had barely water enough for my own parched throat. I had come to be a warrior, now I found my greatest concern was a creature I had not wanted in the first place. As I was worrying over what I might do, the Man from the Valley approached. Again the dog failed to growl. The warrior put down his share of water in its cup. He nodded to Eran.

"He'll be thirsty," he said.

I mumbled some words of gratitude, then asked, did he himself not need to drink?

"Water doesn't quench my thirst," the Man from the Valley told me. And then, for no apparent reason, he said, "Don't go tonight."

Clearly he thought I was a callow boy; to him I was my brother, Adir, who'd been wounded and had little experience in battle. He need not have worried for me. "I've fought men many times," I assured him. "And they've suffered because of it."

He nodded. His glance didn't meet mine. "But this is your first time among us. You haven't been at war. You haven't raided a village."

That was true, the bloodshed I'd known on the eastern side of the Salt Sea had been on the grasslands, along the King's Highway.

"It's my duty to go," I said simply.

I felt his glance upon me, but I looked away now to hide the truth of who I was.

"When the time comes," the warrior all others avoided advised me, "stand beside me."

A MIST had come up to cover the ground as my gray cloak covered me. This was considered an omen of good fortune, for it would allow us to surprise our enemies. My bow was readied as we came down upon the village where the travelers were. The air had cooled, but the ground was still burning from the heat of that day. The earth itself seemed to have a beating heart, and the thudding of my pulse met its rhythm. I saw Eleazar ben Ya'ir in the dark. He was saying a prayer, and he wore his prayer shawl, for he fought for the glory of God. He gathered us together a last time. Before him we resolved to be one in battle. We vowed we would never take slaves.

"We would not want our women and children enslaved," Ben Ya'ir said. "We do the same for those we meet in battle."

People said that our leader had seen those closest to him crucified in Jerusalem, brothers and friends, dying in agony before him. Afterward, the Romans had cut the heads from the bodies and tossed them into the road for the mourners, but without bodies there could be no lamentations, no burials, no peace. Ben Ya'ir spoke the words of our God.

Whoever is disheartened should go back home, for he might cause the heart of his fellows to melt as his does.

But our home was Jerusalem, and Zion had fallen, and not a single warrior turned away from the battle to come. I saw Amram lift his spear along with the others to cheer and honor our leader's words. Only the Man from the Valley did not join them in prayer or in their fevered shouts. Perhaps he had already said prayers of his own. Perhaps the single prayer he recited was a song for the departed. He did not wear a prayer shawl or even a robe, merely a tunic and the metal he wound around his arms. He wanted pain, I saw that in him, and what a man wants he will often manage to find.

We went in stillness as the moon began to rise. I followed near Amram, so that I might keep watch over him, the dog at my heels, the great beast as silent as we were. The heart of the earth was pounding. The world was shrouded in silence until we came upon the guards. Then there was a wild shout and instantly the frantic calls of men in the village. Quickly, the shouting became deafening and the fray began. I went to one knee and began to work my bow, doing my best to ensure the safety of those who went before me. I killed two men right away, and they fell before Amram. Perhaps he thought an angel was beside him, for he gave thanks to God right there.

My dog barked whenever the enemy neared. His warning allowed me to know in what direction I should aim, for there were men approaching from every angle and chaos all around. I might have panicked but for Eran, and I vowed to keep him close from then on.

Our warriors had the best of the townspeople before long; the bodies of the slain were everywhere. I spied the Man from the Valley, a whirlwind with his ax. In the midst of four of the enemy, he brought each one down, then stood among them, appearing to dare their corpses to rise again and battle once more. When yet another villager raced at him, leaping upon his back, he calmly drew his enemy from him and split him open with his ax. The Man from the Valley looked for the next to be slain, diving into the chaos with an intensity that belied the danger around him, his weapon readied. I could feel my blood racing and a kind of joy rising inside me as I shot a man who dashed toward him. I thought that, if my father knew how many had fallen to my arrows, he would be proud to take me to him as his son.

The night was hot with blood, the ground slick, the scent of death everywhere. There were locusts in the air, humming and rising before us. Because I wore silver-scaled armor beneath my cloak, my limbs ached and were heavy, and I was drenched with sweat. I used my head scarf to wipe the film from my eyes, rising from my knees.

In that moment when I lowered my bow, it was as if I had stepped outside the battle. Perhaps I watched as the angels did, removed and distant but holding the ability to see far more than the men who were embroiled in the fight. My hazy vision made me disbelieve what was before me. We had slaughtered the men who had come to defend themselves, along with the travelers in their blue cloaks, men from Moab who had journeyed here to trade spices and dried fruit. There were no acacia branches to burn in their honor, therefore their spirits would not wish to leave their bodies. I was pained to know they would be trapped in a netherworld, far from the Iron Mountain, for no other men would rise from the blood that had been spilled, blood that was as red as ours until it pooled blackly in the earth.

The night had become a dream. The battle now was to force myself to wake from what was before me, for beyond the piles of dead men was something far more terrible than the corpses of warriors. Our men had begun to kill the women who ran from the houses. It was impossible, we did not believe in such cruelty, yet I knew it was true because I heard the voices of the slaughtered. Theirs were the screams of women, and yet there was worse still. Beneath those screams, I heard the cries of children. When I spied Amram, he became a part of the dream, changing before me into a demon, his face a demon's face, his deeds a demon's doings.

Our leader had said there were to be no slaves taken. I had understood this to mean we would let the women and children be, but that was not how warfare was practiced in this sorrowful world. The dog was going mad, yelping and barking, distraught as no beast should be. I held him around the back of his neck and bade him stay, breaking my nails on his rough fur. I felt maddened, as he was, by the sights before me and the wild death calls of the innocent. I nearly leapt in, but on our enemies' behalf, against my own people. I had the urge to fight the men I'd come here with, my brethren. Confused amid the rising bloodshed, I suddenly had no idea why we believed we had the right to take what these people had, other than the fact that we wanted it and assumed we were entitled to what belonged to others, as the robbers had once wanted me and my mother and all we possessed.

I stood there, encircled by the destruction, escaping my own death by the grace of God. I no longer cared to fight, nor had I the stomach for it. I closed my eyes and waited for *Mal'ach ha-Mavet* to come for me, as he was meant to do when my mother and I were sent into the wilderness. Perhaps I was never intended to live past that day when Eleazar's wife disposed of us and had been wrong to elude my fate.

I would never know if the Angel of Death meant to approach on this night of battle, for the Man from the Valley gripped me by my cloak and pulled me after him, out of Death's grasp. Eran and I went with him, even though I could barely breathe, my heart heavy inside me, beating much too fast. I bit my lip until there was more blood to come, until it was my own. I wanted the taste of it. I deserved it.

The warrior led me to a ridge where the haze of the evening had dissipated. He had many wounds from this battle, but he paid no attention to them, just as he made no mention of the fact that I wept. We could see the massacre from here. The houses in the village were made of stone; soon they would be emptied completely. Everything these people owned would belong to us. I took off my helmet and my bloodstained cloak. I understood now that the Man from the Valley had told me not to go because he had known what might happen. He would not murder women and children and refused to see their blood shed. He'd known I was a woman, yet he'd said nothing. He'd known what his commander wanted of him, yet he'd done God's bidding instead.

Of all who were before me, he was the only one I wished to stand beside.

THEY LET the donkeys live, heaping them with the possessions that now belonged to us, the ginger and pepper, the gourds and leeks, all manner of wine and oil and wheat, small amounts of gold, earrings and rings taken from homes and from corpses, heaps of precious cinnamon, lamps, stacks of weaponry. They took the goats and the sheep and killed the chickens. They filled leather containers with water and cheese. Everything smelled like blood.

I went back to the village to gather my arrows. They were easy to find among the slaughtered, a field of red lilies I had left behind. All I needed was to pluck them one by one from the chests and backs of the fallen. I took nothing else. While others gathered the rings from cold fingers, the wine from the storerooms, I washed the blades of my arrows in a bowl of water taken from a rain barrel, reciting a prayer as I did so, entreating *Adonai* not to cause those who had died tonight to suffer any further torment, pleading for Him to keep them safe from the three gates of Gehennom, the valley of hell. I could not look into the faces of the slain women and children, but I began to search among the men from Moab for those I might know.

Amram came by, covered with sweat and dried blood. "Don't bother," he said to me as I turned over the bodies of my sister's father's people. "They're all the same."

BEN YA'IR spoke to the warriors as the last of the night settled around us. I could not abide to be among them. People said that he thanked God, then praised his men for their bravery. He instructed his warriors to say prayers for the souls of the dead and told them that, in another time and place, if our enemies from Rome had not forced us into starvation and poverty, we would have called our victims our brothers.

By that hour we had moved into the high desert, making haste so that we could not be found by any of the townspeople who might have been absent during the raid, returning with vengeance in their hearts. The warriors prayed to God and then killed a goat for their supper. To me the goat's cries sounded like those of a woman. I huddled beside my dog, covering my ears, rocking back and forth on my haunches. The radiance of the Shechinah, the light and compassion of the Almighty, was nowhere near this campground. Here, we were surrounded by what some called the other side, the dark realm, for on this night we had wandered onto the evil side of the world that was also born from creation, that terrible region which could be found at the left hand of God and fed on human sin.

I had planned to lie beside Amram that night after our victory, to bring his hands beneath my cloak so that I might finally let him know who I was and give myself to him, but I did no such thing. I was sick to my stomach and sick at heart. I went into the desert and brought up everything I had eaten since I'd left my mother's house. The taste was sour, as if I had spat out a demon. I was glad my brother had not been among us. Adir, who had such a gentle spirit, yet wanted nothing more than to be among the warriors, had been spared the sight of the cowardly actions of those he so admired.

The white cliffs were invisible in the dark. Everything was hidden. I now understood it was our duty as human beings to see behind the veil to the inside of the world, to the heart of things.

I glimpsed the Man from the Valley and went to stand beside him. There was a circle of thornbushes, and larks were sheltered in the cluster of branches. We heard the others' voices singing, but their songs meant nothing to us. Every bit of the stained earth we walked upon seemed a part of the territory of transgression, where enemies were subdued at any cost. No acacias grew here. There was no way to help the souls of the dead find peace.

Today I had seen my beloved kill a child who could not have been more than four. It seemed nothing to him to do so, but everything to me. Other than the stars in the sky, I could not see any image but the face of the child who'd been murdered, for he now lived behind my eyes and would be a part of my vision forevermore. Every time I looked at Amram, it was that child I would see.

I wished I had been a woman and had stayed at home.

"Did you not think this was what the world was like?" the Man from the Valley said to me.

My dog lay at my feet. There was blood on his fur. By daylight flies would be swarming over him and he would look monstrous. Eran had never once deserted me in the bloody turmoil but had lurched toward anyone who approached me, snapping at them, baring his teeth.

I had never felt as vulnerable, or as flooded with shame. I had lost something so completely, I did not think I could get it back from anything that had been created on earth. I needed to look into heaven. The haze had vanished by this time, and the stars were bright. We saw some drift across the darkness in blasts of light, then vanish, invisible to our eyes. I was transfixed by the sight, and by the goodness of a dumb beast who had never once thought to flee from my side, and by the fact that both I and the warrior I stood beside were still alive.

"Is it not beautiful?" I said of the world around us.

"Is it not terrible?" the Man from the Valley countered.

He gazed at me, and all at once I knew that it was a question and that he needed an answer. I took his hand and pulled him to me, and had him lie down beside me. As he had rescued me, I did the same for him. For one night, when we could still smell the blood on each other, when the night was black and all the world was invisible, we were not alone.

❧

ADIR'S WOUND had healed and his fever had ended, yet my brother limped and seemed frail. My mother worried over him and tried one cure after the next, sifting through her piles of herbs and her recipes for *pharmaka*. Still he was weak. Though she had disapproved of my actions in the past, she agreed I should again take Adir's place when the time came for him to be called back to fight. This was as it should be. I was the better warrior, the one more likely to return. Once again, my mother and I shared secrets. It was a bond we didn't deny, one that was meant to be, for our fate had always been entwined. Whatever bitterness had been between us had dissipated.

Perhaps my father was hoping for a son, as Adir's father had, for Ben Ya'ir had grown reckless when it came to my mother, meeting her in the cistern nearly every night, delighted both with her and with the child that was to be. His own wife was confined, nowhere to be seen. People whispered that Channa was ill again, but I wondered if perhaps her husband had forbidden her to go among the other women. He would not tolerate her interference any longer, for he had given her most of his life. What little he might have left he now claimed for his own.

Ever since our arrival he had been practicing his own form of invisibility, not unlike the skills the old assassin had taught me. He had kept his yearning for my mother hidden right in front of other people's eyes. Indeed, they had looked past what was so evident and seen nothing. He had the right to claim another wife when his own proved to be barren; still Channa had fought him and done her best to trick him, insisting that God had given her the child she stole from Yael.

Now, when it seemed that every day was a gift and another might not follow, as the Essenes had vowed, my father no longer bothered with subterfuge. I had spied him with my mother outside our door, in an embrace so deep it seemed they were drowning. There were evenings when he sat at our table, to join in the meager meal. At such times I remained outside the door, bringing my brother with me into the yard, though he had to lean on my shoulder merely to walk. We sat outside and ate dried fruit and flatbread from our hands. Perhaps my brother assumed I believed neither of us had the right to be in the presence of the great man. But I could not see Ben Ya'ir without my head swimming with the screams I had heard during the village raid. I felt that I had failed him in some way, and that he in turn had failed me. Perhaps it had been better to have viewed him from a distance, so that his flaws were left unseen. I had wanted him to know me in battle and acknowledge me as his own; now I felt invisibility suited me.

And yet one night, as he left our mother's chamber, Ben Ya'ir stopped before us. I had warned my brother what to do if such an occasion should ever occur. We were both to lower our eyes in the presence of our leader.

"When you go into battle again, you may need this," Ben Ya'ir said.

He laid a knife down before us. I spied that the hilt was set in bronze, beautifully decorated with a bower of leaves. *Perac lavan* was engraved upon it. *White flower.* He had carried this knife in honor of my mother and of the lilies she had loved as a girl in Alexandria. I did not agree with all that he did, or his ways in battle, but he was my father. The gift was for a warrior, so I elbowed my brother. Adir mumbled words of thanks, but when Ben Ya'ir left us, I was the one to take up his knife.

*

MORE AND more often, we had our meals in the yard so that my mother and Ben Ya'ir could have privacy. We were not the only ones who knew that our leader came to my mother's chamber each night. Jealousy stalked my mother and mistrust had sifted down upon the mountain. She was a woman who had been in chains, who could call to demons and draw the *kadim* to her. One midnight a quartered dove was left outside our chamber, its beak and feet chopped off, the white feathers dusted black with a scrim of soot. I gave my mother Ben Ya'ir's knife after that, so that she might rebuke any ill intentions. It was a gift from her beloved and therefore rightly belonged to her, for although I owed my mother my first life, I owed my second life to the Man from the Valley, not to Ben Ya'ir. I now felt I had been a fool to think my father had been one of the angels; my true father had been the man on the Iron Mountain, the one who had rescued us and taught me all I'd needed to know.

My mother took the knife, the token of Eleazar's protection. I advised her to lock the door whenever I was gone, and to be more discreet, lest she be the cause of her own prophecy and be brought to ruin by love.

A GROUP of Roman *exploratores* stunned us all when they set up camp in the valley. It happened in our holiest month, *Tishri,* when we celebrate our new year and atone for our sins, the ones we are responsible for and the ones that are to come.

When the scouts arrived, we thought they would be like all the others; they would stand amazed at the position of our fortress, then move on to report we could not be conquered. But this group was different. These soldiers intended to stay. They'd brought urns of wine and oil, herds of camels, and most telling of all, bakers who had settled into their own camp. We could smell the scent of fresh bread baking in their domed ovens.

It was apparent that these soldiers were only the first of what would soon be a legion. Rome was amassing an army outside of Jericho with ten thousand soldiers, along with a thousand Jews who were enslaved and made to serve the Emperor. Our council proclaimed that women were no longer allowed to venture beyond the gates for any reason, to make certain they would not fall into the hands of our enemies. Men who journeyed away from the mountain did so at their own peril. The warriors still went out but more stealthily, taking the serpent's path in the cover of dark or making their way down the back of the mountain, a climb so treacherous, several lost their lives upon attempting to return. Despite the danger, I lived for these nights when the owls glided above us. We made our way past our enemies as though we were mist, freed from our earthly forms.

At night I paced our chamber, wanting nothing more than to go beyond the gates. The only small joys we had were in celebrating Arieh's many accomplishments. He was now fourteen months old. Even those who looked down on a fatherless child admitted he was unusual, handsome and large and respectful. He was so beloved among the women in the dovecote that, each time he ran on the cobblestones or spoke the name *immah* to his dear mother, we applauded as though he had climbed a mountain.

I sat with the women at the looms in the evenings. Though I could not weave, I helped to spin what little wool there was. Beside me, my dog put his head on my knee. Eran and I wanted the same thing, the freedom of the wilderness, but we needed patience. I yearned to be like the Man from the Valley, who slept beyond the fields. I did not see him, or search for him, but I knew he was there. Whenever we were called to go back down the mountain on raids, slipping past the Roman scouts, I made certain to walk beside him, for with him I did not have to pretend to be anyone other than who I was.

*

AMRAM had sent a girl to me to ask why I no longer met him at the fountain. He waited for me in the evenings, but I did not appear. Now he had taken a risk and engaged this child to do his bidding. The girl, not more than four or five, was the daughter of one of the warriors, a friend he trusted from his days in Jerusalem. The child's braid was thick and black, her manner friendly. She reminded me of Nahara, with her bright, knowing eyes. I said to tell the man who'd sent her that a fever was upon me. I flushed with the burden of my lie, and perhaps I appeared aflame, truly overtaken by an ailment, for the child seemed to believe me. Quickly she backed away, then ran to deliver my message.

It was the time of *Rosh Chodesh,* and the priest who watched for the rising moon sounded the call of the ram's horn for us to gather for the Blessing of the New Moon, *Kiddush levanah,* a prayer which grants us favor from God and invites the Shechinah, all that is compassion and wisdom, into our midst. Our people stood beneath the new moon to listen to the priests and the learned men. We rejoiced, celebrating the passage of time with dancing, our musicians taking up rattles and cymbals and bells in defiance of the Romans stationed in our valley. We prayed and danced together, but only the women would not work in the morning, for they were tied to the moon in ways men could not understand, closer to the female heart of creation.

I kept to the shadows so that Amram would not see me, for I had noticed him among his brethren. When I looked at him, I saw not his handsome features but the face of the murdered child from the village, no older in years than the girl who had brought me his message. There was no one with whom I could share the joy of the new month. I yearned for my sister and the way in which we had danced together in the country of her father, though his people did not count their days as we did. Our mother had taught us that when the moon was white, reappearing after its absence, it was showing us that what had been hidden could easily become whole again.

That night in my sleep perhaps I did become fevered, made ill by my sister's absence. I yearned for her, the girl I had brought into this world. I dreamed that there were seven wolves on the mountain, and that each had brought forth a dove in its mouth, and that every one of the doves had seven wings and could fly farther than any others. Seven is the most powerful number of all. The first words of the Torah are seven in number, and the Sabbath is the seventh day, the most holy of all. Now my dream had come to me in sevens. This seemed to me a blessing and a calling, one I couldn't ignore.

I went to the wall to watch for my sister.

I stood there much of the day, convinced my dream had been a pathway, a sign that God knew my sister still belonged to me and that we could never truly be parted. At twilight, the hour between worlds when one's eyes can play tricks and it is easy to see what you wish to view rather than what is before you, I thought I spied Nahara. She was following the thin black goats as they searched in vain for tufts of grass on the sheer, rocky cliff. Below us, in their camp, the Romans would soon enough notice her as well if she went along the mountain while there was still light. Since the soldiers had made camp, the Essenes had not left their cave in daylight. But their provisions would last for only so long if no one came to their assistance. If they had no spring and no well, they would soon die of thirst.

Half of the doves had been taken from us, though my mother begged they be allowed to live. Instead, they had been used for meat. We had but a few baskets of their leavings to feed the earth, and the earth repaid us in kind for our lack of gratitude. In the orchards the leaves that unfurled were spotted; fruit came to us already withered. During our harvest, I gathered what I could for my sister. I could not look across the valley and watch her starve while we could still manage to feed ourselves, however meagerly. I packed dried beans and millet, a small jar of oil we had been allotted. I was willing to be a thief, as I had been willing to be a liar, and a pretender, and a murderer. But there was one offense I could not bring myself to commit. I, who had killed men and had tasted blood, could not bring myself to murder the doves we had tended. I went to Yael, to plead for her help, which she gave me without question.

Together we went to the dovecote. The pale moon watched over us and allowed us to slip through the plaza as nothing more than shadows. We went inside, then crouched upon the straw. I watched as Yael called the doves to her. She raised her hand up, and they were summoned. As each one came to her, Yael sat with it quietly, then broke its neck. She wept as she did so, such was her sacrifice on my behalf. Then she lay their limp bodies on her lap, stroking their feathers before she gave them to me.

She walked me back to my chambers, helping me carry the provisions I meant to bring to my sister. As I had helped her in her times of need, so she was now beside me. I would never have imagined that she who had once been my rival had become a sister to me. If anything, I had imagined she might become my sister through the laws of marriage. Amram and I had always planned to include her in the ceremony, but that time was over. The day after the little messenger girl told him I was ill, Amram came to our chambers and knocked upon the door. My mother was surprised that, as soon as I spied who the caller was, I slunk into the garden. I overheard him ask about my fever and heard her answer that it was my brother who had been ill, not I. Perhaps Amram had complained to his sister, for as we neared the barracks Yael murmured, "My brother says that he rarely sees you. He still wears the blue token."

"That's done in your honor." I kept my eyes lowered. "Not mine."

"Every man changes in war."

From her tone I understood that she knew some part of her brother had been lost.

I DRESSED in my brother's tunic and took a heavy pack upon my back, meant for my sister. Adir was still on his pallet because of his difficulty in walking. When he saw me dressed as him, he was amazed. He vowed he himself would think that I was Adir had he not known better. He hadn't fully understood that he had managed to be a warrior though he still lay in a darkened corner of our chamber.

"They all believe I am you," I admitted.

My brother accepted that I had taken his place and that I had honored his name. This was why the warriors left gifts of oil and myrrh at the door and why people came to offer their congratulations on the bravery of his deeds.

My brother lifted himself up on one elbow to study me. The dog stood beside me, a pack tied to his back, for he was mine when he should have been my brother's.

"Have I done well as a warrior?" Adir wanted to know.

I nodded, embarrassed to have taken so much from him. But he seemed relieved.

"Have I slain many of the enemy?"

"Only when you needed to."

Every time the warriors went out on raids, my brother, you were among them. We attacked at night, splitting into four sections, coming to our enemies in the dark from the four corners of the world. We went to let the Romans know that they had not destroyed us and that we had not disappeared despite their presence in our valley. We went to take what we needed to survive and because our people could not be contained nor denied their right to Zion.

During the nights when you, my dear brother, rested on your pallet, I had gone into the thornbushes and held the man who was unafraid of metal, who yearned for it, as I did, as I had done all my life. Though we were but halves of people, though we had lost ourselves, together we were one, and whole. This is why I was so impatient whenever I needed to remain on the mountain. He was the only one who knew me. He told me that, if I had been a woman, he could not have had me, for he had vowed never to be with a woman other than his wife. But I was something else, a warrior, as he was. We did not have to speak, as those who fight side by side need no words, but instead we knew each other in silence. In that way it was possible for each of us to foretell what the one beside us wanted, whether it was brutal or tender, whether it lasted all night or for but a brief burst of stolen time.

On the day when we repent for our sins, I had left this man to the heartache of his past. On the eve of Yom Kippur, he disappeared into the wilderness. I did not ask to share his sorrows, for that would not have been possible. I waited in the blue night, alone, as any comrade would. When he came back to me, there were strands of thorns fitted across his chest. I offered him water and a share of my supper, and I asked not a single question and made no demands. We had enough adversaries, we did not need to defy each other.

I was grateful, my brother, that you could not see what the world was beyond these gates, as I was grateful that I could close my eyes inside the bower of the thornbushes, that I could moan and thrash as I never did in battle, for in battle, my brother, your reputation was one of silence. You never cried out as you did at night, with only the dog to overhear you as you clung to the warrior beside you. You were young, the slightest among them, but you were a fine archer, perhaps the best of all, known by the red feathers on your arrows that quickened every shot, the weapons becoming birds seeking out our enemies and bringing them to their death. No wild goat could run from you, no rabbit was quick enough.

You often stood at the rear of a skirmish because your vision was so clear you could observe attackers from a distance and fell them before they came upon our men. Because of your skill, several warriors who might have been murdered lived. Amram was once stunned by the rock cast at him by a slingshot, and you, my brother, leapt out to slay his attacker from the hillock you stood upon, your armor burning hot in the sun, leaving red marks along your tender skin.

Afterward Amram came to give you thanks. He called you his little brother and offered you his loyalty. You merely lowered your eyes, as though too impressed by the honor he gave to you to speak, when the truth was you did not want him to see the color of your eyes, or guess at what was beneath the metal and silver scales you wore. All the same, you accepted the gift of his amulet, a silver disk of Solomon fighting a demon on the Temple floor, so as not to offend him. "I owe you protection," he said on that day when you, younger and slighter, had saved him from the Angel of Death that had hovered so near. "My life is yours."

You wore his amulet, so as not to offend him on the battlefield, but you hid it beneath a scarf at all other times. You hadn't the heart to tell him his life was not what you wanted. All you wanted was your own life, the nights in the thornbushes, the days with the warriors.

My brother, your dog was always at your side, as quiet as you were, with a silence he might well have learned from the leopard. When a battle was begun, he broke his silence and roared beside you, for he had no fear of blood or of metal or of death. He was your companion, and slept with you, whether you were alone or with the man who knew who you were, understanding why you set yourself apart under the stars. Though you were dutiful enough when you were needed, willing to carry the other warriors' double-edged swords, their slingshots, their spears, you did not mingle among them.

When you slipped out of your tunic, you disappeared beneath the moon. You vanished into the air and rested there, between the worlds.

That was when I came to take your place.

I STOLE out the South Water Gate with the dog so that I might go to my sister. I had wrapped myself in shawls, for the chill would soon be upon us in the nights. I had brought my sister to life once and would do so again. No guard would stop me, for I was Adir the brave, named for the kings of his father's people, and those posted at the gate merely nodded a greeting to a fellow warrior. My bow was strapped to my back. The dark had begun to stretch across the horizon. Fading light had turned the cliffs red in the distance. Larks and brilliant blue songbirds were crossing the sky, catching the gnats that swarmed in the evening. I made certain to tread carefully, for a single rock might cause the Romans to notice me. I needed to make the perilous climb to the cave of the Essenes.

I was so focused on the Roman camp, I never thought I might be followed. I wasn't prepared when I was grabbed and pulled from the path. I wished I had the knife my father had given to me. In such close battle, my bow was pointless. I turned to fight, but the man who held me was unafraid, as angels and demons are said to be. I battled with him until he overcame me. Perhaps this was not a man at all but one of the seven wolves in my dreams. If so, my dream had prophesied my defeat. I wept at my own weakness. I, who had always been so fierce, gave myself up to him, expecting to be consumed by either light or flames.

I knew him when Eran lay down as though at his master's feet. I saw my follower for who he was, the man who owned nothing but the ax he carried. He said he would accompany me, and if he fell from the cliff we climbed, then it was meant to be, for he yearned for death and had no choice but to court it. If *Mal'ach ha-Mavet* came to him, then what now came to pass was only what he had wished for all along.

I did not wish to put him at risk for the sake of my sister, but in battle you cannot tell another when it is his time to enter the World-to-Come, nor is it possible to keep any man in this world when he wishes to leave it behind. I couldn't argue with the Man from the Valley, that was something a woman might do, and he had vowed to never be with a woman other than his wife. I was his comrade, and as such I must respect his desire. I could not cling to him, for that would show me to be a woman as well. I wore Adir's tunic and carried his bow, therefore I must step aside.

We tied the dog to a thornbush, then went on, the sound of our breathing echoing. The new moon shone with a thin, fine light, but soon clouds moved across so we could slink through the dark. I didn't need to see the Man from the Valley to know he was there, for we were connected by something stronger than sight, and like the king's horses we did not stumble on the sheer cliff. I had half-imagined I might capture my sister, tie her with ropes, and carry her back to the fortress. But had I done so, she would have cried out, as she had called for her father when we left the Iron Mountain. Her shouts would have brought the Romans upon us, and I did not wish to be the cause of my sister's death.

I knew I must let her cause that herself.

Once, as I stared into the dark, my foot slipped and my companion grabbed me and held me close until I could regain my balance. Rocks rattled down into the valley, but in the dark we might well have been two ibex intent on scaling this cliff. As we went on we could distinguish three caves, one for the goats, one used as a storeroom, with another, larger cave in which the Essenes camped.

We had no fear they might attack to protect themselves, for they had no weapons, and no desire for defense other than God's mercy. The stench of the cave greeted us first, and I was astonished that it was worse than any barnyard. When I peered through the dark, I could hardly bear to witness the way in which they lived. The fires inside the cave had blackened their skins, and their linen garments were dusted with ash. Two men came to meet us, frowning, clearly resenting our intrusion into the midst. They were unclean, rail-thin, with the ravished gaze of hunger in their eyes. I recognized Malachi, though he did not know me and seeing my tunic took me for a boy.

"We've brought you provisions," the Man from the Valley said. We set down our packs, the meager fruit, the doves, the flatbread, the grain, the skins of water.

"From the hands of murderers?" the older Essene man said as he considered the provisions we'd courted great danger to bring to them.

"From the hands of your brothers," the Man from the Valley remarked. He was civil, but his tone carried a note of reproach.

I took a few steps forward while the men continued to speak. Through the murk I made out Abba's form; the Essenes' beloved teacher was prone on a ledge, so weak it seemed he'd already passed into the otherworld, though he still drew breath. I saw the women gathered together, gazing at us distrustfully, but I could not tell my sister from the others, nor did she recognize me. I took the scarf from my head and let my hair fall down my back so that she might see me for who I was, the sister she belonged to. Malachi immediately came to me once he knew me, so quick I might have been a black viper, the sort that winds itself around its prey in an inescapable grasp.

"Go now," he said to me, though I had risked my life and the life of my companion to bring them provisions and water. "She cannot see you or think of that other life."

I caught sight of her then, a woman in rags, my beautiful sister, surrounded by the other women, ewes in a pen, no more kin to me than the sheep behind our fences made from the scaly boughs of the thornbushes. All at once I understood Malachi's fear. He had known what I planned to do before I did. For I now called out to Nahara, my voice so plaintive and wretched I barely recognized it as my own.

"Come with me," I pleaded, intent on calling her to me. "You don't belong to them. Leave with me and I'll protect you as I did before you ever came to this place or knew this people."

There was no response, other than the sound of my own cries, for my words fell like stones, they had wrenched tears from me. The Man from the Valley came up beside me. I expected him to admonish me for my actions, for I was nothing but a woman. Instead he leaned in closely and without judgment. "Let me try to speak to her," he urged.

I waited at the mouth of the cave. I noticed there was a shallow pool of still water. Surely the Essenes drank from this pool, though it was not fit for human thirst. In the muddy earth there grew a small acacia tree. Little more than a twig, it was abloom. A thousand bees came to its branches. I closed my eyes and listened to the hum. For a moment I was in the other world, in the grip of my other life, riding over the grasslands. I dreamed that I made a fire and burned a hundred branches and that the sparks flew into the sky and stayed in the heavens to become stars.

I rose when the Man from the Valley approached. I was parched from our journey, but upon seeing him I felt as though something had been quenched. I stood by his side as he told me the Essenes had agreed to accept the provisions. He had been brought before Abba so that a prayer could be offered on his behalf. The ancient teacher could barely speak, for he was so weak that the thread that tied him to this world was wearing thin. My sister had managed to stand nearby. After Abba finished chanting, she had whispered to the Man from the Valley so that he alone would hear. He was to tell me that she remembered me, the fastest rider, her father's favorite son, the sister she had belonged to once, in another time and world.

WE WALKED in silence, as we always did. Our burden was lighter, for we no longer carried fruit and water and millet, as I no longer carried my sister's fate in my hands. I had left her there. Whether or not we were to meet again in this lifetime was not for me to decide. She had renounced the girl I had brought to life, and because of this we were no longer bound to each other. Yet I would think of her not as a woman huddled in a cave, eyes downcast, waiting for the End of Days, but as the only birth I had ever witnessed, God's great glory and miracle.

ERAN was waiting for us. We stopped before we climbed up toward the gate. As comrades, we agreed to do so without a word being said. We knew Rome was approaching, and we understood what this would mean. We took this one night for ourselves, in case there should be no other. We went to the cave where Yael had once told me a lion lived. There was no such lion inside. We made a fire deep inside the mouth of the cave. We knew that others had done so before us, for there were piles of ashes and soot. Perhaps whoever had been here before us had longed for freedom from the mountaintop, as we did. Perhaps they had wished for other worlds and times.

I put my arms around my warrior and drew him near to me and gave myself up to him. I hadn't the strength for battle anymore. I wanted a world that was beautiful, and on this night, he was tender with me in a way he hadn't been before, perhaps because he had seen me weep before my sister. He treated me not like a warrior but like a woman. I knew this was his way of telling me that the world was terrible and that I should prepare myself for what was to come. But I had decided to disregard such fears, as I had cast away my mother's warning that love would undo me. None of that mattered now. We were both wounded, disbelievers in everything we had ever known and seen. We had killed together, and buried the fallen together, and chanted prayers meant only for men to recite. We had been together as animals were, desperate and driven by fierce need, and as lovers for whom the rest of the world falls away.

When we left the cave, morning had opened the far corners of the sky. Dust was rising as the Roman Legion approached. There was a column from the north and another from the east. When the troops joined together, the rising clouds formed not the shape of the boar, the symbol they carried on their banners, but the figure of a lion, the symbol of the ancient tribe of Judah and of the wilderness around us.

"My name is Rebekah," I told him as we stood there together.

As he was Yoav, the Man from the Valley, the love of my life.

Autumn 72 C.E.

Part Four

Winter 73 C.E.

The Witch of Moab

We were no different from the doves above us. We could not speak or cry, but when there was no choice we discovered we could fly. If you want a reason, take this: We yearned for our portion of the sky.

My mother taught me everything a woman must know in this world and all it was necessary to carry into the World-to-Come. By the age of eight I had learned that the leaf of a date palm boiled in water was a cure for a scorpion bite, that the nectar of the spiky blue flower of the hyssop dabbed on the wrist would ward off evil, that the burned, powdery skin of a snake would keep a man from harm. I had the tooth of a black dog strung around my neck as a protection against wild beasts and took care to recite an incantation when I dug around the roots of henbane, the holy plant, for I often buried my mother's amulets as offerings to Ashtoreth, the goddess who watched over us in times of strife.

My mother trained me in the making of fever charms and victory charms, although she refused to deal in hate spells, used to undermine rivals, something that was lacking in my book of recipes. I knew how to cast charms that would dissolve a spell and those which would cure reptile bites. Bits of silver scrolls and scarabs were sewn into the hems of my garments by my mother's quick and tireless fingers. Her great beauty was eclipsed only by her great knowledge. Her name was Nisa, and I thought it was the most beautiful word in any language. The word itself was like the rising of the fountain, the rhythm of rain.

At twilight, when the air in Alexandria grew softly blue, she instructed me in our garden, teaching me Hebrew and Aramaic and Greek, forming the letters in the dirt with a few thrusts of the pointed edge of a stick. No one saw what we did during these lessons, for we did not dwell among the townspeople but in the house of holy women who were available for the priests. In this way we were blessed as well, for the laws that applied to other women did not apply to my mother. Prayers were not forbidden to her, nor was an education, nor was the freedom to allow men into her private chamber.

The entranceway to our house was lined with lanky hedges of jasmine and scented rose trees. In the evening the city itself seemed to turn blue, as if casting our world underwater. Long shadows spread out upon the terra-cotta bricks of our pathway, so no one could make out who entered our door and who left in the middle of the dusky, fragrant night. These shadows served me as well, for I was as solitary as I was self-reliant. The only witnesses to my instruction and my education were the inchworms and beetles. Even as a very small child, I understood that women had secrets, and that some of these were only to be told to daughters. In this way we were bound together for eternity.

In the garden, where I learned my letters, there grew a variety of rare white water lily that gave off a perfumed scent at night.

These blooms have been my favorites ever since that time. A single one is worth a barrel of balsam or myrrh. The wild red lilies of Moab, glorious as they may be, are weeds when compared to these blossoms, their scent mere air when considered alongside the lilies of Alexandria. My mother rubbed their perfume on her wrists, and because of this no man could deny her.

While other women were contained within the walled courtyards of their houses, venturing no farther than the marketplace—and then only accompanied by servants or kinswomen—my mother was allowed to do as she pleased. Every spring she made the journey to visit her family in Jerusalem during the Feast of Unleavened Bread. It was there in that city that my fate awaited me.

IT IS SAID THAT, after the expulsion of Adam and Eve from Eden, two angels offered to enter our world to teach humans the knowledge God would allow us. These angels have eaten meals with humans, fallen in love with them, had sexual relations with them, watched their children be born. Because of this, they can never return to the spirit world. They continue to walk the earth to this day, teaching the wisdom of sorcery to those who yearn to know it. My mother came from a line of women who were willing to listen when the angels began to speak. She kept her most private possessions in a box of carved ironwood, the key to which she wore around her neck on a strand of braided horsehair. The key had been formed into the shape of a snake. When I was a child, it seemed a living thing. Whenever my mother allowed me to hold it in my hand, I could feel it coldly inch across my palm.

Inside the locked box was a notebook of parchment upon which my mother had written the many secrets she had accumulated over the years. It was a recipe book for the human heart, for our people believe that all we know and all we have experienced is contained there.

*

THERE WERE SPELLS on every page of my mother's diary: *For Night Blindness. To Catch a Thief. For Headache. For Fever. For Loyalty. For Love.* While other girls were playing with string or with carved wooden animals, I was learning what had been written by my mother, secrets passed down to me that I would one day entrust to a daughter of my own. The spells themselves were transcribed in code, so that no outsider might understand them or fully gauge their power.

There have always been ancient books of mysteries. Men who practiced magic were teachers who were called *abba,* fathers blessed by knowledge from *The Book of Mysteries.* Even Moses himself was said to have what magicians and great teachers call *The Moon Book,* a collection of magic so strong no other human has ever dared to open the pages, lest he be burned alive by the heat of the words within. There were those who said that Moses could make the sea disappear and that he could have destroyed the whole world had he wished to, or if God had called upon him to do so. Noah, too, had a book of incantations. The voice of an angel in *The Book of Jubilees* recounts that the angels themselves taught Noah all manner of secrets so that he might use the herbs of the earth to heal his sons. Among men it was rumored there was a priceless treasure called *The Book of Watchers,* which offered direct instructions from the Almighty, a mystical treatise so complicated, so hidden and wrapped within riddles, only the wisest sage could begin to understand its meaning.

This was the work of men, of scholars and priests. There were two schools of magic men were privy to, that which the priests practiced publicly, the exorcisms and curses and blessings, and the lesser works crafted by the *minim,* men, be they sages or magicians, who offered magic for payment outside the synagogues. Beyond that, in secret, in the dark, there was the magic women practiced behind locked doors, with our recipe books of *pharmaka,* our medicines, and *philtrons,* our love potions. Women had secret uses for ashes, green bay leaf, blood, sulfur, myrrh, musk, honey, oil and flowers, along with the roots of plants such as the mandrake, *yavrucha,* and that of the *ba'aras,* often called wondershine, red hot and aflame when pulled from the earth. At the Temple it had been decreed that no one should tolerate a sorceress, for such magic was said to be the work of harlots, their wickedness set beneath a mantle of wisdom they should not be allowed. There were ten varieties of wise men known but only two kinds of women who might hear the voice of the Almighty: prophetesses and witches.

For women who practiced in secret, there was no one but Him, our God, the radiant one, who was far greater than any magician. But we did not agree with the rules of men, and we ignored certain decrees, even though the sort of magic women such as my mother were known for was outside the law and therefore considered to be a sin.

We knew why this was so, and why our great goddess, Ashtoreth, both a warrior and a seer, had been defiled and warned against in writings that followed the Prophets. Ashtoreth's presence was denied to us, the images of her form melted down into pools of silver and brass, the cakes we made in her image outlawed, the trees we decorated in her honor torn down long ago. The expulsion of the Queen of Heaven had occurred for the same reason that Samson had once lost every bit of his strength; it was the reason men burned their hair and nails, lest such tokens be used against them in any woman's spell. Women who practiced *keshaphim* were considered witches and punished as such, cast out, burned, defiled. They were powerful and dangerous, and no man wanted such a creature near to him, except perhaps in his bed for a night before he rid the world of her.

Surely this is why women did not often write down their knowledge, to make certain it couldn't be found out and used against them. We told each other our magical recipes, just as we confided the best ways to make a cake of figs, a broth of bones, a stew of apples and honey that would be sweeter than any other. We did not discuss our methods, or make our talents public, yet other women knew. The truth was written upon us, as they say men's sins are written on their bones so that when they die their wicked deeds can be read as if written upon parchment.

We can offer women what they want most of all, cures for the most common ailments of this world. When a marriage is not blessed and demons have attached themselves to a household, a dissolution of the marriage can be found in a spell, which is a legal document of divorce. *I drive you out of their houses, and you should not appear to them, not even in dreams, for I dismiss you and release you by deed of divorce, a letter of dismissal according to the law of the women of Israel.*

When children are ailing or babies refuse to be born, when men are unfaithful, when the sky is empty of rain, when the amulets buried beneath holy walls upon instructions of the *minim* offer no solace and all entreaties to the priests for guidance fail, when the rituals they offer bring no comfort and no consolation, they come to us.

AS A GIRL in Alexandria, I often watched my mother leaf through her notebook when I was meant to be asleep on the pallet at the foot of her bed, which was worthy of a queen, raised off the floor and covered by a fine linen cloth, threaded with strands of purple and gold. My mother looked fierce in the half-light, her black hair falling down her back. In the evenings she burned balsam in an earthenware bowl. The smoke that spiraled up toward the ceiling was pale, much like the inner feathers of a dove's wing. The scent was of lands far away, where the fields were always green and acacia trees grew. My mother had been chosen to go to Alexandria and live among a sect of Greeks and Jews because she was so beautiful and so learned. Because of this she wore secret tattoos imprinted on her skin, intricate designs fashioned with sharpened reeds that had been dipped in henna. These proclaimed her status as a *kedeshah*. After her initiation, she often kept herself hidden, for although her status was revered among many in Alexandria, the Temple in Jerusalem outlawed such practices.

The women who joined in this way of life believed that few were closer to Shechinah than the *kedeshah*. They embraced the feminine aspect of God, the Dwelling, the deep place where inspiration abided, for in the written words of God, compassion and knowledge were always female. This is why the lilies grew in my mother's garden and why she was allowed knowledge of Hebrew and Greek and could converse with any man.

When the priests came to visit, I was sent from the house, and I would go into the garden. Among the hedges, there grew the white blooms of the henna flower that turned a mysterious, sacred shade of red when prepared as a dye. I often spent my time beside a small fountain fashioned of blue and white ceramic tiles. I was not pleased to be sent from my mother, but I occupied myself, a skill learned by children who must sometimes act older than their age. The water lilies rested on plump green pads that trailed pale, fleshy tendrils below them in the waters of the fountain. Birds came to drink, offering their songs in return for quenching their thirst. My mother had told me to be silent, and I did as she asked. I practiced until I could sit so still I became invisible to the birds that fluttered down from the pine trees. Often they would alight on my shoulders and on my knees. I could feel their nimble hearts beating as they sang in sheer gratitude for the shade and comfort of our garden.

Once, when I was little more than four, I was sent out for several hours in the burning-hot sun. I was so angry to have been cast out of our chamber into the brutal heat of noon that I threw myself into the fountain. The ceramic tiles were cool and slippery on my feet. In my childish fury, I leapt without thinking of the consequences. The instant I did, the heat of the day disappeared. I held my breath as I went under. With the green water all around me, I immediately felt I had found a home. This was the element I was meant for. The world itself spun upside down, and yet it seemed more mine than any other place. I wanted to close my eyes and drift forever. I saw bubbles formed of my own breath. All at once someone grabbed for me roughly. The priest ripped me out of the water. He shook me and told me that little girls who played with water drowned and that no one would feel sorry for me if this should be my fate.

But I hadn't drowned, and I looked up at him, defiant and dripping with water. I could feel a new power within me, one that gave me the courage to glare at this holy man. I could see my mother's glance focused on me in a strange manner, her gaze lingering on my drenched form from the doorway where she stood. Her hair was loose, and she was wearing only a white shawl wrapped around her naked body. The henna tattoos swirling across her throat and breasts and arms were drawn in honeyed patterns, as if she were a flower rather than a woman.

Not long after my dive into the fountain, my mother took me to the Nile. It was here, on the shore of the mightiest river, that Moses had inscribed God's name upon gold, throwing it into the waters, begging the Almighty to allow the Exodus of our people to begin. It was a long journey to undertake, but my mother insisted we must go. Our servants brought us there in a cart pulled by donkeys. A tent was lifted over our heads to protect our skins from burning as we traveled. We set off in the middle of the night so that the voyage would be cooler. We rested during the heat of the next day, then set off once again. As I dozed I listened to the wheels of our cart and the drone of our servants speaking to each other in Greek, the language we all spoke publicly, whether we were Jews or Egyptians, pagans or Greeks. Our donkeys were white and well brushed, their gait even and quick. We had fruit in a basket to eat whenever we were hungry, along with cakes made of dates and figs. I wondered if I were a princess, and my mother a queen. The air gleamed with heat, but the closer we drew to the river, the cooler the breeze became.

Morning was rising, and people were already busy in the working world around us. The mass of life was noisy on the road to the river, the air scented with cinnamon and cardamom. There were pepper trees and date palms that were taller than any I'd seen before. I felt a shimmer of excitement, and great satisfaction at being alone with my mother. For once I did not have to share her. She allowed me to play with the two golden amulets she wore at her throat, and the serpent key that gleamed in the sunlight.

My mother wore a white tunic and sandals. She had oiled and braided her own hair and mine, as she would have had we been attending a ritual to make an offering. As we drew even nearer to the river, the hour was still early, the sky pink. There was the rich scent of mud and lilies. Women had brought baskets of laundry to wash and then dry on the banks, and men were setting out in narrow, flat-bottomed wooden fishing boats, their oars turning as they called to one another, their woven nets flashing through the air as they tossed them out for their catch.

My mother leaned down to whisper that we had arrived at our destination. She told me that, if water was indeed my element, I must learn to swim with my eyes open. I must control it or it would control me. To take charge of a substance so powerful, one had to give in to it first, become one with it, then triumph. We went through the reeds, though they were sharp as they slapped against us, leaving little crisscross serrations on our legs in a pattern of X's. I saw herons and storks fishing for their breakfasts. Our feet sank in the mud, and as we went deeper our tunics flowed out around us.

The Nile always grew fat after the full moon in summer, its water a great gift in a time of brutal heat. I could feel how refreshing and sweet it was. I had never known the sense of true delight, how intense pleasure coursed through your body slowly, and then, suddenly, in a rush of sensation. All at once you possessed the river, as it possessed you in turn. I had the sense that I belonged to these waters and always had.

"Now we'll discover who you will be," my mother said to me, eager to see what her daughter might become.

I sank under, my eyes open. I would have blinked had my mother not told me to be vigilant. I trusted her and always did as she said. I made certain to keep my eyes wide. Because of this I saw a vision I would carry with me for my entire life. There was a fish as large as a man. He was luminous in the murky dark. He was enormous, a creature who needed neither breath nor earth, as I did, and yet I had no fear of him. Rather, tenderness rose inside me. I felt he was my beloved. I reached out, and he ventured close enough for me to run my hand over his cold, silvery scales.

I arose from the river with a sense of joy, but also with a melancholy I had not known before. It is not usual for a child to feel such sadness when nothing has changed and the world around is still the same. Yet I had a sense of extreme loss.

When I told my mother about the fish, she said I had seen my destiny. She didn't seem at all surprised.

"Did he bite you?" she asked.

I shook my head. The fish had seemed very kind.

"Well, he will," my mother told me. "Here is the riddle of love: Everything it gives to you, it takes away."

I did not know what this meant, though I knew the world was a dangerous place for a woman. Still, I did not understand how a person whose element was water could stay away from fish.

THEY SAY that a woman who practices magic is a witch, and that every witch derives her power from the earth. There was a great seer who advised that, should a man hold a witch in the air, he could then cut off her powers, thereby making her helpless. But such an attempt would have no effect on me. My strength came from water, my talents buoyed by the river. On the day I swam in the Nile and saw my fate in the ink blue depths, my mother told me that I would have powers of my own, as she did. But there was a warning she gave to me as well: If I were ever to journey too far from the water, I would lose my power and my life. I must keep my head and not give in to desire, for desire is what causes women to drown.

IN THE DESERT, the air burns. Breathe and it flames inside you, for it is strong as iron, as unrelenting as the swirling dust that rises in a storm. Our water comes from the rain, and from aqueducts long ago built by Herod's slaves, wide ceramic tubes which carry the rushing waters of the *nechalim* to us when they fill with sudden streams in the winter months. Still, it is not enough for me. The desert is overtaking me, my strength is dwindling. In water I float, but in the dry inferno of this wilderness, I can barely catch my breath. I dream of rivers and of silver fish. There are those who say our people themselves are like the fish in the sea, nourished by the waters of knowledge that flow from the Torah, and that is why we can survive in such a harsh and brutal land.

I often wake from sleep with a gasp, drowning in the pools of white light that break through the sky each morning. Women carrying new lives within them are especially susceptible to heat. I have felt so afflicted three other times. Once in Jerusalem when I was only thirteen, barely a woman myself. Twice on the Iron Mountain, which was little more than exile to me. And now here, again, in the place where I have found my destiny.

At night I go to the cisterns, led there by the scent of water. To me, this odor is more pungent than myrrh or frankincense. The single thing that can rival it is the fragrance of the white lily that can only be found in Alexandria. People say that I can call down the rain and that water is drawn to me, but they're wrong. It is I who am in pursuit of water, as I have always been. When I dream, I dream of the Nile on that pink morning, and of my mother, whom I have not seen in so long she would no longer recognize me, if she has not already gone on to the World-to-Come.

The stars are reflected from within the black water in the cistern. I find comfort in the omen I glean from this: light in the darkness, truth when it seems there is none. This is the only place where I can be myself, the girl who fell into the fountain, the one who was not afraid of monsters, nor of deep water, nor of drowning. I walk down the hundred stone steps, the granite cool against my feet. I know where love will take me, for on the day we traveled to the Nile, my mother told me that it would bring me to ruin and that anyone I dared to love would be drawn down with me. But even as she spoke she knew, I had no choice but to follow my destiny.

I pause on the edge of the cistern, where the stones have been covered with fine plaster. The white plaster dust clings to my flesh. I watch the shimmer of the heat over the water. It is said that the spirit of God hovers over the water, as it did on the first day of creation. I stand before the glory of what He has created. I remove my cloak, my sandals, my tunic. Other women purify themselves in the *mikvah,* but I need deeper waters. I dive in.

Some people say that this, the largest of the cisterns built by Herod's stonemasons, is bottomless, and if we ever see the floor of this well, we will also see our doom. This pool is deep, but it is not endless. I know that for certain. All things end. I often dive to reach the depths, then keep myself from rising back up by holding on to the rocks piled at the foundation. They are sleek against my hand, smoothed by the endless lapping of the water against stone. I keep my eyes open even though the water is black. There are no fish, no flashes of light, but when I surface, my cousin Eleazar will be waiting.

It was he I saw in the water of the Nile when I spied the fish beside me.

From the beginning until now, that alone has never changed.

He is my fate.

THE SOLDIERS of the Tenth Legion were led through the wilderness by Flavius Silva, the procurator of all Judea, the newly appointed Roman governor. The troops raised a dust storm so enormous it could surely be seen as far away as the Iron Mountain, where I spent so many years in the company of a husband who was twice my age and knew I did not love him, yet he still protected me. He never mistreated me, though he had the stony aloofness of many of the fierce people of Moab, along with a surprising tenderness with his children. His name was Sa'adallos, though I never called him that. If I had, I might have loved him in return. I might have been in Petra instead of at this fortress when the Romans arrived. I might have been walking through that red city with its miraculous carved columns of elephants and camels, enjoying its pool, rumored to be the size of a lake, and the gardens that hang from cliffs, causing men to look upon the mountainsides with awe, amazed to see date trees where in another country there would be only clouds.

Had I loved him, my children would have been safe, my future assured. Instead I brought them to be trapped on this perch from which there was no deliverance. Though the angels might hear us call to them, they could never reach us here on the periphery of the world, even if they wished to save us. I understood this when I threw the bones of the doves, for they prophesied that, just as there was no escape from what had already been written, there would be no escape from this fortress.

Our people gathered to watch six thousand of the legion approach, accompanied by more than a thousand of their slaves and followers. We trembled in silence. What terrified us was not only their number but their sheer determination. They had come for us from Jerusalem, though we were but a few hundred. They had found us as the jackals find their prey, encircling the weakness of their victims, biding their time, ready to leap when the moment is right.

In the dust storm they raised, birds fell from the sky, unable to take flight in the bursts of swirling gravel. Soon the ground was littered with ravens, more in number than the soldiers. The flightless birds transformed the ground into a mournful stretch of black, and all at once it seemed the reaches of the World-to-Come had been laid down before us in a road of flesh and feathers.

"I have seen this before," Revka murmured to me, her face ashen. "We cannot escape from harm."

There was only one reason why Rome should come to try to defeat us when we were so few and their empire so great. They feared we rebels might serve as an ember to reignite the flame of freedom. Disgrace smolders, it burns when you least expect it to ignite. The Romans could not allow this. We were fish in a net, already drawn in upon the rocky shore; all they needed to do was cut us off from the water that sustained us. Already, coins had been printed in Rome to celebrate the fall of Judea. The image of a Roman legionnaire and a captive Jewish woman, humbled and enslaved beneath a palm tree, had been imprinted upon silver. As they had written it, so they wished it to be, as if they and not God alone could create matter out of words and will.

In a land where rebellion has been crushed, there cannot be a single warrior left.

*

IT WAS WINTER and the air was raw. We wore our cloaks drawn about us like armor, shivering in the wind, watching as our fate approached us. The rains had come, filling the valleys with torrents of water. Fish that had disappeared deep within the soil during the arid months appeared once again, magicked into life. Throughout the hills there were wildflowers and honeybees. The trunks of dead trees hummed as if they themselves had come alive. There were greens for the ibex, meat for the leopard. The desert had given the Tenth Legion the most favorable conditions for a crossing. Surely our enemies took this as an omen that they would be the victors. They were hungry, and they were fed. They were thirsty and needed look no farther than the streams that turned into waterfalls.

Perhaps those who were new to Judea wondered how it was that the desert had destroyed so many who had come before them, how the brutality of its fierce heat had changed those who had fought to stay alive in its arms. For this was the merciful time of the year, when birds began to return from Africa and Egypt, when there were herons rather than vultures and the land was plentiful. The army that came to our valley was made up of men from a dozen different lands, all speaking Latin, each one rewarded by Rome with provisions they had not dared to dream of in the poverty of their homelands, for they traveled with camels and donkeys loaded down with meat and dates and leather barrels with enough water to fill ten cisterns.

They approached our fortress with their strength intact, while we were eating grass and doves, sacrificing the sheep for which we no longer had grain, slitting the throats of the goats who no longer gave milk. We had water, what we always longed for, and the cisterns were full, yet we were poor and our hunger throbbed and reminded us of our poverty. So many of the doves had been taken for food and sacrifices, their waste no longer filled our baskets or fed the fields. The orchards failed us, the gardens were empty, the storerooms no longer sustained us. Now when we entered the dovecotes, there was a hush; in place of the song of the doves, there was only a faint cooing.

Our warriors were exhausted. They had been fighting for so long, without reprieve or rest, many of them young and untrained, mere boys, ten- and eleven-year-olds conscripted to stand in the place of the fallen. Yet they hid their fear. They shouted that the legion might bring all of Rome and still they could never scale the mountain to reach us.

But this was the army that had murdered twenty thousand of our people in Caesarea, so that not one had survived. They had dispatched the two other Jewish strongholds, Herodium and Machaerus, where they had slain those they had given a promise of reprieve. Having heard there were those who had managed to escape and were still in hiding, the Tenth Legion had cut down the Forest of Jardes, so there would not be a single tree for the escaped rebels to hide behind. There they killed three thousand more, their bodies left strewn on the field for the birds of prey without even a shred of cloth to cover their nakedness.

Flavius Silva then set his glance upon us. It was said that he was a man without regret, with violent moods and tempers, but with the gift of pure logic when he needed to advance on his enemy. I stood upon the wall with the rest of our people and watched our valley fill with columns of fighting men. Following were those who would bake the soldiers' bread and cook their meals and mend their cloaks, along with the *zonnoth,* women who would be kept in tents for the soldiers' pleasure, and the slaves who would build the camps, dragging enormous timbers from the north through the desert, along with the smiths with their carts of weaponry—spears and shields and thousands of arrows. But there was something more fearsome that arrived with the legion, the sign of our fate, for the Romans had brought a lion on a chain with them. We grew faint when we saw this beast. He, who had once been free in the desert and had ruled the wilderness from his cave, the symbol of the strength of the ancient tribe of Judea, now must do his keepers' bidding. He gazed at us, and in his eyes we saw the Romans' desire.

They meant to devour us.

They attached the poor creature to a metal post, constructed directly across from the palace that had belonged to King Herod. This was where Silva's camp was to be built, in a location that would be an insult and a challenge every time we looked upon it. While they built, we heard the roaring of the vanquished beast.

Yael had confided to me that she dreamed of a lion. As she had feared this creature, so had she been drawn to it. She wept when she told me this, and I understood why she was torn by the meaning of her dreams. A lion may lie beside an ibex in the shade if his appetite is sated, they may even sleep together, their backs resting against each other, but on the next day, if the lion wakes with hunger, then he must serve himself.

Now Yael's dream had appeared before us. She stood beside me and wept to see the lion subdued in his chains, trapped as we were, enslaved by those whose brutality was an affront to nature, and to our people, and to God. After the dust had settled, we could observe him clearly, for there was only the pale blue air of winter before us and the light was clear, the wind fresh. Many said it was possible to view heaven from this mountain of ours, but now we seemed much closer to the first gate of hell. What we heard and what awaited us did not come from the reaches of God. It was below us, in the roar of the lion.

SOON ENOUGH a village was constructed by camp followers, with tents and shacks set up overnight. The scent of food drifted over the valley, cooking meat, bread, spices. We watched, poverty-stricken, starving, like ghosts at a table laden with a great feast. The building went on without ceasing, with slaves working through the night.

This was an endeavor that was meant to last; the Romans were settling in. They would not leave, and they would not admit defeat. They began to build twelve towers, set a hundred yards apart, rising so quickly it seemed they came into being before our very eyes. Once the towers had been constructed, any man wishing to break through to the eastern valley would be running a gauntlet, with guards atop the observation posts. He would never make it to the other side.

As the slaves were completing the camps, more were brought in from the north to give form to a wall of stones. This wall was no worry to us until it began to zigzag into the mountains in a strange design. We did not understand the Romans' intentions, for it seemed a fool's endeavor to set a thousand Jewish slaves to labor throughout the day and night, carrying boulders so heavy many of the workers fell prostrate on the ground. When these pitiful men could not rise again, they were slain and left in the dirt, for it was easier to dispose of them than to heal them. The Romans were intent on this wall they built. We assumed they meant to enclose their camps, thereby protecting themselves from us. Certainly our warriors had plans for raids, however perilous, already in the making.

As soon as he was told of this wall, Ben Ya'ir came to look down upon it. When he took note of the stones cutting across the cliffs, he saw that this was a wall meant to encircle us. It surrounded not only the Roman camps but the entire mountain. It was a siege wall, six feet thick. Our leader immediately understood that its purpose was not to protect the Roman camp but to keep us in.

Some of the warriors laughed at this, for the wall was not so high that a man couldn't climb over beneath the cover of night. They had not yet realized there was another purpose to this endeavor. The Romans intended a crucifixion of the land that belonged to us, each rock in the wall serving as a nail in our flesh. They were telling us that we belonged to them, like the lion on the chain, like the slaves at their bidding, like the six hundred thousand they had slaughtered in their war against the Jews.

They wanted our fear, and that was what they received. Dread went through the fortress as though it was a fever. All at once the blue air seemed difficult to breathe. We had made a world here, one that mirrored the villages where we had once known freedom and the city we loved and hoped to return to. We minted our own pennies, the bronze poured into molds in the palace workshops, imprinted with our dream: *For the Freedom of Zion*. We had our marketplace, our bakers and wine merchants, the potters who fashioned jugs and cooking vessels from the clay that was found below in the *nachal*. As *Adonai* had created us in His image, so we had created Masada in the image of our past lives and the lives we hoped to live again, when we were free.

Now that the siege wall was in sight, people panicked, afraid that Zion would never rise again. They rushed the storerooms, greedy in their fear, thinking only of survival, as the jackal does in the middle of the night when the morning seems such distant territory. But even the jackal shares with his kind, and does not trample them, or forsake them. Our people were maddened by the deeds of the Romans and by their fear of what was to come during a siege that might last months.

Eleazar stood upon the fountain to stop the chaos. His followers had given to him a gold breastplate on which there were four gems of great worth. Although he had accepted this gift, he never dressed in it for battle, preferring instead to take up the same iron mail that his men used. Now, upon the arrival of the Romans, he wore the gold so that he might show the legion, even from a distance, that we were strong and unafraid and that we had been chosen by the Almighty to defeat Rome.

"We have one enemy," he cried out.

People turned to him, as they might turn to a prophet. He was the one who had led them here, who had believed this fortress would be their salvation. The mountain had defended Herod in the time when Cleopatra sought to take this country from him, as it would defend us now. On that point he had never wavered.

"The wall is just a wall, made of stones. But the stones are the stones of Judea. They belong to us, and our enemy only gives us what is already ours. We will not starve, for there is still enough wine and oil for us to make do. Even in a time of siege, we will have enough to eat. Our cisterns are filled with water. Our God is everywhere, on both sides of the wall."

Those who had panicked and been set to trample one another out of fear backed down. We could no longer hear the soldiers in the valley, for like a miracle the wind had shifted and those rough voices disappeared so that we could listen to our leader. The crowd stood close so they might hear the psalm Eleazar now spoke, the words of David, our great king of the past, a warrior who, like any other man, had walked with fear, as we did now, as all men must.

"Because of the voice of the enemy, because of the oppression of the wicked: for they cast iniquity upon me, and in wrath they hate me. My heart is sore pained within me: and the terrors of death have fallen upon me. Fearfulness and trembling are come upon me, and horror hath overwhelmed me."

I remained in the latticework of shadows falling through the boughs of the olive tree in my garden, but my heart lifted to hear my beloved's voice. This was what I had yearned for when I was cast out of Jerusalem, for the way he spoke was a miracle. With his words, he could approach the soul where it resided, a glory to God, for words were what the Almighty first created, after the silence of the world, and they were Eleazar ben Ya'ir's gift as well.

I closed my eyes as though we were alone and those who stood between us were no longer in our path. The world was a river, and I had been led here on its currents, not out of hope but because it was my destiny.

ꕥ

WHEN I first saw him in Jerusalem, I was standing at a well, with a pitcher of water in my hands. I'd been sent to my mother's kinsmen, for I had no father and no *beit avi,* family from my father's line. Though she had to plead to have me taken in, my mother wanted me safely removed from Alexandria, where the *kedeshah* were being cast from their houses. There were no longer to be holy women for the priests, for the ancient laws of Jerusalem had filtered into Egypt. My mother and the other women I had always known as aunts were now called prostitutes and whores, like the women on the streets who had their prices etched into the soles of their sandals so that the men who followed them knew how much they must pay for favors. All at once, what had been honored was reviled. The henna tattoos that had proclaimed them as women of worth now marked them as worthless, and the priests for whom they had sacrificed themselves were the first to accuse them of their sins.

Before I left, my mother had clasped her prized gold amulets at my throat, whispering only my daughters should receive them. She brought out her book of spells from the ironwood box, wrapped the leaves of parchment in linen to disguise it, then gave it to me, filling the box with herbs I might need: black cumin, bay leaves, myrrh. That was when I realized she might not survive the turn against who she was. She who was once exalted was now forced to move through the city in a dark cloak, hiding the swirl of markings that had once convinced me she was a queen, the tattoos which now caused people to scorn her, hissing, as if they were snakes and she a dove, there for the taking. I had already begun the painful and tedious ritual of becoming tattooed before I was sent away, fortunately only on my back and chest, not on my face or arms and legs, as my mother had been marked. No one could see who I was meant to be.

I was twelve on the last day that I saw her, when she stood before me, her eyes welling with tears. That was my age when I went to the well in Jerusalem. I was drawn there because of my need for water, and because I remembered what I had seen in the Nile. My kinsman came to me, searching me out, for I was not allowed to go to the market unaccompanied. I saw that his eyes were silver, the color of the fish. He took the pail of water from my grasp. When he brushed my hand, he assured me that it didn't matter, for we were of the same blood and were cousins. Therefore, as a brother who touched a sister, it was not a sin.

I listened as he bewitched me, for even then he had a way with what God had created first, and his words poured over me like water. But I had bewitched him as well. He was a husband, a young man of eighteen, and I was only a girl. All the same, I felt the power I had experienced when the fish came toward me of its own accord. It had no choice, for it had been written that my cousin and I would find each other, and that our love would ruin me, and that I would not care.

NOW, as I stood and listened to him speak King David's words on the day of madness, when our people were transformed into jackals by their fear, I was again entranced. Like anyone else on the mountain, I was swayed by the splendor of his voice. But the others did not know him as I did. When he recited David's song, I felt he spoke directly to me, for I was his beloved, and had been all this time.

"Oh that I had wings like a dove; for then I would fly away, and be at rest. Lo, then I would wander far off, and remain in the wilderness. Selah. I would hasten my escape from the windy storm and tempest."

From this mountain there was no longer an escape into the wilderness. The six Roman camps with their high towers blocked any passage through the ravines, or down the serpent's path, or along the treacherous southern route of the cliffs on the back of the mountain. This stronghold was the only place where we might abide. Like the lion on his chain, we had no way to run from the force of our enemy. It had been written that we would make a stand here and that we would be the last to do so. The outcome would remain unknown until it was upon us, and all we could hope to do was follow God's path.

"As for me, I will call upon God; and the Lord will save me. Evening, and morning, and at noon, will I pray, and cry aloud: and He shall hear my voice. He hath delivered my soul in peace from the battle that was against me: for there were many with me."

Afterward, when people had grown quiet, their faith restored, the women and children went to gather stones that they might fashion into weapons. These were then thrown down in a volley, like a hailstorm tossed upon the workers below. But the Romans seemed to worry little over the boulders that were catapulted into their midst. The building continued as they raised up their garrisons made of stone. If a slave at work on the wall should happen to die, there would be another to replace him. If a soldier should be wounded and falter, his brother would stand in his place.

In the quiet of twilight, we listened to the echo of the rocks that were lifted upon the wall, and we trembled despite King David's words and Eleazar's fierce confidence. This was the Romans' method, to intimidate and terrify. That night when they fed the lion they gave him a donkey so that he might kill his own meal. We could hear the donkey's screams above the endless clinking of shovels and picks and the raw voices of the men shouting below us. There was a great echo in the valley, and it seemed that the soldiers were speaking directly to us, as though we were the ones the lion had in its jaws.

I gazed down at the cliff to where my daughter was, hidden in the cave with the people she had chosen as her own. It seemed a cave like any other used by the wild ibex for shelter. If the Essenes' presence remained unknown to the Romans, perhaps she would indeed be safer there. There was a bright flash; someone in the darkness of their cave had lifted a bronze bowl that glinted in the dark. I took it to be a message. I imagined it was her heart reaching out to mine. Despite everything, she was still the child I had struggled to bring forth into this world.

IN THE MONTH of *Shevat,* sheets of rain fell. Our people did not plant wheat or barley or flax or venture into the plaza to celebrate *Rosh Chodesh,* but instead peered up at the swollen sky from our doorways, unable to see the new moon and therefore unable to chart the true month, which begins with the moon.

My neighbors stood inside their houses and watched the flooding and breathed in the chill air. They shied from the rain, as I was drawn to it. I went to stand in my garden until I was drenched. I thanked Beree, angel of rain, who came to me when I searched for him, for I had called him to us in the hopes that the Romans would stop their building if the last of the season's violent rainfalls disrupted them. Perhaps pools of mud, deep enough for mules and men to drown, would serve to slow them down.

But if anything the Romans worked harder at their task. Their world was appearing before us. Like the angels, we peered down to see what they were creating out of sand. More Jewish slaves had been brought to the valley, tied together with leather straps, treated as little more than sheep or goats. We could only watch as our brothers who had been enslaved called out for us to save them while they were mistreated and beaten. We heard their wailing, yet could do nothing to ease their suffering. They slept in pens, like the sheep, without shelter from the rain, while the soldiers resided with ease in large tents set upon stone foundations, protected by walls, with guards stationed at each camp's four gates.

I had once believed I could control the rain as I could call upon it, but now, as I gazed upon our enemies, I saw I had been wrong. Only the angel Beree could contain the rain and make it serve him, and then only by the grace of God. What I had called for had enriched our enemies. The Romans bathed in the rainwater and gave thanks to their gods. The myrtle bloomed, and its scent filled the air. Herds of ibex came to lie down before the Roman camps to drink from the pools, though it meant they would be slaughtered, and it seemed that they, too, were a gift from the heavens.

THOUGH he was ailing, I left my son in the care of his sister and asked Yael to accompany me to the *auguratorium*. I had been saving the bones of sacrificed doves, drying them in the sun, so that I might now cast for the future.

We climbed the stairs to the tower. The month of *Adar* was beginning, the time of the blooming of almond trees, and the air was fragrant. From our perch we could see the Roman camp in its entirety, a circle of brutality. The bones I'd brought along in a silk bag had become so white they appeared incandescent in the gathering dark. I thought of the doves who had given their lives, how beautiful they were, how loyal to each other, how unafraid they were of us, their keepers, even when they were to be sacrificed.

Yael cleared the sand, then poured a circle of ashes that would contain the future so it would not spill into the present. She smoothed out the ashes with the knife she always carried in her tunic. As she did so, she recited a hymn to King Solomon. She had a beautiful voice; every chant I had taught her was far more lovely in her mouth than it had been in mine. The purity of her song carried across the valley, and for a moment our brethren who were slaves toiling below us looked upward, as if called by name.

I had taught Yael well, as I'd known I would from the moment I saw her enter the Snake Gate. Though she did not remember me, I had known her long ago. This was the reason I insisted she take the gold amulet my mother had given to me. Before I gave birth to my first daughter and was cast out of Jerusalem, before I was taken to the Iron Mountain by a man I never called by name, before Nahara entered this world, before I had a son who was named Adir, a name his father allowed me, for it means noble to my people, before the doves brought me here, Yael was my daughter, though she was not born to me, and I was her *immah,* her beloved mother, though I was little more than a girl myself.

In Jerusalem I'd whispered the songs of my mother to her long before either of us had ever heard of this fortress. I had combed her hair, and fed her, and watched over her, even though her father had instructed me to leave her hair unplaited and give her nothing but crusts, for he wished that she had never entered this world and blamed her for his grief.

I came to them as a servant, a simple girl with long black hair, so worthless that the assassin never glanced at my face, and knew neither my features nor my history. Had my mother known of my condition, she would have been shocked to discover I had become a housemaid, for I could read Aramaic and Hebrew and Greek and had been trained to speak with the most learned men in Alexandria. In fact, I was relieved to be gone from the house of her kinsmen, who had come to despise me. Eleazar ben Ya'ir's mother was the one who sent me to be a servant. When I first came to her, she brought me to the *mikvah,* for she had the sense that I was *tamé,* impure. As I slipped out of my tunic, I made certain to stand in the shadows, but she saw me for who I was. She drew a deep breath when she spied my tattoos, then quickly murmured a prayer.

My aunt kept watch over her son after that, for she did not trust my upbringing. Soon enough her fear was realized. She knew what was between us from the glances we shared and quickly divined why her son no longer turned to his wife, though they had been wed only a short time. Though my aunt had promised my mother I would be safe in her home, she sent me away, hastily making plans without Eleazar's knowledge, finding me work in a household where the mother had died. It was a place of ill fortune, and no one would work there. That was why I was accepted for the position, though I was a girl with little knowledge of household chores, so young and inexperienced I often cried myself to sleep because I missed my mother so.

Before she sent me away, Eleazar's mother tied an herbal amulet to my cloak and told me it was good luck. I smiled and thanked her, but I knew it was nothing of the kind. She'd gone to a practitioner of *keshaphim* for a charm that would bind me to solitude and keep me from her son. My mother had taught me about such things, and I recognized the root of henbane. As soon as I was sent into the street, I plucked out the thread. I left the amulet in a gutter that ran with filth, for that was where it belonged. I said the prayer of protection, *Amen Amen Selah,* so that He our Lord, blessed be His name, would cast away my aunt's ill will against me.

I WAS SENT to the house of Yosef bar Elhanan, where I was to sleep in the corridor alongside the child I was to care for. She was little more than a baby, forgotten on her pallet, while her brother had his father's favor and a nursemaid of his own. I wiped away her tears when she called for her mother, much as I myself did when I woke from sleep and was startled to find that I was no longer in Alexandria, and that there was no courtyard and no fountain, no white lilies shimmering in the dark water.

Moved by my charge's sorrow, I whispered that she could call me *immah,* even though I was twelve and should have thought of myself as her sister. I knew that in this world every girl must have a protector, for my mother had told me so and I believed all that she said. Although I longed for my mother's wisdom and advice, I had to make my own decisions now. I took it upon myself to watch over this motherless child. I made a vow to protect her as she slept in the corridor that I swept each evening to ensure that the scorpions would stay in the corners.

When the father of the household had the cook leave out only crusts for us, little more than food for the rats, even on the eve of the Sabbath, I took matters into my own hands. I found a silver blessing cup and slipped it into my cloak. Although I knew thievery would bring a curse to me, I brought the chalice into the marketplace, trading it for a new tunic and cloak for the child, along with persimmons and pomegranates and grapes, as well as bedding for our corridor and a dove I planned to roast.

My little charge cried, clinging to me when she realized I meant to kill the dove, pleading with me to set it free. Though she was quiet, she was also fierce when she needed to be.

"If I do as you wish," I warned before I set the bird free, "then you must abide by my wishes in return."

This had been a bargain my own mother had often made with me when I yearned for her favor. Yael gave me her promise, and I released the dove. It disappeared into the sky above Jerusalem, and in doing so it bound us together for all eternity.

We did not have meat for our meal that night, but Yael was pleased. I was equally pleased to care for her, just as I was grateful to discover she was a good sleeper. She never woke when I slipped out at night to go to the well where I had first seen my cousin, so that I might be his. He would talk to me and I would listen—that was how it began. He spoke of his anger at the ways of the priests in the Temple, where there were divisions over who represented the true Israel. He could not abide that the Ark of the Covenant, God's word to Moses, had once been hidden behind walls of gold, when it was meant to be enclosed in a simple tent, as *Adonai* had initially instructed. No wonder it had disappeared from men's sight.

The home of our people was in the word of God, Eleazar insisted, not built of stone or gold. I listened and knew that one day others would listen to him as well, and that they would follow him, and that I would be among them. He was learned and sang the psalms of David, yearning to be in God's favor. I was both his disciple and his cousin. I believed in him and no other, and soon enough I belonged to him. I gave myself away, as my mother had predicted I would.

When Eleazar's wife went to visit her family in the north, near the shore of Galilee, my cousin brought me before a learned man so that we might wed secretly. Then he took me to his chamber where we were wed in deeds as well as words. I burned when I was beside him. I forgot Alexandria and the garden where I had studied with my mother. I never revealed I was learned in many languages, for it was only his voice I wished to hear, not my own. Another man might have questioned the tattoos set upon me and turned from me when he saw them. I told him the marks were the map that had led me to him, and that was enough for him.

He took me as I was.

AS A SERVANT in the house of my master, I was expected to know nothing. My lessons might have never happened, my knowledge turned to ashes. All that was required was that I sweep the floor and care for the child. That was not a problem for me. I was tender with Yael. I learned to be a mother from mothering her. Perhaps I'd sensed that I was with child myself, and that added to my tenderness. Eleazar promised he would tell his family of his love for me, but he could not bring himself to do so. He said his father was a tyrant, but I knew it was his mother he feared. In the night my heart beat too quickly and my blood did not come with the moon. I was hot and flushed, suffering from constant thirst, as I was to be every time I was with child, for each life that grew within me was a fire I had no recourse but to carry and let burn.

When I became so big I could no longer hide my size, Bar Elhanan sent me from his house. The dear girl who had been my daughter clutched my cloak and wept. I assured her that her brother would watch over her, warning him that he must always do so. Yael rushed after me, bringing me water. It was all she had to offer, but to me, in my loneliness, it seemed a great gift. I wept to leave her behind. I told her that if God was willing we would see each other in this world once more before we walked into the World-to-Come.

THE LAST TIME I met with Eleazar in Jerusalem rain was falling. Such a thing was a joy, unexpected and needed. The dust settled, the boughs of the trees lifted their arms to the sky. I became alive again, the girl in the fountain, the swimmer in the river, the one without fear of drowning. I stood in the street outside my aunt's house until I was drenched. At last I saw him, shifting through the yard, liquid in his movements, becoming a part of the torrent that fell upon us, flooding the streets, forcing people to remain inside their homes.

He alone could quench my thirst.

I had called him to me as I had learned to call the rain. There was not a whisper and yet he had heard. I believed that he would divorce his wife and bring me into his home, convinced that, unlike other women who went to the practitioners of *keshaphim*, desperate, willing to pay any price for a charm, I would never have need of love spells.

But Eleazar had come to tell me that his wife insisted she had proof that I had been in his bed. She vowed that the pallet they slept upon had been tinted red from the henna on my skin. My aunt, who despised me, had told her of my tattoos, to forewarn her, and therefore she had looked beneath the blanket she had woven for her husband, and found my mark. My beloved had promised me that I was as much his wife as she was, but now I saw the truth in his expression, his longing for me entwined with sorrow. If the color red had been found in the place where we had lain together, then it had foreseen my fate and was indeed my blood, for my heart had begun to weep.

I was overcome with a kind of dread I hadn't felt before, not even when I left my mother. I remembered what she had vowed on the day I saw my future. There was a part of me that wished I had remained by her side, though I knew our house had been taken from us. New tenants surely stood beside the fountain where the white lilies grew. I cried over those rare flowers when I wanted to cry over my fate. I said I could not live without them. I became frantic, uncontrollable. My cousin was beset by worry; he had me wait while he ran to the market and brought back a vial of perfume. The gift should have pleased me, for it carried the scent of lilies, but the fragrance had come from the red lilies of the fields of Moab, not the ones I had known as a child. I wept even more, for now I understood the loss I had felt when I was only a little girl, no older than Yael, and I saw my future in the Nile.

Eleazar promised he would plead with the elders of his family so that I might be allowed to join their household as his second wife. Such circumstances were fairly common, especially among the wealthy or in towns where there were too few men or if a first wife was unable to bring forth a child. My beloved was an honorable man but young; he not yet dared to defy his parents. He would learn this lesson well as he joined with the Zealots who defied the priests in the Temple, but for now he was at the mercy of his family.

I assured my cousin I would wait for him to come for me, and yet I knew he would not. The marks his wife swore had tainted their marriage bed had ruined me, and no man of any worth could take me for his wife. His family would not allow it.

*

I FOUND a chamber where I could stay behind a house of *keshaphim*. I'd noticed the dim shack as I went through the marketplace, for my mother had gone to such places in Alexandria, and I'd kept this in mind. She had instructed me that I might find refuge in times of trial among women who practiced magic. Three old women who were sisters lived there. They were unmarried, rumored to be witches who turned into dragons at night. In truth, they were kindhearted, poor, but wise in the ways of magic. In return for being allowed to sleep there, I cooked the meals and learned to bake bread in their small clay oven, making certain to always keep aside the burnt offering to sacrifice to God so that He would not forsake me. My cousin did not return. I dreamed about him for days on end, and then he disappeared from my dreams. Now when I woke from sleep I was gasping, drowning in my dreams in the river where my mother had taken me. For the first time I realized that, although the fish had come to me, he had also swum away from me. This had been the reason I was bereft as I stood knee-deep in the Nile.

I begged the sisters for a love charm, for one cannot complete such an amulet for oneself. They fashioned an incantation bowl from white Jerusalem clay, said to be the purest on earth. Before it was fired, I was to write upon it with a sharpened reed. *Holy angels, I adjure you just as this shard burns so shall the heart of Eleazar ben Ya'ir burn after me.*

But in the firing, the bowl broke. We collected the pieces, though they burned our fingers. It was a bad omen, but I took the shards and wrapped them in linen and soaked them with my own tears.

When my time came to bring a life into this world, the three sisters were my midwives. My firstborn's birth was difficult. I was young and frightened. Since that time I have seen a hundred births, but my own blood terrified me, and the tearing heat inside me nearly broke me apart. I wanted to give up, and let the Angel of Death take me, but one of the sisters leaned close to urge me on.

Ehyeh Asher Ehyeh. In the name of I am what I am, the name of God, get out. You have journeyed and now you have arrived. Amen Amen Selah.

I named my child Rebekah and saw that she had her father's eyes. That was all I would have of him. That was my punishment from God.

I WAS CALLED to stand before the elders who were to judge me in the ceremony of the *sotah* in their attempt to prove my guilt as an adulteress. My situation had become a legal matter, for his mother and wife had accused me of adultery and of having sexual relations with demons. They unbraided my hair and let it hang disheveled to shame me and show me as one of Lilith's disciples. They seemed to forget I was only a child, for I had turned thirteen just days before. They wrote God's name upon parchment, submerged in a cup of water so that the word might be erased into the liquid. I would be forced to drink the Almighty's name. If I sickened, it meant my impurity would not accept what was pure. I would then be revealed to be an adulteress.

But water was my element, and it did not forsake me. I drank it all, yet stood before them unharmed and unrepentant. I proclaimed that I had not committed adultery, and that was the truth. Eleazar ben Ya'ir alone was a husband to me.

They held my child up to examine her. She was a small being, with a dark cap of hair. She looked exactly as I had when I was born, my image in nearly every way. Those who judged us were nearly satisfied that there was no proof of any wrongdoing. The dark girl child was mine. There was no sign of the father, whether he be human or some unspeakable creature, no wings, no horns, no demon's mark. They almost let us go. Until they found their proof in the color of her eyes. "The eyes of a demon," Eleazar's wife testified, and perhaps at that moment she believed this to be true.

Eleazar's father had him restrained so that he might not come to me. That night he managed to send a servant with two doves in a wooden cage, trained to return to him, devoted to each other as we were. I took the doves and my child into the cart they used to expel me from their sight. I left my beloved behind, but in my shawl I kept what was left of the incantation bowl. I brought the broken ceramic pieces to the Iron Mountain when I went with the man who paid for me with a few coins. I used turpentine gum to set the ravaged shards back in place. Then I waited. Years passed with waiting, a lifetime. When at last my beloved sent for me, I broke the bowl myself, certain I had no need of such charms anymore.

But when I threw the bones of the doves in the tower so that I might read what was to come, I knew I had been mistaken.

OUR WARRIORS went forth in small groups, with spears, in silence, invisible and deadly. They struck the slaves who built the wall on the cliffs behind us and the soldiers who oversaw them. But as soon as our enemies fell, others replaced them, as though they were not flesh and blood but mere stalks of wheat.

When our people stole weapons, however, those were not so easily replaced. The Romans' anger was brutal at this offense, their retaliation fierce. They showed they would not tolerate our ways, capturing the warriors who had raided their storerooms, swarming upon them in such a great number that our people disappeared in their grasp.

The Roman slaves had set timbers deep in the earth and erected a platform for all to see. They crucified our people in our own valley, then they cut the heads from the bodies, so that our loved ones' spirits would wander. They threw the heads upon the ground and rolled them to the lion. But the beast refused to take them. He lay down and would not touch a single one.

It was still *Adar,* the month of almonds and of good fortune, the time when Yael first came to the dovecote. Perhaps our people were still fortunate. A whisper went up among us that the beast that had been chained was our lion, on our side. Among the warriors a wager went out: whoever freed the lion would give the greatest glory to God. He who did so would be blessed and would bring God's favor among our people.

NO MATTER HOW we might tear at our garments and sing lamentations, there was no end to our grief, for without bodies or bones, we could not honor our people. The families of the murdered shrieked and went to priests, begging for vengeance. There was not a man among us who would not have given his life in exchange for our people's freedom, but a life was nothing to our enemies. We were like the locusts they could kill without effort, with a single slap.

My son tried to drag himself from his bed, using a crutch he'd fashioned from a fallen limb of the tree behind our chamber. He wished to fight alongside his brothers, but Aziza begged him to let her go in his place. She sat at our table and chopped off her long hair, then braided what little was left tightly, close to her head. She instructed her beast of a dog to stand guard and make certain Adir did not leave our chamber. At her command the huge mastiff stood beside the boy, growling, bits of foam flecking the corners of his mouth.

"Am I a prisoner?" poor Adir demanded to know.

He was still a child in my eyes, even though he was the age I had been when I was expelled from Jerusalem to find my way in the wilderness, when I had been judged as a woman and had already given away my innocence.

Yehuda could keep Adir company, watching over him to make certain he would not flee, for the Essene boy would not fight alongside our people, and though he remained with us, and Revka cared for him as if he was her own, he was set apart by his beliefs.

"Are you my jailer as well?" Adir asked his friend.

"I would never be that," Yehuda replied.

The Essene boy rose up and opened the door so that Adir might leave if that was indeed his desire. But Adir was exhausted from our arguments; he leaned back on his pallet, his face ashy. His warrior life had been taken from him; only a part of him remained. Although I felt compassion, I was also relieved. Selfishly, I did not wish to risk my son's life.

My daughter was another matter. She had been cast from iron.

OUTSIDE there was a rising madness. The Romans had begun an attack of fiery arrows that came to us in a blazing hail. A section of the orchard had caught fire, and even when the flames had been put out, our people hurrying to quench them with jars of precious water, the scent of burning fruit drifted everywhere. While our trees were destroyed, while our children breathed in smoke, while our garments singed and turned black with ashes, the Romans set up an arena for cockfights so that they might have some amusement in the evenings. When this bored them, they set their slaves against each other with spears and chains, for to the Romans, slaves' lives were worth no more than the roosters'.

We turned away and did not look down upon them. We covered our ears so that we would not hear the slaves cry out for their mothers and their wives and for their God, who appeared to have forsaken them.

ON THE DAY my son was called to duty, as all warriors were, I walked into the yard with Aziza. Some might say I was wrong to give her up so easily and allow her to fight among the men, but her fate had already been written. Perhaps I might have prevented her call to war had I not changed her name, or perhaps this was her fate no matter what she was named. She was on the path of her element. She had always chosen metal, something cold and sharp. It suited her, as it had suited her to ride in the grasslands.

Before she left, I offered her the second gold amulet of protection that I wore at my throat, but she shook her head.

"I'm protected," she assured me. "Have no fear."

When she lifted her scarf, I noticed the silver medallion with the image of Solomon attacking a female demon. No woman would be allowed to wear such an amulet. Her courage brought me pride, as well as a cloud of regret.

"We should have stayed where we were," I said ruefully.

I had begun to dream about the Iron Mountain. In my dreams there were forty acacia trees, and in each tree there were forty black birds. I was beneath their branches, and I found I could not move. My feet had become entwined with the roots of a tree, my arms the limbs that were covered with yellow flowers. The bees were called to me, and they swarmed about me, and I wept, for I could not taste the sweetness of their honey, though it was all around.

I had done what I could to stop my daughters from following my fate. None of it had prevented what my mother told me had been written before they were born, before I went to Jerusalem and stood at the well and did as I pleased even though I knew where it would lead me. Love would bring about my undoing. That was the reason I had tried my best not to love my children, so I would not bring my curse upon them. In that, I had failed.

"We were meant to be here," Aziza assured me.

Her skin was burned by the sun. I noticed the scar that was beneath her eye shone white in her darkened face. She could have been a beautiful woman, instead she was a warrior. She could have been a boy who walked through the streets of the red city of Petra, instead she was my daughter, who had followed me to this fortress, and whom I loved despite the many ways I had tried not to do so.

When she went to the barracks, I thought of my mother, who had stood in the courtyard beside the fountain to watch me leave Alexandria. Now I understood she had known she would not see me again. My heart dropped because I had viewed my own future and what was to come in the bones I had thrown on the tower floor.

I would lose everything I had.

Something was ending, but it was also beginning. I could feel the life within me move and shift. Creation had begun at the Temple mount, and perhaps it would once again if everything else disappeared. Already, there were men speaking of a third Temple, one that would arise in the future, more glorious than any other. From destruction there would be light, and the first words would again be spoken out of a holy silence, for that is always the beginning.

I walked to the wall, my cloak around me. I rested my hand upon my abdomen, and upon my daughter who was not yet born. My beloved wished for a son, as all men did, but I knew I would have another daughter. I always carried a girl child in the same way, high, under my heart. I wanted another world for her, not this mayhem below us. There were still pools of rain on the valley floor. In any other time we would have been grateful. Wild goats and deer would have come to drink. Falcons and herons would have dropped from the sky to bathe, and the ravens, who had fed Elijah in the wilderness, would have come to us with plums in their beaks.

Now there was only the lion, whose chain allowed him to roll in the water. He was covered with mud, his huge paws leaving cleft marks in the damp earth. I forced myself to look away from this great beast, for I could not bear to see him so debased and tamed. I was reminded of the trained Syrian bears one could see in the alleys of Alexandria and Jerusalem, but this was much worse, for the lion had been humiliated in his own land, dispossessed as we were, the lord of nothing but stones.

I gazed down upon the sheer cliff in my grief. As I did, I spied a black goat along the mountainside, one that had escaped from the Essenes' cave. He was scrambling among the rocks, lost and forsaken, unable to find the rest of his flock.

It was a sign of the darkness to come.

ONE ROMAN SOLDIER noticed the goat, but one was all it took. He told his comrades, and they went after the creature hastily, first in sport, then with the relentless fervor of hunters. In doing so they stumbled upon the camp of those who wanted only peace. Yehuda came to the wall to stand beside me as the Romans began their ascent to the limestone caves beneath us. It was as though his mother, still among her people, had called out to him, as my daughter's heart had called to me. We were helpless to do anything other than watch as the soldiers climbed the cliff. One fell and I was quick to praise God, and I wondered what had become of me that I might pray for a man's death on the rocks, rejoicing at the sound of his cries.

Those soldiers who managed to reach a plateau in the cliff then sent down ropes to ensure those who followed would have an easier time rising up. As it is said of the angels, we could see what was to happen before it occurred, but like them we were unable to change the outcome. If this was what the angels observed when they gazed upon our world, how we might murder each other and cause one another agony, then I pitied them as I pitied no others.

Our warriors came to send down a volley of arrows, but the arrows fell upon the rocks as if they were birds falling from the sky. Aziza, too, had rushed to the wall, but she was dressed like a woman and therefore helpless, though she could not be restrained from throwing down rocks and I heard the war cry of Moab escape from her. The Roman soldiers had entered the cave, and our weapons could not reach them there. Several of our warriors held Aziza back when she scrambled onto the wall in an attempt to leap into the fray beneath us, for a warrior such as my daughter could not stand idly by and was therefore restrained in ropes.

Although the murders were hidden from our sight, they were not hidden from our ears, and we were made to listen to the sound of death, so terrible to hear, all the worse when what you see is inside yourself, the thousand cruelties set upon those you love.

Aziza and I stood together and wept, not knowing if the screams we heard were the voices of those we loved or the pitiless shrieks of hawks above us. We could hold our hands over our ears, we could turn away, but that wouldn't end the horror. The wailing of the dead can be heard in every corner of this world and in the World-to-Come. It does not stop when the sound is finished, it is within you, an eternal part of your being.

BECAUSE she could not be buried, and her bones were left ungathered, my daughter's soul would remain beside her body, lost, desperately trying to reenter herself and become alive once more. The jackals would find her, but her soul would remain in the cave even when they took her in their jaws; she would watch as the beasts shook her into pieces, devouring her. Each of the agonies of the flesh would be hers in spirit. There would be no *taharah*, the purification that readies a body for the next world, no blessed water or oils or aloe to wash away the sins of life on earth. Still the pure of heart were said to be able to see the Shechinah as they were dying, they looked upon the most radiant and compassionate face of God. This was what I could hope for. That at the moment of her death she saw God's light and nothing more.

I wished that the lie the Romans told about Nahara's father's people was indeed true and that her blood did run blue, so that when they cut her down a thousand more would arise in her place. I had nearly died giving birth to her, and would have, had Aziza not been such a fearless child. All of that agony spent only so that I might live to sing lamentations for her throughout the day and night. I tore my garments until my hands bled, keening as I did so. Though I had lost her when she defied me and married Malachi, I mourned her bitterly now. Her blood was on my hands. I did not blame Malachi or the Essenes, for I was the one who had led her to her doom, exactly as my mother had said I would, bringing ruin to all I loved and to anyone who might love me.

When my daughter of Moab was born, her father had waited ten days to see her, as was the custom of his people. He had wanted a son, but when he entered the tent, his face broke into a smile. It was good that a man could not see a child immediately, when an infant was still battered by birth, swollen and blue from the burden of coming to life. To her father's eyes, this girl child was a radiant being. He was a man who did not hide what he felt. He chose her name, and I agreed to his choice, for Nahara meant the light that shone upon great beauty. We agreed on many things, but on this most of all. I wondered if, on the other side of the Salt Sea, my daughter's father knew that she was lost, if he had been waiting all this time for us to return. I wondered if when he found me in the wilderness and took me with him I had been wrong not to love him. At the very least I should have been grateful enough to offer him my loyalty in return.

OUR PEOPLE went out to see the new moon at the time of *Rosh Chodesh*. We offered God our prayers, but we did not rejoice. There was no dancing. The Roman wall had been completed, encircling us like a viper. The camps had risen, several of them larger than most villages. Those who had not come from Jerusalem were stunned by what the legion had accomplished; below them there were more people than many had seen in their lifetimes, the six thousand wearing the white tunics of the legion, and thousands more enslaved to help them with their brutal tasks.

The Romans' main camp, set directly across from the Northern Palace, boasted a tower that rivaled that of any garrison. There was another large camp behind us, guarding the treacherous eastern slope, and six more smaller camps set in a circle. Beyond Silva's camp there was the village of followers, where people led their daily lives, raising chickens, taking women for their pleasure, praying to their gods. I considered each one to be the murderer of my daughter.

I went out at night to the wall where I had drawn spells before, and there I took a dreadful oath.

I invoke and beseech the Most High God, Lord of all spirits and of the flesh, against those who treacherously murdered or killed, who spilled innocent blood in an unjust fashion. Lord who oversees all angels, before whom every soul humbles itself, may you avenge this innocent blood and seek justice.

I wrote these words upon parchment, then burned them so they might rise up to the Almighty. I called down the angels of *Chimah*, the messengers of wrath and of vengeance. *Chimah* is also said to be the name of the stars in the sky that are the seven sisters, who look down upon us in times of sorrow. As I beseeched the angels, I took a knife to my flesh and sliced along the palm of my left hand, though our people were not allowed to cut ourselves, or harm that which God had created. I cut deeply as I offered myself in a bargain to keep my surviving children safe from every living thing, and from the demons who were so close by, and from the lion below us.

OUR ENEMIES studied our ways. To them, we were nothing more than a scorpion placed under glass. They wished to gauge when we would next sting. Each time they attempted to scale the serpent's path, we poured boiling oil onto them. Our archers were perched in the olive trees and along the wall, ready to shoot down whoever might try to pass. The path was narrow, and the legion was wide, an easy target when they tried to scale the mountain.

We thought they would see how dangerous a scorpion could be, despite its small size. But if anything, the Romans decided that the best way to catch a scorpion is to crush it in its own garden. To destroy us, they needed to reach us. They began their own path, a wide ramp built at the western slope and rising toward the North Gate. Barrel upon barrel of earth was brought to raise up this ramp, which took the form of a white mountain. We thought they were mad to attempt to create what only God could form, a cliff reaching two hundred cubits from the valley from which they could pursue us. But there were so many slaves and the work was unceasing, and before our eyes the cliff appeared, so white it burned with brightness. At night it seemed the world had overturned, and the stars were beneath us, rising up to us, threatening to burn us with their light.

The men at the synagogue met to discuss whether or not it was truly possible for this ramp to reach our walls. But in the time it took for them to debate this matter, the ramp rose so high that we could plainly hear the workers. The Roman soldiers were able to swing javelins and spears that took several lives. We were stunned by what our enemies had accomplished, and how, like our Creator, they had built a mountain overnight.

IN JERUSALEM I had seen my rival only once, as I stepped into the cart on the day I was driven out of the city. The wooden cage of doves was in my hand and I carried my child, who wailed in my arms. They forced me to go barefoot, as was the custom; when my feet bled, one more sorrow would be added to my punishment.

I remember that Ben Ya'ir's wife was wearing fine sandals, made of goat leather, clasped with brass buckles. She wore necklaces of lapis and carnelian and turquoise, with gold bracelets on her arms. I had only a black scarf wound around myself. As my enemy watched me climb into the donkey cart meant for hauling ewes to the butcher, I thought not of the torments of the wilderness, nor of the vultures and ravens that would follow us. I was not occupied with the heat that would bring us low or the jackals that would not be content to wait for our death so we might be their meal. Instead I was ashamed of my bare feet.

Now, after all this time, she came to my door on the day the Roman ramp was completed. The ramp had fallen short, and for this we were grateful. But we shuddered to think of how the Romans might amend this, and how intent they were on reaching us, even if that meant they must float through the air.

The dog who watched over my son howled when Channa approached, as he might have had the Angel of Death knocked upon our door. Dogs are said to know of such visitations. In Alexandria I had witnessed a priest's dog howl at the moment of his owner's death; the grieving creature was then put to death himself so that his body might be buried beside his master's. I held our watchdog by the neck and opened the door so that I might gaze upon my caller with loathing. I had already faced her once on this mountain, and she had no more power over me.

At least she knew well enough not to cross my threshold. I took in my rival, her pinched face, her sorrowful eyes, and in return she stared at me. By then there was no disguising I would soon bring another child into this world. But it was a world torn asunder. To me, birth seemed less like a gift to the soul I carried than it did a curse.

The dog pulled back his lips and showed his teeth to my visitor.

"I only want a minute," Channa said hastily.

I loosened my hold on the dog, and he snapped his jaws. Perhaps Eleazar had once mentioned she was afraid of dogs. Perhaps that pleased me.

"I thought you wanted my life," I remarked.

"No." She shook her head. "I wanted my husband."

"Then go to him," I suggested.

She was hesitant. Not until I began to close the door did she speak out, her words flowing.

"Only you can grant me the protection of his life."

We gazed at each other over the threshold. I wondered if it was possible that, even now, as Rome was besieging us, Channa might be trying to ensnare me, hoping to have me brought before the council and tried as a witch. Still I listened, for this woman and I had been tied together as the night is tied to the day, never knowing each other yet never eluding one another.

Perhaps I wanted to see her beg for something. The idea of her bleak pleas and her remorse was compelling. I sent the dog inside, then stepped into the yard. In any other year, this season would have meant the start of planting, but our fields lay fallow. There were no seeds and no men to work the plows and no beasts to assist them.

"I am not a magician," I told my rival. "I can't grant you anything."

The almond trees were in full flower, and the hyssop bloomed. Channa had finished the cure I had sent to her and was once more prone to difficulty when she drew in deep breaths. I did not mention that hyssop grew nearby, along my wall. I let her puff and pant.

"Tonight the warriors are going out to try to stop the building of the ramp. They will not all return."

I was resolved not to let her see how this news affected me. If she thought I was indifferent, she would not have the power to break my heart.

Channa went on when I was silent. "I dreamed he would return only with the help of a black bird."

"I'm not a bird," I said, though I was alarmed by this news, for I, too, had dreamed of a black bird, a raven, such as the one that had visited Elijah and fed him when he was lost in the wilderness and had no sustenance. "Why come to me?"

She was gazing at the child within me. "Is it a son?" Her voice was plaintive.

"Now you think I'm a witch and can divine God's will. You think I'm many things, it seems. Did you ever think I was a girl who was sent into the wilderness? Did you see that my feet were bare and that the vultures followed me and that I was alone, sent to die? Maybe that was why your dream came to you. Perhaps you're meant to choke on feathers."

"Save him, even if it's for yourself," Channa said to me then.

She raised her eyes, and I saw the truth, that he was her husband and that she was willing do anything to rescue him. I took a step away. I knew then that she had power over me still, and that her power came from the fact that she loved him.

"I should have brought you into our home," she went on. "Then your children would be mine as my husband was yours. We might have carried our burdens and joys together, as sisters."

I marveled that she had the courage to speak to me in this manner, that she hadn't been afraid to court my hatred of her and my spite. Because of this, I softened in a way I hadn't thought possible. Perhaps it had been written that she would ruin her life and my own. Perhaps she, too, had no choice but to follow her fate.

"Don't do this for me," Channa said. "Do it for the one you love. Our husband."

I watched her hasten away, following the wall, although arrows flew close by, some set on fire. She didn't shrink from them; perhaps she no longer cared about matters such as her own safety. I noticed that her feet were bare, and that she had wound a black scarf around her shoulders, and that she was now in the wilderness herself, and that everything she had said was true.

*

I WENT to the Snake Gate and asked the guard to let me by. I understood why I had dreamed of forty acacia trees surrounded by bees. The dream had been given to me by the angels and by the Almighty. What had appeared to be a puzzle now formed itself into a path.

The guard might have refused me, but Amram passed near, and I turned to him to plead for help. He was arrogant and impatient, half-dressed in his silver-scaled armor. His hair was long and plaited, ready for war.

"No woman goes through the gate," he told me coldly, girding himself for the coming night, when the warriors meant to attack the slaves who were building the ramp. He had no idea that I had known him as a spoiled and sweet child, favored in his father's eyes. Now his demeanor was harsh, and I saw something dark within him, a blackness of spirit that wasn't there before. Some whispered that the raids of our people had included the murder of women and children. They swore our warriors had no choice, that it was all for the cause of the true Israel and the one whose name can never be spoken aloud, *I am I*. But war brought such changes to all, and with those changes it brought a loss of *lev*, the true heart, especially for those who had betrayed God's laws, and who knew that they did, and who told themselves they acted as they must.

"Perhaps you've come because your daughter has a message for me?" he asked.

Aziza had spurned this warrior without granting him a reason for her displeasure, and his hurt was evident. She would not speak of him and seemed to have no interest in him.

"Are you her messenger?" the warrior wanted to know.

He used the word *mal'ach*, which although it can mean messenger can also mean angel. Perhaps this was his way of calling her a *shedah*, as many before had, or perhaps he believed I had called the angels of wrath upon him, that it was my disapproval which had caused Aziza to turn from him.

Yael had spied us from the plaza. She wore a tattered gray cloak that was too large for her frame. She came forward, concerned, when she saw her brother's bitterness. "Shirah is not the cause of her daughter's actions," Yael reminded him gently.

"Or am I, it seems," Amram said in a heated tone. "She can no longer even see me."

"Be patient," Yael suggested. "She may return to you."

Amram reached out to make a quick sweep of the chaos below us. "I have no time to wait."

Yael had taken note of the basket I carried. She threw me a quick look, then asked her brother if we might gather herbs from the hillside.

Amram shook his head, for this was not allowed. "Not on this day."

"My brother," Yael teased, "must I remind you that I can remember when you slept with your thumb in your mouth and feared the scorpion in the corridor?"

"Yaya," he said, shaking his head, smiling in spite of himself. "I cannot let you go."

"We'll be careful," she vowed. "Some things are meant to be," I heard her whisper to Amram. "I'll look for an herb that will bring you luck."

He was still her brother, willing to listen to her demands. He spoke with the guard, who let us slip out the gate. The daylight had stretched itself into long shadows, which allowed us to press ourselves against the cliffs and go forth unseen. I had meant to be alone, but now I had no choice in the matter. Perhaps it was fitting that Yael should accompany me, for she had learned the spells my mother had taught me and would have no fear of what we must accomplish.

We made our way along the hillside together, then slunk down toward a damp ravine between two caves. Once, gathering kindling nearby, I had spied bunches of fragrant pink blooms set upon spindly green limbs. They were wild cousins of the rhododendron, a flower my mother had pointed out in Alexandria so that she might warn me of its dangers. Like the *ba'aras* root, which could draw out an enemy's soul, the leaves and roots of the rhododendron were forbidden but often used for *pharmaka* in matters of love and of revenge. Of all the parts of this toxic plant, the flowers were the most potent.

We crouched low and listened well, the mud of the *nachal* slippery under our bare feet. We were protected by the wind. It seemed we were in another world entirely, one in which we might remember how beautiful the wilderness could be. We would soon be approaching the Feast of Unleavened Bread, and the sun was strong for the season. The rhododendron flower was the potion I had come to find, one I did not need to concoct or create, for it was already part of creation. Spells and charms were not enough to protect my beloved. It was poison I needed.

I held up my hand so that Yael might bend her ear toward the echo that rumbled nearby. Beneath the never-ending noise of the Romans, rising up as they toiled with shovels and picks, was the sound of bees. In spring they often swarmed in these hills, traveling here from Egypt for the last flowering of the desert before the heat arrived. We followed the buzzing to a fallen log, wherein yellow honey was dripping forth, what some among us call *debas*, and others refer to as *manna*. The food of the bees was often salvation to those in the desert, praised by man and beast alike. But this honey was like no other, for it was gathered from the deadly pink flowers that grew in the ravine; only a small taste would drive a man mad for hours, perhaps for days.

I shrugged off my cloak and insisted Yael stand back. I alone was safe from the bees' stinging wrath, for I had poured salt upon my skin, so that they would not light upon me as I reached inside the log to draw out the honeycomb. Before our warriors went to destroy the ramp of the Romans, the soldiers of the legion partaking of this tainted honey would be maddened. When evening fell, they would not be able to divine whether they were dreaming or if indeed our men had fallen upon them. In their confusion, like men made drunk, they would fail to draw their swords.

Yael and I huddled beside a cliff as bees circled around the honeycomb. I sprinkled salt upon it, forcing the bees to float away, back to the deadly pink flowers, where they gathered more nectar. When I described my intentions, Yael was not surprised. She admitted that she had come in search of me, for she had heard a voice calling to her, telling her what she must do. She was the one who would bring the poison to our enemy. That was the reason she had chosen to leave Arieh with her father, and why she'd dressed in the assassin's cloak, slipping it from a hook in his chamber to serve as her armor, flimsy and thin as it might be. When she drew it over her head, she all but disappeared before me. The cloth was the color of the pale sky, and of the stones, and of the thin sunlight that fell upon us. Even her scarlet hair faded beneath the hood; her face disappeared and became a mist.

I had planned to deposit the tainted *manna* for the Romans, but Yael insisted the voice had spoken to her for a reason. I did not wish to let her go, or to be the cause of any harm that might befall her. I pleaded with her, but she would not listen. She believed she had been called to take the honey from my hands. In truth, I understood, for in my dream she had been beside the acacia trees. She had lifted her arms to heaven as she'd stepped into my place.

I appreciated why Yael had given the slave the gold amulet of protection; we were all comforted to think of him finding his way to his own country, where the snow was spiraling down. Still, she was in need of protection. I fastened the second gold amulet around her throat, despite her pleadings that she wasn't worthy. I knew that she was meant to be sheltered by the sign of the fish, and by the promise of water, and by the grace of the Almighty.

I WAITED in the fading daylight as Yael went on alone. We had entered the hour that opens the heavens to our sight, a time when holy men insist it is possible for them to witness the throne of God. I saw only the cliffs that were before us. I dared not raise my eyes to the cave on the sheer cliff where the Essenes had died, for my daughter's spirit lingered there, cold and alone. The wickedness of the world was a part of creation, I knew this, and the Angel of Death had been created on that day when life first appeared, yet I was embittered. I wept for what I had lost and what the world had lost and would yet lose again.

Yael was quick as she made her way down the mountain. I barely managed to observe her form beneath her cloak as she approached the white ramp that led to hell, for that is what we called the valley that had once been ours and had come to belong to Rome. When she neared the building site, she immediately left the honeycomb on a ledge of rock, placed carefully, so that the soldiers who oversaw the slaves would be sure to find it. The sweet scent would call to them, and they would devour the poison as our people enjoyed the bounty of *manna* when we were released from bondage in Egypt. Our warriors would then have a measure of safety when they attacked.

The curtain of night would soon be upon us, the honeycomb was in place, yet Yael tarried. I grew cold watching the stars appear, still she did not come. I began to worry and pace, for she seemed to have vanished. Though she wore the gold amulet of protection, God alone could protect her in this valley. As the hour grew late, I became frantic, nearly overcome with the fear of what might have happened to her. Then I saw a flicker of mist.

In the darkness, Yael had managed to slink down beside a rock and remain hidden as the Romans in the field practiced for the warfare to come, setting to with the swords and javelins they would use against us when the white ramp was completed. When the soldiers at last went to their barracks, Yael rose up from beside the rock. I couldn't fathom the meaning of her movements as she left the safety of her perch and continued to go forth. I wondered if perhaps she had eaten from the honey and if she herself had gone mad to think she could enter the valley floor of the Romans and survive. Still she moved forward.

The pool of mud was before her, and beyond that lay the lion.

In all the valley this beast alone had spied her, or perhaps he had picked up her scent. Yael had gone to the *mikvah* that day, and when stench is everywhere, the scent of what is pure is most noticeable of all. The lion raised his head and gazed across the pool as Yael made her way, wading carefully. I could not abide the thought of seeing her torn apart, ravaged and devoured while I watched, the little girl I had loved as though she were my daughter when I was but a girl myself. My grief was enormous as I stood alone in the falling dark, weeping for all I had done in the world and the many people I had wronged. I thought that perhaps I was witnessing the End of Days and that the Essenes had been right all along, and we had been merely too foolhardy to listen. I thought of what the bones I had thrown had revealed, and the future I had seen and all I had yet to lose in this world.

Yael had come to stand before the lion. He could have easily reached to attack her, yet he did not move. His tail switched, nothing more. Yael drew closer still. I could see them through a layer of mist. A fierce creature, a pool of water, a woman who was unafraid. Perhaps because she had once been bitten by a lion, she imagined she was immune to any further bites, as some who are attacked by bees never again react to their sting.

No one in the Roman camp had paid attention to the lion for

some time, or had even thought to feed him since their arrival. One donkey was all he'd been granted. He had been mistreated, half-starved, made to stay unsheltered from the burning sun, unable to flee the torrents of rain when they came. He had served his purpose, to frighten us, and now he was abandoned. Ravens came close, but he could not reach them. Ibex and deer and sheep had been roasted over the fires of the Romans, but the lion had not been granted a shred of their meat or bones.

He did not move as Yael approached, nor did he shrink from her. Perhaps he did not maul her because he had been broken, taken from his land, abused, unable to act like a lion. Or perhaps he was merely waiting for a messenger from God, as we wait for Gabriel.

Yael now came close enough to unhook the brass buckle which fitted the creature's collar to his chain. I could not breathe or move. I imagined he would turn on her then and I would see her death before my eyes. Instead the lion rose to his feet and stood before her. He stared at Yael with his yellow eyes, more curious than ferocious. He may have thought she was one of his own kind and wondered if she meant to accompany him. He may have believed she was a dream, for if lions dreamed it would surely be this, freedom in the night, hands that unleashed you, the mountains before you.

Yael lifted her arms, as we do to bid the doves to take flight. The lion turned to run across the valley, disappearing into the cliffs, his dun color the cloak which allowed him to vanish before our eyes.

I knew then I had witnessed a miracle. I waited where I was, praying, offering gratitude to the Almighty, my faith renewed, while on the valley floor the bravest warrior among us made her way back to our mountain, invisible to all men beneath her gray cloak, but radiant in the darkness, a shining star before the eyes of God.

*

OUR WARRIORS went out that night to find the soldiers of the legion intoxicated, maddened and half-asleep, for they had mixed the toxic honey with wine to make a mead, and many had drunk from this poison. Our men killed as many as they could before the cries of the slaughtered brought hundreds of soldiers racing. By then the warriors of Masada had begun to climb back up the cliff. Several were lost in the fray and were carried upon the shoulders of their brothers. At least we had their bodies and could prepare their earthly forms for burial. In Jerusalem we would have taken our dead to the caves of our fathers, then a year later collected the bones to be stored in stone ossuaries. Here there was no time for such practices. Though the Romans had retaliated with a storm of burning arrows, we gathered in the plaza to sing lamentations and tear at our garments and lay the dead to rest.

In the midst of our mourning, some among us looked down upon the valley. They saw that the lion had been freed from the chains of Rome to return to the cliffs of Judea. There were shouts and prayers. Crowds gathered, mystified, wondering if it had been Gabriel, the fiercest of the angels, who had brought this omen to us, for surely no man would have dared to approach a lion.

STILL THE ROMANS built their white ramp, still it rose higher. Though we sent down hot oil, stones, arrows, they continued on, a machine of death intent on victory. In weeks, the ramp was a few arms' lengths from our walls, and the damage their soldiers could now manage was great. We had many losses and fires occurred every day. Whatever they destroyed with stone and flame we rebuilt, but we hadn't enough hands, and there were ruins all around us. No one dared to leave the fortress now, or even venture close to the wall. We huddled together in the wind. There was a great silence over us. It was despair, and it passed from one to the other more quickly than a fever.

When Eleazar came to me at night, he did not speak. Though words had always bound us together, they were not enough to save us now. Below us, there was a blur of movement, faster all the time, more purposeful and more brutal. We were reminded of the way in which bees could create entire cities overnight in their hives. So, too, could the legion. Where there had been six thousand, ten thousand now stood before us. The Romans were like an endless swarm. You could not outfight them or outrun them. The only choice was to put salt on your skin, though it might pain you to do so, to cover yourself with a cloak, so that you might disappear.

My beloved cousin had told our people the Romans would move on once they understood a siege could not take us down. We had enough to sustain us, we would be hungry, but it was possible to live in poverty and survive for a year on rations, perhaps two. Surely Rome would tire of us and decide to use the legion's power to a better purpose. Now that the ramp had risen so high on the western slope, my cousin no longer spoke of such things or gave us false hope. The Angel of Death has a thousand eyes and no man can outdistance him. There have been stories of men who have ridden all night to escape their fate, only to arrive in a far-flung village where the Angel waited, knowing his victim's destination before the rider himself did. *Mal'ach ha-Mavet* would find his intended no matter how fast a victim might ride, even if his horse was as swift as my husband's had been, the great Leba, who held the heart of a thousand horses.

Eleazar and I went to the cistern together after darkness fell, no longer caring who might accuse us of sin. As Death saw us, we saw him in return, even when we closed our eyes. In the water, I embraced my beloved in silence; he winced, for he was freshly wounded and had paid no attention to this injury. I wanted to dress the cut with *samtar,* but he told me there was no time. When he said this I began to weep, as I had on the day in Jerusalem when it rained and he went to the market to find me the vial of perfume scented with lilies. That had been the last time we saw each other until he had called me to this mountain. Now I was losing him again.

"Don't," he said to me as I cried. "There's no time for that either."

He had been hardened by his years of fighting. He had been not much more than a boy when I first knew him, now he had killed so many that his hands were stained. Yet tears could undo him and remind him of how human we were. The suffering of the world weighed heavily upon him. I dried my eyes because he asked me to do so. I had always done as he asked, not because I was bound to do so by duty but because I saw the depth of who he was and how he himself suffered. When I gazed at him, I did not see the brutal face his enemies looked upon, or the heavy arms and back of a warrior who carried armor and steel, but the young man at the well who had seen beyond my henna tattoos. He had always known who I was.

Eleazar gathered my hair and lifted it so that he might kiss my throat. Without my amulets, I was unprotected. I felt myself burn. I believed myself to be safe with him. He who was so cruel in the field of battle, was still the boy he once had been, so eager for me that his wife and father and all the laws of Jerusalem could not keep him from me. He whispered that he would prefer to spend what little time we had left in each other's arms. *Let us not speak, or tend to our troubles, let us lie together and forget the world, remembering only each other.*

The Romans would find us, as bees did; they would swarm upon us and the salt would fall from our skin and we would be naked and defenseless before them, as we now were with each other.

❧

WHEN WE rose from our restless sleep, we found that the ramp on the western side of the mountain was already completed. It was a cool day, misty and blue. Already the month of *Nissan* was upon us, when our people celebrated their freedom. When we opened our eyes, it was as though the ramp had always been there, magicked into being, more real than the mountains that had stood since God created them.

On that same day the dust rose up along the desert floor when a group of travelers from the east arrived. I saw that many of their cloaks were blue. They belonged to the people of Nahara and Adir's father, nomads from the hills of Moab. They had brought all manner of spices and treasures from Petra and had come to offer their help to the Romans, with whom they had a treaty of peace. When I regarded these men, my heart fell, for I knew how fierce they were and how difficult they would be to defeat.

My hair was damp from my night in the cistern, my arms ached from holding on to a man who always left me while I slept. I would awake on the edge of the well, beside the deep water, a scrim of plaster dust flecking my skin, and I would be alone. Despite my enlarged belly, I had grown thin. The man who had been my husband in Moab would have noticed, he would have been certain to feed me dates and figs, for he thought a thin woman was like a thin horse, too weak for the hills of his country. He had loved me, though he never said so. He had watched me all the while we were together, as if his eyes could not get enough of my form.

Eleazar had not noticed that my ribs could be viewed, or that the bones at my shoulders and backbone were rising through my skin. He did not see that the poor diet of roots and beans had caused my hair to be less glossy, for I plaited it into braids, then clasped it atop my head with two pins made of horn. To him I was the girl with the sheet of black hair at the well in Jerusalem, just as he was my beloved, the man who stood with me in the rain and took me to him, the one I had been pledged to throughout time.

*

WE NO LONGER took note of the laws of men, only the laws of God. Day and night, prayers were said. The old men gathered in the synagogue, and by the flickering light of what little oil we had left, they begged for God's forgiveness and His favor. Timbers had been laid into the Romans' ramp to support the barrels of white earth the slaves continued to pour upon it. The ramp was now so close the Romans could speak to us, and Silva himself came to shout for Ben Ya'ir. Some of our men shouted back that our leader would never speak with demons, for a demon could take your soul from your words. It was true, we knew, for when we listened to the demon who commanded the Tenth Legion, he had brought us clouds of terror. We covered our ears, yet we could still make out Silva's words. *Surrender now and we will let you go free.*

Exactly what they had told the warriors of the fortress at Machaerus before murdering every one, leaving them for the jackals so that their bones were scattered through the forest, as if they had never been men at all but had come into this world as stones.

BEN YA'IR gave no answer to Silva but instead sent a hail of arrows set aflame. I saw the finest archers upon the wall, my daughter among them. She used so many arrows that soon enough she had no more. That night she taught Adir how to fashion these weapons, how to keep the flint straight so he would not scrape his hands raw as he struck the thin metal tip against a stone, how to wind the sharpened tip to the wooden shaft with a thin strand of leather. Because Yehuda could not by faith touch an instrument of war, he collected feathers from the doves, to attach to the arrows so they might fly straight from the hands of my daughter to the hearts of the enemy.

Aziza took me aside before she returned to the wall with her basket of newly made arrows. She looked so strong, her muscles fine, her face beautiful and harsh and dark. My daughter told me she would attempt any tactic to save our people, except for one. She would not shoot any man in a blue robe. One among them might well be the man who had been Nahara and Adir's father, my husband once, who for a very long time had forgotten that Aziza was not his true-born son.

I gave her my blessing, casting powdered snakeskin into her short, black hair for her protection. I felt my love for her in the back of my throat. I could not say it aloud for fear I would bring her doom to her, but I embraced her and she knew what she meant to me, as she had known I'd depended upon her to help me bring Nahara into this world, as I'd had faith enough to allow her to ride with the men in Moab. Once I had given her a name that would help her to be fearless in a world commanded by fear. That was my greatest gift to her.

FORTUNATELY there was still a space between our cliff and the white ramp. Every time more earth was heaped upon it, the end of the ramp collapsed in a landslide. Although the slaves had brought up huge battering rams, as large as the trunks of date palms, those last few yards could not be forged, and therefore they could not break through the wall. Though King Herod had been wicked in many ways, we were grateful for the wall he had built and for the stones that bore his mark. We thought the legion's inability to build the ramp to meet the king's wall was an omen of our assured success, and we prayed and thanked the Almighty.

It would soon be the eve of the Feast of Unleavened Bread, the day when our people were freed from slavery in Egypt. We thought of Moses in the desert, and how there had been faith even when there was no hope, how he had led his people despite their agonies.

We thought our celebration would bring us fortune in the future. We did not understand that, much like the ninth of *Av*, when both Temples fell, when Moses broke the tablets, when sorrow reigned across our world, some days were meant to make us remember that the past was with us still.

The Romans were relentless, and a king's wall was nothing to them as they worked for the glory of their Emperor. They threw up an enormous platform that rose to more than two hundred cubits. The wood had come all the way from Greece, shipped across the sea, hauled here on the backs of slaves; the timbers carried the scent of the forest. Revka said they had been fashioned from cypress, and she wept in remembering. We stood watching as the platform was completed and the soldiers scrambled upon it and called out curses, quickly letting go with volleys of burning torches. All we could smell then was fire; the fragrance of sweet cypress was like a dream that had once clung in the air.

When the platform was still not enough to breach the distance between the ramp and Herod's mighty wall, the legion extended it with huge stones that fitted together. Then came the worst creation we had ever seen, one invented by Vespasian, then used by Titus, and now by Silva. It seemed this work of warfare had been fashioned in the demon world, and a thousand evil spirits had constructed it. We stood in awe and in despair. Even grown men had tears streaming down their faces. A metal-plated tower nearly a hundred feet tall had been set upon the wooden platform so the Romans could attack us yet be protected from our slingshots and arrows and darts. From this tower they were able to set forth huge boulders, striking the king's walls that were meant to last for all eternity.

So it began. The mountain shook and the birds took flight, the ravens and the larks, the sparrows and hawks, every winged creature fled from us, save for the doves in the dovecotes, who had no choice but to remain. I felt the child inside me shift as I sat upon the rim of the fountain. All around me there was madness. Children of the ages of three and four were scraping the blood from spears that had been cast into a pile, pulled from the bodies of the slain. Our dead were so many they were brought into the field where the almond trees flowered with both pink and white blooms. There the dead were washed with rainwater and oil, then wound in sheets of linen.

When we had no more linen and still more dead, we used our own shawls to wind them in. Two of our young warriors, mere boys in armor, slipped through the gate to fight the soldiers on their own. Their heads were cut from their bodies and thrown up to us by catapult, their eyes still open. These boys' mothers tore at their own flesh, horrified, caught in the nightmare that was our waking life.

Revka and her grandsons had come to stay with me, along with Yael and Arieh, for their chamber was too near the wall; their neighbors had been killed as they slept when an arrow soared through the slit in stone that had served as a window, setting their pallets on fire. Certainly, we had room enough. My daughter Aziza had set a tent in our yard. She no longer wished to sleep indoors and, like the warrior that she was, stayed beneath the stars. The Man from the Valley came to take his meals with her, and they sat there like brethren, not speaking, yet not lacking for comfort. This man's sons, Noah and Levi, peered out at this grave warrior, for he had become more a legend than a man to them. Once I noticed his glance flicker over to them. His expression softened and something seemed to stir within him, but he turned away, attending to the meager meal of beans and lentils Aziza had cooked for them to share.

Revka had confided that on the day of her beloved daughter's death, her son-in-law vowed two things: As long as he was in the world he would not take another woman into his bed, and he would never again cut his hair. But one night when he came for his meal,

Revka groaned when she saw him, then hurried away. She stood with her back to us, shaken. Her son-in-law had cut his hair, then shaved his head. I followed Revka and took her hand in mine as she wept. It was over, she told me, this life of ours on earth. Her son-in-law had shorn his hair because the time had come for him to leave this world behind.

That same night I saw my daughter embrace this warrior in our garden. He seemed a brutal being, covered with scars, metal strands embedded in his flesh, his only clothes made of metal scales. Yet in that single embrace I saw what I had never seen between my daughter and Amram. I saw that love had led her not to ruin but to her own destiny. I could never have hoped to stop the path she was meant to be on. The Man from the Valley had vowed not to love a woman, but he had never sworn such an oath about another warrior. In becoming a boy, Aziza had allowed him to love her.

This was why so many had believed my daughter was a *shedah*, for when she cast her arms around this man who bound himself with strips of sharp metal, it was as though she was one of the thousand messengers who watch over us, sent to take him in her wings. I turned away when I saw him weep, for I knew what Revka said was true. This world was vanishing.

It had already been written.

WHO CAN SAY at what hour Herod's wall was breached, the wretched moment when the first stone fell? It had been raining, but as the rain cleared, there continued to be thunder. Then, all at once, we understood it wasn't thunder, but the battering ram continuously crashing against the wall. We stood and watched as God abandoned us, and then we did the best we could. There was chaos as the men raced to the plaza to build another wall, quickly, with mad fury. My cousin wanted a wall that would stand behind the stone wall the legion had broken through, one made of mud and grass so that it might sway with the battering ram rather than break apart. In a storm a blade of grass can withstand the fury of winds that bring the palaces of kings to ruin. There wasn't a person who didn't assist in building this second wall, for terror stirred in us all. Even Yehuda, the Essene boy, and my son, Adir, on his crutch were there, eager to help.

It was God's will that we should have rainfall, and therefore there would be mud, pools of it, quickly hardening once the sun came forth, forming the second wall. The children all were covered with mud, toiling among us despite the arrows set aflame that landed to singe our cloaks and set fire to our roofs and gardens.

Our every action seemed to occur in a dream that had descended. I saw a child catch on fire and die in his own mother's arms, and men give up their lives without complaint. I saw the legion leap up like a beast made of metal, with no heart or spirit as the wall of mud was shaken, yet it did not fall, for it was stronger than Herod's wall though it had been built by old men and children. I saw the Angel of Death perched beside my daughter as she lifted her bow, running his hand over her radiant flesh. I saw the ghosts of those who had been murdered in the Essene cave walking the paths of the cliffs like black goats, their souls rising before them. My cousin broke away from the crowd when he realized how many had died and must be laid out in the field. When I followed him, I found him sobbing in my garden.

In that moment I saw the prophecy that had come to me when I threw the bones in the tower. They had recounted that I would drown, exactly as the priest had warned I would when I was a child and had leapt into the fountain of my mother's garden. Not in water but in my own blood.

FOR NIGHTS ON END I had dreamed of the child I carried. In my dream she was immersed in water, her eyes open, for water was her element, as it had been mine. If we were all to be slaughtered, and if I was to be among the dead, I wanted to make certain this child came forth before she entered the World-to-Come. That was the only way I could ensure she carried a name, which would allow God to call her to Him, unlike the unborn, unnamed souls who must wander without direction for the rest of time.

I knew it was time for my daughter to come into the world, for soon enough there would be no time left at all.

I boiled a tea of rue, meant to cause miscarriage, and quickly drank a cupful. This mixture would bring my child before her time. I walked the floor of my chamber while Adir and Yehuda and everyone with any strength worked feverishly to restore the damages to the second wall. I called Yael to me, for she had promised to help me in my time of need. She left Arieh in Revka's care and brought me a basket of leavings from the dovecote to lay upon the fire. As I had taught her how to attend a birth, so she would now bring my daughter to life.

I stood over the smoke so that it might open my womb. Yael crouched down on her haunches, singing the infinite one's name backward and forward until it formed a single letter in her mouth, rising and falling, a sound so ancient no man could understand its meaning. I focused on the image of Ashtoreth on the altar. I had brought her from my mother's chambers, wrapped in linen along with her book of magical recipes, hidden in the doves' cage beneath a handful of straw.

All that I needed I had been given by my mother. All that I knew, I knew because of her. But all that I sacrificed was for my daughter.

I had poured an offering of olive oil before Ashtoreth and covered myself with pomegranate oil and the perfume of the lily in her honor. It was the last of that fragrance in my possession. I knew there would be no more. I imagined the lilies beside the fountain in my mother's garden. They appeared to grow up between the black and white mosaics that tiled my chamber's floor. I concentrated upon them until I saw only those invisible blooms and the rest of the world fell away. I labored hard and did my best to make no noise, so that no one would be called to us. I bit down on my arm and drew blood. Despite the hour and the circumstances, I was alive, still able to give life.

As time went on and the child did not appear, I was afraid that the daughter I was about to bring forth would be weak because she was so early. There was a drum of panic beating at my throat. The council might decide to set her outside the wall to perish before she was named. I vowed this would never happen. There would be no wilderness for this child, no ravens, no unburied bones, no soldiers of the legion, no jackals appraising her with hunger. Her spirit would not be trapped in a cave or wander through the valley but would instead remain in God's hands and under His careful watch. This was why I would bring her into this world before her time, so that she might know more than sorrow and bask in the Almighty's radiance, in His favor and His wisdom, even if it was for only an hour or a day.

My daughter came at dawn, after many hours, and much blood. Too much, pouring out of me, but it was the price to be paid for her birth. Although she was early, she wasn't weak. She cried out and my heart opened. Her eyes were gray, as her father's were. Her hair was pale, much like the feathers of the dove. We took her into the field, so that we might bury the afterbirth, though the last of the almond trees had been chopped down for wood to build the wall. We thanked Ashtoreth and *Adonai*. I removed my cloak to stand naked before them, though I was exhausted, and seven days had not passed. We did not know how many days were left to us, and because of this I could not wait to name her.

I called her Yonah, for she had come into the world because of a message brought by a dove.

My wife, my beloved, my daughter, my world.

ALL THROUGH the night our people reinforced the second wall, our only defense against the abyss. They lashed together the boughs of the almond trees that had been hewn so hastily, chinking the open spaces with mud so that the new wall would be pliant, moving with the thrusts of the battering ram. The Feast of Unleavened Bread would be celebrated the following day. On all other such festivals, our people would have gathered together to give thanks for our freedom from Egypt. Now we did not have time for anything except the prayers we carried inside us.

But the wall that could not be broken could be burned. The scent of almonds rose in a bitter cloud. The Romans lit our wall on fire, and there was a ring of flame around us.

In my doorway, I gazed upon my daughter in my arms as I heard the men chanting, for the chants had lifted above the sound of warfare. I heard women crying. As I gazed upon our sorrow, I turned to take note of a shadow in my garden, a raven crouched down among the rows of vegetables I had grown, all burned to ash now, the mint and rue, the coriander and the hyssop mere twigs. I went into the garden that was no more.

Channa had come to see the child. She was gaunt, as we all were, but her face lit up when she spied the infant in my arms. She vowed that she had told no one about the birth, not even our leader, so as not to distract him. She whispered that the doves I had released had returned to tell her of the birth, the ones in the cage behind her house who had visited me in the land of Moab.

I signaled to her, and she came as a dog might, trotting over, head down. She was captivated instantly, her face eager as I lifted up the child for her to see. I watched as my enemy stood there weeping, not with sorrow but with joy.

She had sent me into the wilderness, but I did not remember how my bare feet had burned on the stones. She had disparaged me and ruined me, but I did not recall the words that had been used against me or remember the years I had spent in Moab. The garden was burning, the air sparked with specks of flame as they say it will be in the World-to-Come when we walk beside the angels and have no fear of their illumination or of their might.

I let her hold our daughter. We rejoiced together over the beauty of our husband's child, for she was like a pool of water, still and beautiful. We were submerged, our thirst quenched, though there were fires and bursts of flame everywhere, on leaves and rooftops, falling upon us like rain. We sat there, our heads close, as others hid in their chambers or worked furiously to put out the flames. We were no longer thirsty, and no longer had any need of fury or revenge, for we were enemies no more.

HOURS LATER, the entire wall caught fire. It encircled us as a snake would, meant to devour us. We believed our time had come, but then God sent us the wind from the north, and the blaze blew back to the Romans. It burned their soldiers alive and caught their battering rams aflame. Our people came to watch and sank to their knees in gratitude.

But what we are given is taken as well, so that we know God's glory comes to us from His will alone. The rescue was temporary. The wind changed direction again; it came from the south and was our enemy once more. Our people ran, in fear for their lives. They soaked themselves with what little water they could find in an attempt to withstand the blaze of heat. Everyone could hear the Romans' cheering and their bloodthirsty cries. They posted a thousand guards in the valley, so that none of our people might slip over Herod's wall and escape.

We gathered in my chambers, covered with soot. Yael's boy, with his dark and beautiful eyes, was quiet; he seemed to sense the terror that had come upon us and dared not cry. We poured water over our heads from a pitcher, in the hope no sparks would light upon us. I nursed my child and thought of how Nahara and Adir's father had not seen his children for ten days after they were born, the practice of his people. Only now did I realize this law was not merely to prevent the father from seeing the child in a bruised condition, the price of the journey of being born. Rather it was to ensure that a father waited until it was more certain that his child would live. To be attached to what is bound to die made no sense to the fierce people from Moab, for they rode with death and pitched their tents with death. They knew that flesh was not lasting in this world.

I would follow their law now and keep my daughter from her father's eyes so that he would not have to love something he was bound to lose. As I held her inside my cloak, two hearts beat against my chest. But no creature can contain more than one heart. I knew that one of us would live and one would die. I wept to think I would not hear my child call me mother.

THE SECOND WALL had been breached. That rough edifice we had built until our hands were ravaged and bleeding, until there was no longer a single tree standing in the field, had cracked under their battering ram, the dirt spilling out, the pliant limbs of the almond trees splitting, turning to dust. Our people had done all they could to fight the tide of what was to come, the soldiers that would climb through, the bloodshed and the torture and the murder on the day of our greatest feast. Eleazar came into the plaza. We were brought there by the sound of the ram's horn, used to call us to prayer. I made my way among our people, though I was still weakened from childbirth, the infant hidden in my cloak. I left a trail of blood on the stones, which turned black as it fell away from me, an omen I understood well.

From my place on the edge of the crowd, I could see women whose children I had helped bring into the world. I saw my daughter with her bow, mud streaking her arms and legs, and my son, ruined by battle before he was a man, and my people in the throes of sorrow, and the man I had loved since I had first seen that he would come to me.

"We resolved not to follow the Romans and to follow God alone. Now the time has come for us to prove our faith. We cannot disgrace ourselves in the eyes of our Lord, or submit to slavery. If we fall into Roman hands, it is the end of everything, not only our lives but the life of Zion. We had the privilege to be the last stronghold, and as God has favored us so, let us return the favor and die nobly as free men."

People began to panic at Ben Ya'ir's words. It seemed that some might attempt to flee. But there was also a surge forward of the most loyal, those who had burned for freedom and could not turn back now.

"By daybreak, our enemy will be upon us, and we can hold them back no longer, but we are free to choose to die with honor, in the arms of those we love. We cannot defeat the Romans in battle here on this earth, but we can deny them a victory."

Women wept on either side of me. I pitied Eleazar that he must speak these words.

"We have done everything to claim our freedom, and we cannot stop now. We do not know why God let His city burn to the ground, why He has let our people be chased into extinction, why we must die today. Our freedom is our winding sheet, and it is more glorious than any other. We will leave nothing behind for our enemies, and the taste of their victory will be bitter, and they will not be able to cut the heads from our bodies and leave them for the ravens."

The women wailed, and some of the men joined in. The flames around us were a blessing, for they roared and made it difficult to hear the peals of agony and grief.

"Let our wives die unharmed, our children without the bitter mantle of slavery. Do you want them half-devoured by wild beasts, tortured by fire and whippings, enslaved? Let us make haste. Let us avoid the evils of mankind. We prefer death before those miseries. Let us go out of the world with our wives and children in freedom.

"Let our story bear witness that we perished out of choice, a choice we made at the beginning, to chose death rather than slavery."

Warriors were sent to set fire to the storerooms. The heat was worsened so that it became an inferno. We seemed to have fallen headfirst into the month of *Av,* that time when the sorrows of our people blaze, when God tests our faith and our duty and our belief in His greatness.

WE LISTENED to Eleazar as we might listen to a dream, one we could not stop, one from which there was no waking. I felt my love for him so deeply I thought I might break as the boughs of the almonds had, my ardor the knife that pierced me. People began to run to their houses, not to escape but to gather their worldly goods so they might be destroyed rather than fall into the hands of the Romans. A great bonfire was begun, and all we owned was heaped upon it, garments and sandals and wooden bowls and yards of wool. The goats and sheep that were left had their throats slit, and their bodies were placed upon the fire as burnt offerings sacrificed to God, for there would be no need of meat or milk, only of God's grace. There was no Temple standing and this would be our last sacrifice.

Eleazar's men, his favorites, warriors who had fought beside him, men scarred by battle who had journeyed from Jerusalem to become hawks in this desert, came to him to encircle him. Some of them sobbed and were consumed by grief; others no longer felt the pains of the world, for they were in a state of sacrifice, as warriors were before they entered into battle. There were fifty or more, Amram among them, and these men brought broken pottery pieces, *ostraca,* upon which their names or initials were written. The weeping grew more furious as the lottery was begun. The priest and his learned men began to pray and chant, rocking back and forth with the passion of their prayers.

Ten men among them would be chosen. They would do the deed and dispatch with the rest of us. They would bear the burden as death-givers so that we did not have to carry the sin of harming ourselves, which was forbidden. When the time came they would slay each other, until only one was left. That man would hold the weight of all our sins, and would be commanded to enter through the three gates of Gehennom, the valley of hell, where he would suffer the torments of demons for all eternity.

"Why should we fear death when we do not fear sleep?" Eleazar cried out, in a frenzy, in such a pure rapture that none could look away. I saw him as he was at the well, furious with all of men's wrongdoings, assured he could set things right in the name of God. "Death allows freedom to our souls. It takes true courage to find true freedom and to be called to God's side. It would have been better if we had died before seeing Jerusalem destroyed. Now our hope has fled, but we can avenge the enemies of the holy city, and show kindness to those we love, and not see them led away in slavery and be witness to the torture and violence that awaits our wives and our children and our dearest friends."

Husbands and wives were embracing, mothers had taken up their children, sons ran to search out their fathers so they might die side by side. The ten men were chosen, our saviors and our executioners. Ben Ya'ir took his sword to make his pledge upon the weapon he had used to fight for God, and for his nation, and for us.

"We were born to die, as are all who are brought into the world. This even the most fortunate among us must face. This is our fate, and our fate is now upon us."

My fate was upon me as well.

I quickly signaled to Yael and Revka. We made our way back to my chamber, pulling Revka's younger grandson, Levi, along, lest he be taken up by the crowd, with Noah following behind. Revka herself all but fainted in the crush.

Yehuda was in my chamber, wrapped in his white garment, reciting the prayer for the souls of the dead. Adir was nowhere to be seen.

"Where is he?" I was so distraught I caught the poor Essene boy by his prayer shawl. Revka, who had come to consider Yehuda as her own, came to coax the frightened boy into speaking.

"He was worried for Aziza. He said she was in his place, and he would find her and bring her back here."

I ran to my cabinet for my mother's book of spells, my two hearts stirring inside me. There were screams echoing from the plaza, for the death-givers had begun their work and some of the dying could not bear to see their families slaughtered, even at the hands of our own men, angels of mercy, the messengers of our fate. My hands were shaking. Perhaps it had been written that I would be redeemed. Perhaps love would not be my undoing but my salvation.

I cast my mother's book into Yael's hands and insisted that she must keep it safe. I noticed that she wore the collar of the lion twisted around her arm, and then I knew I had been right to choose her, for she was as fierce as she was loyal.

Revka was huddled with her grandsons, keeping Arieh on her lap. He was little more than a baby, but he was sensitive and knew when silence was needed. When Revka held a finger to her lips, he hushed and leaned against her. She then patted Yehuda's shoulders as he wept, guilt-ridden for having allowed Adir to leave. He was only a boy, and his mother had left him in our care so that he might be safe from harm. They all huddled together on the tiled floor fashioned for a king's kitchen, a room that had turned fetid, burning hot, like a grave in the sand.

The child who was my heart cried. I took her from beneath my cloak and gave her into Yael's hands as I had given her the book of spells. I went to my ironwood box, which had come with me from Egypt, the one my mother had locked with a key in the shape of a snake, a snake I'd thought came alive to inch across my palm when I was only a girl. Inside the unlocked box were ingredients I had been storing for the worst of times: snakeskin for the black viper that sleeps between the rocks, ash from the fire of a sacrificed dove, crushed lapis from the stone that is stronger than all others, strings tied in precise knots, all of these meant to weave a web of protection. I took what I needed. I was going to find my children in the plaza, then I would go to Eleazar. Panic was beating inside me, for I knew, no matter what I did, I would indeed drown on this day. That was the fate that had been cast by the bones in the tower.

Yael put her hand on my arm, attempting to stop me as I went to the door, insisting it was too late for me to go.

"What would you not have done for the one you loved?" I asked her.

"I am doing that now," she answered, as if she were indeed my daughter. "Don't go to him."

She had promised me once that she would do as I asked. I reminded her of this as I gave her the last piece of fruit I had saved, a pomegranate, the same fruit I had given her at our last farewell. She knew me then as the girl who had cared for her in Jerusalem. She threw her arms around me, and we might have wept if there had been time. Instead, I drew away and told her what she must do. I hoped she would obey me as she had when she was a child. If she saw a sign from the doves, she was to ask Revka where she first saw me as I am. She was to go there without hesitation.

*

THERE WAS chaos everywhere. I did my best to make my way. Those who say you cannot see *Mal'ach ha-Mavet* could not be more wrong. I have seen him standing right in front of me, his twelve wings blackened by fire, his thousand eyes seeing all that we are and all that we do. I was grasped in the grip of his darkness, a violation of God's radiance and His glory. We must suffer in his presence, we must stand before him, but I was not ready to face him until I found my children.

The Romans had already begun to lay down planks so they might walk across our wall in the morning. It was the night before our forefathers' escape from Egypt, the night when our death began. There were husbands and wives lying down side by side on the blood-soaked cobblestones so that they might find their death together; children lined up, wailing. The ten executioners were at their sorrowful work, going from house to house, as the Almighty had done on the night of Passover, when Jews painted their doors with bloodstained hyssop flowers allowing *Adonai* to know them as true believers and pass them by so they might live.

I went through the Western Plaza, then down the steps toward the Northern Palace. My chest was aching, and drops of blood fell from me, but I went on. Above the chaos, I heard my daughter's dog barking. I ran, following the echo of that desperate beast, avoiding all men, staying to the shadows until I saw figures near the entrance to a small pool where the king had once bathed in cool water surrounded by white lotus lilies he had brought from Alexandria. There, on the stairs, Amram had come up behind my daughter. Her arrows had fallen around her as he grabbed her at her waist and slit her throat. In doing so he had her for himself at last, but while she gasped in his arms, he had seen the silver medallion at her throat. When I spied him he had clasped her to him, his grief enormous, for he knew her for who she was for the first time, the warrior who had fought beside him and saved him. He cried out for what he had done, mourning all that had died with her.

Adir came rushing at Amram as I watched. My son hadn't a spear or a sword, only his crutch, which he used to beat Amram, for he had seen his sister murdered and was standing in her blood. Amram turned and pierced him through, then finished his work with one swift cut at my boy's throat. He wore his prayer shawl, as all the death-givers did, the garment which was always to be made of linen with a single blue woolen thread to remind its wearer of heaven and of God's commandments. But Amram's prayer shawl was stained, and appeared brown as the blood upon it clung to the linen.

I watched in a dream, as if I had seen this all before and had come here as a witness so that my children would not be alone in the hour of their death. I prayed to God that they would be embraced in the Shechinah, the dwelling place of the Lord.

My son was no warrior, only a boy. My warrior was a woman who would not have expected an attack from someone who had loved her so well.

The dog was wild over the injury to his mistress, wailing as though he were a man rather than a beast. He would not stand down when Amram turned to shout at him; he straddled Aziza's fallen body, protecting her still form, his jaws snapping, flecked with foam. Amram kicked at him, then charged, but the dog stood his ground. He was a beast who craved revenge, more loyal than the warrior who now stabbed him through, time and again.

The mastiff refused to die, the guardian of my daughter, who in her death revealed herself to be only a young woman who had shorn her hair and worn men's garb. Her red feathered arrows fallen around her, her field of flowers, her last farewell. Though mortally wounded, the dog grabbed on to Amram and refused to let go, his teeth sinking into his enemy's flesh. I watched the struggle in a haze of grief, until both dog and man were so wounded neither could go on, yet neither one would die.

The Man from the Valley should have been at his leader's bidding, for he was one of the chosen ten. Instead, he had come for Aziza. When he saw what had happened, he slit the dog's throat so that the beast could die with honor, thereby releasing him from pain and from his duties in this world. But the warrior stood over Amram and watched him in his throes, offering no solace and no assistance. The man who had been Revka's son-in-law when his name was Yoav, when he still had compassion and faith, let my daughter's murderer die in anguish.

When Amram was no more, the Man from the Valley cut off the dead man's armor to further dishonor him, so that the ground was littered with silver scales, and it could be known to God that here lay a coward unworthy of being called a warrior. Then the Man from the Valley took off his prayer shawl and covered Aziza, as though she were a man, a warrior who had fallen in battle. Perhaps that was what he wanted to believe. He could not bear to see her as a woman he had loved, a girl made of flesh, not iron, who had loved him in return.

When that maddened warrior had slipped back into the turmoil of the plaza, I hurried to my children. I closed their eyes and prayed for their spirits. I washed their feet and hands with water from the pool, though ashes had turned the water black. I wound the spells I had carried with me through the strands of their hair, so that they might be protected, if not in this world then in the World-to-Come. I thought of the moments of their births: Aziza's in a chamber in Jerusalem where the women who worked at *keshaphim* urged me on to bring forth her life. Adir's in a tent on the Iron Mountain, where I waited for my husband to ride his horse from the eastern reaches of Moab so he might be there on the tenth day to see his son and to name him a king of his people.

THE TEN went on their murderous rampage for our honor and for the Glory of God, and in this they had succeeded. As I made my way up the stairs to the plateau atop the mountain, there were bodies everywhere, those who loved each other, those who despised each other, those who had believed there would be freedom in Zion, those who had followed a husband or a brother, those who had been born on this mountain, those who had dreamed they would die here, all in a jumble upon the stones. I saw the raven in a black shawl who had cast me into the wilderness curled up in her garden, and I wept for her spirit. I saw Yael's father, the assassin who had killed so many in the courtyards of the Temple in Jerusalem, splayed out near the barracks, his blood as bright as any flower.

I went to the dovecotes and opened the doors of the first two, at last coming to the stone *columbarium* that was shaped like a tower, the place where my daughters had most often worked beside me, where Revka had come in her mourning, where Yael had called the birds to her without a single word, as I knew she would when we'd gone to the marketplace in Jerusalem and she'd begged for a dove's freedom and in return had given her promise to do whatever I asked.

I chased the doves out, shaking my shawl, whistling, as the hawk does, forcing them from their roosts. They lifted into the blackened sky all at once, flecking the darkness with their radiance, delivering the message that there was a time to die and a time to rise up.

THE MAN I loved met me at the door to my chamber. No one else was there, only the two of us, as there had been on the day he took me into his bed, when I left a scrim of vermilion on the bedclothes, not henna but blood. The others had fled. Yael had kept her promise. She'd done as I'd asked.

I let go of everything but my beloved. I did not care if there was blood upon him. I didn't want to know how many he had slain, or if he had embraced his wife before he made quick of her or even if he'd asked for her forgiveness after all this time.

"Death walks beside us, but not with us," he said to me as he took me into his embrace.

I was glad he hadn't seen his new daughter. Had he done so, it would have been too painful for him to leave her, and I never wanted to be the cause of his pain, as I knew he never wished to cause me any grief. My mother had warned me what love would do to me. I hadn't cared then, and I didn't care now.

His eyes were gray, like the dove, like the mist that cleared when the world was first begun on the day God gave us the word and we could speak and our words turned the world into what it has come to be. I could have howled at fate and covered my head. I could have begged for more time, pleaded with him to flee with me. But perhaps I had been granted all that I had needed in this lifetime. My beloved was a stubborn man, a true believer. He was more complicated than any man I had ever known and the only one who could have called me to cross the Salt Sea and leave behind my husband and the green hills of Moab.

That was what my mother meant when she told me love would be my undoing. Love made you give yourself away, it bound you to this world, and to another's fate. I lay down beside Eleazar. We were together as we had been even when we were apart, for we were one person, wed by more than our desire.

We had our last moments of life in this world, but I would have died a hundred times to have had his love. I kissed him in a way I would never kiss another. His spirit entwined with mine as he entered me and took me to be his. If I wept, it was only because water was my element, what I yearned for and needed most of all. When he was done, I still wept to give him up, although it had been written that I must. I loved him even now, as he took a knife to my throat, as I drowned in blood, as I whispered, *Cousin, you were wrong. We were born to live.*

Nissan the 15th, 73 C.E.

Alexandria

77 C.E.

They call me the Witch of Moab.

So it was written in the Book of Life. Before I was born of a woman who was already dead, before I left Jerusalem and was bitten by a lion, before the Romans came to destroy us, it had already been determined that this would come to be.

Once I was certain I would never again know the pleasure of the simplest things: a loom, a table, a comb for my hair. I thought my life was over and the angel with a thousand eyes was at my door. But I was wrong. I have a house made of white stones. Workmen labored to build the fountain in the center of the courtyard deep within a walled garden where there are date palm trees and pots of jasmine and the white lilies that can be found in no other land, except, perhaps, in the fields of the world beyond our own.

When Mal'ach ha-Mavet came for me, flecked with the blood of my people, I was wearing the cloak of invisibility. I had journeyed so far down into the earth he would have had to have taken a hundred steps before he could spy me, though he possessed the vision of an army. Despite his gift of sight, I still would have been hidden from view, for it is said that Death must close his eyes when he enters into water, and I was submerged in a cistern, a well so deep there are those who believe that it has no bottom, that it reaches to the center of the earth, back to the foundation stone in Jerusalem, where creation began.

It was water that saved us, protecting us from the flames that flickered and from Death's grasping hands. We had hurried down the stone steps, breathless in the dark, as Death surged above us, before we slipped into the water, as though we were fish, for our people are sister and brother to such creatures, and that is why we can endure where others are doomed to perish.

In Alexandria, the mornings are pale, the air so damp it seems a world of water until the sun breaks through in yellow bands of light. I can see the harbor as I prepare cups of black tea, sesame candies, sweet oranges cut in quarters. There are three black goats in the barn, a dozen sheep behind the fence, a white donkey who is so swift he raises clouds of red dust when he runs. There have been disruptions in this city for our people, but we have managed to remain.

Arieh and Yonah play in the garden after their lessons, hiding in the reeds beside a pond where herons come to feed. There is a white ibis who has laid claim to our fountain. She stands on one slim leg and drinks water, lifting her head to the heavens. Perhaps the one we left behind has come to us in the guise of this creature, for she observes us carefully, and with compassion.

Revka's grandsons are no longer children but men whose shadows are so tall I am startled they belong to those who were once the boys to whom I told stories so they might sleep through the night. Now it is Revka and I who toss and turn as we dream of men who refused to surrender and women who were ruled by devotion. We remember everything they were fighting for and everyone they loved and were loyal to. We remember the way the world looked when it was ruled by war.

In the evening when the sky is struck with gauzy vermilion light, in the hour when the space between worlds opens before the inky blue night sifts down to earth, women come to the back gate to ask for the

Witch of Moab. They wear their finest clothes, leather sandals that hush their steps, gold signet rings and bracelets adorning their slim fingers and wrists, black kohl rimming their eyes. They offer me gold and silver coins, strands of pearls. In return they ask that I throw the bones of birds to divine their futures. They ask for marjoram and rue, for amulets and potions, for good health, for children to be born and enemies to vanish. Always, they ask for love. I open the book where these recipes are written, the ink still fresh even though the parchment has turned brown, as if I held a sheaf of leaves in my hands.

The women who arrive call me clever, cunning, beautiful, wise. They tell me their secrets and speak of violations and of dreams. They confide what they would never admit to another even though I am a stranger. I do the best I can on their behalf. I have learned divination from a wise woman, but I learned how to listen from a ghost.

I often take the winding cobbled road to the harbor to watch the great lantern that is lit there in the evenings in the lighthouse on the island of Pharos, one of the seven wonders of the world. I look for the ships that come from Greece, blowing across the sea, their huge white sails filling with wind from the four corners of the earth. Water surrounds us. When the Nile overflows, the fields turn green and there are great celebrations, lanterns strung from trees, drumming all night long, dancers in veils and long skirts. The river runs every shade of blue that has ever been known to humankind: ink and turquoise and lapis, indigo, teal, cerulean, and ultramarine. Yet what I long for most is the desert. Ivory, alabaster, the rocks that caused my feet to bleed, the knife to mark off days, the man I loved. In the evenings the scent of that arid land comes across from Judea and reminds me of who I used to be. My hair is perfumed and braided, but at night I remove the pins and let it fall loose down my back.

When I sit in the darkness, the birds come to me. They still know me for who I am.

I am the girl in the desert, even though I am so far away.

I am the woman who was saved by doves, for when I saw them rise up in a cloud above Masada at the hour when darkness reigned, I knew that we must escape.

We were in the kitchen of the palace, waiting for Mal'ach ha-Mavet to walk through the door in the form of one of the ten death-givers who would come to us to slit our throats. Revka and the children were huddled together, listless, as dumbfounded as the sheep who edge toward the butcher when called and herded by bells. I paced the black and white mosaic floor, then went to the door, eagerly scanning the crowd. I was hopeful that Shirah would soon appear, returning to us with Aziza and Adir safely retrieved from the mayhem. But the more I watched the more I trembled, for bodies were piled up in the plaza and the blood was like a river, a tide that fed the olive trees and the date palms and the garden that had turned to ash. There was incessant wailing, but soon the echoing cries gave way to an uncanny silence. Shirah had once told me that silence was the only thing we had to fear. It was our true enemy, signifying that, like the footprints that were swept away in a storm, we had disappeared from God's sight.

Yonah cried suddenly, breaking the silence with the sweet voice of one who demands to be fed. I still nursed Arieh, and when the newborn cried, I felt my milk come in. In that instant I knew that, despite the death that encircled us, I was still alive.

The fortress was burning from the inside out, ravaged by our own people. Every home had been lit aflame, every possession cast upon a bonfire that flared up with the wind and was quickly burning out of control, the sparks smoldering on rooftops and in the leaves of the few trees that had not been cut down to build the inner wall. Many bodies had already burned to ash, and those ashes rose up to bring about a night that was the darkest we had ever known. It was the eve of Passover, but there was no manna as our people had known in their escape from slavery in Egypt, only the black sky and a scrim of smoke. We breathed in the bones of our people—their desires, their petty differences, their faith—all martyred, vanishing into the dusky, murderous air.

There were no stars, and darkness reigned, as it did before the first day of creation. But then the doves lifted upward through the smoke, as though they themselves were stars. I wondered if manna had appeared in this way as our people wandered in the desert for forty years, if it had floated above the earth as a dove might, a message to let us know we were meant to survive.

Because birds do not fly at night, I knew the doves in flight were the sign Shirah had vowed she would send to me. She, who had cared for me when I was a motherless child in Jerusalem, once again watched over me. She had opened the doors of the dovecotes, as we were now to open the doors for ourselves.

I took Shirah's daughter in my arms and held her along with my son. To me, they might have been twins, the one newly born, the other twenty months in this world, one no dearer to me than the other. I instructed Revka to stop weeping, for we must flee. We had no time for death, I told her, surprised by my fierce certainty.

Revka stared at me, thinking I had gone mad, for we were the captives of the Romans and of our own people and of fate. We had been told to be indifferent to the world we had no choice but to lose and to embrace death. But the children in my arms were squirming, alive, destined for something more.

We had been commanded to sacrifice rather than surrender, and

I might have complied, if not for the children. Once I explained myself, Revka was quick to agree. We would do anything to save those in our care. Revka had done so at the waterfall when death stalked her grandsons. As for me, I was not about to lose another lion. I could not yield to our leader's commands. If this was treachery, then I was a traitor indeed.

But I had broken laws before, and God, who had witnessed my sins, had forgiven me.

I hurried Revka and the children. Yehuda hesitated, for he had been taught not to combat violence but to accept it and was troubled to think he might disrespect his people. I spurred him on by reminding him that his mother had entrusted him to us so that he might live; that was her intention and he must honor her will above all other motives.

I raised a small rug to reveal a door that had been fashioned in the floor of the kitchen, meant for the escape of the king. Aziza had once confided to me that she'd used this exit in order to meet Amram. No one knew of this doorway but the king who had been gone for a hundred years.

We entered the space below the floor, hushed, slinking into the shadows. I pulled the door closed behind us, shutting out every glimmer of light. We took the stairs into the cellar. Holding hands, we moved in the dark, swiftly and in silence, as the rats do. Noah and Levi were used to silence, for it had become part of their nature. Yehuda was diligent and hushed. Even Yonah and Arieh seemed to sense that without their silence we would be caught up in death's net. They did not whimper or cry but instead clung to me without complaint.

I could not help but think of my brother, one of the ten who had been chosen by our leader. I wondered if he still wore that square of blue silk on his armor, if he remembered the day I had come to him beneath the flame tree and begged him to put away his knife. Perhaps that knife was all he had now, the only thing he cared about or trusted or was loyal to. I said a prayer for him. I think I knew the answer to my questionings, because the prayer I murmured on his behalf was a lamentation sung in memory of the dead to bring peace in the World-to-Come.

We went through the stone chamber, breathing in the dank air, not stopping until we came upon another set of stairs, which would bring us to a heavy wooden door. That door, once pushed ajar, led us into the open air. There we stood, the bitter reek of smoke claiming us, the wind in threads carrying sparks of the fires that had been set, along with the writhing spirits of the dead.

Revka took my arm, and we gazed at each other, needing no words to understand the pact made between us.

We intended to live.

I kept Shirah's newborn girl wound in my shawl so that she might remain quiet and unseen, while Arieh rode upon my hip, his dark eyes wide, his hands clutching tightly to my tunic. When we emerged into the night and the door to the tunnel had shut behind us, it was as though we had entered through the first gate to Gehennom, the doorway into the valley of hell. The scene we had stumbled upon hardly seemed like earth but rather a world that was aflame with punishments for the wicked. Or perhaps this was a test for the faithful. Could we face hell and walk through fire without hesitation, or would we sink to our knees and give up the life God had granted us?

We could not go back now. Our world was ravaged, it had disappeared from God's grasp. Revka and the boys were reluctant to go on, for there were crowds all around and they were afraid we would be sighted. Stay in the shadows, I told them, for that was what I'd done in the wilderness when I wished to go unnoticed by the birds who came to me.

I asked Revka where she had first seen Shirah, for that was where Shirah had instructed me to flee. I assumed she meant for us to run to the dovecotes and hide there, or wait for her by the Snake Gate, but Revka whispered a location that surprised me: She had seen Shirah many times, but she had not clearly seen her for who she was until she stumbled upon her in a cistern, the largest one, situated in the deepest cave carved into this mountain, down hundreds of plaster steps, set in the farthest field. That was where Shirah meant for us to go.

We made our way through the madness around us. Edging around the barracks, we passed the bonfire that was flaming out of control. Bodies had now been heaped upon it, alongside provisions and the remains of animals, all that we had in our warehouses and storerooms. Though the smoke was acrid, I stopped, stunned, for it was there, beside the piles of weapons, that I saw my father for the last time, lying among the slain soldiers.

I went to him and knelt beside him so that I might close his eyes. From his expression I understood that he was now beside his beloved wife, the woman with the flame-colored hair who was also my mother. We had that, at least, in common. Beside him on the ground lay the gray cloak. He might have attempted to escape his fate, but he had taken off the cloak so that he would be seen for who he was, the assassin Yosef bar Elhanan, who had been my father and who would remain so for all eternity.

As I studied his face, serene for the first time, I recalled what he'd said about his talent of stealth. Men often failed to catch sight of what was right before them. They searched for secrets and for what was buried, but what was openly before them in the light blinded them so they could not see. A mouse who went quickly across the table was less likely to be caught than one that stationed itself in the corners of a room, where mice were expected to huddle. An assassin who walks into a room may easily look like any common man if he does so with confidence, with every right to do as he pleases.

I took my father's cloak. The others followed, and we moved together as if we had formed a cloud, a mist, nothing human. Quickly, we made our way through the orchard where there had once been almond trees, where pink flowers had floated in the air when the kadim wind arose. Nothing remained here, not a branch, not a bough, although the ground was littered with sparks that glowed with the incandescence of white moths that had been set before us, fallen to the earth.

More than mere trees had been felled in this now barren orchard, with blood flowing rather than sap, and strands of hair rather than flowers. Corpse after corpse littered the field.

Revka told her grandsons and Yehuda to think of the dark shapes on the ground as fallen trees, not as men and women and children with their throats slit. The deeds of the death-givers were nearly completed; soon they would set upon one another, for they had stood beside the Water Gate and drawn lots to see who would be the last warrior, the man to take all of his brothers' sins upon himself and finish the other nine before turning the sword on himself.

Yet there were still some among our people to be dispatched, and the violence was not completed. We saw a family with four children waiting on the steps of a burning storeroom, silent as ghosts, though they were still in the world of the living, bleary-eyed and trembling. The father of the family was the first to offer his throat to one of the death-givers, as if to teach his children, as he might instruct them on how to gather sheep, or shoot an arrow, or begin their morning prayers with the rising of the sun. But this was not a lesson of beauty or knowledge, only an ugly moment of horror. The children swarmed around their dying father, grasping at his cloak as though by doing so they could retrieve his spirit from the World-to-Come.

The death-giver was Uri, the warrior who had come for my father and me in the desert, the boy who had been my brother's friend, a mild young man who had been so awed by this fortress as he described it to me in the greatest detail while we sat around a fire in the wilderness, eating a meal I had procured, a bird I had called to me.

He had told me of the frescoes of the seven sisters painted by the finest artists from Rome, the baths that were heated by ceramic pipes, the gardens that clung to the cliffs, the palace that faced north so that anyone who resided there would always be gazing toward Jerusalem. We had sat together in the desert in the dwindling light, the scent of the myrtle around us, watching the fire as though observing a fate we didn't yet understand. We were young, and the desert loomed with its unearthly beauty, the stars glittering above us in such great number we grew dizzy with their light.

Now the stars were hidden by the rising billows of smoke. Uri murmured the prayer for the dead for the man he had killed. The slain man had been one of the bakers in our marketplace. Revka hesitated when she saw the white apron beneath his prayer shawl as it turned scarlet. It was as though a flag of despair had been waved at her. I grabbed her arm and forced her to follow me, as I followed the doves who were fleeing from the only home they had ever known. Already the baker's children on the stairs were being dispatched by Uri's knife; they had gathered together to oblige their slayer, for there was nowhere for them to run.

Perhaps Revka uttered a groan as she turned from that scene of death, perhaps one of the boys stepped upon a stone or Shirah's daughter, who had been named for a dove, whimpered and cooed inside my cloak. I hushed her as I hurried the others along, but it was too late. The echo of noise caused Uri to spy us through the dark. He finished his business on the steps in haste—they were only young children, and once they were gone, their mother gave no fight but flung her cloak open so that she might be taken from this life.

Uri came after us, spurred on by his duty. We ran, urging each other on, the boys darting out in front. Our breath was hot, and we all gasped as we ran for our lives. Noah and Levi stopped when they realized their grandmother was no longer among us. Revka had fallen back, unable to keep up. She shouted for us to run on, insisting that we forsake her though Uri was upon her, already restraining her, pleading with her to accept what must be as she fought him off. I wondered if she had stumbled on purpose, to keep the young warrior from gaining on us.

I told the boys to go forward and handed the babies over to Yehuda before running back to Revka.

"Go on," she shouted, waving her arms the way she might have if I were one of the doves who refused to leave the nest.

She hadn't thought much of me when I had first come to the dovecote, and she'd been right to be suspicious of me. I hadn't been anyone worthwhile. A thief who hadn't known what love meant, a fool with no understanding of what a lion could do if you lay down beside him.

I'd been a girl from the desert willing to do anything to survive.

I ran up behind Uri as he held Revka in his grasp. I rushed at him so that I might come at him with more strength, but also so I would not have to see his face. I had the knife that had belonged to Ben Simon, the one he had used on behalf of Zion, given to me to protect myself when he knew that he would die, and that we had sinned, and that I must go on without him.

I used the dagger before I could consider the weight of my deed, before I could feel the heat of Uri's blood. When I had trapped the doves in the desert, their deaths had seemed like drifts of white smoke, swift and silent. This was an inferno, an explosion of blood and heat. Uri released Revka and turned to me, stunned, his gaze fixed upon me, as if I were the murderess and he the bird in the net. He moved to grab me and take me down with him, but before he could grasp me, he was struck from behind and he stumbled, lurching forward. He seemed a pale sheaf taken from the furrows of the earth, cut down in harvesting. He fell to the ground like the almond trees in the orchard.

The Man from the Valley had come upon us. He was nearly unrecognizable, his countenance resembling a beast as much as a man. That was why the Almighty had given us prayer, to distinguish men from animals, to leave the beasts inside of us locked away, as demons are locked in lead jars. This warrior wore nothing but his metal bands of agony and a tunic that was sodden with blood.

But no matter his appearance, the Man from the Valley was indeed human, though he himself might deny it. When Uri reached for me again, grasping at my leg, the Man from the Valley shouted at me to dodge backward. He made a quick sweep to complete Uri's death, so swift it seemed his ax was made of light. Perhaps Gabriel, who was the lord of fire and of vengeance, did indeed walk beside him.

After the Man from the Valley had slain the younger warrior, he knelt to sing our song for the dead, which many said was the only prayer he would offer up to God. He chanted, in a trance. When he rose, I saw that he had been marked with the letters of the Almighty's name across his chest and arms, for he was the last of the ten, the one who must slay all of the death-givers and then bring upon his own death.

Once he had been a learned man and a scholar, he had been a man of faith. He had partaken of a lottery to see who would be the last man, and God had chosen him for this terrible last task. Of all the death-givers, he was the most fierce, for his rising indignation over the condition of his kind had left him without fear. He was inured to violence; whether it was inflicted upon himself or upon another made no difference to him now.

At that moment I was unsure whether he would be our murderer or our salvation. The children had stopped in their path, watching with horror. The boys knew their father and called out to him, but he did not answer. Instead he gazed at me, unguarded, and in that moment I saw the man he had been, the one he would be again when he walked into the World-to-Come and bowed before the Creator of all things.

"I leave my children to you," he said, his voice hoarse. "Wherever they go my wife abides."

Even now he could not forsake her, or lose her to the beasts who took her down. If he'd been another man, he might have come with us to hide from this mayhem, for I murmured that we were making our escape. But he had been searching for Death for so long he could not linger among us now. He was finally about to meet the one he had been waiting for, his ax ready to take up against Mal'ach ha-Mavet in the only way he could ever win this battle, against himself.

He breathed into his hand, then took my hand in his and told me what I must do.

I ran to those who awaited me. We hurried to the cistern and took the steps as quickly as we could. There was darkness before us, and the echo of the water beneath us. At the mouth to the cave, I paused to tell Revka she must kiss my hand, for this was what the Man from the Valley had commanded of me. When she did, I told her of her son-in-law's gift to her. Neshamah, the breath of her daughter's soul, was returned to her, to keep for all eternity and to take with us, wherever we might go.

Our footsteps pounded as we went down into the earth, but only to our ears, for there was no one else left to hear. We could feel the silence of the dead, but it did not follow us. There was only the languid echo of still water, splashing as rocks fell from beneath our footsteps. When we reached the bottom of the well, the white plaster ledge shone and led the way. It seemed that the stars had fallen underground.

We slipped into the water, and that was where we hid from death. We were there on the sixteenth of Nissan, as the day of Passover dawned.

The heat of the fires above us passed over us. As our people were saved when the Angel of Death passed over them when they were slaves in Egypt, so, too, had we eluded him. We slept at the mouth of the well, for we were exhausted and had spent hours in the water, paddling, holding on to the sharp plaster ledge until our fingers bled. We then had pulled ourselves from the cistern so that we might rest alongside the mouth of the well and not drown in our state of exhaustion. There we lay, spent, our hair trailing in the water, our fingers raw, our tunics drenched.

Perhaps we dreamed that those who had died lingered nearby, for they whispered to us in the night. We were so close to the dead we could hear them in the way it is possible to hear wind in a storm even when you are safely hidden away. When we woke, we marveled that we were still living. The black ash had been washed from us during our hours in the cistern, and we could see bands of light streaming from above, for it was morning, and another day had come.

We gazed up in alarm when we heard muffled voices. We thought they were the voices of the dead and perhaps we were among them and hadn't recognized the World-to-Come, taking it to be the world we had always known before this murderous night had fallen. For all we knew, we, too, were among the dead and had not yet realized we had left our bodies, lingering as the dead often do before they can move on. Fainthearted, we bowed our heads.

Levi and Noah feared that demons awaited us, for they had seen such beings at work. They held each other, readying themselves for whatever terrors would next be inflicted upon them. Yehuda insisted that the End of Days had come, and that his people had arisen from their graves and from the mountain where their bones had been scattered by the jackals, and would soon come to join us. He began to pray, facing in the direction of Jerusalem, for though we were beneath the earth, he could divine the location of that holy city by the placement of the rays of light as the sun rose above the cistern.

Steps clattered down the stairs, down into the earth where we awaited whatever was to come. The noise made me think of the king's horses, how they had fitted themselves onto the narrowness of the serpents' path because they had no other choice, how they were blind to the dangers around them.

Four soldiers from the legion came to us, their faces registering shock when they saw us. One grabbed Yehuda and pulled him to his feet. I rose up with a shriek. My hair was the color of blood, and I was flecked with the blood-hued spots that had always marked me and by the bloody slaughter of my people.

The soldier stood back. Perhaps he believed in ghosts.

What are you? he said. He spoke in Latin.

I pretended not to understand.

Are you alive? he asked.

And then we knew we were, for he could see us and he was made of flesh and blood, clothed in the white tunic of the legion, carrying a spear that had been readied to use against us. But the spear had gone slack in his hand, for he knew not what we were, and ghosts could not be killed with weapons made by men.

If circumstances had been different, surely we would have all been slain, but now the soldiers' expressions were confused, for they were unnerved by what they had witnessed on the mountain above us, the hundreds of charred bodies, the burning of all we had been and all we had owned.

What of all the others? the same soldier said.

I had assumed they had captured more survivors, those who had hidden in their chambers, or had crouched beside the wall.

We have searched everywhere and found nothing but the dead, he went on.

We realized that we were the only ones, and that we alone had the story to tell.

They lined us up and gazed at us, afraid that we were indeed ghosts, and they treated us as such, their respect fashioned from their fear. There was blood on the soles of our feet and on the palms of our hands. One of the soldiers had brought a rope to tie us with, but the one who had spoken to us first slapped the rope away.

Where would they go? he said. How would they escape?

We followed the soldiers, our eyes cast down. The day was chalky and dry, but we were still soaked from our time in the cistern, water streaming from our hair and our sodden tunics. We looked like creatures that had been brought up from the bottom of a river in a net, pale fish who had emerged from the waters of hell.

The stench of charred flesh made us dizzy and faint. Many of the soldiers covered their mouths and noses, many were ashen. Flies were swarming everywhere, and above us there were clouds of ravens and birds of prey. The Romans had been prepared for a battle, never imagining they would have to cross over a field of martyrdom. Nine hundred, burned, slaughtered. Worst were the children and the women and the babies in their mothers' embrace, their pale, young bodies in clutches of blood, bees circling round as if their remains were sweetened by the honey of their youth. Such deaths were a disgrace to the legion, and the soldiers took no joy in this surrender. Men who feared spirits and ghosts stood on the periphery when we were brought to the plaza. Men who feared their gods imagined that it was a sin for them to walk upon this ground.

I bowed my head before the legion, not to honor them, not as their captive, simply because I could not bring myself to gaze upon the faces of those who had led the battle against us. The children did as I did, and after a moment Revka did so as well, though I knew it was a violation for her to bow before Romans. I hoped she would not judge me. Certainly, I would not judge myself. I left that to the Almighty. We had a reason to go forward and much to protect. We were still in this world, the one we knew, the one we clung to though it was filled with sorrow, the world our fathers had created.

Silva, the great general, came before us. The soldier who had found us gave a shout, and we sank to our knees.

We lowered our eyes to the dust. Still we saw Silva's shadow; he was the force behind the siege, the commander who had built the wall and the ramp, the one who had murdered our people. It was impossible to interpret his demeanor, whether he intended to run us through himself or order our crucifixions or leave us to the jackals. Panic was beating in my throat. I felt chilled though the air had grown hot, bloodstained, moving in red waves as the sun rose higher.

My veiled eyes flickered over Silva's form. He was a tall man, dark in complexion, stern in aspect. But he was more than muscle and sinew. He was the monster without mercy. All the same, the longer he took to study us, the more I came to believe that had he intended to kill us, he would have done so already. The general was not often seen by common people, and the fact that he had come to appraise us made me grasp the notion that we might matter more than I had dared to imagine. Perhaps we had something he wanted.

Revka held Arieh, and I had Yonah in my arms. The commander may well have thought the newborn girl to be an angel, the cause for our survival, for he commanded us to stand so that he might look at her more closely. She was only days old, not a winged messenger, only a human child with a cap of silver-blond hair. Silva's eyes then went to me, the flecks of red on my skin, my hair the color of the flame tree, darkened by the water of the cistern until it seemed made from strands of flowing blood.

I returned Silva's gaze. He reminded me of the leopard I had once seen in the desert, the one who might have slain me and devoured me had I not stood upon a rock and made myself larger than I was, waving my shawl in the air, growling as if I were a beast as well.

I heard one of Silva's men suggest that we were nothing, whores and their whelps deserving any death they gave to us. The general's man said although my hair was the color of the rose, I was a weed, to be plucked out and burned. He spat after that word, and his spittle fell on me. He spoke in Greek. I knew this because Shirah had taught me the language during our lessons. This soldier suggested that his men take care of us, not bothering to waste the nails and wood to crucify us, merely running us through. He would see to it himself, a servant to his general.

There is always a moment when something begins and something ends. I could feel the weight of Shirah's daughter in my arms, a gift and a burden, my child now.

A weed feeds sheep far better than a flower will, I said in Greek.

My voice pierced through the men's discussion. Silva turned to me, surprised by my knowledge of that language and my nerve to speak before him.

I continued in Latin, for Shirah had taught me the language of the empire as well. A flower lasts an instant, a weed can plague you for all eternity.

What happened to your people? Silva asked. Where is the man who led you?

I raised my chin and studied the general who had destroyed us. He was just a man like any other. What would he do if he had to stand before a lion without a spear or a sword to protect him? Here was my secret and my strength: I had spoken to the lion, and this was the reason I lived when I faced him. I had told him that I belonged to him. I had given him my name, and in return he was mine.

He is murdered, I said. Lying among the dead of our people.

How could he be murdered? Silva demanded to know. We had not yet come over the wall and the dead were already everywhere.

She knows nothing, his second in command remarked coarsely. What would she know of their leader or their plans?

This soldier cast his eyes over me. I could see he had an idea of what he might do before he murdered me.

I reached for Ben Simon's knife. It flashed as I cut my flesh. I held my arm out and let my blood drip into the sand, staining it, claiming it. A murmur went up among the soldiers. I had always believed, if I were to be wounded, I would rather see to it myself. Now I realized when I had cut myself in the desert I had done so not merely to mark the days I had spent in the wilderness but to remind myself that I was alive.

Eleazar ben Ya'ir was my kinsman, I announced. I knew him as no other, for I am his cousin. I am Shirah, his closest companion. I alone can tell you the story of this fortress.

In that instant when I changed my name, I changed my fate.

I will give you the story, I promised. It will be the truth and you will be able to tell all of Rome what happened here today. I ask only for one favor in return.

There was laughter from the men. I could feel Death walking close by, peering at me with his many eyes. I can say with certainty that his eyes are cold and that his glance can freeze the heart. I drew the assassin's cloak around myself so that I might vanish from Mal'ach ha-Mavet's sight. I thought of the leopard I had chased off when I was only a girl in the desert, and the lion I had lain beside and the one I had freed when he was chained without mercy. Since that time I had worn the beast's collar around my arm, as a bracelet and a token. There were those who vowed that lion's blood provided the power of persuasion over princes and kings. I removed the collar and held it up, for the lion had struggled in his captivity and his blood was upon it.

Do you not recognize this?

Several of the men did indeed know the collar for what it was, and they stood back, stunned. Since the day the lion had been released, there had been talk of witchery.

Silva walked to me and took the collar, then returned to where he had stood on the wooden platform. He examined the collar and found it had been marked with the insignia of the Tenth Legion. I could see he was puzzled, though his expression was veiled. He signaled for me to come closer. I recognized his gesture, the same one my father had used when he wanted me to follow, as he might have signaled a dog. But a dog is often beaten once he has performed his task, so I stood in place, not yet willing to yield and approach the general.

I have need of your favor, I said. And you of mine.

Silva's eyes flitted over my form. One favor, he agreed, perhaps imagining that I was only a simple woman with simple desires, and would ask for bread or water. Only one, he warned me.

I asked for him to let us have our lives.

He stared at me and remarked that he wished to know who I thought I was to ask for such a reprieve.

I said I was the Witch of Moab and that it was written that I should be here to tell the story of what had happened on this day in the world Adonai had created, while the doves flew above us. I told him that no one would know how Rome had come to us, and how we had trembled before the lion who was enslaved on his chain without the story I told.

You will say that you were unafraid, he responded, thinking of how my story would defame his empire. You will recount how you went to the lion and he bowed before you.

Only a fool would be unafraid of a lion, I assured him, remembering the man who had once escaped a lion that had slain nine men before him. I was simply too bitter for his taste, I said.

Silva nodded, compelled to hear more. Why should I grant what you want?

Though we were merely women and children, we were the only ones who had lived through this tide of death. We had heard Eleazar ben Ya'ir speak to his followers and had memorized his words. We alone would be believed when this night was spoken of, for we were the only witnesses. We had heard the cries of those who knew they had no chance of victory against Rome.

I bowed my head then, for I had said enough. A story can be many things to many people. I would give him the story he wanted, but like the scorpion who is hidden in a corner, my story would sting. I knew not to speak of how our people had chosen their death rather than be enslaved. Nor did I suggest that we would be strengthened by my story if I lived to tell it, and that Rome would be haunted by the ghosts of our people, and that a ghost could be stronger than an empire, for it could move people not only to tears but to action.

The general gazed at me. I knew he wanted to hear more of what had happened. How could our people slay themselves and everyone they loved? It was a puzzlement, and even fierce men can be intrigued by a puzzle, though once joined, the pieces may serve to defy them.

When he agreed to my bargain, I approached him.

He told me to speak, and I did exactly as he asked. I told him what he wanted to hear.

We came to Alexandria, because it was there the Witch of Moab belonged, the city she had yearned for when she dreamed of the great river and of her mother and of the white lilies that grew in this city's gardens. We were brought before the legion in Jerusalem, so that our story might be recorded and written down and sent to Rome. We told it many times, and though we bowed to the strength of the empire, each time we told it a thousand more people learned of the night when we refused to be defeated. The story became a cloud, and the cloud a sheet of rain, and rain fell throughout the empire.

We were released outside the walls of Jerusalem. It had become a city we no longer recognized, and our people were not allowed inside its gates. I sold the gold amulet of the fish to pay for our journey. It had protected us, delivering us from our enemies, and in doing so had served its purpose. I thought of the slave from the north and prayed that his amulet had done as well for him so that he had found his way back to the land where the snow lasted most of the year, where stags that were as swift as the leopard ran across grasslands, where he could be free.

Yehuda traveled with us and lived in our house for several years, but when he became a man he was called to his people. The Essenes had gathered in the north, near Galilee. There were those left among his people who still believed in peace and in the principles of pure devotion to the Almighty. On the day he left us, Revka wept, for she loved him as though he was her own.

Noah and Levi soon enough became young men. Both had honey-colored skin and dark eyes; they were handsome, devoted to their grandmother as she aged. They might have become scholars, as their father had been before fate changed him, but instead they learned the trade of their grandfather. Every morning we were awakened by the scent of bread baking in the domed oven in a shed at the edge of the garden. There were times when I found people at the gate early in the morning, weeping, led here by the scent of bread that reminded them of the bread of their youth, when Jerusalem was ours. Now we are citizens of the world, and the brothers' bread reflects this: the honey is collected from Egyptian honeybees, the coriander and cumin from Moab, the salt from the shores of the sea the Witch of Moab crossed because she was fated to do so.

As for my son, he is quiet and fearless. He is an excellent student, and speaks four languages, but he is plagued by nightmares. It is only to be expected after all he witnessed, though he would never complain about such things. I discovered his difficulty sleeping because there are nights when I rise to find him sitting in the dark. Sleep is still an unfamiliar country to me, as it is to my son. Perhaps his father speaks to him in his dreams, as mine comes to me. I still possess the assassin's cloak, the one that is said to have been woven from spiders' webs, which concealed him from all eyes. I have forgiven him, as I hope that in the World-to-Come he has forgiven me, for I was not blameless. If I was brought before him, I would honor him, for he gave me my life, and for that I will always be grateful.

Every year on the anniversary of the day when the fortress fell, I recount the part of the story I did not tell Silva, although my children know the tale by heart. How the soldiers captured the lion and kept him on a chain and tormented him, how he bided his time, lying in the mud until he was released, how he was set free into the desert, and how he is there still, alone and lonely.

I say that this lion is the king of nothing other than his own freedom. Whether or not the third Temple rises, whether men build palaces or bring cities to ruin, it is the lion who will have to fight for a land of stones. All things change, for that is the way of the world we walk through. But some things remain constant, even after they are gone. I tell my children that we once had a thousand doves and that we set them free, but if we look at the sky we can still see them, even though we are so very far away.

Each year, in the month of Nissan, Yonah and I go to the river on the night before the feast that records our people's journey out of Egypt, a journey we hope to make again someday when Jerusalem is ours once more. It is a long voyage that we undertake. On this year we celebrate the Blessing of the Sun, for that glorious orb is in the exact same place as it had been during Creation, when God brought forth good and evil, imbuing our world with both at the same hour when he created the word and brought us out of silence, so we might make our own choices. We ride the white donkey we keep in the shed. Revka and I make certain this creature is well cared for, ready if we should ever need to depart suddenly. Our people never know when we may have to flee. Everything that is important we carry with us, whether or not it has been written down.

Yonah is a beautiful child, although with her pale hair and gray eyes she looks nothing like her mother. Still, she is called to the water. I could not keep her away if I tried. I have found her splashing in our courtyard fountain where we keep fish. They do not flee from her, but instead gather around her, as the doves once came to me. That is her element, one she shares with Shirah, who did everything she could to bring this girl forth into this world, even though it was not yet her time, far too early to do so with any assurance of safety. Shirah bled so badly after the birth she would not have survived even if the Angel of Death had not walked among us on that terrible night. We both knew this would come to pass as she drank the rue and stood over the smoke that would begin her labor. She gave her life so that Yonah would have hers. For those who say that the Witch of Moab never loved anyone, that she was selfish, concerned with her own fate alone, I can only say that she was ruined by love and delivered by it and that she left something glorious to the world, a child who loves to stand in the rain.

Our bare feet sink in the mud as we make our way into the waters of the Nile. The river is ink blue. There are sharp, green reeds, and the scent of balsam floats in the air. Women wash their clothes and leave them to dry on rocks along the shore. The men have pulled their boats in, lifting them upon their shoulders and carrying them up the sandy paths. We walk until there are shadows of silver fish darting close by. As the twilight sifts down, we set a candle on a lotus leaf that floats out with the current and watch as it disappears into the dark. This is the reason we are here, to give thanks to our mothers, who are watching over us in the place where we will join them one day, in the World-to-Come.

ACKNOWLEDGMENTS

The Dovekeepers is a novel set during and after the fall of Jerusalem (70 C.E.). The book covers a period of four years as the Romans waged war against the Jewish stronghold of Masada, claimed by a group of nine hundred rebels and their families. The story is taken from the historian Josephus, who has written the only account of the siege, in which he reported that two women and five children survived the massacre on the night when the Jews committed mass suicide rather than submit to the Roman Legion. It was they who told the story to the Romans, and, therefore, to the world.

I was inspired by my first visit to Masada, a spiritual experience so intense and moving I felt as though the lives that had been led there two thousand years earlier were utterly fresh and relevant. The tragic events of the past and the extraordinary sacrifices that were made in this fortress seemed to be present in the pale air. It was as if those who had lived there, and died there, had passed by only hours before.

In the Yigal Yadin Museum at Masada many of the artifacts mentioned in this novel can be found: a tartan fabric belonging to a legionnaire conscripted from Wales; the sandals and hair of a young woman whose remains were found beside a fountain, alongside the skeletons of a young warrior and a boy, with silver scales of armor surrounding them. An amulet in a museum in Wales is the one given to the escaped slave, Wynn, and the incantation bowls, amulets, and spells in the novel can be found in museums in Europe, Israel, and Egypt. The names found on *ostraca* at Masada—including Yoav, the Man from the Valley, and Ben Ya'ir, the leader of the rebellion—which may have been the lots drawn by the last warriors, are also on display at Masada. Several skeletons were discovered in the cave below the fortress, and although no one can know if Essenes were at Masada, their scrolls have been unearthed there. Magic was a secret endeavor, but as often as possible, I have threaded found archaeological remains into the story of *The Dovekeepers*.

I am indebted not only to Josephus's account, but to Yigal Yadin, the archaeologist in charge of the Masada project, author of *Masada*, the courageous story of the excavation of the fortress. Although there are debates regarding the history and archaeological findings, I have always deferred to the initial findings and interpretations at the site.

I have researched *The Dovekeepers* for many years, but I am not a historian or a religious scholar. As a novelist I worked as best I could within the confines of reality. Although some of the characters are based on historical figures, the stories of women have often gone unwritten, and *The Dovekeepers* is my attempt to imagine those stories. My hope is that in doing so, I can give voice to those who have remained silent for so long.

I would like to thank my earliest readers, Maggie Stern Terris, Daniel Terris, Pamela Painter, and Sue Standing for their insights and invaluable comments and for their friendship and support during the writing of this book. I would also like to thank my uncle and aunt, Ashley and Harriet Hoffman, early readers as well, for their continuing kindness in both my writing and real lives. Thank you to Mindy Givon, my sister-in-law, for being an early, supportive reader, for traveling through Israel with me, and for being a great friend. Gratitude to the Women's Studies Research Center at Brandeis for my appointment as a visiting scholar, with special thanks to Shulamit Reinharz, and to my wonderful student researcher, Deborah Thompson.

Thanks to Susan Brown for copyediting that was both meticulous and tolerant. Thank you to Gary Johnson and Julia Kenny at the Markson Thoma agency for their continuing support, and also to Paul Whitlatch at Scribner for help throughout the publication of this book. My thanks to Camille McDuffie for her friendship and for many kindnesses over the course of many books. Gratitude to Joyce Tenneson, whose glorious photograph inspired me as a symbol of the courage and grace of women in the ancient world.

I am indebted to my brother-in-law, Menachem Givon, who was my guide in Israel and whose knowledge was invaluable to me in his thoughtful reading of the manuscript. It would have been impossible for me to have ever researched all that he knew by heart and was kind enough to share with me. I am also deeply indebted to Richard Elliott Friedman, an exceptional writer and scholar, whose wise and careful reading of the book was extremely helpful, and whose brilliant insights into the world of the Bible were both fascinating and invaluable. Thank you both for being generous, patient teachers.

I would especially like to thank Elaine Markson, my extraordinary agent and friend; she believed in this book from the very start, and has always believed in me. Many thanks also to my long-time agent and dear friend Ron Bernstein for his wise counsel over the years. I am grateful beyond words to have worked with Nan Graham as my editor and Susan Moldow as my publisher. They, too, believed in me and in this book and embraced it. In doing so, they changed my fate. Thank you also to Carolyn Reidy for her kindness and support.

I am indebted to my husband, Thomas Martin, who journeyed to the desert with me, despite the sorrows we encountered.

Lastly, my greatest debt is to my mother, Sherry Hoffman, who I miss every day. I hope you forgave me, as I have long ago forgiven you.

FURTHER READING

The Jewish War, Josephus, Penguin Classics edition
Masada, Yigal Yadin, Welcome Rain Books
Ancient Jewish Magic, Gideon Bohak, Cambridge University Press
Magic in Ancient Egypt, Geraldine Pinch, The British Museum Press
Every Living Thing, Daily Use of Animals in Ancient Israel, Borowski, Alta Mira Press
Daily Life in Biblical Times, Borowski, Society of Biblical Literature, Atlanta

More historical information and a glossary can be found on the author's website: www.alicehoffman.com.

A SCRIBNER READING GROUP GUIDE

The Dovekeepers by Alice Hoffman

A NOTE FROM THE AUTHOR

Once in a lifetime a book may come to a writer as an unexpected gift. *The Dovekeepers* is such a book for me. It was a gift from my great-great grandmothers, the women of ancient Israel who first spoke to me when I visited the mountain fortress of Masada. In telling their story of loss and love, I've told my own story as well. After writing for thirty-five years, after more than thirty works of fiction, I was given the story I was meant to tell.

I was initially inspired by my first visit to Masada, a spiritual experience so intense and moving, I felt as though the lives that had been led there two thousand years earlier were utterly fresh and relevant. The tragic events of the past and the extraordinary sacrifices that were made in this fortress seemed to be present all around me. It was as if those who had lived there, and died there, had passed by only hours before. The temperature was well over a hundred degrees and the horizon was shaky with blue heat. In that great silence, standing inside the mystery that is the past, surrounded by the sorrow of the many deaths that occurred there, I also felt surrounded by life and by the stories of the women who had been there. In that moment, *The Dovekeepers* came to life as well.

TOPICS & QUESTIONS FOR DISCUSSION

1. The novel is split into four principal parts, with each of the main characters—Yael, Revka, Aziza, and Shirah—narrating

one section. Which of these women did you find most appealing, and why? Were you surprised to find you had compassion for characters who were morally complex and often made choices that later caused guilt and sorrow?

2. Yael describes her relationship with Ben Simon as "a destroying sort of love" (p. 46). What does she mean by that? Are there other relationships in the novel that could be described in the same way?
3. From Yael's setting free the Romans' lion, to Shirah's childhood vision of a fish in the Nile, to the women's care of the doves, animals are an important component in the book. What did animals mean to the people of this ancient Jewish society, and what specific symbolic forms do they take in the novel?
4. The figure of Wynn, The Man from the North, who comes to serve the women in the dovecote, is based upon archeological finds at Masada. In what ways does Wynn come to bring the women together? Compare Yael's relationship with Ben Simon to her relationship with Wynn.
5. How do spells function in the novel? What is the relationship between Shirah's Jewish beliefs and her use of magic? If you have read other Alice Hoffman novels that include mystical elements—such as *Practical Magic* or *Fortune's Daughter*—how do they compare to *The Dovekeepers* and its use of magic?
6. How do Shirah's daughters react to the intimate friendship that develops between Yael and their mother? Is Shirah a good mother or not?
7. What do you make of Channa's attempt, essentially, to kidnap Yael's baby Arieh? Is Channa different from the other major female characters in the book? Do you find your opinion of her changes?
8. "You don't fight for peace, sister," Nahara tells Aziza. "You embrace it" (p. 343). What do you think of Nahara's decision

to join the Essenes? Is she naïve or a true believer? Do you see similarities between the Essenes and the early Christian movement?

9. Why is the Roman Legion preparing to attack the Jews at Masada? From historical references in the book, as well as your own knowledge of history, explain the roots of the conflict. Do you feel the lives of the women in *The Dovekeepers* echo the lives of women in the modern world who are experiencing war and political unrest?
10. Revka's son-in-law, the warrior known as The Man from the Valley, asks Aziza, "Did you not think this is what the world was like?" (p. 378). Describe the circumstances of this question. After all her training for battle, why is Aziza unprepared for the experience of attacking a village filled with women and children?
11. In the final pages of the book, Yael sums up those who perished at Masada, remembering them as "men who refused to surrender and women who were ruled by devotion" (p. 478). Do you agree with her description?
12. For the women at Masada, dreams contain important messages, ghosts meddle in the lives of the living, and spells can remedy a number of human ills. How does their culture's acceptance of the mystical compare to our culture's view on such things today? Do mystical and religious elements overlap? How do they compare to your own views?
13. In the note on page 507, Hoffman explains that the historical foundation of her story comes from Josephus, the first-century historian who has written the only account of the massacre. How does knowing that the novel is based on history and archeological findings affect your reading of the book?
14. Women's knowledge in *The Dovekeepers* is handed down from mother to daughter, sister to sister, friend to friend. Why do

you think it is so difficult to know what the lives of ancient women were really like? Do you see any connection with the way in which your own family stories are handed down through the generations?